Ira Morris

THE CHICAGO STORY

BY IRA MORRIS (I. V. MORRIS)

THE CHICAGO STORY

COVERING TWO YEARS

MARCHING ORDERS

LIBERTY STREET

THE TREE WITHIN

THE CHICAGO STORY

a novel by

IRA MORRIS

Garden City, New York, 1952

DOUBLEDAY & COMPANY, INC.

The characters and the incidents in this book
are entirely the product of the author's imagination
and have no relation to any person or event in real life.

LIBRARY OF CONGRESS CATALOG CARD NUMBR 52–5531

contents

part one 1905

THE GILDED HERD

KONRAD FAMILY TREE

ADOLPH
d. 1950
m. Wilma
Busch
d. 1936

- **WILLIAM** m. Gladys Hastey
  - WILLIAM, JR.
  - SUSAN m. James McCormick — 2 children

- **RUPERT** m. Helen Mason
  - COSIMA
    m. (1) Sam Luke
    m. (2) Lincoln Rice
    m. (3) Stan Harding
    — Patricia d. 1950

- **CECILIA**
  m. (1) Justin Judson
  m. (2) Gerald Foyles
  - CECIL m. Elizabeth Page — 2 children
  - HENRY m. Louise Hansen — 1 child
  - MABEL m. Alan Armitage — 3 children

- **BEATRICE**

- **FRANCIS**
  d. 1926
  m. Maureen McKenna
  d. 1948
  - FRANCIS

one

The carriages were driving up and away. Adolph Konrad, standing by his steaming punch bowl, breathed easier at the thought that the long ordeal was almost over. Who *um Gottes Willen* had invented New Year's Day receptions anyway! He supposed they were one of the tributes exacted from the wealthy by the goddess of chance, but for whose favors the elect would be drinking beer instead of champagne, and perhaps doing it in poverty-stricken Schwabenland, rather than Chicago. A consolation was that they came but once a year, thought Adolph, glancing about his parlor, crowded with chattering ladies, and gentlemen whose names he did not recall.

"A delightful party, Mr. Konrad! And a happy New Year to you."

Adolph, recalled to attention, stretched out his hand with a gruff "Come again!" but in a moment Wilma had hurried up with her warm, quick smile.

"How kind of you to have called!" she murmured, pressing the tiny hand in the glacé glove. "We certainly wish you a happy New Year. Hauptman, will you call Mrs. Chauncey Armitage's carriage?"

The stony-faced butler nodded and slipped away, and a moment later his voice could be heard above the buzz of conversation and the crackling of the big logs in the fireplace.

"Mrs. Armitage's carriage! Mrs. Chauncey Armitage's carriage right away!"

"Do be more careful, Adolph," Wilma whispered, as she returned from seeing the star guest to the door. "Be very polite to everyone. It's safer—much safer!"

"They can go to hell," Adolph angrily whispered back, incensed at the suggestion that a man who was the third power in the Stock Yards world should have to make up to anyone. But then he turned to the next

9

of the departing guests and said, "I am pleased, sir, that you came!" It happened to be one of his own plant managers whom he yelled at every other day of the year. The fellow was so surprised that he forgot to thank for the party.

"Papa, can I ask a favor? I want to invite Gladys Hastey to stay on for supper."

The young man with the morning coat, white carnation in the buttonhole, resembled his father at first glance, but on analysis, there were more points of difference than of similarity. He had the same heavy build, but with him corpulence was turning to flabbiness; big nose and strong jaw gave him a similar profile, but in the deep-set eyes was none of the fire or the power that caused Adolph Konrad at forty-six to be one of the most respected and most feared men in Chicago. "Ve have supper guests enough. For vhy should I feed an army after pouring drinks down their throats?" grumbled Adolph, and William was already looking resigned when Mama came to his help.

"You let him ask her, Adolph, if he wants to. Gladys is a nice girl," Wilma said, and in her voice was the vocal equivalent of a wink. "One more or less, Adolph. Does it matter?"

"Vell no, perhaps not," Adolph agreed, still reluctant, but having remembered that this same Gladys was his sole link with a Stock Yards family even more powerful than his own. Apart from her, no Hastey had yet been in Sans Souci, nor had Wilma and he been invited to the mansion on Prairie Avenue on whose front door was arrogantly carved the Hastey escutcheon: two unicorns holding between them a shield. Not astonishing, seeing that his own escutcheon, had he had one, would most fittingly have represented a pig and a steer holding aloft a silver dollar!

"Carriage for Mr. Schultz! Mr. and Mrs. Sauerwein's carriage!" Hauptman's voice kept sounding from the front doorsteps, and now the crowd was beginning to thin out; only the supper guests and a few hopefuls angling for invitations lingered on in the plush parlor, heavy with cigar smoke. The maid, casting a questioning glance at the punch bowl, received a negative sign from Wilma; there would be no need to pour in more champagne. Rupert, Adolph's second son, noted the gesture and quickly replenished his goblet before the supply ran out. His

10

brother William scowled at him disapprovingly as he led Gladys Hastey out into the conservatory; wiping off a marble bench with his handkerchief, he invited the young lady to be seated beneath a spreading rubber plant.

Adolph, who had been shaking hands and sweating under his morning coat for the last three hours, slipped upstairs to take off the stiff collar which was biting into his neck. Arrived in his and Wilma's room, he tore off the offending article, ripping it angrily in the process, and flung the two pieces in the wastebasket. Then he undid his white stock, took out his old corduroy jacket, and selected a comfortable shirt with shoestring bow tie to go with it. He felt more like himself as he stood passing the brushes over his thick hair.

Going to the window, Adolph peered down at the little cluster of carriages drawn up before his stables. Earlier in the afternoon there had been a long row that lined the snow-sprinkled driveway right down to the wrought-iron gates giving on the road; there had also been two or three automobiles and one of those high-roofed "electrics" that were becoming fashionable in Chicago at the time. Now there remained but a scattering of inelegant carriages, their horses shivering in the evening chill, with no coachman at hand to throw monogrammed blankets over their backs. There wasn't one vehicle left whose owner's position demanded Adolph's presence in the parlor! These twopenny guests could be taken care of by Wilma.

Adolph Konrad sat down on the stool by the window and let his big head fall on his breast. He was not dozing, simply giving the empty battery inside him a chance to recharge. Gradually, very gradually, he felt the cells filling up with that power that had carried him over every obstacle on the grim road to success; the power that had raised him from a penniless immigrant, son of a pigherd, to millionaire and industrial giant; the power that blazed in his black eyes and filled his great guttural voice. Reaching for a birch stick on the window sill, he began to whittle away with a knife, pulling the blade down the wood with sharp, decisive movements. He felt happy and relaxed at his favorite occupation. The little white shavings flittered to the floor, forming a pattern that may have been the pattern of success.

There was the sound of a door opening in the corridor, and Adolph

11

could make out the swish of a skirt in the neighboring room. From one second to another anger filled him. His big lips pouted; his nose twitched. Rushing into the room where Wilma stood bent over the bed of their youngest son, he was trembling with rage.

"Und for vhy are you here?" he shouted, as the frightened boy pressed closer to the wall. "Mit guests downstairs, you come running up in de middle of the party. For vhy you keep babying the boy? Is it I vhat should do your vork for you, like always?"

Wilma started guiltily when Adolph's tall frame appeared in the doorway. Long experience with his tempers had taught her how best to avoid a scene before the boy.

"But, Adolph, almost all the folks have left by now," she answered composedly. "And everyone said that our party was just dandy. Do you know that there were over two hundred guests? What do you say to that, Adolph?"

"Ush! I don't gif a demn." He stood chewing his nether lip, while curiosity gradually got the better of him. "Two hundred? Und how do you know?"

"Because I counted them as they came in."

"Hu! Spongers und riffraff come to gobble up my sandvitches. I'd like to know vhat it all cost. Und now get downstairs mit you, Wilma," he said, the anger drained from his voice. "How often do I have to tell you, there's nothing the matter mit Francy?"

Wilma smiled down at her son, then bent and tucked in his sheet. The boy's wan face was turned towards her, soft eyes filled with tears. The little weakling! thought Adolph unhappily. At this boy's age he was earning his living in the lace shop, working twelve or fourteen hours a day. If Wilma only stopped mollycoddling him, the lad would be forced to get well, Adolph reflected as he stamped out of the room. He would tell O'Grady not to listen to Wilma, and to see to it that the boy got out of bed.

She joined him in the corridor a few seconds later, lines of worry visible in her face. She looked old suddenly (or ageless might have been a better word), like the farm woman she was, at grips with the elemental problem of sickness. The purple lace dress hung limply from her shoulders, and now it seemed to suit her singularly ill.

"Adolph," she said, "Francy is sick—real sick. His fever is up. I can feel it on his forehead."

"Fever? Nonsense!" Adolph had raised his voice again; it echoed down the staircase of Sans Souci to where the last guests were gathered in a group. "For vhy you keep bothering me? Is this the time or the place?"

"Yes, it *is* the time, *and* the place," said Wilma, halting at the head of the stairs and fixing Adolph with a gaze so pleading that he could not step by her. "He is your son, Adolph. And mine. I want you to call a doctor tonight . . . for I am scared. . . ."

"You are scared? But doesn't O'Grady say that the boy is okay?"

"He says it to please you. He'd say anything to please you, Adolph— haven't you understood that yet? Let me call in a good doctor! I beg you."

"Absolutely no!" Adolph's shout was so loud that one of the parting guests peered up curiously before hurrying into the vestibule. "O'Grady is my friend. Und he's a fine doctor too. If he's good enough for me, he's good enough for my boy. That is final, Vilma!"

For a second Wilma stared at her husband, rebellion flaring in her eyes. Words never before spoken rushed to the fore; she was infused with the reckless courage of a primitive woman fighting for her young. But when she opened her mouth, strangely enough no phrase issued forth. Adolph was watching her. She began to tremble and threw her hand before her lips.

"I know best," Adolph was saying. "To please you, I'll ask O'Grady to look at Francy tonight. He is staying for supper. Now are you satisfied, Vilma? Are you satisfied?"

A moment passed before Wilma replied, a moment in which was compressed a whole lifetime of suppressed desires, of reluctant obedience, of silence.

"Yes, Adolph," she whispered. "Yes, yes, Adolph, I am satisfied."

two

Amidst the remains of the dead party, amidst the empty glasses and the filled ash trays, Dr. O'Grady sat trying to make conversation with a bony man in an ill-fitting morning coat. Of all Adolph's guests that day, no two could have been more contrasting. Florid, jovial, and expansive, the Irish doctor was the very antithesis of the bleak Scotsman who shared with him the signal honor of being invited to stay on for supper. It was one more mark of the favoritism which Adolph had been bestowing of late on Angus McKenna, one of the managers in his big Stock Yards plant.

"I'm tellin' ye, Angus, there's no one like Adolph when it comes to stickin' up fer a friend," O'Grady was saying, while his warm eyes followed the curvaceous figure of the maid as she stacked empty goblets. "Loyalty is Adolph's middle name. Ye ought to be happy, workin' fer such a king of a man."

"Ay," said McKenna. "Ay. No doubt you're right."

It was impossible to tell whether he was assenting or dissenting.

"It's twelve years now since I've known Adolph," O'Grady went on in his enthusiastic way. "Twelve years our friendship has lasted, an' I owe him everythin' in me life. I was a poor man when I met him, an immigrant newly arrived from the old country. Did ye know"—he lowered his voice, casting his eyes about furtively—"did ye know that I started life as—as a veterinary?"

"No, O'Grady, I didn't know," said McKenna, obviously caring less.

"Me family had no money to finish me medical education in Dublin," O'Grady explained, toying with the elk's tooth swinging from his massive watch chain. "We were respectable folk, we O'Gradys, but dead broke, like all the Irish. So there I was in Chicago, back in the year '93, trying to make me livin' out of the aches and pains of the four-footed species, and havin' a square meal maybe once a month. One avenin' as I was addin' up accounts an' won'rin' if it wouldn't be simpler to put

14

a bullet through me head, comes a ring at the doorbell. I goes to open an' sees a man standin' there—in a terrible state of agitation."

"It was Adolph Konrad," guessed the Scotsman. Mean in conversation, as in everything else, he refused the speaker the minute pleasure of creating a surprise.

"It was indeed," the doctor admitted, almost reluctantly. "Adolph in his hip boots and black string tie and that big shaggy head of his bared to the winter breezes. He was fairly shakin' with excitement.

"'C'm on, you son of a gun!' yells he. 'Hurry up, God damn ye. Me best carriage horse's gone an' slipped on the ice, an' he's cracked his foreleg. Ye've got to patch him up for me, an' ye'd better make a good job of it, I'm tellin' ye.'

"So I followed Adolph out on the street," said O'Grady, fixing the listener with his bloodshot eyes. "An' there was the horse lyin' stretched out between the car tracks. It was a beautiful gelding, honey-colored and sleek, with the traces of the buggy still attached to him. He looked up at us, entreatin'-like, when we came close. Adolph knelt in the snow an' began strokin' the beast's muzzle, gone as gentle as an old woman with her ailin' cat. I even saw there was a tear glistenin' in his eye." The doctor's own brown Irish eyes dampened sympathetically. "But I saw, too, that there was nothin' to be done. The horse's leg was busted, that was evident, an' the kindest thing was to dispatch him. Just as I was about to administer the hypodermic."—O'Grady held up an imaginary syringe and demonstrated by wiggling his forefinger back and forth—"I felt a yank at me collar. Before I could say knife, Adolph'd swung me to me feet.

"'What're ye doin' with that instrument?' he shouted in a fury. 'I told ye to fix me horse, not to kill him. Take that!'

"An' with a swipe of his big hand, he'd knocked me right into the gutter."

"Ay, ay, that's a good one!" The Scotchman looked interested for the first time; he even let a feeble smile creep into his big-boned face. "And what happened then?" he asked, moving his chair to make room for the maid to walk by with a tray of used glasses.

"What happened then?" O'Grady reached out to snatch a half-filled goblet before answering. With his other hand he administered a sharp tweak to the girl's rotund bottom, and then continued, unfazed by her yelp of dismay. "Why, it all turned out for the best. Can ye believe it that that horse's leg was not really broken after all, thanks be to Mary, Mother of God! It was just badly sprained. I transported the beast to an empty stable behind me house, an' there I took care of him like a baby. Every mornin' and avenin' Adolph used to drop in to see how his pet was gettin' on an' watched me massage its ankle with Sloan's liniment. I do believe it was Adolph's great strength of will made that leg to heal. For Adolph is a battler for life! In one month that beast was as right as rain, an' next spring he won a prize for buggy horses at the Chicago horse show."

"Lucky you didn't give him that hypodermic," McKenna remarked.

"That it was. I never would've become friends with Adolph, an' he never would've leant me the money to finish me medical education. . . . After that one blow of his fist, we got on—oh, swimmingly! We understood each other. When Adolph called for his horse a month later, he took me back to his house for supper. We sat talkin' till one in the mornin' in this very room, an' next day he mailed me a check for me tuition fee at the medical college. D'you understand now that I swear by Adolph? Best friend a man could have."

The Scotchman nodded. "Ay, ay. A good friend. A good enemy too, if he feels that way. Believe me, O'Grady, that's the secret of any man's success: to have the strength to love—and the strength to hate. The fact is, one of them's of but little use—without the other. . . ."

"And what are you two gentlemen talking about so seriously?"

The young girl whose question had interrupted them obviously had no desire to be answered. Her wandering eye and the vacuous smile that flirted about the corners of her mouth evidenced a constitutional lack of concentration; only the jutting jaw, the dominant nose, marked Cecilia as one of Adolph Konrad's children. And in her case those features betokened stubbornness, not strength.

"Why, girl, we was sayin' some fayne things about yer father," O'Grady explained, jumping up from his chair and offering it to Cecilia.

But, ignoring the gesture, the young girl took his arm and, while

16

her eyes continued to circle the room, said urgently, "Oh, Dr. O'Grady, may I say a word to you? It's important—most terribly important. Will you excuse us, Mr. McKenna?"

McKenna nodded and strode off towards the conservatory, his stolid expression unchanged. Whereupon Cecilia sank her voice to a whisper.

"Something terrible has happened! Oh, Dr. O'Grady, you have to help us—you have to do something before Papa comes downstairs."

"What's the matter, me girl?"

"It's—it's about Rupert. Oh, if Papa finds out, gracious knows what will happen!"

"An' what has that brother of yers gone and accomplished?"

"He's—he's—oh, Dr. O'Grady, I'm afraid he's—drunk too much punch! Isn't it terrible?"

O'Grady's round face blossomed in a smile.

"More terrible things than that have happened," he promised her. "Yer lead me to him. And don't worry yer pretty head."

Cecilia took the doctor's arm and led him through the vestibule into the small library on the other side of the house. Stretched on a couch lay young Rupert, his eyes closed; beside him reposed necktie, stiff collar, and gray morning coat. Beatrice, his younger sister, started up from the floor with a little cry as they entered. She was holding a damp towel in her hand.

"Don't be frightened, me pet. It's only O'Grady," said the doctor, patting her arm. "And now let's see what the matter may be with the handsome young invalid."

Bending over, he raised one of the boy's eyelids, then let it drop back. Rupert did not stir.

"Be gorry, he's pretty far gone," said the doctor, chuckling. "Never fear, we'll bring him back among the living. Go and fetch me some smelling salts, will ye, Cissy? And you, Bee, try and find some aromatic spirits of ammonia. Remember, if your father comes in, say that yer brother's had a faintin' spell—the heat an' the crowd an' all that."

"Oh, Dr. O'Grady, aren't you just wonderful!" Cecilia exclaimed.

"Yes," said the doctor. "Why yes, I suppose I am."

Left alone, O'Grady took the towel, wrung out the wet end, and gave Rupert a smart flick across either cheek. The boy stirred on the couch, then raised himself with a jerk. He stared at the doctor through bleary eyes.

"Hello, ye blitherin' young fool!" O'Grady greeted him unceremoniously. "Ye might have chosen a better spot to get soused in, than the parlor of yer old man's house."

Rupert blinked his eyes confusedly and stared about him. He was a handsome lad of twenty, the best-looking of the five children; only the surly, self-centered expression marred his natural attractiveness. As with the other four, he resembled Adolph, although lacking that special quality that made their father a dynamic personality.

"I'll get drunk where I like," he mumbled back with the bravado of a spoiled youth. "Yes, I'll drink and I'll drink. Just let them kick me out," he said, trying to focus his glance on the doctor, "let them do it, and see if I care!"

"Ye shouldn't speak like that about yer own parents," said O'Grady severely. "Ye've got the grandest old man a boy could have. Where'd ye be, but for him? Herding pigs, most likely, like yer grandfather an' his father before him."

"Oh, what a splendid thing!" Rupert hiccoughed. "Pigs, pigs—how I love pigs! Isn't it just wonderful that I can spend the rest of my life in the Stock Yards of Chicago?"

"Ye're a mean little slut!" cried the doctor, and it was clear now that his ire was roused. "Oh, I know that ye're riled at bein' snapped out of college an' put to work in the business instead. It's no one's bloody fault but yer own! If ye'd studied a bit, as ye were meant to do, yer old man might've let ye stay on."

"Studied? So you really think studies had something to do with it?" In his excitement, Rupert sat up on the couch, but, growing dizzy, he lay down again. "Why, studies weren't the reason I was yanked out of college at all! If I told you, Dr. O'Grady . . . if I told you . . ."

But whatever Rupert was about to tell, the moment proved unpropitious. In the entrance had appeared Rupert's two sisters, tiptoeing along, each with a small bottle in her hand. And at almost the same instant the dinner gong in the hallway began to sound. Through the doorway they could catch a glimpse of Hauptman, the butler, calling the elect to another in the series of overplenteous meals that he had been serving twice a day for the last fourteen years.

The sound of the gong rang through Sans Souci, carrying into the conservatory where William was mumbling sweet nothings to Miss Hastey, and upstairs where Adolph sat whittling away at his stick, and into the parlor where Angus McKenna and his wife perched side by side on the sofa in stony conjugal silence. It was more than a summons to dinner; it was the music of respectability and affluence, a triumphant tattoo announcing the reign of prosperity and plenty in Adolph Konrad's Drexel Boulevard house.

three

Supper was half over. The soup had come and gone, likewise the patties, and now everyone was awaiting Hauptman's entrance with the *plat de résistance,* that regal dish without which no self-respecting dinner was complete in the year 1905 in Chicago: the fifteen-pound roast of beef. An expectant and respectful hush had fallen over the company.

Not that it could be said that conversation had been either scintillating or fluent hitherto. People came to the Konrad board to eat, not to talk. If anything was said, apart from an appropriate comment on the food or a hushed request for the salt or butter, it usually came from Adolph himself. Ten to one it consisted in the recital of some Stock Yards incident which had taken place earlier in the day. The other members of the family, including Mama, occupied the roles of listeners or appreciative commentators. And when, as today, there were guests these also assumed a deferential attitude, awed by the big shaggy-headed man who (they were not allowed to forget) had provided every scrap of the food and bought the very chairs on which they were sitting!

Now Adolph was testing the carving knife by running its edge over his thumb, which was remarkably well formed and sensitive for the son of a peasant. Soon that knife would slice through rare beef, and Adolph in anticipation was already experiencing the sensuous sensation of severing the tender meat whose nature he knew so well. He had heard it said about him that he could tell at a glance whether a given cut came from a Texas steer or an animal from Missouri or from Illinois; and while he realized that this was not strictly true, he had taken it as a compliment. It seemed to him that for a man connected with the Stock Yards world it was as absurd not to love meat as for a glazier not to love glass, or a carpenter not to love the raw wood with which he spent his working hours.

And yet, he thought, his glance skimming the faces of the diners, of these nine people only Wilma knew the first thing about meat, even though their lives were bound up so intimately with the Stock Yards. McKenna, that sallow-faced Scotsman, would as soon have been eating oatmeal; his terrified wife looked as if she subsisted on carrots. His own sons and daughters had a secret scorn of roast beef, no doubt because they had eaten it too often and begun eating it too early in their lives. The same held true of Gladys Hastey. But had not her expensive gray dress been paid for with the lives of hundreds of Stock Yards steers? Had not his son's solid morning coats and his daughters' party frocks been paid for with sheep and hogs?

The door opened and Hauptman stepped into the room, his expression that of a priest bearing in the Host; in his two hands he held before him the great salver on which reposed a mighty joint, its steam spiraling to the ceiling. Following after with the vegetables was Hulda, the maid, a quaking altar boy, terrified by Hauptman, by Adolph, by the unknown faces, by the boisterous O'Grady, given to pinching her on the behind. Solemnly Hauptman lowered the platter before Adolph, signaling Hulda to find place for the vegetable dishes further down the board. There lay the great roast beef, the end product of twenty-five years of slaughtering and quartering, the symbol of hundreds of thousands of dead animals, the badge of achievement and success!

Not a word was spoken as the master plunged his carving knife into the roast and began hewing off slices, each as thick as a fair-sized plank. As Rupert gazed in repulsion, O'Grady in expectancy, Molly McKenna in awe, and Mama in devout adoration, Hauptman distributed the over-laden plates along the length of the table. For the next moments the

20

scraping of silverware against china, the shuffle of Hauptman's shoes across the parquet, and the munching of nine mouths, alone interrupted the ritualistic silence.

Yes, nine mouths only, for Rupert had not yet brought himself to take a single bite. It wasn't only the fact that he was rather drunk that caused his gorge to rise; roast beef had always had that effect on him. Ever since his father forced him to give up the study of philosophy for the study of butchery he had had a feeling of personal enmity toward the great hunks of meat that appeared so consistently on the family board.

Perhaps that feeling was heightened by the fact that a certain young lady was a vegetarian, and that he loved this young lady better than the rest of the world. Now, as he stared at his meat, he kept thinking of the professor's daughter and of their brusquely interrupted love affair. In the six months since his father had decided that it would be dangerous to let him return to Harvard, Helen Mason had become the embodiment of everything that Chicago was not; the more Rupert loathed the Stock Yards, the more he adored this exquisite girl whose life centered on her piano and who was ethereal as a nightingale. When he spoke her name he heard rippling music and felt the touch of a silk dress. Suddenly the dirty walls of the packing plant would melt away, disclosing a blossoming apple tree; the sickening reek would be replaced by the odor of lavender; and in his ears, instead of the mooing of moribund animals, he would hear Helen's voice asking him, "Rupert, what are you doing so far away . . . ?"

He roused himself with an effort, aware that he must make inroads on the great mountain upon his plate, aware also that he was not up to the task. He put a little mashed potatoes in his mouth and gulped them down. At least they didn't have the taste of animal and blood! Aware that his sister Beatrice was making signs at him, he cut a small bit of meat and forced himself to swallow it almost whole. At once he felt fiercely nauseated. He closed his eyes, for the room was circling about.

When he opened them again he saw that second helpings were already being served. Without the formality of questions, Hauptman was taking each plate in turn and carrying it to the head of the table, where Adolph, back bent over the platter, loaded it with a hunk weightier and even bloodier than its predecessor. Rupert knew that he was beaten.

As he heard Hauptman's footsteps approaching, he had a sinking feeling connected only remotely with the excess of champagne punch in his stomach. A moment of agonizing suspense followed, as Hauptman, already reaching for the plate, halted his hand with the index finger curved in the form of an indignant question mark.

"Rupert! Vhat's de matter mit you?"

The voice was Adolph's, of course. (Who else ever raised his voice in that room?) There was no anger in it as yet, only surprise, incredulity. Never had it happened before that a member of his family had refused two servings of beef!

"Nothing's the matter." Rupert's voice sounded unfamiliar in his own ears. "I'm just—not hungry."

"Not hungry?" (It was as if Rupert had casually announced that he was not sane.) "Vhat do you mean, not hungry? There is nothing the matter mit that meat. You couldn't get a better cut in all Chicago. Hurry und eat now. Qvick!"

Rupert stared down at his plate. Of their own volition his fingers reached for the knife and fork, then halted their journey halfway. A revolt, long brewing, seethed up inside him, and alcohol broke down the barriers.

"No," he said, and put down the knife and fork. "I don't want any."

Had Rupert announced his intention of murdering the assembled company, or flung at his father the bronze centerpiece, depicting Cupid aiming his arrow at a coy Psyche, he scarcely could have created more of a sensation. A complete silence followed his remark. Everyone had stopped eating with the exception of William, who continued cutting up and chewing his meat as if nothing had happened. His smug expression said, "At least *I* know the value of good roast beef and I disassociate myself from this rebellion." Under the table, Rupert could feel his sister Cecilia's warning kick, but he paid no attention. Beneath his soft exterior, he, too, was a fighter, and he knew that the battle was on.

Adolph, standing at the head of the table, carving fork in hand, glared down at his son. As always when temper overcame him, his mouth worked in and out and his black eyes blazed furiously; but Rupert held their gaze without flinching. And suddenly Adolph realized that this was far more than a dispute with his second son as to whether or not he would eat up his dinner.

"I don't vant my good food to go vasted," he said, pointing at Rupert's plate with his knife. "I guess you're in love, eh? Is dat the trouble?"

Now it was Rupert's turn to go white. That reference to Helen Mason touched him at his tenderest point; all his resentment at being yanked out of Harvard, at being put to work at a dull job in the Stock Yards, at having Helen's letters intercepted and read, found expression in one infuriated shout.

"You shut up, will you!"

Mama gave a little cry of dismay. With her frantic glance traveling from husband to son, she murmured, "Now, Adolph! Now, Rupert! Please!" But it was clear that neither of them heard her.

"I shall shut up, shall I?" Adolph was shouting. "You sit there und tell your father to shut up! Ve'll see who shuts up. You get out of de room this minute, you—you *Lausbube! Teufel Hohl dich! Donnerwetter noch einmal!*"

The two girls were trembling in their seats, on either side of the renegade. Often they had witnessed their father's anger, but never had they seen him like this, waving the carving fork and shouting wildly in German. O'Grady had pushed back his chair and seemed ready to leap between the two disputants; poor Molly McKenna looked as if she were about to burst into tears; even William had stopped eating at last and was staring at his younger brother with unconcealed disapproval. Only Gladys Hastey sat watching Rupert with her lips twisted in a funny little smile; she looked as if she were enjoying the whole proceeding.

Rupert jumped up from his chair, which toppled over behind him on the floor.

"Yes, I'm going!" he cried. "I'm leaving and I won't come back either. I've had enough of being ordered about like a little boy. I'm—I'm almost twenty-one!"

He had taken two steps toward his father and stood there, shouting as loudly as Adolph. A strand of black hair had fallen over his pale forehead, and he looked (Gladys might have been thinking) extraordinarily handsome.

23

Just at that moment the French windows behind him blew open. He must have brushed against the catch as he strode past, and now a blast of winter air rushed into the room, carrying with it an odor unmistakable for any inhabitant of Chicago: the faint, sweetish smell of blood and of death. Rupert swung around. He pointed with one finger out into the night, a violent gesture, like the aiming of a loaded revolver.

"That's what I hate, I am telling you!" he cried. "The Stock Yards! The bloody Stock Yards! I'm never going back there as long as I live. And I'm never going to eat roast beef again, so help me!"

With a swift movement that no one could have foreseen, he snatched up the carving knife. He held it poised before him for a second, then brought it down into the meat with a mighty jab. Gravy besplattered the tablecloth, and a few drops even leaped over Adolph's white shirt front; the knife's bone handle swayed giddily to and fro. But at almost the same instant Adolph's palm flashed out, and the crack of a blow resounded in the room. Rupert took a step backwards, his eyes set on his father in hatred; across his cheek, white as the tablecloth, could be seen the fiery mark of a hand.

For a moment father and son stood glaring at each other across the table with its sadly besplattered cloth. Then Rupert flung his hand to his cheek and rushed wildly from the room, while his two sisters, now that the strain was over, burst into tears and flung themselves in their mother's arms. It was a period scene, worthy of the pages of any Victorian novel. In the midst of the weeping girls, the frightened women, the indignant gentlemen, lay the roast of beef, pierced to its red heart. The long bone knife swayed back and forth like a clock's pendulum, measuring off the early moments of the new year.

four

Next morning Adolph Konrad awoke before dawn with a sour taste in his mouth and a feeling which he might have analyzed as depression, had he ever heard of the word. Like all intelligent people, he instantly remembered the happenings of the night before, remembered them and at once put them out of his mind. The new day claimed him the moment he threw off his covers, and its urgent demands left no time for reflections on the old. Having stepped out of his flannel night-gown into an icy tub, having dried himself and shaved and put on his clothes, Adolph clumped downstairs in the hip boots he had been wearing almost every day for the last twenty years. Had Chicago not been Chicago, those boots and the lumberman's shirt and the black shoestring tie would have seemed strange in that quarter-million-dollar Drexel Boulevard house.

He was glad to see that every sign of yesterday's festivities had disappeared (though it was not yet six) and that the house looked as on any other morning: no empty goblets, no cigar ash, the lights of the chandelier glinting on the armored figure at the foot of the stairs. Adolph stopped to raise the warrior's visor, which had a habit of falling down over the wax face, and as he did so, the butler Hauptman stepped out from the pantry with a feather duster in his hand.

"Goot day, Mr. Konrad," Hauptman murmured, freezing to attention in the German manner, duster held stiffly before him, like an army rifle.

Adolph passed him with scarcely a nod. Accepting deference as his due, it did not strike him as strange that he should be worshiped as a slave by a man who with better qualifications might have become as wealthy as he. For by a curious coincidence it happened that this Hauptman had emigrated to America, the land of golden opportunity, from the very same section of Schwabenland as Adolph Konrad. That circumstance constituted a bond, never mentioned yet at the same time never wholly forgotten. To be sure, Hauptman would not have dared to speak to Adolph in German; he had tried it a few times and been met by a frigid stare. Even Hauptman's occasional reliance on German words irritated his master, who sometimes yelled at him, "Gott demn, vhat are you trying to say? Can't you speak English, *Dummkopf?*" And yet it was known by one and all that Hauptman's position in Sans Souci was as permanent and secure as that of the metal-clad warrior on the stairs.

On the breakfast veranda William sat swallowing porridge, his stocky body seeming to expand a little with each mouthful. Adolph, as he took his place beside him, felt reassured, yet at the same time vaguely irritated, by his eldest son's smug concentration on the task at hand.

He'll never disobey, never get mad, never be late for an appointment, thought Adolph, remembering the fiery scene of the night before. Yes, yes, he tried to console himself, my William is a good boy.

"I like that friend of yours, Gladys Hastey," he remarked a little later, wanting to reward William for his obedience. "You can ask her here again."

"Oh, thank you, Papa!" William beamed. "Very well brought up, isn't she? I hope that she wasn't too disgusted at Rupert's behavior."

Adolph scowled. He certainly wasn't very bright, this eldest son of his! How was it that William never knew what not to say and when not to say it?

"Rupert didn't sleep at home last night, Papa. His bed is still made. I wonder where he could have gone to?"

"To hell, I hope," growled Adolph, pushing back his chair. "Vell, are you ready already? Come along now, Villiam. Come along."

"Yes, Papa. Right away!"

William gulped down the last of his porridge, his eye set yearningly on the bowl. As Adolph rose, he quickly helped himself again and bolted another plateful in a second; a little blob of oatmeal and cream went slithering down his chin.

Beneath the portico of Sans Souci, Hirsch was flapping his arms in the black chill morning. He had on his long coachman's overcoat, while the horse, Bismarck, was protected from the cold by a blanket with the initials "A.K." upon it; with the animal's every breath a plume of mist was sent out into the darkness. Hirsch ran to open the buggy door.

"Cold day," said Adolph, climbing into the carriage and letting Hirsch hand him the reins.

"Yes, Mr. Konrad, it sure is," Hirsch agreed, as he glanced towards the sun, just visible over the horizon. Perhaps he was wondering why a multimillionaire felt compelled to set out at this hour of the morning, but he knew better than to ask. "Good morning, Mr. William," Hirsch added as the eldest son hurried out in his bowler hat and black bulky coat. "And isn't Mr. Rupert coming?"

Without giving William a chance to answer, Adolph cracked his whip, and the buggy's wheels began to grind over the frost-covered gravel and then down the driveway leading to the road. They passed a gardener busy sweeping loose snow from the drive, and a glasshouse, its windows covered with straw thatching. Adolph did not speak, and William, holding his bowler hat with one hand, could think of nothing to say that would not remain as well unsaid. Having reached the wrought-iron gates, Adolph pulled on the reins to bring Bismarck to a halt before swinging into Drexel Boulevard; he never knew nowadays when one of those newfangled automobiles would go tearing past at twenty miles an hour, and Bismarck, winner of two red ribbons for carriage horses, was a frisky, high-tempered beast. Adolph made William jump down and have a look to right and left to make sure that the coast was clear.

As they were trotting down Forty-seventh Street snow began sifting down from the gray sky, while an icy wind blew on them from the north. William, shivering in his greatcoat, wondered how it was that his father never seemed to feel either cold or heat, nor to experience any of the other physical discomforts, such as fatigue and hunger; William had known him to go forty-eight hours without a meal, which to his way of thinking was more remarkable than any other of his father's exploits. Here he was now, clad in nothing heavier than his old corduroy jacket, and as usual without a hat, his big head thrown back so as to get the full blast of the wind. He kept Bismarck to a trot, although fresh snow had fallen during the night and had not yet been swept away; it would soon be weather for a sleigh, but he knew that even then Adolph would drive to his office every morning, clad exactly as in summer, but for a checkered scarf around his throat. William had never ceased to be amazed at this constitutional robustness, so singularly lacking in his four brothers and sisters, and in himself.

They met a horse-drawn streetcar filled with early morning workers, some of whom pressed their exhausted-looking faces against the panes to watch the smart buggy swish past; in comparison to the two hacks pulling their rumbling conveyance, Bismarck was a beast from another world, a winged Pegasus! A little later they saw a long line of workers heading towards a factory whose warning whistle was shrieking as they passed. The men were ill clad, more miserable-looking than the

27

favored group riding in the streetcar; with his quick eye Adolph placed them as sweatshop workers, less strong, hence lower-salaried than the big Polacks and Hunkies whom he employed in his own Stock Yards plant. The whole lot of them together weren't worth one hair of Bismarck's mane, reflected Adolph, and flicked the sleek flank of his gelding with the whip.

Father and son had not yet exchanged a word when Adolph drove his buggy through the Stock Yards entrance, saluting the gateman by a flourish of his whip. It still lacked some minutes to seven o'clock, and only the vanguard of the thirty thousand workers had streamed into the yards, specialized employees for the most part, together with some riffraff headed for the various employment bureaus. Adolph always made a point of getting to his office before the rest of the staff, aware that it put him at a tactical advantage. However, the cattle market had been under way for a good hour, and the sharp cries of the buyers rose above the lowing of animals which seemed to form an aural counterpart to the noisome stench hovering over the yards. Rich, sweet, and sensuous, that typical Chicago odor was concentrated in this square mile where it had its origin.

Adolph had to draw up at the railway tracks to let a late cattle train rumble past, and through the slats of the boxcars he and William could see the animals standing so tightly packed that it would have been hard to squeeze a cat among them. All through the night those trains had been clattering into the yards, coming from Kansas, from Iowa, from Texas and the Far Western states; they carried with them the ten thousand cattle, the ten thousand pigs, the five thousand sheep required to fill the daily wants of this brick and iron monster.

When the train gates were raised, Adolph drove on past the pens, raising his whip in salute to various drovers and cattle brokers circulating on horseback between the enclosures. Occasionally he recognized one of his own buyers, and would stop to exchange a word about the day's transactions; William would lean forward with cupped ear in the buggy seat so as not to miss a word above the mooing and bleating and squealing of the multitude. Instructions noted, the buyer would go galloping off to some designated pen, and a moment later his strident voice could be heard bidding against competitors in a code language

28

that would have been gibberish to an outsider. Only to Adolph's ears did those sharp angry cries have all the beauty of an aria swelling and fading on a grand opera stage.

They left the pens and Bismarck trotted past the smoke-stained buildings that comprised the huge Hastey plant, and then those of Armitage and Company, almost as extensive. Smoke was already pouring from the tall chimneys, joining overhead in that gritty cloud which forever veiled the sky from the denizens of this mechanized city. Now and then the wind would come, to gather up handfuls of smoke and fling them over the buildings; it seemed at such times as if a heavy natural mist had settled over the whole area of the yards. As yet the chutes connecting the pens to the slaughterhouse were empty, but soon the streams of condemned beasts would begin to flow along them, a stream which would eventually emerge from the same building transformed into ham, beef, mutton, and the innumerable subsidiary products of the yards.

Now Bismarck was picking his way without direction between the buildings marked "Adolph Konrad Company," his delicate nostrils quivering, as though under the conglomerate stench he were trying to make out the happy smell of the private stables where he would spend his day. At the entrance of the General Office Building his master brought him to a halt, and at this point William was entrusted with the reins. Adolph gave Bismarck a lump of sugar, his son a wave of the hand, before stepping into the little world which he had set into action through the sweat of his brow, the brilliance of his mind, and the creative capacity which has nothing to do with either intelligence or effort, but is the monopoly and the hallmark of genius.

five

Angus McKenna was sitting in his office, filing correspondence, as Adolph passed down the corridor. The sight of that bony head bent over the papers gave Adolph an unpleasant twinge. It was not so much the fact that McKenna had again beaten him to the office, as the impression he received that it was a mechanism rather than a man sitting there, sifting correspondence with the impersonality of those elaborate machines in the packing plant that sorted out meat according to size and weight. For some reason he found this machine-man rather terrifying.

"Mornin', McKenna," Adolph said, as he peered through the half-open door. (Strange that he could not bring himself to call the man by his first name! With others who had not been with him half so long he never hesitated.) "I see that a late night doesn't faze you vone bit."

"Late night?" McKenna seemed scarcely to remember there had been one. "Oh no, indeed. Mrs. McKenna and I enjoyed ourselves very much," he added, being always carefully polite. Then he went on with the relief of a specialist returning to his field, "Mr. Konrad, there's a letter here we ought to discuss."

"A letter? How d'you get it? The mail hasn't come yet," Adolph shot out suspiciously.

"It was left with the watchman last night. A New Year's present from the union, Mr. Konrad. They're complaining again."

"The union! Alvays that demn union! Gott demn their souls!" cried Adolph, flaring up like gunpowder at contact with a match. The word "union" always had that effect on him.

"They're complaining about conditions in the pickle rooms," said McKenna, having waited for the first blast to pass. "It's signed by that man Gogerty."

"Demn fool! Demn fool! Ought to have his cheeky mouth stopped up!"

"They'll always get someone to write their letters," McKenna said dryly. "Gogerty's of no importance. If he were, we'd have fixed him long ago."

"Und vhat is it that Mr. Gogerty complains about today?" Adolph asked acidly.

"Oh, you know—the usual line. What they call health conditions! He says the pickling solution's an inch high on the floor and it eats through the shoes; says there're cases of men who've had to have their toes amputated. He speaks of the pneumonia rate too. To believe him, you'd think it was suicide for a man just to step into a pickle room!"

30

"He can go to hell. Yes, to hell! Listen, McKenna, you tell that cheeky bastard that he can go straight to hell. D'you hear me?"

"Yes, Mr. Konrad," McKenna replied.

But Adolph could detect a note of doubt in the voice, and he began to get mad at McKenna also. If there was one thing he disliked, it was having his paid employees telling him how to run his business!

"Vell, vhat's the matter, McKenna? Spit it out, man! Don't sit there looking like Jesus Christ on the Cross. Spit it out!"

"If you ask my advice," McKenna said, stroking his chin, "I'd be for giving them a civil answer. The fact is, as you know, that we've been meaning to install new drains in the pickling rooms. It wouldn't cost much, and it'd take the wind out of the union's sails. We'd have a stronger position when it comes to fighting them on something more important. That's what I think Mr. Konrad."

"Und not me!" Adolph shouted at the top of his lungs. "No, Mc-Kenna! Positively no! Give them vone finger und they'll vant the whole hand. Pickle on the floor, eh? Vhy shouldn't there be pickle on the floor? D'you t'ink when I vas a kid vorking in a factory in the old country, there vas somevone to sweep up the floor for me? Don't make me laugh, McKenna! You write this man Gogerty und tell him that if the pickle men vant to quit, it's okay mit me."

"They're sending a delegation this morning, Mr. Konrad."

"Oh, they are? Then tell the delegation chust vhat I said. Und I don't vant to see them," he added almost in panic. "I hate those demn union men. You speak to 'em, McKenna."

"Very well, Mr. Konrad," McKenna answered after a pause. "You're the boss, sir. But don't forget that we're living in the twentieth century."

"Oh, that's okay, McKenna." Adolph smiled for the first time. "I'll lick the twentieth century just like I licked the nineteenth. See if I don't! You bet your bottom dollar. Ain't vorried, are you?"

Angus McKenna, peering up through pale eyes, gave a shrug of his shoulders. It was a typical gesture, meaning either affirmation or negation, as you wished to take it; perhaps it implied a combination of the two. But you only had to look at McKenna's stony face to know one thing for certain: he was not worried for himself.

31

In Adolph's own office, at the end of the corridor, the man called Chippy was dusting the furniture. Neither office boy nor secretary, neither watchman nor reception clerk, Chippy's position was as indefinite as his age. His height was about four feet six, his weight under a hundred, and he had drifted into Adolph's life entirely by chance, having been discovered one winter morning by Max Heinrich, head manager at the time, three-quarters frozen, on the doorsteps. Heinrich had taken him upstairs and thawed him out at Adolph's stove, whose close vicinity he had scarcely quit since, spending his days in the corridor and his nights on a cot dragged into the office. He received no fixed salary, but did get an indefinite amount in tips, including an occasional ten-dollar bill when Adolph was feeling good.

"Mornin', boss," the little man greeted Adolph in his high squeaky voice. ("He sounds like a scared chipmunk," someone had once said, and since then the nickname "Chippy" had stood.) "Cold day, boss. Mighty cold day. B'r'r."

"It'll put hair on your chest," said Adolph vaguely, which, if true, would have been a compensatory dispensation, for certainly there was none on Chippy's bald head.

"That's right, boss," Chippy said, and being sensitive to his employer's moods, he scurried out into the corridor with his broom and duster. He could be heard out there, sweeping away like mad and whistling "I been workin' on de levee" through the gap between his two remaining teeth.

To Adolph Konrad running a business really meant *running* it. Despite the growth and spread of his company, he still maintained the same personal control as when he stood quartering hogs purchased before dawn at the maimed-animal market. At that time he had functioned in a ramshackle shed, disposing of perhaps six carcasses a day; gradually he had expanded, taking on a few more workers one month, a few more the next, renting a brick house, finally buying it, then buying another. And in the end he had seen the business mushroom into what it was today: a vast concern employing over three thousand workers and occupying nearly a dozen different buildings.

Of course he could no longer supervise adequately the various divisions of his huge plant. Not even with the help of his two sons could he have checked on the work on the killing floors, in the refrigerator plants, in the barrel factory and cannery, in the cooking and pickling rooms. It had to be left to the managers, and to the section bosses under the managers, and to foremen under the section bosses. A huge organization was functioning that called itself Adolph Konrad Company, but every string of control was still held by the man with the great shaggy head who this morning sat whittling a stick in his untidy office. Seeing that he no longer could be everywhere at once, he had his foremen report directly to him, and it was during these morning hours that he received them, each at his appointed time.

"Hello, Seversky. Vhat's new on the big floor?" he greeted the man in charge of the great room where steers were dispatched and their hung carcasses bled, decapitated, gutted, and skinned. And as Seversky reported on the number of animals handled (mentioning the fact that one steer had broken loose and gone charging about until dispatched by a bullet), Adolph sat whittling his stick, eyes set hard on the foreman's face. Through Seversky he was able to project himself onto the slaughtering floor; listening to that guttural voice with the Polish accent, he could hear the bellowing of the cattle and the heavy thud of the sledge-hammer blows that rained on their heads; he even heard the rush of the blood as it torrented out of the cut throats onto the killing-room floor. It was the next best thing to being present on the scene. He had elevated Seversky from the ranks, and he had confidence in him; watching the man's eyes, he would have known at once if all was not well on the slaughtering floor.

The door of Adolph's office creaked open, and in the slot showed a bald pate and a worried weasel's face.

"Sorry, boss," Chippy squeaked. "Awfully sorry, boss. There's someone out here wants to see you, and he won't go away."

Adolph's black eyes flashed fire.

"Gott demn you, Chippy! Haven't I told you a hundred times that I don't vant to be disturbed? Vhat good are you, anyvay—you demn fool!"

"Sorry, boss. Sorry. But . . . but it's Mr. Heinrich."

Adolph brought his fist crashing down on the desk. Now Chippy knew that the boss was really mad; it showed in the pouting of his lips and the twitching of his big nose. There were several stages to Adolph

Konrad's furies, but this was the worst. Chippy turned to scurry into the corridor and beg the visitor to go away, but already the man called Heinrich had stepped past him. Almost double Chippy in height, his tow hair falling down his broad forehead, the tall fellow walked up to Adolph's desk.

"Adolph, I've got to talk to you! You've got to listen to me, Adolph."

Adolph stared up without answering. His face was expressionless, but the knife in his hand kept whittling away, sending splinters flying through the air. Chippy, watching from the doorway, saw that he was drawing the knife *towards* him, rather than away, and he knew that that was a bad augury for Mr. Heinrich.

"I t'ought I told you not to come back here!" Adolph said after an icy pause. "Your memory must have got pretty punk, Max Heinrich. Never vas no demn good, as I recall."

The big man took the jibe without protest; he even let a smile creep into his face, as though by agreeing with Adolph he might slip into his good graces. It was a gentle smile, gentle and somehow ineffectual.

"My memory's good enough to remember that," he said. "I'll remember it all my life. You can bet that I never would have come back, Adolph, but . . ." The smile faded, and now the expression of his face became taut, harassed. ". . . but this is a question of life or death! My wife's life or death," he added, lowering his voice and sending a glance towards Seversky, who sat there stolidly in his checked shirt and dungarees.

But Adolph refused to take the hint; that would have made it too easy for Heinrich.

"Spit it out!" he shouted. "Spit it out qvick, Heinrich! I haven't got all day. Und Seversky he stays right here."

Heinrich put a big hand on the desk and leaned across it, his eyes seeking Adolph's in vain. Adolph was staring straight over the tall fellow's shoulder.

"I'm broke, Adolph," he said. "Dead, stony broke. Haven't got ten dollars—haven't got five dollars to my name. I haven't had a job that you could call a job since you kicked me out of here. Without your okay I haven't a ghost's chance of getting one. And my wife"—he lowered his voice again—"my wife is going to have a baby."

34

Adolph remained immobile; but for the play of the hand that held the knife, he was like a figure hewn of stone.

"Yes," he said finally, still without moving his eyes to meet Heinrich's. "Yes. Und vhere do I fit in mit all this?"

"A word from you, Adolph!" The big man was speaking urgently, desperately now; drops of sweat had sprung out on his forehead and he wiped them away with the back of his hand. "You're my oldest friend in this city—only man I could count on, I always thought. You saved my life once, when I lay sick on that boat coming to America. We were partners, Adolph, and . . . and I worked for you for fifteen years."

There was another pause, and gradually into Heinrich's face crept the expression of a man who knows he is beaten; his big hand on the table slid away and fell down by his side. Seversky, in the meanwhile, sat there with jaw protruding and a glint in his eye; it was clear how he despised this fool who had committed the unpardonable fault of getting on the bad side of the boss.

"That's right," said Adolph finally, and he gave a nod. "I saved your life vonce, Heinrich, but I von't do it again. Vhat's the point of saving the life of such a veak, gutless fool? Vonce a veakling, alvays a veakling! If you'd had any guts, you vouldn't have let me buy you out of de business, und then come right back on my pay roll. Is that how a *man* acts? But I still liked you, Max Heinrich! I liked you real vell. That's vhy I don't like you now. You vent against me, und that's vone thing I'll never forgive from any man vhat I pay."

"Went against you? No, Adolph, you're wrong!" Heinrich was making a last effort, but it was clear he had small hopes of success. "God knows," he said, "I've been loyal to you since the day we stepped off that ship. Didn't I stick to you through hell and high water? But there are different ways of showing guts, Adolph! When it came to sending rotten meat to those soldiers in the Caribbean (yes, stinking, rotten meat that was going to lay hundreds of them out like rats) . . . Well, Adolph, a man's got to draw the line somewhere!"

But Adolph had jumped up, and his face had gone white and his big lips were working out and in furiously.

"You get de hell out of here!" he shouted. "I told you before, Heinrich, I don't vant never to hear about that demn meat again. Did I know that it vas rotten? It vas the business of them vhat bought it, und a hell of a lot they cared. You say that you're in trouble? Vell, get some demn fool like you to help you out of your trouble. Not me!"

For a second Heinrich stood there, staring at his former boss. Chippy, peering in through the doorway, felt his throat tighten because of the unhappiness in that nice Mr. Heinrich's face. But then an unexpected thing happened: Heinrich smiled. The same smile as before, gentle and ineffectual, chased away his expression of defeat: one would have said that he was almost pleased with the outcome of their conversation.

"Okay, Adolph," he said. "I'm going. But before I leave I'm going to tell you one thing, for it's a thing you ought to know, Adolph. One can't keep treating men as you do! Men aren't pigs, Adolph Konrad. Remember that! Men are men."

Chippy was still peeking in from the corridor, and now he noticed something that surprised him through and through; for the first time in his experience, the first time in these long years that he had known Adolph, the boss seemed at a loss for words! He stood there, scowling and glaring up at Heinrich, but for a moment he did not speak. And that silence, brief though it was, told Chippy something about Adolph that he had never known. So the boss was not invulnerable! There was a chink in the armor, after all! Like a rodent hiding away nuts, Chippy stored away his discovery for possible future use.

But even before Chippy had got over his shock, Adolph became his own self again. Pounding his fist on the desk top, shouting at the top of his lungs, he seemed bent on erasing the memory of that moment of weakness.

"You get de hell out of here," he screamed at Heinrich. "Vhat the devil d'you mean, anyvay, breaking into my office und carrying on? I'll teach you for vhat's vhat. Son of a bitch, you. Come on, Seversky, throw the bastard out of here!"

Seversky had only been waiting for those words. Leaping from his chair, he made a dash for the intruder, who was almost knocked off his feet. Pinioning his arms behind his back, he rushed him to the door, and with a hefty shove sent him crashing into the corridor. Poor

36

Chippy had to dodge away, lest Mr. Heinrich knock him over in his fall.

As he scurried into a corner the terrified little man cast a quick glance across his shoulder. For the fraction of a second he could see Adolph standing by his desk—the fraction of a second only, but long enough for Chippy to receive another shock. Whether or not it was his imagination, he could have sworn that Adolph's eyes, set on the fallen Heinrich, had in them a sad, almost a tender look! Then the door banged to, and a grim silence followed. Chippy, listening to that silence, his little heart aflutter, could think only of one thing: of how Adolph Konrad had stared and stared at Mr. Heinrich, and had not found a single word to say!

six

Stepping off the train in Back Bay station, Rupert Konrad experienced a sensation of pure delight. It was, he thought, exactly like coming home! The clean, quiet station, the polite attendants, the orderly rhythm of New England life, all enchanted the young man and evoked comparisons between this cultured New England city and the vulgar capital of the Middle West.

Through the window of his closed horse cab, Rupert looked out on the Charles River, and a little later onto well-proportioned Harvard Square. They trotted past some of the college dormitories, including the one where he had spent three happy terms, then down a street with several famous clubs. Bitterness at his father flared up anew as he reflected that he should by rights be dining in the most select of those establishments at the moment.

In his imagination Rupert saw himself seated at a delightful dinner table, surrounded by well-bred people for whom Stock Yard smells, coarse German accents, and tasteless furnishings were things to be read about and avoided with horror. There were not only pleasant young men at Rupert's grand table; among the diners were lovely women as well, and at the head sat the most exquisite of all, her lithe figure swathed in green silk, her pale hair worn deep on her neck in an elegant chignon. He did not have to look at her face; he knew that one woman alone could occupy the position of honor at that idealized dinner table that appeared ever and again in his day dreams. That woman was Helen Mason!

Rupert's excitement had reached its peak by the time he stepped out of the brougham before Professor Mason's pale yellow house. Prim and discreet it looked behind the well-trimmed box hedge. As he was taking out some money the sound of piano music reached him across the snowy lawn. Rupert stiffened into immobility, the dollar bills suspended on their journey to the cabman's palm. Those tinkly notes sounded like icicles shattering on the frozen ground, or like water running in a mountain brook. The music, austere and pure, filled the young Chicagoan with exultation. Now he understood that the decision which had pushed him onto the train and sent him rocking across a third of the American continent had been inevitable; standing there on the New England road, he reaffirmed what he had first determined in his father's dining room, trembling and insulted, with the sound of a brutal blow echoing in the air.

She was seated at the piano when the maid showed him in, half turning towards him, one hand on the keys. The late afternoon sun fell through the window, glimmering on the blond hair that she had gathered in a low bun on the nape of her neck—perhaps because he admired it that way. Pale, pale, was her hair—almost silvery—and it seemed to Rupert that Helen, too, had a silvery sheen. In the split second before she rose to greet him she looked a little uncertain, a little frightened, he thought. Perhaps it was that quality of suppressed panic that made the professor's daughter seem so beautiful, so eminently desirable that day.

"Rupert!"

"Oh, Helen! Thank the Lord, oh, thank the good Lord that I have found you!"

They did not kiss, though they had been on kissing terms for over a year. Both realized that this was no occasion for embraces; it had about it an atmosphere of fatality that caused them to look at each other as though they were doing so for the first time. As Rupert took her hand

and led her to the window alcove, Helen never moved her eyes from his face. Perhaps she was thinking that Rupert, with his pale harassed countenance, the high forehead, and those burning black eyes, was handsomer than she had ever realized before.

They sank down by the window, on the farther side of which a young boy and girl were passing with skates on their shoulders, while Whip, the professor's terrier, could be seen chasing an uninterested-looking poodle across the lawn. Rupert was still holding her hand.

"Helen," he said, "I've left them—for good."

"Your—family?"

He nodded.

"I couldn't stand it any longer—the killing, the smells, the blood. And our own home; just an annex of the Stock Yards, with my father, the head butcher, presiding. I'm never going back there again."

"It was brave of you, Rupert! Very brave. And what will you do now?"

"I'll look for a job, here in the East. Anything—it doesn't matter. When I've saved some money I'll go into the diplomatic service. You know that's what I've always wanted—to see strange countries, meet fascinating people. But it all depends on you! That's why I came here, Helen. I had to ask you . . ."

"What?" There was fright in her voice now; it could be seen in her eyes too, and in the corners of her unformed mouth. "What did you have to ask me?" she whispered, dreading his answer and longing for it as one longs for one's unavoidable fate.

"To marry me," said Rupert after a pause. "That's what I came to ask you today."

There was a long silence in the little room. The sun had fallen under the horizon, taking with it the vivid colors of the curtains and of the cut flowers in the vase; Helen's pale hair was like a silver crescent glimmering in the dusk. Now the snow on the front lawn looked like sparkling diamonds no longer, but like a sheet of dull metal, bluish-gray in color. Across it came trotting Whip, with a frustrated gait, having given up his chase of the joyless poodle.

"Have you really thought it over?" Helen asked finally, but it was only to gain time. "Do you think we are suited for each other, Rupert?"

He answered quickly: "I know that you are made for me. How can you have doubts? You love me, Helen. You wrote me . . ."

She pressed his hand, not knowing how to answer. Yes, she did love Rupert, it was true; when he spoke to her, or when he held her in his arms and kissed her, she felt that her love was deep and that she wanted more than anything in the world to have Rupert for her husband. And yet there was that uncertainty in her heart, never quite stilled, that little warning bell that ever gave forth a tinkle when she thought of joining her life to his.

"I do love you, Rupert," she said, putting conviction in her voice. "You know that! But do you really want a wife for whom children, and the home, and even her husband, won't be the beginning and end of her world? There will always be my piano, you know. I'm warning you."

"I would always want there to be," Rupert answered. "Do you think I'm so old-fashioned not to want a wife with a career?"

"Of course not!" She was superficially reassured. "You are sweet, Rupert. And I do love you."

"Then—it's decided?"

At the last moment she stopped herself from nodding.

"Let us think about it," she said. "It's so—so sudden, isn't it? You must let me get used to the idea. . . . Ah, there's Father coming across the lawn!" She broke off and pointed through the window with a gesture that had in it something of relief. "I told him that you'd be staying on for supper. But it'll be a very simple meal, I'm afraid—just waffles and syrup. You don't mind not having meat?"

He began to laugh.

"Oh, Helen, if you knew how many tons of roast beef I'd trade for one helping of New England waffles! Especially *your* waffles. I think that when we're married, I shall become a vegetarian too. . . ."

A moment later Professor Mason could be heard knocking the snow from his galoshes in the vestibule.

"Down, Whip!" he was saying. "That's enough now, my friend. Haven't I taught you better manners?"

Rupert began to feel ill at ease almost instantly. Helen's father

40

seemed to him almost as terrifying in one way as his own father was in another. Under the professor's vague, gentle manner lay an indomitable will inherited from generations of staunch forefathers. He was a New England perfectionist; just as he demanded of Whip the obedience suitable to a dog, so he demanded of Helen the high achievement and moral integrity befitting the daughter of a teacher of philosophy in Harvard University.

"Good evening, Professor Mason," said Rupert, forcing a natural tone to impress Helen.

"Ah, Rupert." The professor eyed the visitor over the top of his bifocals, then walked over slowly to shake hands. "A pleasant trip on the train?"

"Very pleasant," said Rupert, feeling that he was falling into a deferential manner despite himself. "It's nice to be back here."

"Is it?" inquired the professor in a tone of mild surprise. "You left us rather sooner than expected, didn't you? I'm sorry you didn't stay to take a degree. It's a bad thing to give up any journey at the halfway mark—bad for the voyager, I mean. A person should always go through with what he—or she—has set out to do," concluded the professor, accompanying that last remark with a significant glance at Helen.

"It wasn't Rupert's fault, Daddy." She came to his rescue. "Rupert's father wouldn't let him come back, though he wanted to very much."

"Yes, yes, I remember." Still the professor did not seem to believe this, or only to half believe it; that was evident from the quizzical glint in his eyes as they analyzed Rupert. "Well, it's a shame anyway," he said. "You should have told your father that there are more important things in life than making another million dollars. He's a clever man. You might have impressed him."

"I'm afraid not," said Rupert. "My father's a clever man, as you say, but he's stubborn."

"He wouldn't have made a fortune if he hadn't been," Professor Mason agreed. "But there is the maid calling us in to dinner. Daughter, will you lead the way?"

During dinner Rupert's main task consisted in keeping his eyes from wandering, thus giving away the fact that he was less interested in the professor's conversation than in his daughter. Demure in her black

41

dress, she sat, picking sparingly at her waffles and acting the part of hostess in an unobtrusive yet utterly gracious fashion. Whence had she got that superb elegance of hers? Rupert kept asking himself. He supposed it was from her mother, now dead, who had been of aristocratic Austrian descent and been known as a violinist of talent. Whether or not it was she who had bestowed on Helen grace and distinction, the fact remained that it was there. Watching Helen from the corner of his eye, Rupert again saw before him that dinner table of his imagining, which was *his* dinner table, with Helen at the head, exquisite in a gown which fell in folds from her shoulders, swathing her in soft green.

Dinner over at last (they seemed to Rupert to have taken an inordinately long time to consume some waffles and maple syrup), the professor burrowed into a corner with a book. Helen and Rupert found themselves free to go for a stroll down the snowy road. Both young people were excited, and though they talked of other things, each knew the thoughts that were passing in the other's brain; unspoken questions and answers accompanied them on their walk as closely as the professor's terrier trotting at their heels. Sensing Helen's reluctance to continue their afternoon's conversation, Rupert concentrated on his favorite subject: himself. Unconstrained for the first time in months, he recounted the painful history of his Stock Yards interlude, describing so vividly the gruesome sights and sounds and smells that he began to feel sorrier and sorrier for himself. Through the very act of listening Helen seemed to grow closer to him, the fact being that Rupert Konrad had a constitutional need of female sympathy.

When they came back to the house they found the professor still buried behind William James's *Principles of Psychology*. He looked up and gave Helen one of his gentle smiles.

"Nice walk, Daughter? Whip looks as if he'd enjoyed it."

"Well, he certainly doesn't get out on many walks with his master!" Helen leaned down to kiss the top of her father's head. "How long since you've been further than from here to the class hall?"

The professor made a vague gesture and mumbled something about taking up walking in the spring. Helen gave a hopeless shrug which

42

told Rupert better than words what she and her widowed father meant to one another.

"I like the professor. I do truly," Rupert said, as they made their way into the music room next door. "I'm sorry that he disapproves of me."

"Oh, he doesn't really. He just disapproves of your being a Konrad. Besides, he disapproves in principle of anyone who doesn't meet his own terribly high standard. He's against people who can't perform miracles!" said Helen.

In the young girl's voice was a bitterness that surprised Rupert, so recently reminded of her daughterly affection. There was resentment here: the resentment of the pupil against the teacher who demands accomplishments beyond his strength.

"But what does he expect me to do—give away my money and become a pauper?" cried Rupert, giving vent to his indignation at last.

"He doesn't expect anything. He just keeps making one feel ashamed of oneself, because he's so wonderful himself. If I told you some of the things Daddy does! You know how badly off he is, on an assistant professor's salary, but at this moment he's supporting three other people who aren't even related to us. Without the slightest hesitation he takes on every new burden that comes his way."

"They're new burdens for you too," remarked Rupert.

"Oh, of course. No wonder we haven't been able to take a holiday for the last four years! I know I shouldn't complain, and I do admire Daddy more than anyone, but sometimes I feel that there are limits to what one should demand of oneself—and of other people. Mama was a gay sweet little woman, but Papa never let her laugh, and in the end, she stopped laughing. Some people can't live without laughing! He's trying to do the same to me. Daddy wants me to be not a good pianist, but the best woman pianist in the world. I practice six hours a day and always feel that I ought to practice six more. I can't do it!" cried Helen, with desperation in her voice. "I want fun too. I'm no different from anybody else."

"Of course you aren't, my sweetheart," Rupert said. "And if you let me, I'll give you all the fun you want. Six hours a day! My goodness, what does the man want? I think it's simply wonderful that you play as well as you do. Matter of fact, I wish you'd play something for me right now. I love listening to you."

"Oh, Rupert, you know how I feel about playing for people!"

"So I'm 'people' now!"

"No, silly, naturally you're not. But I've already told you that Madame Lubokova, my wonderful piano teacher, has made me promise never to play just to *entertain* anyone. She says it would be a 'betrayal of the piano.'"

"She certainly must have a lot of respect for your playing, Helen!"

"Well, she does say I've made progress. She's really encouraging. Does that sound conceited?"

He smiled, thinking how far she was from conceit. And he should have known, coming from Chicago!

"She says that she wants me to give a concert next year," Helen told him. "She's going to arrange the whole thing—get a hall for me in Boston, and see to publicity and so on. You can't imagine how exciting . . ."

Suddenly she noticed that Rupert was tugging away at his ear lobe. His favorite gesture, it always meant that he was not listening to what one said. When she stopped speaking, he came out of his thoughts quickly and put on a semblance of enthusiasm.

"Why, Helen, that certainly is exciting news! By the way," he went on, "I wish you'd tell me what you were playing this afternoon as I came up the drive. Couldn't I hear it again?"

Helen hesitated a moment, then sat down and played a movement from Beethoven's "Appassionata." She had considerable virtuosity and a great deal of feeling for her music; Rupert could not have known it, but he was listening to a rendition that might have won her the acclaim of an exacting audience in a concert hall. He clapped when she had finished, and Helen, who was not only an artist but a woman, was as gratified by that applause as she had been by the praise of Madame Lubokova, one of the finest piano teachers in the East.

Much later she accompanied him across the lawn and they said good night in the shelter of a snow-sprinkled shrub bordering the road. All evening they had not kissed, but now Rupert put his arm about her waist, and at once Helen came into his embrace, not diffidently, as she used to do, but as if she had been looking forward to this moment. She turned up her face, and when their lips met Rupert knew without the shadow of a doubt what her answer would be. Scarcely would he have to repeat his question.

seven

Back in the hall of the inn a single light was burning and a man with a mop and a pail of soapy water was scrubbing the floor. Ten-thirty, Rupert noted, glancing at the clock above the reception desk. He was about to climb the stairs when he caught sight of a familiar figure in the leather armchair facing the entrance doorway. With a shock of dismay, Rupert recognized his own mother dozing there!

His first thought was to turn and tiptoe out of the inn. He felt trapped, and the thought came to him (he used to have it sometimes at college) that he was not like other boys—a person who could disappear in the crowd. The Konrad money branded him, as might a title, or some physical defect. Even before his mother had opened her eyes Rupert knew that it was too late to escape—that it always had been too late to escape.

"Rupert!"

He halted with one foot on the stairs.

"Mama! How on earth did you know . . . ?"

"Because I love you," Mama said simply. "Where would my boy go, if not to Cambridge? And where in Cambridge, if not to this inn? Aren't you going to kiss me, Son?"

He came back from the stairs and walked over to Mama's armchair. She was looking tired, he saw, and there were deep lines of worry about her mouth; probably she had scarcely closed her eyes since he left the house two days before. The thought not only moved Rupert but gratified his deep-seated desire to occupy the center of the stage.

"Mama," he burst out, having given her a peck on one cheek. "Mama, I do think I'm old enough to take a little trip when I like. I'm

45

almost twenty-one, please remember! What do you want of me, anyway?"

Mama did not get up from her chair. Usually so full of energy, she acted tonight like an exhausted old woman; the look that she turned on Rupert was an entreaty, not a challenge.

"What I want? I want you not to make a fool of yourself, Son! I want you to apologize to your father."

"Apologize! Was it *I* who hit *him?*" Rupert cried.

"Who was to blame is no matter," said Mama wearily, still sitting hunched up in her chair. "I don't care if you were wrong, or maybe Papa, or maybe the two of you. What I do say . . ." Suddenly Mama's voice had changed, had become forceful, almost violent. She jerked forward in her chair and her eyes darkened. "What I do say is that we can't have a quarrel in our family! Where there's a split, there is weakness. And our family must remain strong. Strong! Do you understand, Son? It is important, what I say."

Rupert was astonished at the change in his mother. He was used to thinking of her as a timid person, cowed by the force of his father's overwhelming personality. Now her eyes blazed, and the mauve bonnet had slipped down her forehead, giving her a quite terrifying appearance.

"Then tell Papa not to keep treating me as a child," he said querulously. "I'm not going back to the Stock Yards, and he can't make me. I hate the place! I hate it with my whole soul."

For a second an expression of horror suffused Mama's face. To her ears those were blasphemous remarks, the Stock Yards as an institution being as sacred for her as her own Lutheran-Methodist Church. But for its existence, might they not still be a group of poor German immigrants, eking out a miserable living in some forgotten back alley? Through the blood and the stench of the abattoirs had her husband established a family in the full sense of the word.

But Wilma was a woman who believed in first things coming first; she had never let her own feelings, her happiness, even her safety, stand in the way of the precious unity of the Konrad clan. When she spoke again there was conciliation in her voice.

"About that we'll speak later. I have taken your side before, haven't

46

I, Son? Perhaps I can persuade Papa to let you go back to college. But first you must come home! You must apologize to Papa. Then we'll talk about other things."

Rupert began to pace the deserted hall of the inn. Nervously he twisted his ear lobe and wrinkled his heavy eyebrows. This certainly was no place for a discussion, yet he knew that it would be better to have matters out before his courage failed. Closing his eyes, he took the leap from the tower.

"Mama," he said, "I am going to marry Professor Mason's daughter."

The silence that followed was broken only by the disagreeable swish of the porter's mop and a splash as he wrung it out in the pail. Rupert was still striding up and down, white in the face, and shaken. He realized now that he had half expected Mama to faint, or at least to burst into tears; either attitude would have been less disconcerting than the calm with which she accepted the most sensational announcement of his life. When she finally did speak, her words startled him far more than he had succeeded in startling her.

"Well, well, I'm not saying that it's a bad thing. I'm not saying yes and I'm not saying no. I'm not saying nothing at all! You are young, Son. But Papa also married when he was young. Of course this young lady isn't the sort of girl we'd have picked for your wife. With our position, you could have married a real rich girl in Chicago, someone like that Gladys Hastey, who comes from a family that counts. If you marry now, why you won't even have a job. Think of that, Son! Not even a job!"

"Helen and I will manage," Rupert replied, pretending that this did not strike home. "I'm going in the diplomatic service, and then I won't need help from anybody."

Mama nodded her head in that wise way of hers, saying much without using words. She made a point of never contradicting her children.

"Of course you'll manage," she agreed. "I'm not saying nothing at all. Still, it's too bad you can't talk it over with Papa. It's hard for a young fellow to start out nowadays. You know, Son, it's real hard."

Rupert gazed at his mother, seeking for words to convince her, for arguments to show her that nobody and nothing could dissuade him from an action as inevitable as next day's sunrise.

47

"Listen, Mama," he said, and he was conscious of the ring of sincerity in his own voice. "I need Helen. I need her—to complete my life. Try and understand me when I say that I'm not just a boy who's fallen in love with a pretty girl; I am a person *in love with his life.* I can see it lying before me, like a picture made up of many pieces— sort of like those big picture puzzles we used to lay out in the parlor. You remember how we could never finish the picture before fitting in the key piece. In my life Helen Mason is the key piece! Don't ask me how I know. I do know, Mama, and you must have faith in me. You had faith in Papa when he dreamed a dream which nobody thought could come true. My dream is different, but for me it is just as important—and just as beautiful."

Wilma looked up at her son slowly. She had grasped only part of what Rupert said (she was a countrywoman and highfalutin language was beyond her), still she did understand instinctively that this marriage was bound up with Rupert's most deeply felt ambitions. As his mother, it was not up to her to stop it! And now there came into her eyes the look of a tried politician, ready to compromise, ready to make concessions, if through doing so she could but save what was essential.

"Rupert," she said innocently, "and what if I should see this lady who you tell me is so important? It'd be right sort of convenient, wouldn't it? I'm here in Cambridge and it's not likely I'll be here again."

Rupert suppressed a yelp of joy. Never had he imagined this as the happy upshot of a conversation on which he had embarked with such painful doubts.

"Not a bad idea!" He tried to sound rather casual. "You'd like her, Mama. I know you would! And when you get back, perhaps you could speak to Papa—about our getting married."

"Speak to Papa? Why, sure!" Mama's face brightened, but almost at once she let it cloud over; slowly and sadly she shook her head. "Land's sake, Son, I couldn't do that! You know Papa. Why, he wouldn't even listen to me before your quarrel got patched up. It's a pity. It really is!"

"But, Mama, don't you think——" Rupert began, only to be cut short by Wilma's, "Don't let's say another word about it, Son. It wouldn't work. And I don't suppose I'd best see your young lady either, come to think of it. Papa would be good and mad, you know. Real mad!"

For a moment, and a moment only, Rupert wavered. Pride and self-will pulled him in one direction, his good sense in the other. He knew this was the moment to mend the rift and get Mama on his side; yet the thought of crawling back to Chicago and submitting to William's jeers made his blood run cold.

"And if I do go back, Mama—*if* I do—could you, would you, speak to Papa about her?"

Mama gave her shoulders a shrug. She looked suddenly less tired, less harassed, Rupert thought. She looked—why, she actually looked young!

"Maybe," she said, "I could at that, Son, though I'm not making any promises, mind. Why, I haven't even seen the young lady yet! Still I might be able to do it—*if* you come home. I'm not saying yes and I'm not saying no." Mama straightened her bonnet with an almost jaunty gesture. "I'm not saying nothing at all."

eight

Adolph Konrad was in one of his ornery moods. This new year, 1905, certainly had started off on the wrong track! To begin with there had been that fracas with his cheeky son, which had ended by Rupert's tearing off to Cambridge and Wilma's following on the next train without so much as a by-your-leave. (She must have gone plumb crazy! thought Adolph, this being his usual explanation for disobedience to his commands.) Then there had been the trouble with the workers in the pickle rooms. And this morning, on arriving in his office, who should he find joining the forces of revolt but little Chippy, than whom there surely was none humbler among his three thousand employees! It was almost as if one of the Konrad pigs on its way to slaughter had got up on its hind legs and begun to protest.

"Boss," squeaked Chippy, sidling into Adolph's office, "boss, cin I trouble you fer jist a minute?"

At first Adolph thought that Chippy had come in to empty the cuspidor, and he waved him away impatiently. But as the little man kept standing there, waiting for attention, he looked up and asked, "Vell, vhat is it? Spit it out, Chippy! Spit it out."

"Sorry, boss." Chippy was shifting about on his feet and was puffing out his little chest to give himself confidence. "Sorry, boss, but it's five years since I been here—five years come February. I done all right by you, boss, ain't I? You're satisfied wit' me okay?"

"Ya, ya. Okay. Sure," said Adolph, still not understanding what the fellow wanted. He had given him a ten-dollar bill before Christmas, but decided now that he may have been a bit stingy. Pulling out his wallet, he extracted a fiver, whereat the surprising Chippy put up his hand in refusal.

"Boss, that's not what I mean. What I mean is—well, it's something like this, boss: don't you think it's about time I started—gettin' a salary? Every week, I mean. Somet'in' like that. Sorry, boss, sorry."

Adolph slowly put back the five-dollar bill. He kept staring at Chippy, whose face had gone as red as the frayed woolen sweater which constituted the top part of his winter garb. (It was a castoff sweater of William's, given him at Christmas four years before.)

"Vell," said Adolph after a moment. "Vell, I'll be switched. You little son of a bitch, you!"

Chippy nodded, as if in complete agreement. He seemed to have shrunk in the last seconds; his pouter-chest had collapsed.

"Vhat d'you mean by asking me such a t'ing? Who's been talking to you—the unions?" Adolph exploded as the full extent of Chippy's effrontery struck him. "You have a good chob here in my own office. I took you in out of de gutter. Und now you come und vant for me to give you—a salary!"

Chippy himself seemed aghast at this unheard-of effrontery; he kept nodding in agreement. During the days that he had been screwing up his courage to address Adolph, the bold step had seemed quite feasible. (He kept remembering that moment when Adolph had remained silent, defeated before Max Heinrich.) Now that he had bearded the lion in his den, it was proving a different matter.

"Boss," he managed to mumble, "it's like this. I'm cold at night here

—awful cold. And in summer it smells somet'in' fierce in your office. You know that yourself, boss. I can't sleep wit' dat sweet Stock Yards smell in me nose! Now if I got, say, twenty bucks a month, I could hire meself a little room. Even fifteen bucks steady . . . wit' tips . . ."

Adolph snorted. "You t'ink I'm made out of money, don't you? You're all the same—all of you. I've got a good mind to kick you out of here for good!"

Chippy, looking frightened, began to back towards the door. "Don't do dat, boss. Please don't do dat! Don't be mad at me, boss."

"Get out!" Adolph shouted. And Chippy scurried out of the room so precipitately that his impetus carried him halfway down the length of the hall.

Left alone, Adolph sat scowling to himself, his anger at Chippy expanding into a more general feeling of annoyance at the various people who had set themselves up against him in these last few days: Rupert; Max Heinrich; Gogerty, the union boss; the recalcitrant workers in the pickle rooms. He sensed a relationship between these various revolts, and the knowledge made him vaguely uneasy. The very fact that there was discontent in the air and that it had sifted down through the various strata, commencing with his own son and ending with Chippy, the lowest of the low, evoked forebodings for the future. He remembered how McKenna had reminded him that they were in the twentieth century.

Picking up a birch stick that he had cut from one of his own trees, Adolph began to whittle away. But today he drew the blade of the knife towards him rather than away, an infallible sign of ill-humor. On his desk lay two telegrams, and had Chippy known their contents, he certainly would not have chosen this, of all days, to ask a favor of Adolph. From Wilma in Cambridge came the first, announcing that she and Rupert were returning to Chicago that afternoon. (But not a word to explain her sudden disappearance without his knowledge or approval!) The second was signed "Gogerty" and dealt with the strike in the pickling plant. This was the wire that really had upset Adolph, for in it the union boss stated that the pickling strike would continue until "safety" conditions had been improved. Curt, almost threatening, the message was like a slap in the face.

Snip! Snip! Adolph's penknife whittled away at the birch, each thrust like a stab at the body of that impudent fellow who had dared set himself up against the powers that be. What did the man mean anyway? Didn't he realize that he would be broken, crucified, like so many before him who had dared oppose the forces of the Stock Yards world—mighty organizations which counted the city government and the police force among their allies and could even name justices of the city courts. Why, the little man didn't have the chance of a snowflake in hell!

But then Adolph remembered that this Gogerty was not really a man at all: he was the personification of another organization, powerful also, and with its authority rapidly mounting. The union, that mysterious entity which drew life from its thousands of constituents—there was the enemy! Gogerty himself, the signer of this telegram, was a nobody, a little man in a cheap suit, a third-rate paid organizer. He was, as McKenna had said, of no importance. But the union itself *was* important, and Adolph realized that fact with the instinctive knowledge of an elemental man in the face of danger.

After a few moments Adolph Konrad jumped up, thrust what was left of the birch stick in his pocket, and with rapid strides left the room. The first of his morning visitors was coming down the hall, but Adolph called out that he was busy and that the man should return later in the day. Past the offices of McKenna and the other managers he strode, then took the steps of the iron staircase two at a time. A moment later he was striding across the empty space before the office building, his hip boots making deep tracks in the new-fallen snow. He headed straight for Building No. 3, with the pickling and canning works, nor did he stop till he stood on the floor of one of those pickle rooms whose workers, backed by the union, had insulted him by walking out the day after New Year's.

The huge room was cold as an icehouse, not surprising considering the lack of heating and the subzero temperature outside; each time Adolph breathed, a little cloud of steam formed in the frigid air. The smell here was overpowering, combining the familiar Stock Yards aroma with the peculiar acrid stench of the pickling solutions, in which meat was marinated before canning. Around one of the huge vats which formed the sole furnishing of this chamber of horrors, a handful of men were at work. By means of huge forks they were transferring the contents of the vat into a half-empty truck which presently would carry it off to the canning plant. The men wore sweaters or overcoats; several had woolen mufflers tied about their necks.

The floor boss caught sight of Adolph and came hurrying up, slipping and almost falling on the wet cement in his haste. His great boots were none too stout, for it did not take the pickling acids long to burn through leather and attack the toe bones with devastating results. A muscular Polack with a heavy mustache, his name was familiar to Adolph, like that of each of the fifty-odd floor bosses in this ten-building plant.

"Hello, Milwyzki. Vhat's de matter mit that outfit of yours? Do they think they're on a picnic, or vhat?"

"Sorry, Mr. Konrad." The boss threw out his hands in a hopeless gesture. "They're no good, and I know it. But they're the only men who showed up today, so what can we do? We're running quarter capacity as it is."

"Und it's them vhat I'm payin' double wages!" fumed Adolph. "Vhy, they're not vort' a nickel an hour! Gott demn that blasted-to-hell union!"

"Yes, sir! And if it weren't for the double wages, even these fellows wouldn't have come. They all think they're going to get their blocks knocked off."

"Blocks knocked off? Demn fools!" Adolph went red in the face. "Don't they know dat ve've been promised police protection? Haven't you told them, Milwyzki?"

"I have, Mr. Konrad. But the police can't protect them back in their homes. That's where most of the beatings-up went on this morning."

"Vell, you tell them again, Milwyzki. Tell them the police chief has promised to look after this matter himself. Tell them that. Go ahead und tell them!"

He watched the man rejoin his gang and explain to them what the big boss had said, but there was scant response on their part. They continued ladling out the great sides of beef; but so clumsily and slowly that Adolph's fingers itched to seize one of the forks and demonstrate how it ought to be done. Damn fools! he thought as he watched them. Scum and no-good riffraff! The world wouldn't be much poorer if they got carried away by pneumonia and the other "occupational diseases" the union was always wailing about.

Leaving the room with the bungling workmen, Adolph walked out of the door of Building No. 3, head bent and scowling. He was not happy with what he'd seen, nor with the thought that the union, through decreeing this strike, had as good as paralyzed the whole pickling business. For it had spread well beyond his plant! Since yesterday pickling workers had quit in the Hastey and Armitage establishments, and this fact, far from consoling Adolph, only increased his anxiety. It showed what a force for evil that hated union had become. What power might it not wield in the future?

It wasn't until he stood on the floor of the main slaughtering room in another, larger, building that Adolph's scowl melted away. Here work was going on full tilt, a couple of hundred workers straining themselves for the ultimate aim of adding to the revenue of Adolph Konrad, which of course was as it should be. This great room was still the center of his plant, as it had been since the company's foundation; despite the rise of subsidiary enterprises ranging all the way from sausage making to can and barrel making, it was around the slaughter of cattle that the packing business had been built. And within these four walls was the killing accomplished, at the rate of four hundred or more every hour.

There was a bellowing and stamping here that drowned out the sound of human voices, and every few seconds came the heavy crash of an animal, felled by a sledge-hammer blow. Intersecting the room were the long belt conveyors from which the dead and dying steers hung suspended, and beneath them worked men with long knives, slicing their throats, and decapitating and skinning and gutting the beasts. Each worker had one specific task which he accomplished with the precision of an automaton, and, like automata, these killers had no individuality, having taken on the dulled expression of mass-men. The floor was an inch high in blood and manure, and as the men waded through it they splattered each other with the sticky brown mass. Each time the throat of a new animal was cut, a fountain of blood would gush out, often dousing some worker not nimble enough to step aside. Then a volley of curses would be heard above the bellowing of the animals.

Scarcely would the spectacle have been found attractive by the average man. Only someone like Adolph, whose life had centered around livestock, could have understood that this mass killing and mass preparation of meat had about it something satisfying, almost grandiose. After all, man was a carnivorous creature, and through the ages had depended for survival on the consumption of animal flesh. Here in the Chicago Stock Yards the process of turning beasts into food had reached its ultimate stage. Never before had it been done on such a vast scale, with such efficiency, such economy, such speed. Here was butchery raised to a science, if not an art; here was the quintessence of butchery.

Perhaps it was reflections such as these (not worked out but instinctively known) that caused Adolph's spirits to rise as he watched the functioning of the elaborate machinery of annihilation. Or perhaps the change in his mood derived less from abstract reflections than from the ever-recurring realization that he alone was responsible for the existence of this huge plant which functioned with such clocklike precision; that he, Adolph Konrad, the poor boy from Schwabenland, had out of nothing created this miracle. The strike in the pickle rooms was forgotten; after all, it was no more than a temporary disruption of one branch of his huge factory. The frenzied activity on the killing floor, the screaming of cattle, the flash of bloodstained knives in the sunlight, told him that fundamentally all was well in the world of Konrad.

In a calmer mood he retraced his steps to the office building, prepared to tell McKenna to carry on the fight with the union, with no thought of the smallest concession. He felt a new awareness of personal power that made the still undeveloped power of the union seem puny, almost negligible in comparison. Alone he had built up this business, and alone he intended to run it. He would take advice neither from Gogerty nor from McKenna nor from anyone else. This was *his* show! With firm steps he mounted the iron staircase, the echo of his boots on the metal carrying a message ahead of him down the corridor:

"Here comes a man!"

nine

William and Cecilia had been invited to supper at the Hasteys'. It had proved no easy task to secure their father's sanction, in the first place because he rarely approved of his children going out, in the second because the date and the very hour corresponded with their mother's return from Cambridge. Hirsch would be taking the brougham to meet her at the La Salle Street depot, while Adolph would not yet be home with the buggy from the Stock Yards. Only when Gladys Hastey offered to call for them in her family's "electric" had Adolph given his reluctant consent. As William had pointed out, one had to think twice before refusing an invitation from the Harold Hasteys!

"Oh dear, what can be keeping her!" Cecilia fretted, coming back from her third trip to the front door. "D'you suppose that silly electric has broken down? They always do. Perhaps we ought to telephone."

"Mr. and Mrs. Hastey have not installed a telephone," William reminded her, with a satisfaction derived from the knowledge that some people were as conservative-minded as himself.

"Then there's nothing to do but wait. Oh dear! I only hope that she'll show up before Mama. I don't want any fuss at the last minute."

"And there'll be one all right—if Mama catches you in that getup," William warned her.

"Getup! What's wrong with my getup?"

William, searching for words, found it hard to answer her question. The pink organdy frock was pretty, to be sure, but it was too fancy for a little supper with friends; the silk scarf exaggerated this effect, besides clashing in color; the coral necklace, bangle bracelet, and cameo earrings were—too much of a good thing. His sister Cecilia was dressed in impeccable bad taste.

"The Hasteys are very conservative people," William remarked stodgily. "They are at least three times as rich as we, but Gladys doesn't even wear a ring. People whose ancestors came over on the *Mayflower* don't need to make ostentatious displays of wealth."

56

"Meaning that I'm vulgar, I suppose!"

"Well, Cissy, you could do without those earrings. If one has a father who speaks with a German accent, one's got to be doubly on one's guard. You know perfectly well that Mama would make you take them off. I bet Justin won't appreciate them either."

Justin Judson, Gladys' cousin, was to be one of the supper guests, and William shared the general knowledge that Cecilia was keen on him. Indeed, the dashing daredevil, Judson, had already captured many a heart since his expulsion for misconduct from Princeton University. But if William had hoped to persuade her, he had not reckoned with Konrad stubbornness. Cecilia's prominent jaw shot out, and a hard look came in her eyes.

"You mind your own business, smarty! You don't look so marvelous yourself, in that ridiculous high collar. You'd have to be a giraffe to be comfortable in it; it's cutting right into your neck."

"Oh, is it?" Uncertainly William's hand went up to the towering collar whose ultraformal appearance appealed to him. "Perhaps I'd better go up and change. Why didn't you tell me before?"

"Because you couldn't improve matters much, whatever you did," said Cecilia.

William went up to make a change, but before reaching his room stopped off on the first floor to see Francis. Pressed for time, he had neglected to bid his sick brother good night, a lapse which now disturbed his sense of decorum; conscientiousness was his salient virtue. He found Francis sitting up in bed playing Black Peter with Beatrice, their younger sister. That was against doctor's orders, he remembered, but on reflection decided that it would be easier to say nothing.

"Good night, Francy," William called out from the doorway. "Cissy and I are going out for supper."

"Where are you going, Will?"

When Francy smiled, as he did now, his face had a sweetness shared by none of the Konrads. It was plain at such times that he alone was his mother's child.

"I'm going to Mr. and Mrs. Hastey's, on Prairie Avenue, almost the richest people in Chicago. They have three flunkies in plum liveries to wait at table and they eat off solid gold plates."

57

"You said two flunkies last time," his sister Beatrice remarked. She had been in a sour humor all evening because of being only sixteen, and left out of the festivities.

"Oh, two or three, Bee—as if it mattered," William said airily, just as there reached them the sound of wheels on the frozen driveway.

Rushing to his room, William wondered why he always had to bungle things at the last minute. Here everything had been so beautifully planned, and now, a stickler for punctuality, he was going to make his best girl wait! Might Gladys think him too unreliable to be taken seriously as a suitor?

But when he came downstairs it was obvious that the spoiled Gladys had scarcely noticed his absence; her tiny body almost lost to sight in one of the many huge armchairs, she gave the impression of being bored even before the evening had started. Cecilia, on the other hand, poking at her hair and self-consciously toying with the bodice of her dress, was obviously in a spin because of the unexpected arrival of Justin Judson with Gladys. It appeared that the electric had balked just as Gladys was about to drive off with the coachman, at which moment Justin had arrived to set things right and accompany Gladys to the Konrad house.

"Yes, an electric's far too complicated to be handled by a coachman," Justin resumed after William had greeted the arrivals. "I'm going to say so to Uncle Harold tonight. He really ought to get a qualified chauffeur to run it, and to see that the batteries are in order. In my opinion," Justin declaimed, twirling his guardsman's mustache, "the time will arrive when there'll be almost as many chauffeurs as coachmen in this city. You can't stop the march of progress."

"Fiddlesticks!" William broke in. "They'll never perfect those silly contraptions, and as to gasoline-run automobiles, they're only good for empty country roads."

"Do you call Fifth Avenue, New York, an empty country road? You may not know that they're using automobile omnibuses on that route. William, you're old-fashioned!"

"Well, maybe I am. I'd rather be old-fashioned—than plumb crazy!"

There was so much fire in his voice that William himself was surprised. He would have found it hard to explain why newfangled ideas

—automobiles and telephones, short engagements and quick divorces, strikes and socialism—all aroused in him an equal degree of hostility. As a life principle, the maintenance of the status quo seemed to him eminently desirable.

"Tell me, Cecilia"—Gladys roused herself from the boredom produced by this male conversation—"tell me, is it true that your brother Rupert is getting back from Cambridge this evening?"

"Who told you that?" William exploded.

"Oh—I really don't remember." Gladys' odd little face screwed up in a smile that made her look almost Chinese. "It must have been some little bird," she said in a teasing voice.

"I don't know if you've heard"—William turned to Justin in embarrassment—"my brother made an awful fool of himself the other night. It's most mortifying, but the fact is that he got quite drunk and was rude to my father. Please don't let it get about, Justin."

"I couldn't." Justin gave out the satanical chuckle which had earned him his reputation as a cynic and a rake. "There's practically no one in Chicago doesn't know about it already. They even know the name of that young lady in Cambridge: Helen Mason."

"Who must be highly seductive," Gladys remarked, smoothing a wrinkle in her expensive frock. "I wonder what it would take to make *you* stand up to your papa, William? Certainly no Helen Mason. Perhaps Helen of Troy . . ."

William cast a sharp glance at Gladys, obviously shocked at this attitude on the part of such a well-bred girl. Why, she actually seemed to admire Rupert's misbehavior! What was happening, anyway, to this younger generation of which he reluctantly formed a part? Sourly he pulled a watch out of his waistcoat pocket.

"Goodness gracious, do let's be going! I loathe unpunctuality more than the devil himself."

They filed out of the front door, held open for them by the dour Hauptman, and climbed into the electric, which Justin started by jerking down the flexible steering rod. William, squeezed into the back seat with Gladys, felt so nervous that he scarcely noticed that his arm had found its way about his partner's shoulder; craning forward with eyes glued on the driveway, he asked himself if Justin could possibly negotiate the first curve at their breakneck pace. Why, the speedometer marked almost fifteen miles an hour! Would the electric go cavorting off into the rhododendron bushes? Oh, that reckless daredevil, that hotheaded fool, that irresponsible Justin Judson!

And then his worst fears were realized, even before he became aware of specific danger. There was the glimpse of horses' manes seen over the bushes, the crunching of carriage wheels, and a panicky yell which William recognized as coming from Hirsch, the family's coachman.

"Ho there, Schiller! Ho, Goethe! Gott damn! An electric!"

The next instant Justin had crashed his vehicle full tilt into the side of the carriage, to the accompaniment of splintering woodwork, terrified neighing, and the hysterical screaming of young ladies in party frocks.

William pushed open the door of the electric and plunged out, landing on his big stomach in the middle of the bushes. When he recovered sufficiently to look back, he saw to his surprise that Gladys was still seated in the electric, bent double with laughter; for once she was not looking bored. Cecilia, minus her salmon-colored cape, one shoulder strap of her organdy dress snapped in two, was being helped out of the electric by Justin, cool and collected as ever. Then his eye swerved to the carriage, and through the dusk he saw Rupert and Hirsch surveying the wreckage; the left front wheel had been knocked clean off and the fore part of the brougham now rested on its axle.

The face of Mama appeared at the window. Her black traveling bonnet had been jolted awry, but otherwise she appeared none the worse for the shake-up; she was even smiling. William's amazement mounted as he realized that she, like Gladys, was more amused than distressed by the accident.

"My goodness!" Mama cried. "You must be in a terrible hurry, Mr. Judson. And where were you going with all that speed?"

"To Mr. and Mrs. Hastey's for supper. But now I'm afraid that we'll be late, and what's more, we'll never convert William to automobiles."

"You certainly won't," William said, brushing the snow from his overcoat.

Gladys, in the meanwhile, had alighted and walked up to the carriage window to greet Wilma. (What perfect manners she had! thought William, gratified.) But he found himself biting his lips as she stepped towards the front of the carriage, where Rupert stood examining the wheel. Apart from the accident, William had reason to wish they had got away before that handsome brother of his appeared on the scene.

"A good clean job!" said Gladys, pointing at the severed carriage wheel. "I guess this is the age of the machine, all right."

Rupert straightened up and pushed back the mesh of black hair that had a habit of falling over his forehead; it gave him a romantic appearance that actually did not correspond with his character in the least.

"Oh hello, Gladys," he said vaguely. "At least you are still alive."

"Very much so," Gladys said. "Alive and kicking. I hope you had a nice trip to the East."

Rupert gave his shapely shoulders a shrug. He was not the sort of man to forget his own problems for long, and neither the shake-up nor Gladys' query had penetrated the shell of his self-absorption. His mind was concentrated on the approaching conversation with his father, rather than on a young woman whom, to tell the truth, he had never found particularly attractive.

"Listen, Rupert," Gladys went on, "Cecilia and William are having supper with us tonight. At least they are if we ever manage to get home! Why don't you join us? I'm sure my parents would love to have you."

But Rupert shook his head.

"No thanks," he said. "Couldn't manage it tonight."

It was too dark for him to see how Gladys' thin lips pressed together. It did not even occur to him that he might have made some excuse. Only from the note of relief in his brother's voice did he sense that there had been a minor crisis in the making.

"That's right," William said, "Rupert couldn't possibly leave the house tonight. My father wants to have a talk with him."

"In that case," said Gladys icily, "let us be getting on. Shall we trust Justin to handle the electric—or had I better phone someone to rescue us in a carriage?"

William reflected for a moment. He certainly did not trust this electric, but neither did he have much confidence in Mr. Bell's diabolic system of communication.

"You three go ahead in the electric," he decided finally. "And God be with you. As to me, I shall run all the way to Prairie Avenue. It's only about a mile, and the exercise will do me good. In all likelihood I'll be there long before you arrive."

ten

It was the third week of the strike in the pickling rooms. Muggings had become everyday affairs, broken jaws abounded in the packing-house district, and it had become increasingly difficult to enlist men for work in Building No. 3. Yet the strike was no nearer settlement than the day it broke out. Already the disruption of work had cost Adolph thousands of dollars, and each day added to his loss.

The situation was one of the worst headaches that he had had for years, and not the least galling part of it was the fact that it could so easily have been avoided. Putting in new piping would have stilled the men's grievances, as well as given an increased value to the building. As usual, McKenna had proved right. And this knowledge hurt Adolph even more than the monetary loss.

"Vhat's de matter, McKenna?" he roared at him extra loudly, aware that he had himself to blame. "Vhy can't ve settle this Gott demn trouble mit the pickle men? It's gone on long enough. Vhy don't you get busy, for Christ's sake?"

"I am busy, Mr. Konrad. But it's taking a little time. These union bosses are acting pretty tough."

"Shut 'em up! Buy 'em up!" shouted Adolph. "Vhat d'you t'ink I pay you for, anyvay? Vhat I vant is results."

But even as he bullied McKenna he realized how dependent he had grown on this dour Scotsman. He himself was incapable of dealing with the unions; it implied a kind of negotiating to which he could not adapt himself. It did no good to shout at the union bosses as he shouted at his foremen and managers. To beat the unions required an impersonal, calculating brain like this man McKenna's, who treated the whole thing rather like a problem in mathematics. In the first place McKenna was

not a packer. He might as easily have gone in for the selling of buggies;
it was mere chance that had steered him towards the Stock Yards and,
once there, into Adolph Konrad's private office. Strange, thought
Adolph, that the men who *did* things, those who had put up the buildings and hired the workmen, those, in short, who had created the nation's industries, were relying more and more on this manager type,
who somehow had the knack of holding the whole complicated structure together.

One Sunday the telephone rang as Adolph was eating his breakfast.
The caller proved to be O'Toole, the police chief of the packing-house
precinct, and it was clear from the man's ingratiating tone that he was
the conveyer of bad news.

"Mighty sorry to tell you, Mr. Konrad, that those hoodlums at the
yards have been at it again. They've gone out for bigger game this time.
It's too bad, Mr. Konrad."

"Spit it out, O'Toole! Spit it out!" shouted Adolph.

"It's one of your floor bosses, sir—man in charge of the pickling
rooms. Milwyzki's his name—sounds like a Polack. Poor fellow's been
beaten pretty near to a jelly. He's lost the sight of one eye."

"Demn scoundrels und no-good punks!" Adolph screamed into the
mouthpiece. "Vhat's the matter mit you fellows in uniform, for Jesus
Christ's sake? You don't know your business! Vhat ve need is a new
police force in this city."

"I know how you feel, Mr. Konrad. But Packingtown's a big area,
you know. One can't be everywhere."

"Everyvhere? Vhy, you shouldn't be anyvhere, Gott demn you to
hell!" was Adolph's reply. And he knew that O'Toole could not have
answered even had Adolph not flung back the receiver on the hook. For
O'Toole and his subordinates all held their positions through the good
will of the packers, and any one of them might be looking for a new
job within twenty-four hours.

Later that morning he sent word to Hirsch to bring around the
buggy, having decided to pay Milwyzki a call. Demanding utter loyalty,
Adolph always had offered the same in return, and it seemed to him
perfectly natural to devote his leisure morning to this errand. Apart
from that, his journey had a second motive as well: being really happy

only in the vicinity of the Yards, he seldom let slip a pretext to visit them on the so-called day of rest.

Milwyzki lived in a two-story frame house in a tenement district "back of the Yards." As Adolph steered Bismarck down the mean street between the ramshackle houses, he was shaken about until he had to cling to the sideboard of the buggy for support. This was "made land," created some years before by the dumping of garbage, a fact corroborated by the uneven roadway and the penetrating fetid smell; mingling with the reek of the Stock Yards, it formed a peculiar and quite overpowering aroma. In the course of years the roadway had settled several feet below the level of the houses, and as Adolph bumped his way along (avoiding ice-covered pools and the more vicious of the ruts) he had the impression of driving down a deep ravine. Cracking his whip to scatter children and loafers, Adolph drove to the address he had obtained from O'Toole.

A gaunt-looking woman, very tall and of indefinite age, opened the door to him. She looked as if she had not had a good night's sleep since she was a small girl.

"I'm Adolph Konrad. I've come to see Milwyzki."

The woman's gaze did not soften; she gave no sign of being impressed by this visit of the all-powerful to her sordid dwelling. Somewhere inside the house an infant began to howl, and the quick swerve of the woman's head was more of a reflex than a deliberate movement. Without a greeting, she opened the door sufficiently for Adolph to walk in.

"Second room on the right down the corridor."

Milwyzki was lying on an iron bedstead in a bare room with a mousetrap in one corner. His head was heavily bandaged, with but one eye visible, that now focused its gaze on Adolph in an expressionless cyclopean stare. One arm was in a sling; the other hung laxly by his side.

Adolph walked over to the iron bedstead and stood looking down at Milwyzki; reaching for the wounded man's hand, he pressed it hard. A gruesome thing happened then: tears sprang into Milwyzki's remaining eye, overflowed, and ran down into his thick mustache. Apart from that there was no change, no movement, in the battered, swathed object on the bed.

64

"Can you hear me, Milwyzki?" Adolph said, raising his voice so that it would penetrate the bandaging.

There was a nod of the head. The tears had stopped flowing now; the single eye stared up at Adolph, solemnly, impersonally, like a glass eye in an optometrist's window.

"Milwyzki, I'm sorry for vhat happened to you," Adolph said, as always speaking spontaneously, without forethought. "Those dirty bastards got you, und got you good. They'll pay for it. I vant you to know that I'll spare no expense to track down the men vhat did this. Und vone more t'ing: your chob vill be vaiting for you vhen you are vell."

Milwyzki's head remained motionless for a moment; then it moved slowly down, and again up. He had understood. And now there was no more to say. Adolph, peering into Milwyzki's remaining eye, wondered what thoughts were passing behind those layers of bandages and behind the pool of jelly that once had been a human eye. Was this simple Polack aware that he had played a part, albeit a futile one, in the unfolding conflict between two great forces in the industrial world? That conflict, Adolph realized, was still in its preliminary stage. Only gradually would it take on full dimensions, to thunder through the successive decades of the new century and shake the foundations of our world. And here lay Milwyzki, the dumb victim of circumstances whose cause and import lay far beyond his power of comprehension! How many Milwyzkis must suffer and endure before a settlement was reached?

Adolph pressed for a second time the flaccid hand that hung dangling beside the dirty blankets, resembling nothing so much as one of those great hunks of meat that it had been handling for years. Head bent, he stalked out of the bedroom and down the corridor. By the front door the tall woman was still standing, her face as inflexible as that of a woman hewn from stone.

"I saw your husband," Adolph said, stopping with one hand on the doorknob. "Those devils! They'll pay for this!"

The woman did not move, nor speak, for several seconds. Her head turned slowly and she fixed Adolph with a glance that seemed to come from a great distance.

"They're not devils," she said, her flat voice tinged with the guttural accent of the Poles. "They're poor people, those who did it—like us. Like you were once too!"

Adolph stared at her as one would stare at a madwoman. He had expected tears or, failing that, grim silence. More than once had he been to the home of some foreman gored on the killing floor or laid low by an industrial accident. Never until today had he encountered enmity in people so dependent on his help.

"For vhy are you sorry for them?" he asked, fighting down the anger that was ever latent inside him. "Hooligans vhat beat up your man und vould perhaps kill us if they got de chance. No-good scum are they!"

"Like us," repeated the woman in her expressionless voice.

There she stood, grim and implacable as the figure of Nemesis, accusing Adolph through her very refusal to accuse those responsible. Did she consider him guilty? And guilty of what? As he stared at her with the hot fury rising in his throat, he realized suddenly that this tall woman looked like someone he knew, someone who had accused him, as she now accused him.

"One can't treat men as you do," he heard Max Heinrich's voice in his ear. "Remember, Adolph Konrad, that men aren't pigs. Men are men!"

He stamped out of the house and climbed into his buggy without glancing back. But as he jogged along the frozen road that ran like a black snake through Packingtown, the gaunt woman with the bitter eyes rode with him; she stood beside him in the carriage, arms folded over thin breasts, mouth set in the hard smile of accusation.

She's crazy! Adolph tried to tell himself. They beat up Milwyzki, and that's too bad, but who can blame me? I did everything to prevent it, even told O'Toole to put extra men on those beats. That damn union's behind it, just as they're behind this whole trouble in the Yards. It's they put up the pickle men against me! I pay good wages. If those picklers don't like it with me, they can go look for jobs elsewhere.

The buggy passed over a bad bump and Adolph came near to being flung from his seat. Jarred from his reverie, he grew aware that Bismarck had instinctively headed for the Stock Yards, whose outlying buildings were already visible at the end of the road. Today no smoke

66

belched from the chimneys, and absent was the noise of the rumbling cattle trains that brought raw material for these factories of death; a Sunday quiet had settled over the whole region of the Yards. Only the faint lowing of the cattle from the pens beyond the train tracks bore evidence that the work of slaughtering was merely suspended. Tomorrow at this time those animals would already be transformed into so many hundredweight of meat, hides, offal, and the innumerable side products of the Stock Yards industry.

My industry, thought Adolph, stopping his buggy by the entrance gate. I was as responsible for its building up as any other person in this city. Only old man Armitage and Harold Hastey played as big a part in the history of the Union Stock Yards as myself, who came to this country with a capital of five dollars sewn into the lining of my coat. When I die, these buildings will stand as my monument. Could any man have a better?

But as he gazed at the buildings of which he was so proud, it seemed to Adolph Konrad that the grim figure of Milwyzki's wife interposed itself. She fixed him with her bitter and accusing stare. By her side, other shadowy figures reared themselves, men and women in the shabby costume of workers, which varies little from state to state, from country to country; they might have been Pennsylvania charcoal burners or Schwabenland lace workers as easily as toilers in a Stock Yards plant. And at that moment Adolph understood that he was being accused of—treachery! This gaunt woman hated him, not because of her husband's injury, but because he, who had been a worker, now profited from the sweat and tears of thousands of Milwyzkis, bound together in the brotherhood of the exploited.

Of his own will Bismarck had begun to move down the frozen road skirting the Yards. Adolph made no effort to guide him; for once he felt relieved to have a decision taken from his hands. As they jogged along slowly, his big head fell forward on his breast; he gave himself over to his thoughts. There are times in the lives of the most active when the impulse to achieve is temporarily stilled and the need for self-justification grips the mind. Old doubts, long resolved, reassert themselves; old memories are revived. The great question which may have been lying dormant for half a century suddenly presents itself with undeniable urgency: What, after all, has been the purpose of my life?

I have fought a battle and have won it, Adolph answered without the slightest hesitation. In this world you have to conquer or go under, and it so happened that I had the stuff of which conquerors are made. Money is the measure of a man's success, the measure of his power. That is why I have amassed wealth, not because I was a miser or a buyer. Of course they hate me, those defeated fools, coughing and spitting in the pickle rooms! And the other fools, stamping about all day in blood and manure. And my bosses and foremen and my managers too. I have no illusions. They hate me, just as I hated rich men when I was poor. Only it happened that I was cleverer than the rest, so now I'm holding the whip over their heads. Cracking it too! Is there one who wouldn't do the same if he could? Dog eat dog! Dog eat dog! Wasn't I poorer than any of them thirty years ago . . . back in Germany . . .

Back in Germany! He sees the hill, and the factory on top of the hill: that huge pile of red bricks and black mortar which dominates the surrounding countryside like a medieval cathedral and, like a cathedral, draws sustenance from the lifeblood of the countrymen. He sees the line of workers tramping upwards through the misty dawn, shadowy and grotesque figures in the early morning light; impossible to tell which are children, which ones stunted or misshapen adults; as they bend forward in their climb, all seem to be carrying great loads upon their backs.

He sees himself in that endless line, a spindle-legged, ragged boy, weighed down more heavily than the others. And in his case by a living load! It is his brother Franzy that he carries, for the tiny boy is tight sleep and he does not want to wake him before arriving at the factory; he knows that Franzy, like himself, has slept far too few hours the night before, and for many, many nights before that. In his sleep Franzy's arms cling to his older brother's neck, and today, thirty-four years later, Adolph can still feel them there next to his skin, thin as ropes, cold and hard as the arms of a dead boy.

He sees the workroom in the factory, sees the benches, sees the children sitting in long rows. They look not like children at all, but like little old men and women, bent deep over their tasks. On each child's lap lies a high pile of lace, and it is the loose threads left by the machines that the children are drawing out. For that work no intelligence is required, merely many pairs of deft, sensitive fingers; ideal work it is for children of six and upwards who can be made to work twelve to fourteen hours a day at a wage of a few marks a week.

He sits at one bench, Franzy at another, where his shaven head can be seen between the backs of two children. How frail, how vulnerable, it looks—like an eggshell that can be cracked by a small spoon! Beneath Franzy the "lace mistress" has put a pile of sacking so that he will appear as tall as the other children in the unlikely event of an inspector's visit. For Franzy is only five, and even in that paradise of unhampered free enterprise which was Germany in the mid-nineteenth century, a child of five was held unequal to working fourteen hours a day.

He sees the "lace mistress," black-clad and dour, in her hand the long stick with which she prods the backs of her wards when they fall asleep. At this moment Adolph can feel the stab of the pointed stick on his spine, the sting of the harsh words in his ears. *"Schafskopf! Dummkopf! Pass auf, Knabe!"* He sees the overseer, with his red cheeks and black beard, walking towards Franzy, crouched low over the lace. Again he experiences the old agony of suspense as he watches Franzy's fingers moving numbly, too slowly, over the spiderweb lace and realizes that the bearded man is about to land a cuff on his brother's ear. There it comes! He can still see the surprised jerk of the shaved head and hear the small cry of pain. In the evening his brother keeps rubbing his ear, and as they lie in the same bed at night young Adolph can hear him whimpering in his sleep.

He sees that bed, set high on its posts and covered by one of those huge feather bolsters that in Germany take the place of top sheet and blankets and quilt. But now it is his father who lies under the bolster, in his eyes that same faraway look that had been in the eyes of Franzy, as he lay coughing away his life a bare year before. His father has been felled by a great pulley that dropped on him in the iron foundry where he worked, and he groans incessantly; something is broken inside him, something essential to the functioning of the underfed body, stunted and worn by a lifetime of work, first as pigherd on a landed estate, later as worker in one of the innumerable factories that sprang up as a result of industrialization.

He sees himself standing beside the bed, gazing down at the pinched white face, the sunken cheeks, the straggly mustache which, like its owner, seems never to have had a chance to reach its normal development. Young Adolph can think only of that mustache as his father speaks to him.

"To America, boy! Do you hear? You shall get to America. Mama is to write down your name when the contractor comes, and he will take you to America on a great boat. Life may be better there. It is—it is my last wish."

He sees only the mustache, the weak mustache, the sad mustache. He has never loved his father, but strangely enough, at that moment he has a feeling almost of love for the tired, the defeated mustache.

"You must be strong, boy," his father is saying. "Yes, strong—strong. Strength is the one thing that counts. Don't let the fools and the pastors tell you anything different. Franzy died because his body was not strong enough. And now I shall die because the spirit within my body was not strong enough. Otherwise I, too, would have reached America, the golden land. But you, Adolph, must go forward! Fight your way on, beat down the others, climb high on the bodies of the failures."

And as his father speaks to him, he realizes suddenly that the potatoes on the stove are burning. He knows that he must stay by his father's side, and he knows that he must go to the stove to take off the potatoes. A conflict rages inside him, but only for a moment. Has not his father himself said that he must be *strong*? He turns his back on the dying man and walks heavily, unhesitatingly towards the potatoes, towards food, towards the substance of life. . . .

The wheels of the buggy crunched over gravel, and Adolph looked up, to find that the horse Bismarck had made his way home unaided through the empty Sunday streets. Having turned into the driveway of Sans Souci, the gelding was now drawing the black and red buggy up the hill. Adolph tightened his grip on the reins and flicked his whip across Bismarck's mane, sending a shower of snowflakes to the ground. Then he noticed for the first time that it had begun to snow and that the driveway, the bushes, Bismarck's sleek back, were all covered with a film of virgin white.

He left the buggy beneath the portico for Hirsch to put away, walked into his house and up the broad staircase. His mind still dwelled in that past which, with the advent of middle age, had often come to seem to him as near and familiar as the living present. Now he found his footsteps passing by his own room, to halt instead before that of Francis, the youngest of his sons. For a moment Adolph waited, hand on doorknob, then gently pushed open the door and stepped inside.

The small boy lay sleeping lightly, stretched on his back with his hands twisted on the coverlet. The cretonne curtains were drawn, and in the half-dark Adolph could barely make out the exhausted face upon the pillow, mouth open in labored breathing, drops of perspiration spotting the forehead beneath the fine light hair. The little face was no more than an oval blur on the white square of the pillow, familiar from his earliest memories, infinitely dear. Was it the face of Franzy that he saw (he, a boy of twelve, gazing protectively at his younger brother in a smoke-filled cottage in Schwabenland) or was it that of his son Francy, marked with the same signs of weakness, of early suffering and early death? Franzy—Francy. The dead boy and the sick boy seemed to have merged into a single personality.

He was filled with a fierce longing to give to this lad the strength he required to fight the merciless battle of life. He, Adolph, who had taken his father's advice to beat his way upwards, he, Adolph, who was strong and knew the importance of strength, wanted to forestall the foreordained failure of this child. Impulsively his hands knitted themselves into fists. How he would have liked to fight Francy's fights for him, smoothing his path, taking on himself the burden which this frail back could not bear! He felt strong as a giant, able to perform miracles by a mere effort of his will. . . .

But as he bent low over the ailing body of his little son, as his lips approached the humid forehead, a wave of profound sadness swept over Adolph. He straightened up without having made the gesture of tenderness that he had been withholding for so long. It was not because of hardness that he refused to pamper this lad, and that Wilma complained of his paternal severity. The memory of Franzy, and of Franzy's defeat, was ever in his mind. Perhaps one day Francy would under-stand. He hoped with all his heart that the boy would never hate his father for having loved him in a way that precluded tenderness.

He walked out into the corridor and pulled open the door of the big room that he shared with Wilma. Wilma was sitting by the window in a rocking chair, doing some mending. No doubt she had just returned from church, for her German-language prayer book lay beside her on the table. She looked up quickly at Adolph's entrance and the usual warm smile came to her lips. But Adolph walked up to her and absently took from her hand the jersey she was mending. Fixing Wilma with his great burning eyes, he said earnestly:

"Listen, Vilma! I vant for the boy to get up from bed. For three months now he's been lying here, lying here. I can't stand for to see it any more. Tomorrow he is to get up, I say. Positively!"

"Oh no, Adolph! No!" Wilma jumped to her feet and stared at Adolph; to judge from the look in her eyes, one might have thought she had received her own death verdict. "It's too soon, Adolph. The boy's still sick, mighty sick. Don't you see that he's weak as a kitten?"

"And it's not by lying in bed that he is going to get stronger. Vonce he gets up, he vill have to get vell. He *vill* get vell! O'Grady thinks so too."

"Oh, Adolph, how often have I told you: O'Grady thinks what you tell him to think! Don't be hard, Adolph. Leave Francy for just one more week!"

"My mind is made up, Vilma. Don't argue. Tomorrow the boy's to get up, und I'll tell O'Grady to give him a tonic! Ya, a new tonic to put flesh and blood on our Francy. It doesn't matter if it costs a t'ousand dollars a bottle, two t'ousand dollars. Vhat good is a fortune . . . ya, vhat good is a fortune, if a rich man can't make his own children strong?"

72

eleven

There was a luncheon visitor in Sans Souci that snowy January Sunday. Helen Mason had arrived to spend some days as the Konrads' house guest, the astonishing aftermath of Wilma's journey to Boston. Little had Rupert guessed, on catching sight of his mother in the hall of that Cambridge inn, that he was about to gain an invaluable ally. As events proved, their conversation had convinced Wilma that the family could be held together only by the sanctioning of this marriage on which Rupert had set his heart. Better have an unwanted daughter-in-law than lose a son, she had told Adolph on her return. And then she had tried to remember what Rupert had said about Helen's fitting into the big picture puzzle that was his life, but unfortunately the complicated imagery had proved too much for her; she got confused and gave up the effort.

"It doesn't matter. It doesn't matter, Adolph. What's important is that you don't go against him. You let the boy do what he wants! He's *your* boy and he's got a will of his own."

"Und so vhat do you vant? That I ask the young jackanapes' forgiveness?" Adolph had stormed. "That I should go on my knees to him, perhaps?"

"No, Adolph, he's already asked forgiveness of you, and it was mighty difficult for him to do it. Let's invite this Miss Mason to visit us for a few days, and then you can judge her yourself. If you don't like her—well, land's sake, if you don't you'll still be free to say no to the marriage."

So in the end Wilma had had her way, and the invitation to Helen had been dispatched. It was not what Wilma wanted, and it certainly was not what Adolph wanted, but it was better than losing a son altogether, which was the other alternative.

Rupert, driven by Hirsch, had been down at the station to meet her, and the expensive-looking brougham with initials painted (a bit showily) on the door, had been Helen's first contact with the fabled Konrad millions. As she stepped into the carriage she was acutely conscious of her cheap little traveling garb, of her clumsy suitcase, which in fact belonged to her father, of the old-fashioned umbrella which had once been her mother's property. And yet this modern Cinderella was not really frightened in the least for, strangely enough, she knew how to behave: the knowledge lay in her blood, transmitted from her mother, together with a love of music, an appreciation of nice clothes, and that natural elegance which had so attracted Rupert from the start.

"You seem speechless," Rupert said as they drove down glittering Michigan Avenue. "Don't be taken in by this false front. In spirit Chicago's no more than a big sprawling village, as you'll soon find out."

Helen laughed. "Now you are trying to make me feel at home. I'm glad you realize that I'm only a small-town girl."

Which of course was the truth. But for trips into Boston, she had scarcely left Cambridge all her life; she belonged to a household that spent in a year what Rupert's family probably spent in a week. Not a day passed without her father's reminding her that each penny she squandered was snatched from the hands of some needy person. How was it, then, that she found it so natural to sit on green broadcloth behind a high-trotting horse, and to have her companion call out, as Rupert did now, "Give him the whip, Hirsch! We're in a hurry to get home. Come on, man, let's make a little speed!"

"Home" was in line with the brougham, only a hundred times more overpowering, more hideous, and more lavish. She had never realized that such tasteless furnishings could exist, despite Rupert's warning that Sans Souci was a "museum of monstrosities." She tried not to betray her feelings and, as she had savoir-faire, actually succeeded. But her inclination was to turn and rush out of this house, with its great heavy draperies, its mounted steers' heads and bulls' heads, its excess of knick-knacks and its absence of books—to rush right back to Cambridge, and into her father's arms. She kept remembering his quiet voice and serene smile as she met Rupert's elder brother and his sisters (all of whom talked too loudly and made far too little effort to hide their animosity), and finally met Adolph himself, when he stamped downstairs before luncheon, wearing hip boots and a lumberman's shirt with black shoe-string tie.

74

But towards Adolph she felt entirely different. The minute she saw him she recognized him as a personality; there was something satisfying about Adolph, whether or not one liked him. He fitted, she thought, among these monstrous furnishings and statues which commemorated the fortune he had amassed; there was a visual harmony between the man and his possessions. Only his children, supercilious but uncultured, seemed almost as out of place here as they would have been in her own father's house.

A little later the great gong sounded, and Helen followed her hostess into the dining room, finding a chance on the way to send Rupert a smile, for she knew that he was even more nervous than she. As always when his face had gone pale, he seemed particularly good-looking; that rebellious mesh of black hair lay over his forehead, giving him a distraught, almost desperate appearance. He reminded her of Heathcliff in a dramatization of *Wuthering Heights* that she had once seen in Boston.

Poor dear, he is not only worrying about what impression I'm making on them, but about what impression they're making on me, she told herself. He is worrying about what I think of these heavy chairs and plush furnishings and what they think of my cheap little dress. She had an intuition that throughout his life Rupert would always find something to worry about, and always find someone like her on whom to throw his worries.

That Sunday luncheon, like so much that had happened since she stepped into the gleaming black brougham at the station, was a new experience for Helen. It was a revelation for her that people could eat so much, so lengthily, and in so solemn a fashion. Back in Cambridge she and her father had most meals alone, but never were they at a loss for conversation; here a pin could have been heard dropping on the carpeted floor. Through their glass eyes the mounted animals on the wall surveyed the ceremony, perhaps finding consolation in the memory of how they, too, had been devoured with gusto—and with Idaho baked potatoes.

Now she was looking straight into the eyes of an Angus bull, belonging, so Adolph had told her, to the first herd of these cattle ever imported from Scotland. So melancholy was their gaze that Helen wondered if in the dead animal's brain there still lay memories of lush grass and heather and some silent loch in the highlands. Perhaps he heard the splash of a salmon leaping high into the air, or the sucking sound made by his wives' hoofs plowing through the marshy strip beside the water . . .

And suddenly a melody began playing. It was a very faint melody, and as it was playing far inside Helen's head, naturally it remained inaudible for the others. But for her it sounded as clear and as pure as though it came from a tiny flute right by her ear! Hardly daring to breathe, she gave ear to the reedy music which came to her from the Highlands through the medium of that hairy monster on the wall.

Ah, now it was growing louder! Behind the flute she could make out the notes of a pipe, shrill and unearthly, as if it were being played by a Caledonian Pan with cloven hoofs and horns on his head. She longed to jump up and run to a piano, there to give form to the ghostly melody that was running through her head. In her excitement she half rose from the table. Her hands went out, as though reaching for the keys . . .

And then she realized that Adolph Konrad was watching her. Those burning black eyes were set on her face with a look that drew her straight back into the world of reality, as far from the sound of pipe and flute as was this solid mahogany table from the lochs and heather of Scotland. Steady! they said. Steady, my girl! You'll have to learn sooner or later, and it might as well be now, that an Angus bull represents a specific number of dollars, rather than a link with a romantic dream. We live in a world of dollars and cents, of pounds and hundredweights. You'd better begin to measure and weigh and evaluate, my girl, if you know what's good for you. Now you stop this silly nonsense about being a vegetarian and hurry to eat up your meat!

The music had stopped. In its place she grew aware of a silence louder than sound, and she wanted to cover her ears so that she could hear the melody again. But Adolph's eyes were on her, the hard eyes of reality warning her that she was at a luncheon table with people engaged in the solemn consumption of roast beef, in which task she ought to join with the appetite appropriate to a young woman who might eventually become the mother of Konrads yet unborn. As Helen took up her fork, her glance sought Rupert's. He was looking out of the window at the falling snow, and it seemed to her that he refused to meet her eye, knowing what she was thinking, and realizing that when all was said and done (his own revolt notwithstanding) Adolph was right.

twelve

Lunch over, they returned to the parlor, where Adolph buried himself behind the voluminous pages of the Sunday *Tribune* and Wilma settled in her favorite chair, her crochet work on her lap. The young people grouped themselves at the other end of the room, the three girls on the sofa, William sitting stiffly on a straight-backed chair, Rupert stretched languidly on the bear rug at Helen's feet. It was then Helen realized how deeply her presence was resented; in no subtle way Rupert's brother and sisters were impressing the fact that a small-town girl did not belong here, nor ever would.

"How I hate Sundays!" Cecilia cried, unfastening and fastening the ornate earrings that dangled by her cheeks. "So deadly dull! But then I don't suppose Cambridge is very lively at any time, is it, Helen?"

"Ah, but it certainly is! There are concerts or recitals quite often, not to mention all the musical events in Boston next door."

"My goodness, that certainly does sound exciting!" said Cecilia sarcastically, and William added, as he bit off the end of a cigar, "Of course we're spoiled, living here in Chicago. If you stayed on awhile, you'd realize this is the finest city on the continent. One day it'll be bigger than New York, so the experts say."

"The experts? What experts?" Rupert demanded. He had not protected Helen hitherto, but now that he had a chance of lashing out at William, he did. "Oh, you professional Chicagoans!" he cried. "You make me sick. A hick town, that's what this is. Wild and woolly as a bucking steer!"

"It's good enough for me," William boomed solemnly.

"You've said it," Rupert agreed.

"Why don't we play some sort of game?" Bee broke in, her fingers toying with a coral brooch in the shape of a bee, her own emblem. Though only sixteen, she had all the instincts of a ward politician, ever anxious to arbitrate and ingratiate herself with both sides. "Charades or truth and consequences or something like that."

"Or we might persuade Helen here to play the piano," Rupert took the opportunity to suggest.

"Oh, let's do something amusing!" Cecilia cried, before Helen had the opportunity to decline. (But she sent him a reprimanding look, for he knew very well that she refused to play before anyone.) "What I'd like is to go see people. How about calling up Gladys Hastey?" Cecilia said.

"The Hasteys don't approve of telephones," William reminded her rather grandly. "Besides, Gladys is going to Jane Atwill's birthday party this afternoon."

"Oh, a party, a party!" Cecilia sounded ecstatic, parties already having become the aim and justification of her life. "Let's drop in on Janie and wish her many happy returns."

"Not I," said William stodgily. "She could have sent us an invitation."

"And would have if she'd thought of it," Cecilia brushed his objection aside. "Oh, come on, come on! Janie'd love to see us. It's snowing so hard that lots of her guests may not show up. She lives way out on the North Side."

"Then let's ask Papa if we can take the sleigh," Bee, the politician, suggested. "We can say that we were out on a sleigh ride and just driving by."

Rupert shot Helen a glance and was relieved to see her face as bland and untroubled-looking as ever. Thank goodness, he thought, that she did not understand the equivocal position of a Stock Yards family of German descent in Chicago's self-conscious society!

But perhaps it was lucky for Rupert's peace of mind that he could not read Helen's thoughts as she mounted the stairs to get ready. She was not horrified by the Konrads, nor did she despise them; she had merely realized today that they were as foreign to her as Zulus. Her father had taught her ever since she was a child that there were certain rules of conduct, observed with greater or less respect by all civilized people; the Konrads acted as if they had never even heard of such rules. Seeing

Rupert in the family circle helped her understand his revolt and at the same time pointed up the alarming resemblances between these despised relatives and himself. Uncontrolled, moody, and tempestuous, Rupert was saved only by his personal charm from being a typical Konrad!

Helen's room lay at the top of the stairs. Stepping through the doorway, she found that the curtains had been drawn, letting in but a sliver of daylight. Very soothing she found this darkness after the garish parlor, where electric illumination mingled with the gray winter light. How she would have liked to stay up here for the rest of the afternoon, rather than to join these hosts of hers, with whom she had so little in common! But she had better get ready or they would soon be calling her in their strident, impatient voices. She stepped over to the window and gave a tug at the tassel, which brought light streaming in. It disclosed a table and a bookcase that had not been there before; it disclosed a sofa and a bed, and—Helen gave a start—it disclosed a little boy sleeping in the bed!

He lay with one cheek resting on the palm of his delicately shaped hand, an expression of profound unhappiness on his face. The fragile beauty of the lad captured Helen's attention, and now she stood there entranced, her eyes on the finely shaped head which rested on the pillow like some fragile object on a nest of cotton. If this were Francy, about whom Rupert had spoken, she wondered how he could be so different from all the rest of the family. There was in his face an ethereal look which contrasted with the expressions of the other Konrads—yes, even of Rupert, if one looked under his handsome exterior. This tender lad had been cast in a different mold.

As she gazed down at the fine forehead, a little damp in sleep, at the sensitive mouth and the uncertain chin, Helen experienced a curious feeling of kinship with this little boy. It seemed to her that he fitted in this great ugly house as little as did she! The unhappy expression of his face testified to that, and the distraught quiver of his eyelids in sleep. Suddenly she wanted to snatch him in her arms and flee—flee far away in order to protect him from the onslaught of bad taste and wealth which would break upon him.

Boy, boy, she thought, you and I do not belong here! We are in danger—yes, both of us—in grave danger!

79

She tiptoed from the room, keeping her eyes upon him until the last minute, aware that she would never forget that perfect little face with its expression of childish suffering. It would, she knew, come back to her ever and again, and each time she would feel this urgent desire to protect, knowing that it lay beyond her power to give protection.

The snow was coming down heavily as Hirsch drove the team of dappled grays through the gate and headed in the direction of Lake Michigan. Squeezed on the back seat between Cecilia and Bee, Helen tried to enjoy the occasion. Certainly it was fun swishing through Chicago's streets in a luxurious sleigh, bound for a party where laughter and gaiety awaited her; it was the sort of fun her mother had longed for ever since her marriage, and perhaps for want of which she had sickened and died. And yet she could not imagine doing this sort of thing very often! It was much like going to an amusement park: a distraction to be indulged in only once in a long while.

Yes, yes, she thought, even as she snuggled back on the cushiony seat, her father had been right. This world of luxury was not hers! Hers was the world of music and contemplation, of hard work and of spiritual satisfaction: a world inhabited by people like her father and Madame Lubokova, not by wealthy parvenus who went to parties to which they had not been asked. It would be a relief to return to Cambridge in a few days' time, to get back to her work and her practicing. She wished that she were in the chilly music room at this moment, her notes before her, her every effort concentrated on understanding and interpreting the noble achievement of a fellow artist. The very thought of it sent a wave of happiness washing over her. She sat there thinking of her piano, aware only of the snowflakes falling in her face, of the swishing sound of the runners and the high tinkle of the German sleigh bells in her ears.

And then the Highland melody came back. At first she could hear it but faintly, merging as it did with the sounds of the sleigh, but gradually, note by note, it pieced itself together. Again she listened to the reedy notes of the flute, and to the shrill pipe sounds that appeared and disappeared like a gay motif in a colorful Scotch plaid. Now the jingling sleigh bells had joined the unseen orchestra, giving body to the music, which swelled and ebbed as the sleigh sped along the lake front between the tall buildings and the choppy sea. She hummed the melody beneath her breath, hummed it higher as it grew familiar, until she realized all at once that she was singing aloud and that Cecilia had turned to stare at her.

"What a queer song, Helen! What is it called?"

"Oh, I don't know. Just something I heard," said Helen, falling silent.

But Cecilia's interest had been piqued, and she insisted. "Sing it again, Helen. How does it go?"

"I've really forgotten," Helen answered, which was the truth.

"Then why don't we sing something else? 'Jingle Bells' or 'John Brown's Body.' All together!"

Helen shot Rupert a glance, hoping that he would understand and save her. Instead, it was he who chanted the first line of "John Brown's Body," and in another moment all four Konrads had joined in, singing at the top of their lungs with the abandon of unmusical people. Helen felt her little tune withering away at the sound of those crass young voices.

They crossed the Chicago River and found themselves on the North Side, a district which, Rupert told her, was now the fashionable center of the city. It was clear from his voice that he resented the fact that his family still lived on the South Side, but William, as ever a conservative, assured her that the North Side was not all it was cracked up to be, being vulgar and "nouveau riche." The brothers were still arguing the point when Hirsch drew up before an imposing building of brownstone, and the five young people descended from the sleigh.

"Remember now, we just happened to be sleighing by and thought we'd drop in to wish Janie a happy birthday," Bee whispered as they stood in the hall taking off their wraps. From beyond the door came the sound of voices and occasional snatches of laughter, to prove that a party was in swing.

"Well, I wonder what Gladys will think," said William uncertainly. "I have a good mind to wait for you all in the sleigh."

"Don't be a spoilsport!" Cecilia snapped at him. And then she added, rather to Helen's suprise, "Jane'll be tickled to death. After all, her

81

father doesn't amount to a row of pins; Papa could buy out his whole business and never notice the loss."

In the meanwhile Rupert was helping Helen off with her cloak, and when she took off her snow hood, disclosing her hair, she could sense his surprise and pleasure. Before leaving, she had fashioned it into one of those low chignons which she wore only on special occasions. (They looked silly, she thought, in a professor's house in Cambridge.) That was the way her Austrian mother had worn her hair, and as she caught sight of herself in the mirror she was surprised once again to see how it changed her. Instead of a demure little New England girl, there looked back at her a woman of breath-taking distinction.

"You look beautiful, Helen! You look divine!" Rupert whispered, just as Jane Atwill appeared in the hall to welcome her uninvited guests. Whether or not Jane's cordiality was linked to her father's "not amounting to a row of pins," Helen did not know; at any rate she greeted the out-of-town visitor with a warmth that helped dissipate Helen's embarrassment. Whisked off on a round of introductions, she was surprised at the feeling of self-confidence which came to her the moment she stepped into the crowded room and sensed the eyes of all men turning towards her. Never had Helen been to such a party, yet here again she knew instinctively how to act. Forgotten was her feeling of constraint in the Konrad house. She was happy to be here, and accepted with delight the special attention that Chicagoans shower on visitors, finding a ready answer to compliments and a polite one to the oft-repeated invitations that she stay on for good in this most wonderful town of the continent, if not of the entire world.

There was only one person whose attitude differed markedly from the rest. At first contact Helen had sensed enmity in Gladys Hastey's slanting eyes, and now wherever she moved, she could feel their disapproving gaze upon her. William, she noticed, had attached himself to this dark-haired girl, and hovered by her side, ready at a hint or a glance to dash off in search of some more angel cake or to replenish her dish of tutti-frutti ice cream.

"William is sweet on Gladys," the wise Bee informed her. "He'd give his life to marry her, but Gladys won't make up her mind. Her family are terribly wealthy. Is she pretty, do you think?"

82

"Well no, not pretty. But she has an odd little face—quite bewitching."

"Well, she's certainly not half as pretty as you," said Bee, gazing at Helen with her lying green eyes. "Rupert's a much smarter judge of women than William."

"Aren't you a bit young to know?"

"Oh, there's not much that I don't know!"

As she stood there, fingering her coral bee, the little girl struck Helen as being about double her age.

Rupert came walking towards them from across the room, where he had been standing talking to Janie's mother. Helen realized that he was pleased that their "dropping in" had passed off so successfully, and particularly pleased that she, his guest, was proving the sensation of the party. There was nothing Rupert enjoyed like limelight, even limelight reflected from someone else.

"You are a great success, Helen! Everyone is crazy about you. Now aren't you glad that you came out to Chicago?"

Janie had put a record on the victrola, and a gay polka boomed forth from the instrument's great metal horn. Rupert led Helen to a far corner of the room, where the carpet had been rolled back, and he polkaed off with her. She could feel that he was dancing his best because of all the eyes upon them, and his best was very good indeed. It occurred to her all at once that this trip to Chicago was going to turn out pretty nicely after all.

"Oh, I wish you'd never leave," he whispered in her ear. "You're so beautiful, and sort of silvery, with that pale hair of yours shimmering! Won't you let me stay near you forever?"

She smiled at him, struck, as always, by his amazing good looks.

"Can I stop you?" she said, still making her answer as ambiguous as possible.

The tune had come to an end. Helen walked back with him to the buffet, where Cecilia stood speaking to Justin Judson, who was twirling his mustaches and looking highly seductive in his sleek Prince Albert coat.

"Nice work, Rupert!" Justin called out. "Don't you feel giddy after all that twirling about, Miss Mason?"

"Giddy? Well, I do. Quite giddy, in fact!"

"You'll give me the next dance?"

"Of course I will," Helen said, and noted with amusement Rupert's jealous glance.

The phonograph started again, this time booming out a Vienna waltz. Helen, as she took the floor, remembered that back home Vienna waltzes were still thought a bit daring, the New England matrons considering that the partners as good as embraced each other on the floor. To judge from Mr. Judson's conversation, he would not have been averse to doing so in earnest!

"You dance beautifully, Miss Mason," he murmured as he swung her about expertly. "I must say, you have it all over our Chicago girls. You're elegant! You're charming! I suppose you've noticed how madly jealous of you they all are."

"Really?" said Helen innocently. "No, I hadn't noticed."

"Then just take a look at that bevy of beauties over there!" Justin said in the daring manner which accounted for much of his social success. "Look at Cecilia, for instance. No wonder she is biting her lips. She's in love with me, you see."

"Do you expect me to say, 'Lucky girl'?" Helen asked, emulating his way of speech. Obviously this Mr. Judson was rather a cad (who else would hold a young lady so tightly?) but she found him amusing, and by this time she was in the best of humors.

"Well, that depends on how my finances hold out," Justin answered, not disconcerted in the least. "To tell the truth, they're pretty rocky right now. Yes, I really might marry Cecilia in the end."

"I think that you are a very immoral man."

"So I am," Justin agreed, and he squeezed her a little tighter. "You see, nobody takes me seriously, so I can afford to be honest. Between you and me, I'm an adventurer at heart, though I come from a very good family. In fact I'm related to the Hasteys, the stuffiest of the Stock Yards millionaires, and New England descent, like yourself. Just look at old Gladys scowling at us, by the way. She really does hate you, Miss Mason."

"But whatever for?"

"Do you have to ask me?" Justin detached himself from his partner

84

long enough to peer into her face. "So you honestly and truly don't know? It's amazing!"

"Don't know what?"

"Why, that Gladys is taken with Rupert Konrad. She's had her eye on him for years."

"You're joking!" For the first time Helen felt something more than amusement at Justin's audacious sallies. "Why," she protested, "I've just been told that there was a romance on between Gladys and Rupert's brother."

Justin gave his malicious chuckle.

"Romance! Do you really think that word suits William? Can you imagine anyone, especially a smart girl like Gladys, dallying with William Konrad underneath the palms? She may marry him in the end (for her beauty's so strange that she's considered plain ugly by most Chicagoans), but if she does, it'll be a *mariage de convenance,* believe me. Wealthy people are drawn together, perhaps because they're always suspicious of the motives of everybody else. But it's Rupert she wants! And she's never going to forgive you if you steal him away from her. Mark my words, Miss Mason!"

The waltz ended in a high flourish of the violins and a crescendo of twirling by Justin.

"Whew! I am hot," he said, taking a handkerchief from his Prince Albert. "Do let's have something to drink. The fruit punch is well spiked. I can thoroughly recommend it."

"Not for me," said Helen, laughing. "I have never had an alcoholic drink in my life."

"Can such a thing be possible?" Justin looked at her in mock dismay. "In that case is it not time you sampled one of the great pleasures of life, exquisite Easterner?"

With a shake of her head Helen turned to accompany her partner, and it was at that moment that an accident occurred. Gladys Hastey had been standing close by, a glass of sarsparilla in her hand. Now, as Helen moved, they collided, and some drops of sarsparilla spilled over Gladys' dress. Before Helen had had time to apologize, she received a venomous look from eyes that had narrowed to mere slots.

"Well done, Miss Mason," Gladys said coldly. "That's a clever way of ruining a two-hundred-dollar dress."

The attack was so uncalled-for that for a moment Helen thought she had heard wrong; then she realized that she had been insulted, and the blood went to her face. Meeting Justin's sly eye, she realized that he had taken it all in and, what was worse, was feeling sorry for her.

"That was a dirty dig," he said angrily. "Only a thwarted rich girl would have been mean enough to make it."

"Oh, I don't even know what she meant," Helen replied with a shrug. "But I'm sorry that I spoiled her dress—if I really did."

"You know perfectly well that you didn't spoil her darned dress. And you know what she meant, too—the vixen!"

Helen smiled and patted her hair. All her joy in the party had fled, but she certainly was not going to let on to Justin. What did it matter that she had made a success, seeing that she had just been reminded that she belonged to a different world? Well, thank goodness that this new world of Rupert's was not her natural environment! Thank goodness, she thought (as she swallowed the tears in her throat), that she did not live with people like Gladys, for whom material wealth was the sole criterion of value.

But Justin was holding out a goblet, the sardonic smile on his lips.

"Let us drink—to manners," he said. "You certainly have them, Miss Mason. Would Rupert be angry if I told you that I admire you very much?"

Helen remembered what Justin had said about the punch being spiked, but at that moment nothing much seemed to matter. Accepting the glass, she downed its contents in a few gulps. Almost at once things began to happen. Through her body went a sensation of warmth, and with it her self-confidence flooded back. She had never imagined that there was so much comfort to be obtained from one little glass of liquid! Suddenly Gladys' rudeness seemed to her utterly unimportant, something to be laughed at and forgotten. With an expression of curiosity, she finished her glass and it did not occur to her to protest when Justin took it up to refill.

But Rupert had seen what was happening. Now he came hurrying up, eyes ablaze, and with one jerk had pulled the pitcher from Justin's hand.

"What do you mean by giving this young lady alcoholic beverages? We've had enough of your cheap tricks!" he cried (though he kept his voice fairly low, having no desire to create a scandal). "No wonder they kicked you out of Princeton University. You are no gentleman, Justin!"

"So you've just found that out?" Justin retained all his composure. "There's no harm done, Rupert, I guarantee. Did you, Miss Mason, find this beverage particularly unpleasant?"

Helen refrained from answering. She could not admit that the effect of the punch was highly desirable, soothing and calming her, when a moment before she had felt painfully shaken. For a young lady of 1905 there were many subjects on which honesty was out of order, which is why she turned her back on her tempter and walked away. But as she was about to dance off with Rupert, her eyes met Justin's over her partner's shoulder. Was it her imagination, or did he give her—a collusive look? Long afterwards Helen would remember that look, and she would ask herself if Justin realized that day that he had initiated her into a secret.

"I should have warned you," Rupert was saying. "That fellow Justin just isn't to be trusted. Imagine him doing such a thing in a respectable household!"

"Oh, I don't think he meant any harm," Helen said, savoring a little-known feeling of satisfaction in the moment at hand. (As a rule, she had felt torn, whether seated at the piano, with one part of her rebelling against her father's tyranny, or when *not* seated at the piano and feeling that it was her duty to be practicing.) "Don't be angry with him, Rupert!"

"Not angry with him! After watching him dance with you as no decent man should do, then try to make you inebriated with that spiked punch! D'you know that I have half a mind . . ."

Helen began to laugh.

"Why, Rupert, I do think that you are jealous of Mr. Judson. Yes, you really are!"

Suddenly she began feeling completely, quite ridiculously, happy.

Being feminine, she interpreted Rupert's jealousy as sure proof of his love, and being the slightest bit tipsy, she no longer saw any obstacle in letting him love her. He, who could have had a wealthy girl like Gladys Hastey for the asking, had chosen instead the daughter of an indigent professor. Could the professor's daughter refuse? He was ready to open the door to a world of which she had had her first glimpse that very day: a world of daring men and smart women, of footmen and sleighs and beaver rugs; a world where people lived gaily and one didn't have to worry about perfecting oneself as a musician— or, for that matter, as a human being. It was a world she had never known, but for which one part of her had longed ever since she was a small girl dressing up her dolls in snippets of gay silk.

And as they drove home in the sleigh a little later, this feeling of present happiness and wild anticipation was still with her. She sat holding hands with Rupert under the rug, and each time he gave her fingers a squeeze, she squeezed back, meaning yes. The future seemed to her rich and exciting, like an exotic country whose borders she had passed at night. She was riding into it in a golden sleigh behind two dappled mares, and presently the sun would go up and a fantastic landscape would be disclosed to view. The sound of the runners driving over the snow told of their swift progress. But tonight that sound was not transmuted into the eerie music of Scotch glens; it ebbed and flowed like the tones of a languorous violin, while the clip-clop of the horses' hoofs beat in her ears the rhythm of a lilting Vienna waltz.

thirteen

When the sound of the sleigh bells had passed down the drive, Adolph put aside his *Tribune* and sat staring into the fireplace; calming to his nerves was the silence that had settled on the house with the departure of the young people. Wilma had gone upstairs to make sure that Francy was asleep, and presently she came back, carrying a pile of clothes in need of darning. She was a little ashamed to engage in this task before her children, although she found it more enjoyable, and certainly more useful, than her finicky crocheting. Indeed, she had to stop herself from doing many things when the children were about, such as wearing bedroom slippers, or making herself a cup of coffee in the kitchen, or using homely, countrified expressions in her speech.

"Well, Adolph, how do you like our Rupert's young lady?" she asked at length, as she drew her needle through a woolen stocking that belonged to Bee. "A real nice girl, ain't she?"

Adolph looked up from the fire slowly. There was a thoughtful expression on his face, and Wilma knew that his active brain had been ranging far afield as he sat there staring at the flames.

"Ya, Vilma." He nodded. "A nice girl. A little dreaming, perhaps—not enough feet on the ground. At lunch today she had a look on her face like vh~· she vas a t'ousand miles avay. Still, she vill maybe make the boy a good vife. Rupert needs somevone—a little special."

"You're right, Adolph," Wilma said, careful not to let on that it was she who had put this idea in his head.

Adolph reached for a birch stick on the mantelpiece and pulled open the blade of his knife. He began whittling the point of the stick, sending the shavings flittering into the fire. Wilma saw that he was drawing the blade of the knife towards him, and as always when this happened, her thoughts went to him in solicitude.

"I know what you're thinking," she said, dropping the unmended stocking in her lap. "You are thinking that Rupert hasn't turned out just like we wanted. It makes you sad, Adolph."

"It is not your fault, Mama. Rupert is Rupert."

"Yes, yes, Adolph. One's got to take people as they are, as my papa used to say. Rupert's still young. Perhaps this Helen Mason can help him. That's what I was hoping when I took the train for Boston."

Adolph gave a grunt. He hadn't forgiven Wilma that journey to the East, and she knew it had been foolish to remind him of her first rebellion in twenty-seven years.

"Perhaps our William will marry that young Hastey girl," she hurried on, so as to change his mood. "It would be a grand match for him. And a real boost for the family."

"Ve don't need no boostin'," Adolph said testily. "Villiam is good enough for the Hasteys or for anyvone else."

"I should say he is! Still, it would be pretty nice, wouldn't it, Adolph? Just think! One of the best families in the city, almost as rich as the Fields and the McCormicks. We couldn't go higher, Adolph. We couldn't go any higher."

"No," Adolph agreed, "it's a fact—ve couldn't go no higher."

He tossed into the fire the remains of the birch stick, no longer than a pencil now, and at the moment that it burst into flame, a smile lit his face. Wilma, watching him, knew that she had struck the right formula.

"Not such a bad match for the grandson of a Schwabenland pigherd!" He chuckled. "Vhat do you suppose my papa vould say, if he still vas alive? Or your papa either, vhen it comes to that! Listen, Vilma, if I ask you a qvestion, vill you give me an honest answer?"

"I have alvays been honest with you," Wilma said, taking off her glasses and gazing at Adolph with her steady blue eyes. (Without her glasses she looked ten years younger, a still handsome woman with blond hair and round cheeks.)

"I know you have," said Adolph. "So tell me this. The day I left your papa's farm in Ohio, back in '76, I had exactly tventy-two dollars to my name. Tventy-two dollars und that little tray mit my peddler's vares! Vhat vould you have t'ought then, if somevone had told you that our son vould marry the daughter of a bluestocking millionaire?"

"Why, land's sake, Adolph, I wouldn't have been one bit surprised!"

Adolph reached out to pat her hand.

"I knew that's vhat you'd say. Ach, Vilma, I can alvays count on you! Still, I can't help vondering vhat gave you so much confidence in me. Vhat vas I, anyvay? Chust another poor boy from the old country, trying to make his vay. I vas chust seventeen, vorking my vay to Chicago mit a few shoelaces und buttons as vorking capital. A peddler, no more!"

"Yes, Adolph. But such an unusual peddler! I knew it the first day I saw you. The very first minute! Do you remember? Oh, Adolph, do you remember . . ."

He remembers lying in the meadow on that far-off July day. It is so warm! The branches above his head throw shadows on the grass, on his cap lying by his feet and the wooden box which holds his stock of peddler's wares. He has just made an inventory, and the box still lies open, with the celluloid combs, the ribbons, the handkerchiefs and the painted toys all flashing their colors in the sunlight falling through the trees.

He feels very happy, for he has sold better than he hoped when he started off, and he is more than halfway to Chicago. Already his six grim months as a charcoal burner have receded into that past which he can think of only as a long stretch of slavery; whether he toiled in the lace factories of Württemberg, in the sweatshops of New York, or in the coal mines of western Pennsylvania, the aches and the misery were the same, and the dream of freedom, ever nurtured in his heart, was also the same. And now in another month he will be walking into the city whose streets were either still unpaved—or paved with gold! He smiles to himself, reflecting that either alternative holds strong possibilities for gain.

There is a stirring in the bushes. A rabbit? he thinks, and holds his breath so as not to frighten it away. But then he sees the bushes part, and between them steps a young girl in a blue dress with her blond hair in braids. She looks like a real German peasant girl! When she sees him, she stops short, and he is sure that she will hurry away. However, she catches sight of the open box, and now curiosity masters her. She steps closer, peers down at the ribbons and the lace strips with a childish expression of delight. One finger reaches out tentatively and touches the edge of a pale green ribbon, then pulls back in alarm.

And at that he puts out his hand and he calls to her in his broken English, "Ach, please, miss, do not go avay. Vill you allow? *Gestatten Sie, bitte?*" he goes on, falling into German. And, reaching for the ribbon, he holds it out to her with the tip of his fingers.

She hesitates. Will she hurry away? Will she take the ribbon? He lies there with beating heart, and then he sees her hand slowly, cautiously, moving towards his, until her fingers close on the band of cloth. He draws back his arm. And suddenly the realization comes to him, novel and altogether startling (like a realization that he has been endowed with a sixth sense), that he has actually *given* something away.

Not sold. Given! From the farmhouse above the meadow a voice is calling:

"Wilma! Wilma!"

"Vilma, ach, Vilma," Adolph said, "do you know how long ago that vas? Tventy-nine years! But sometimes it seems like yesterday. I bet if I walked into your papa's farmhouse this minute, I'd remember each crack in the kitchen table and the chips on every plate. I can still see the old Cherman cuckoo clock on the vall, right beside the cloth you'd embroidered mit 'Home, sveet home.' That house was real home for me! Those two months on the farm vere my first holiday since I began vork in the lace factory, vhen I vas six years old."

Wilma smiled.

"Holiday? A funny holiday! Why, Adolph, you were up before any-on- in the morning, and at night you stayed awake doing lessons. Even Papa said you were worth any two other hands, and Papa sure made our hands work. I don't wonder that he wanted you to stay on."

"Don't say that, Vilma. Your papa vas good to me. The first man vhat ever vas good to me! Vhere vould I be now if he hadn't taught me how to read, how to write? I love his memory. Not yet do I understand vhy he took to me such a liking."

"And why shouldn't he have, I'd like to know?" said Wilma huffily. "Wasn't he as good a judge of a man as his daughter? He knew a smart boy when he saw one—a fellow who was going to make a success of life. Mama did too. But she was scared that you'd steal her daughter away."

"Und how right she vas!"

Adolph pulled Wilma up from her chair and made her sit on his knee. His arm was about her waist. As he gazed into the fire, it all came back to him: the pond where they had fished and he had put the worms on the hook for Wilma; the path up the meadow where they gave each other the first kisses; the hayloft where they lay with their young bodies intertwined and their lips finding each other in the dark. The summer smells were in his nostrils: the smell of alfalfa and of fresh milk and of young sun-warmed flesh. He could hear the sound of water being pumped into a pail, and of an ax striking wood, and of

92

the gilded herd

Farmer Busch's cattle stamping down a sun-baked road, the surrounding trees echoing their hoof-falls . . .

And Adolph remembers the September evening when he lay in the meadow again and, falling asleep, had a dream. It was a very important dream, setting as it did the pattern that he had been following ever since. Or perhps the pattern was already there, and this was no dream at all, but merely a revelation of events to come. Often since he had pondered this very question: whether all he had ever done, his whole life's work, in fact, had been a series of willed and deliberate actions— or else merely the attainment of objectives set out like milestones on his way (neither way nor milestones having been alterable from the day of his birth). With each succeeding decade he was more tantalized by this imponderable problem.

In this dream, or vision, of thirty years back, Adolph saw Farmer Busch's herd of cattle, but now instead of thirty cows there was a giant herd, which grew and grew, even as he watched it. Until at last the whole field was filled with cattle! As far as the eye could reach stood the sleek, browsing beasts, and in the dream their tawny hides had taken on a beautiful golden sheen. . . . Suddenly the animals began streaming from the field. Rapidly, ever more rapidly, they moved down the broad road leading to the city, the smoke of whose chimneys billowed up in the distance, shot through with clear golden flames. He could hear the stamp of hoofs hammering in his ears, and it was like the beating of great kettledrums.

With a feeling of exultation, young Adolph had swum out of his dream, back to reality. And now he had had the sure knowledge that the time had come for him to move—on, on to Chicago! He must follow the path of those stamping cattle. Westward had been his direction ever since he boarded the train back in Germany, in charge of the contractor who was to take him to America. New York, Pennsylvania, Ohio had been steps along his way, but not yet was his journey over. It was in Illinois that those cattle would be transformed into gold, with which he would fill his pockets until they could hold no more!

As he rose from the field the sun was dipping low in the western sky, and it, too, like the cattle and the pillars of smoke, had an unearthly golden color. He walked back to the farmhouse, prepared to get his wages from Farmer Busch and to bid Wilma good-by.

"Oh, I was sad when you had gone away!" Wilma sighed as she peered into the fire. "How long the days were! I thought your first letter would never come, and when it did, I began to long for the next. I was afraid I'd be an old woman before you came back to fetch me to Chicago."

"But you alvays knew that I *vould* come back?"

"Land's sake, Adolph, what a question! But sometimes I thought old age would come for me first. A year went by, and then the next . . ."

"I wrote you tvice every veek. I spent more on postage stamps than on fun. In fact I didn't have no fun."

"I know, Adolph. But it wasn't alvays easy to wait. I wasn't exactly —an ugly girl."

"Ach, but vhat you say, Vilma! Ugly!"

"And there were other fellows . . ."

Adolph took her hand and carried it to his lips. He was in one of those sentimental moods that were rare for him, and it seemed to him in looking back that his and Wilma's love had been more perfect than any romance written about in books. For thirty long years, ever since emerging from childhood, they had been completely loyal to each other. And in all that period, the nearest they had come to a misunderstanding was in connection with Rupert, this very month!

Being egocentric, Adolph did not stop to reflect that this accord had been achieved largely because Wilma always gave in to him. He knew that he had loved her more than anything in life—that perhaps she was the one thing (apart from his business) that he really had loved. Without this ally, could he have won through to victory in the fierce battle of the Stock Yards? Without this helper, could he have survived the backbreaking days, the sleepless nights, the constant tension and the constant struggle? Without this mate, could he have welded into reality a dream dreamed thirty years before?

He sees himself standing beside her in an empty lot south of the old city limits, Wilma dressed in a country girl's best (blue cotton dress

with lace collar, and a funny straw hat looking rather like a "boater"),
he in a brand-new black suit, new boots, new shirt, new everything.
For they have been married only the day before, and have just arrived
by train from Ohio. Both are carrying suitcases, Adolph having suggested that she would see the city better if they walked to their hired
rooms near the Yards instead of taking a jolting (and expensive) horse
cab.

And now he has been escorting her for an hour and a half, through
the Loop, down Michigan, across the slum district by Indiana, finally
to arrive in the open country east of Prairie Avenue. Here Adolph has
led the surprised Wilma across a field used as a dumping lot and a
larger field where brambles clutched at her skirt and grazing goats
looked up at them as they passed. He has halted at the foot of a long
bare hill and is pointing towards its summit.

"That," he informs her, "is vhere ve are going to live, Vilma."

"Oh, Adolph! Tonight?" she asks, obviously prepared to pitch a
tent on that bare knoll.

"No, no," he says, laughing. "Not tonight. But here is vhere I am
going to buy land vone day und put up our house. It's a good spot, not
so, Vilma? High up, so it can look over everyt'ing, und mit plenty of
room, so it can be a really *big* house. For I vant for my house to be as
big as any other man's! It vill be tall und solid, und have a mansard
roof und bow vindows out in front."

They stare up at the empty hill, empty no longer, but crowned now
by a house that is as real for both of them as if the last tile had been
laid. They see the curving driveway, flanked on either side by a sloping
lawn, the stables on the left, the hothouse on the right, beside the
flower garden with its even rows of blooming plants. Everything about
their future home is actual and complete, down to the children playing
tag beneath the arched portico. Do they not know that with Adolph
conception carries within it the seeds of accomplishment?

"What a lovely house it will be!" Wilma whispers in delight. "A
real palace, Adolph!"

And Adolph agrees, as a smile floods into his face.

"Ya, ya, a palace, Vilma—a palace for new royalty: the Konrads of
America. So let's call it Sans Souci, just like the Kaiser's fine palace in

95

Potsdam. It's pioneers like us vhat have built up this country mit our brains und our sveat und our lives. Ve are the rulers! This is our country! Chust let anyone try to take it avay from us!"

There was a peal of the doorbell that rang through the house, urgent, almost imperious. Adolph gave a start. That summons seemed to call him out of the nineteenth century right back to the twentieth; it was as if someone were shaking him by the shoulders and shouting in his ears that yesterday was gone beyond recall, that, as always, it was today and today's problems that must be faced. A moment later Hauptman entered the room.

"It's Mr. McKenna come to see you, Mr. Konrad."

Adolph and Wilma looked at each other. What on earth could McKenna be wanting here on this snowy Sunday afternoon? Adolph sensed that Wilma's whole body had tensed, and he was aware once again of the inexplicable antipathy that this man aroused in her. Then he realized that he, too, was bracing himself for the interview.

But when McKenna walked in, he wore the matter-of-fact air that was as much a part of him as his snub nose or his thin sandy hair. His very first words should have laid Adolph's suspicions at rest.

"I have news that is going to please you, Mr. Konrad. I've just come from a meeting with Gogerty, the union boss. Excuse me for bothering you on the Sabbath, but I thought that you ought to know just as soon as possible."

"Know vhat?"

"Why, that the pickle-room strike is over," said McKenna, not looking as if he were either pleased or displeased. "And we haven't made the slightest concession! All the concessions come from Gogerty's side, and the other union bosses will fall in."

"So Gogerty sold out?"

"Of course," McKenna said.

But even now Adolph derived no satisfaction from the victory. He had been wanting to hear this for weeks, yet now he could only reflect that his manager's success was the corollary of his own failure to subdue the union. And what implication, he asked himself, did that success and that failure hold for the future?

96

"So you don't even stop vorking on a Sunday!" he grumbled, determined not to give McKenna the satisfaction of hearing praise. But it was evident that the realistic Scotsman had expected none.

"Ay. Got to keep on the move, Mr. Konrad," he said, rubbing together his bony hands. "Despite my Presbyterian upbringing, I've found Sunday as good a time as any other to strike a bargain. A little better, perhaps. And now, Mr. Konrad, I'll be taking my leave and not disturbing you and Mrs. Konrad any longer."

Adolph felt that something was called for at this juncture. Should McKenna be invited to have a drink before he plunged back into the snowstorm? But then McKenna did not drink, and one had the feeling with him that he was almost insensible to cold or to heat. Should he be offered a cigar? He knew McKenna did not smoke.

"Vouldn't like a cup of tea, vould you?" he suggested, figuring that at least Scotch people did drink tea.

"Thank you, no," McKenna said. "I shan't trouble you. I've got a two-mile walk before me, and I'd best be getting started before the storm gets any worse."

"You mean to tell me you came all this vay from Packingtown on foot?"

"Certainly, Mr. Konrad. Why spend money on a streetcar? The exercise'll do me good."

"Vill it?" said Adolph. "Vell, vell."

Gazing at this joyless, penny-pinching man from the North, Adolph Konrad had the feeling that here finally he had met someone who was his match: his match for toughness, his match for ruthlessness too. And he had a moment of acute distress because his sure instinct told him that there was no room in the same business for two such single-minded individuals. One day, he realized, a showdown would be called for between his manager and himself, so perhaps the most sensible thing to do was to kick the fellow out now, while the kicking was good. Or could it be (the thought flashed through his mind and was gone) that Angus McKenna already had made himself indispensable to the proper functioning of Adolph Konrad Company?

Adolph watched McKenna being helped into his overcoat by Hauptman and tried to think of something to say which would re-establish the proper relationship between boss and paid employee. After all, the man did still receive his pay check on the first of each month, with Adolph Konrad's signature at the foot of it. Somehow McKenna seemed able to rise above such considerations.

"You remember that proposition ve spoke about last veek?" he asked, reverting to his everyday business manner. "In connection mit our buying Building No. 2 of the old Hastey cannery? I've been t'inking about it und, you know, I like the idea, McKenna. Ve haven't stopped expanding yet! I vant for you to get the facts und figures down on paper, und for Christ's sake get a viggle on. Let me know chust as soon as you're ready."

"I'm ready now, Mr. Konrad," answered McKenna blandly. "I looked into all that last week and even found a chance to drop a hint to Mr. Jones. I believe we can swing a deal."

"Oh, you do, do you!" Adolph said, the wind taken out of his sails. "Und who the devil is Mr. Jones?"

"You've met him, Mr. Konrad: Mark Jones, the Hasteys' plant manager. You know how difficult Harold Hastey is. It's simpler and easier to do business with Jones."

"I see," said Adolph, wrinkling his brows. "I see."

And he thought, *Ach mein Gott!* Yet another manager. Where is all this going to end?

Hauptman pulled open the front door, and McKenna stepped out into the blistering afternoon as casually as if he were stepping from one room to the next; walking stiffly as an automaton, he made his way down the drive. Before Hauptman could push shut the door, an icy blast had swept into the vestibule, bringing with it a flurry of snow. The cold air even swept into the parlor, where Wilma was sitting so cozily before the fireplace. When she looked up quickly, her anxious gaze met Adolph's across the hall.

"Close it, *Dummkopf!*" Adolph shouted at his butler. "Close it! Close it, I say!" His voice rose to a pitch of fury approaching desperation. "Vhat d'you vant—that me und the missus should get blown right out of our own house?"

part two 1920

THE TWO-HEADED TURTLE

one

The late afternoon sun slanted through the window, gilding the lace curtains, the camel-hair rug, the thin blond hair of the young man who lay dozing on the sofa. Francis Konrad stirred uneasily and threw his arm before his eyes. As he lay, half awake, half asleep, a dream had flitted across the surface of his mind, like the shadow of a great bird passing overhead. The memory of it was still there, mysterious, vaguely terrifying.

He had been riding over a boulder-strewn trail along the side of a great canyon, his horse picking its way forward with no guidance on his part. Far beneath him a dried river bed twisted like a black snake between the blood-colored cliffs; the air he drew into his lungs was of incomparable purity. Suddenly he noticed that the trail before him divided, one fork heading downwards, while the narrower path zigzagged upwards along the sheer side of the cliff. Gripped by indecision, he remembered with relief the mountain horse's unerring judgment. But at that moment he grew aware that he was on horseback no longer. In terror, he realized that he was making his way towards the point of decision on bare bleeding feet.

Francy sat up and stared about him. His heart was pounding, as it always did when he awoke from one of these frightening daydreams; his whole body was bathed in perspiration. Only gradually, as he recognized his own intimate surroundings, did the feeling of panic wear away. The lithograph of Goethe; the well-loved books that filled the bookcase; the framed college diploma on which stood out in Gothic script the words *summa cum laude*—all these were safe and familiar objects, assuring him that there was no cause for fear.

His eyes moved to the armchair, on which two sets of clothes were laid out side by side: the one a suit of dark blue serge, the other consisting of a pair of worn flannels and a tweed jacket. They reminded him that he was expected at his brother Rupert's house, and that he meant to go on from there to a literary gathering on the far North Side. At that the feeling of uncertainty flooded back, though without the anguish attendant on it in his dream. While he wished to look his best at Rupert's, he certainly could not turn up at Andy Bogarty's "bohemian" party in a conventional blue suit! Oh, why, why, is nothing simple in my life? thought Francy as his glance passed from the double-breasted jacket to the sports coat with a button missing. Before him he saw again the mountain trail with the two diverging forks.

A half hour later he was walking down the staircase with the dark suit on his back, in his hand a traveling bag into which he had flung the other. He felt pleased with this compromise and exhilarated at the prospect of the exciting meeting towards which he hurried. A tune was on his lips as he skipped down the broad steps two at a time, stopping on the lower landing to adjust the visor of the armored figure that had stood there since before he was conceived. This was the year 1920 and Francy was twenty-four, but no one in Adolph's household had yet contrived a means of keeping that visor from slipping down over the crusader's wax countenance.

As he continued down the last flight, Francy heard a voice call out to him from the parlor, and caught sight of Dr. O'Grady through the doorway. He was lolling in an armchair, his feet on the sofa, in his mouth one of Adolph's best cigars with the Havana band still on it.

"Where are ye off to, young fellow me lad?" O'Grady cried, while the cigar in his mouth moved up and down like a sensitive antenna. "Why the great rush, Francy?"

"I'm looking in on Rupert," Francy replied, as he halted between the sliding doors. "And I'm afraid I shall be late," he added, with a glance at the old-fashioned clock upon the mantelpiece that had ticked away the decades under its glass dome.

For already he was conscious of his old feeling of constraint with the doctor; their relationship was as clouded as a muddy brook. O'Grady it was who had treated him for rheumatic fever as a child, and whether it was owing to his ineptness or to his desire to please Adolph, he had consented to the sick boy's getting up from bed well before his fever had dropped back to normal. Thanks to that fateful mistake, Francy's heart had been permanently weakened, so no wonder that in his presence the doctor now acted like a guilty man. He talked and he laughed too much, and he kept boasting until the listener felt acutely embarrassed for his sake.

"Late? Come, come, what d'ye mean, late?" O'Grady was winking and beckoning to Francy, who reluctantly stepped into the room. "Why, it's barely six, me boy, an' yer brother Rupert never serves dinner before seven-thirty. European habits! He's far too grand for this wild an' woolly city. I ask meself why that young diplomat didn't stay abroad for his long holidays, instead of comin' back to Chicago an' actin' the grand seigneur."

"After twelve years abroad, I suppose even Rupert got homesick," Francy suggested.

At which the doctor declared, "Not Rupert!" He waved his cigar about in circles, sending the ashes flying. "Rupert always hated Chicago an' everythin' about it. No, he came back to dazzle us all and to prove he was a real success. Particularly to prove it to William! His main aim in life is convincin' William that he's the cleverer, the more successful and the more glamorous of the two!"

Francy had to smile. The doctor's theory certainly went far to explain the pattern of his brother's life!

"Well, admit," he said, "that Rupert has set the city on its ears. He's getting more publicity for giving parties than my father ever did for making a fortune."

"That's right, me boy." O'Grady chuckled. "I suppose you'd call Rupert a success: he hobnobs with the elite in th' capitals of the world and thinks nothin' of givin' a dinner party for princesses and prime ministers. He's got the life he always longed for, an' if you ask me, it's ninety per cent thanks to that nice wife of his. Smartest thing he ever did was to marry Helen."

Francy felt his heart beginning to pound. Every mention of Helen's name had that result, and in vain would he attempt to look uninterested, as befitted a man hearing about his brother's wife. He had the feeling at such times that every eye was on him, probing his secret, analyzing his thoughts, accusing him of having fallen in love with his own sister-in-law!

"Well, now I really must be going," he broke in, and snatched up his bag desperately. "I've got to get way up to the North Side and I'm going to be late."

But again the doctor tried to dissuade him, as if to prove to himself that he felt at ease in his ex-patient's presence.

"And how's your poetry coming on, me boy? Still scribblin' away?"

"Oh yes, always scribbling," answered Francy, and he smiled awkwardly to hide the fact that this was yet another subject that he wanted to avoid.

"I hear ye're thinkin' of takin' up poetry as a career," the doctor went on, with his infallible instinct for saying the wrong thing. "Damnedest career I've ever heard of for the son of a meat packer, but I'm wishin' ye luck. Your dad showed me one of yer poems that wormed its way into an anthology, and if you don't mind me sayin' so, I failed to see what ye was drivin' at. Not that it's yer fault, me lad. I used to write poetry meself when I was a young man, and pretty good it was too. Everybody praised me up to the skies—they called me the white-haired boy." (O'Grady said this without blinking an eyelash.) "But in those times we artists used to say what we meant, or tried to anyway. Well, I dare say ye'll find people willin' to puzzle out what ye're aimin' at."

"Oh, I hope so," said Francis, completely flustered. Then, mortified and unhappy, he waved an overcordial good-by and hurried from the house.

It was March, that betwixt-and-between month when a young man's body is stirred by vague desires, though still gripped with the lassitude of winter; his metabolism has not yet attuned itself to the new season. As Francy made his way past the flower beds he saw that the crocuses had begun to open their leaves; against the black earth they formed a brilliant pattern of purples, yellows, and whites. He thought of picking a few to take to Helen, then decided against it. She would think him raving mad, and with right, if he arrived with a bouquet, like a young swain courting his beloved!

Outside the old stables Hirsch was clumping about in rubber boots, aiming the jet of a hose against a great Pierce-Arrow with the initials "A.K." on the door.

"Good evenin', Mr. Francy. Will you be using the Ford car tonight?"

"No," Francy said, "I'm taking the trolley. I'm having dinner at Mr. Rupert's on the North Side."

"And why go bumping across town in a trolley, you with your bum heart? Why not ask Mr. Konrad if you can take the Ford?" Hirsch suggested. And then he answered himself, "Or don't you want to ask your own father a favor?"

But Francy had strolled off down the drive, swinging his bag and whistling a tune. As Hirsch watched the slender figure vanish around the bend, he pushed back his chauffeur's cap and gave his curly head a scratch. Mr. Francy had always puzzled Hirsch, a practical North German—puzzled him and worried him considerably. Of the five Konrad children, Mr. Francy alone seemed to have inherited none of his father's common sense—in fact simply did not have his feet on the ground. Mr. William was a good businessman with a Packard; Mr. Rupert had two Mercedes-Benzs abroad; Miss Cecilia had a handsome husband and a Nash, whereas her sister, Miss Bee, had gone in for politics and a Hupmobile. Only Mr. Francy had no car and no profession. He said he was a poet, but who had ever heard of a millionaire's son writing poetry? Hirsch shook his head. At heart he was very fond of Mr. Francy.

When Francy stepped off the La Salle Street trolley it was already darkening; the lights were beginning to go on in the apartment buildings, and dusk masked the hideousness of the Chicago streets. From the direction of the lake a spring breeze blew towards him, carrying, thought Francy, the vague scent of apple blossom to mingle with the city smells. That put him in mind of flowers, and now he regretted not having taken the crocuses after all. Catching sight of a flower store, he went in and looked first at the roses, then at some pink carnations. He would have taken the roses, except that they were expensive and it was against his very nature to make a display of wealth. But as the girl was wrapping up the carnations he thought, What difference can it possibly make? As if I were fooling anyone except myself! I mustn't let my actions be controlled by these sterile guilt feelings.

105

She was lying on the sofa by the window with a book open in her hand. But obviously she had not been reading. It was too dark, for one thing; and from the slow way she turned her head, he understood that she had been far away. Only when she sent him her warm smile was he sure that he was not intruding.

"Hello, Francy. How sweet of you to have come!"

Francy walked over to the sofa slowly. He was thinking what a beautiful color combination her mauve velvet dress made with the sofa's green brocade and with her pale hair, which in the half-dark seemed to have a silvery sheen. Each time he saw her Francy was overcome by Helen's lightness, her grace; he always felt that she might float out of the room at any moment. It was this ethereal quality in Helen that had moved him ever since he was a boy.

"Oh, you have brought me red roses!" she said. "I love red roses better than anything in the world."

"I thought you did," said Francy, putting his bouquet into the open hands she stretched up from the sofa. Detaching a rose, Helen pinned it to her bosom with a little amethyst clip and stuck the rest of the flowers in a pitcher. Then Francy noted for the first time the whiskey bottle beside the couch, the half-empty tumbler, and the ash tray littered with stubs.

"But could you afford it? Admit, Francy, that you've been terribly extravagant!"

He laughed, pleased at the assumption that he had to think of economies; most people took it for granted that as the son of a rich man he could spend as much as he chose.

"Don't worry about that. I finished another stanza of my *Stock Yards Ballad* this morning, and if it isn't worth a dozen roses, then I ought to give up writing forever."

"Ah, that's exciting!" She sat up on the sofa, and her hand went out to give his a little squeeze. "When will you let me hear the new stanza?"

"When will you let me hear you play the piano?" he countered. "I've been waiting ever since you came to Chicago, more than a month ago."

But now Helen shook her head, and there came into her face the distraught look that Francy had seen each time he mentioned her playing. Her forehead puckered above the sensitive little nose.

"I wish you wouldn't ask me again. Do me a favor, Francy! I've told you already that I never play for anyone, and if I still practice, it's for my own enjoyment. As a musician—I am a failure."

Failure! Francy found himself wincing at a word which had always struck him as the most frightening in the language. Could it have been his dread of artistic failure for himself that caused him to cry out, "That isn't so! You must never, never say that again. I absolutely refuse to listen to you"?

"Why, Francy, what's the matter?" She was smiling at him from the depth of her sofa. "My goodness, what a violent person you are, beneath all your gentleness! But it's true, you know—what I said. Why should it upset you?"

"Just because it *isn't* true! You are a real artist, Helen. One knows it just by watching you, by looking into your eyes. I have never heard you play, but I know that if you wanted to enough—you could play wonderfully."

The smile lingered on Helen's face. It had taken on a wistful quality now; it was turned in upon herself.

"Could have, once upon a time," she said. "But that's a thing of the past. In fact I don't want to talk about it. I'm fond of you, Francy. You know that. But you are a young man of twenty-four, and you can't possibly understand my life."

At once he grew contrite. It was as if she had reminded him that she was the wife of an elder brother, that she was ten years his senior, and consented to see him only to fill in a few empty half hours. There came into his face that embarrassed grin which always seemed to imply the opposite of what he meant.

"You're right, Helen, utterly right! Forgive me! It's just that I can't bear the idea of—of wasted talent. Wasted talent's a crime against nature. Don't worry, though! I shan't say another word."

"But you have just said another word!" cried Helen, half laughing, half seriously. "And, what's more, you'll keep saying other words. In the end I'll have to ask you not to come here any more."

"Oh, don't do that!" He ran a hand through his thin hair in a distracted gesture. "Whatever you do, don't do that. If you only knew how much our—our friendship means to me."

Helen turned her head on the pillow so that their glances met. Francy was gazing at her with an expression that bordered on dismay; had it not had in it the tragic intensity of youth, it would have been almost comical. And it struck Helen, not for the first time, that it really would be safest if she told this naïve young man not to come here any more. She knew, she knew all too well, the danger of these meetings in the late afternoon when boredom ravaged her and the realization of the dreariness of her life came sweeping over her like a wave.

And there came back the memory of a whole series of such afternoons, in Vienna and in Berlin, in Cairo and in Teheran. Always there had been a young man somewhat like Francy, sensitive and artistic and understanding, with whom she had shared those melancholy hours. (Antonio Lazari playing the violin for her, his aristocratic fingers looking almost too delicate to hold the bow; Anton Holbein, the young Austrian painter who had consumption; Pahlevi Azad, the Persian boy with the tragic eyes who committed suicide later on.) What had she wanted of them? Not love. Certainly not mere distraction. Perhaps it was reassurance that she had sought from them: reassurance that there still existed another world, apart from the two-dimensional diplomatic world to which she and Rupert belonged.

"My dear brother-in-law, you had better show me a bit of respect," she said, adopting a bantering tone. "Remember I am an old lady, and now stop lecturing me. Tell me instead when I am going to hear your new stanza."

"Oh, whenever you wish!" The relief in his voice was touching. "As a matter of fact"—he patted his breast pocket—"I happen to have it with me now. I'm going on to Andy Bogarty's place from here. (As I told you, there's a group of us get together there every Wednesday.) Andy phoned me this morning to say that Edgar Lee Masters had promised to drop in tonight. We're all going to read him bits of our poems and we hope he'll give us advice."

"Oh, Francy! Aren't you excited?"

"No. It's much more exciting just reading to you."

He drew from his pocket the sheets of foolscap, scribbled over in his large untidy hand, and sat down on the edge of the sofa. Helen switched on the standing lamp, flooding their corner of the room with a mellow light. Smoothing out the papers on his knee, Francy began:

> *"On the floor of the abattoir*
> *Grows a red flower.*
> *It is nurtured by blood,*
> *Its aroma mingles*
> *With the reek of corruption,*
> *With the smell of fresh death*
> *That blows through the yards*
> *Like a poisoned sirocco . . ."*

As he read, Helen lay watching him through half-shut eyes. What a sensitive, frail face he has! she was thinking. It really had not changed since that long-distant day when she stood gazing down at it, having wandered by mistake into the boy Francy's room: and, as on that day, its unhappy expression aroused in her the maternal instinct—stronger than ever now, because she was a grown woman, with no child of her own to cherish and protect. His was the face of a person who has known long illness, and the terror and loneliness which are the inseparable companions of illness. It sometimes struck her that no two brothers could be more unalike than Rupert, with his striking good looks and physical charm, and little Francy with the face of a dreamer and the soul of a distraught idealist.

> *"The flower of the stock yards*
> *Has petals of crimson* [Francy was reading],
> *With edges sharp as a killing knife,*
> *Its roots grope under the cement foundation,*
> *In the black loam of Illinois."*

As he went on, Francy's voice gained intensity. He was bending forward over the paper now, squinting a little because of his nearsightedness, and his gentle voice quivered with emotion. She knew how deeply the subject moved him. His hatred of the Stock Yards was not, like Rupert's, based on aesthetic grounds; it derived from his consciousness of the exploitation and sordid dishonesty connected with the rise of the big packing interests. The very thought of the Stock Yards aroused in Francy horror and a deep-seated feeling of guilt.

She heard the sound of the outer door swinging open, and firm footsteps in the hallway. Ah, there was Rupert now, she thought. He always had had a knack of appearing when not expected, as if to give himself a chance to use the assortment of meaningless apologies that are every diplomat's stock in trade. She imagined him stepping through the hallway, nervous fingers automatically straightening his dark tie, ears alert to catch any interesting and possibly useful tidbit of conversation.

"Go ahead, go ahead!" He had tiptoed into the room and laid a kindly hand on his brother's shoulder. "I had no idea, Francy . . . but for heaven's sake, don't let me interrupt."

Francy folded together his poem and stuck it awkwardly into his pocket.

"Oh, that's all right, Rupert. As a matter of fact," he lied, "I'd just come to the end."

He took two steps away from his brother and then began toying with the lid of a cigarette box to explain the instinctive withdrawal. But Rupert was hurt and Helen saw that old look of self-pity come into his eyes. Poor Rupert! He really did try to be nice to people; he was considerate, kind, and even understanding; most women and many men found him charming and attractive. It would have been impossible to explain to him why Francy (and incidentally herself) felt so ill at ease in his presence.

"How about staying for a bite of dinner, old man?" Rupert's voice was still cordial, even affectionate. "We're having a quiet evening for a change. No guests to speak of. Cecilia and Justin are dropping in for a little game of bridge later on, that's all."

"Really? I thought you didn't approve of our brother-in-law, Rupert."

"Let bygones be bygones," said Rupert airily. "I certainly wouldn't have picked Justin Judson for my sister's husband, but he's changed considerably since his marriage. Cecilia's had a wonderful effect on him, and everyone seems to have forgiven him his youthful aberrations. There's no doubt that they go around with the best people in Chicago."

"The best people are going to be your death someday," Helen murmured, so low that Francy could scarcely hear her. He noted the gesture of exasperation with which she reached for her highball glass and emptied the last of its contents.

"Well, old man, I guess that the company doesn't tempt you?" Rupert said.

"Oh, it isn't that," Francy answered, "but I've got another engagement. Anyway, we'll be seeing each other at Mama's 'chocolate party' tomorrow, won't we? Before I go," he said, and then grinned in embarrassment, "would it bother you if I changed my suit in the washroom?"

"Go ahead! By all means! Putting on your glad rags, Francy?"

"Glad rags? Well, not exactly. Or perhaps you could call them glad rags at that," said Francy, walking towards his suitcase with the worn jacket. He stopped in the doorway and looked back at Helen. "Thanks for listening to my poem," he said. "Thanks, Helen, a thousand times."

two

For Helen this so-called holiday of theirs had been the most trying period of her marriage. During its fifteen-year span she and Rupert had had homes in half a dozen countries, yet their life always had forged on of its own momentum. What, after all, was the difference between a dinner party in Rome and one in Teheran except in the accents, and possibly the complexions, of the guests? They always had managed to build up a set pattern of existence, with the same sort of friends, the same sort of bridge parties, luncheon parties, week-end excursions. Only in unsophisticated Chicago, freed of the round of duties that fill the diplomatic day, Helen had found herself with time on her hands: time to think; time to remember. Dangerous leisure for a woman of thirty-five.

Yes, thirty-five, thought Helen as she sat doing her hair for Mama's party. Her face in the mirror certainly showed her to be a very youthful thirty-five, but that very fact bespoke the emotional sterility of her life. One day she would no longer be thirty-five, and then what would she have accomplished? Precious little, to judge from present indications! With all her fine dreams, her rich hopes, her elevated ideals, she had

111

succeeded in giving no meaning to her life. Close to the border of middle age, she found herself leading a worldly existence with a man whom she no longer respected. She drank more than was good for her, and sought other solace in a series of platonic friendships, none of which gave her what she sought. And in the meanwhile she kept practicing daily for a concert that she would never give! Oh, it was not much to show as achievement by the daughter of Professor Mason!

Downstairs the clock struck four. Helen half rose from the chair, telling herself that she must hurry to the piano. Then she sat back with a sigh. How ridiculous it was, really, to have carried these habits of her girlhood into her present life! That was the hour that her father had fixed for her practicing, and though there no longer was the slightest reason to observe it, she found herself going to the piano at four o'clock. Now it seemed to her that she was back in the pale yellow house in Cambridge, back in the chilly music room. Once again she felt that special atmosphere of austerity, of suffocation. So would a man feel, Helen thought, standing in the rarefied air on top of a mountain peak. There was rebellion in her heart, rebellion against her father, the taskmaster, against the difficult notes, against the empty piano stool demanding her presence. She could not, no, she could not endure this slavery! But as she stood there, torn between feelings of rebellion and guilt, she heard her father's footsteps approaching: measured, disciplined, purposeful. She knew that she must obey, and that it was right that she should obey.

Now, fifteen years later, Helen Konrad took up her bag and gloves and walked slowly down the stairs. The past was still there, she thought. It would always be there, like a ditch running alongside the highroad of her life. She kept slipping into that ditch at unwary moments, and emerged therefrom, feeling a bit shaken as a rule, and determined to keep her feet firmly on the cement. But before she knew it she would be down in the ditch again—that long ditch growing ever longer. . . .

In the taxi, traveling to the South Side, Helen remembered that she had not bought Mama a gift. True, Rupert would be bringing something from them both, but that would not be the same thing at all. She decided on the spur of the moment to stop at Marshall Field's to buy something. Helen had a very warm spot in her heart for Mama; she had loved her ever since their first meeting in Cambridge, fifteen years before. Indeed, of all the family, it was only Mama she did love—Mama, and of course Francy. They had something in common, Helen thought, remembering the sweetness in Mama's eyes. She had always felt that Francy was Mama's child, rather than his father's. Oh, Francy! Francy! she said to herself, and knew that a smile had come to her lips. In a few moments now she would be seeing him again, hearing his voice, looking into his gentle eyes. "Francy, oh, Francy!" she said.

Marshall Field's was as crowded and noisy as ever. Often though she had been there, Helen had never mastered the labyrinthal intricacy of the great department store. It was beyond her capacity to retain such directions as to proceed to the third aisle on the left, from there take the second to the right, and then head for the fifth counter from the corner. She had always ended up in the toy section when she was looking for lingerie, or in the bookstore when she wanted to buy herself stockings, and today was no exception. She had thought vaguely of getting Mama a little brooch, but after wandering through the entire length of the store, found herself finally in the art department, surrounded by paintings and etchings and unattractive little busts in terra cotta, set out to entice the art-conscious buying public of Chicago.

She was standing before one of those Persian-style prints that were coming into vogue at the time, this one representing a turbaned prince of antiquity driving his lance through the body of a gracefully kneeling deer. The prince had marvelously aristocratic features, tragic eyes, and a lithe girlish body clothed in beautifully embroidered silk. He looked like . . . he looked like . . .

Ah, there she was, down in the ditch of the past again! What little discipline she had when the sight of this cheap reproduction of a reproduction could summon to mind a whole chapter of her life and transport her in a flash to the very opposite corner of the globe! It was not even as if this Persian nobleman of a bygone day really looked like her friend Pahlevi—excepting perhaps for those tragic eyes. Pahlevi Azad had lived in modern Teheran and had been dressed not in silks but in a well-fashioned London suit. How proud he had been of his Western education, of his blue MG roadster, of his ability to play cricket! ("I used to be handiest at mid-gully, Helen, and I could bowl a fast googly

113

ball too," pronounced in the purest of Oxford accents, with those expressive oriental hands weaving.) And yet it was that very conflict of loyalties, isolating him in his own neurotic world, that had led to his undoing.

Strange, she thought, gazing in absorption at the lithograph, strange that she could remember just where she had been standing when she heard the news of Pahlevi's suicide. It was on the terrace of their apartment in Cairo, where she and Rupert had been transferred a few months before, and they had been having drinks with a Belgian diplomat just arrived from Teheran.

"You remember that nice Persian boy you used to know, the boy with those fantastic dark eyes? Pahlevi Azad. He shot himself last month."

She could still hear Monsieur Lemayeur's suave voice as he recounted this item of gossip, and then passed on to a description of a garden party at the British Legation. She could relive her own feeling that she was hearing something she had already known, and then the feeling of guilt that overwhelmed her. Somehow this, too, was her fault, as had been her father's death a few years before! It was true that she had not promised Pahlevi more than understanding and sympathy, yet he had been deceived in her—bitterly deceived! So it had been with her father, become a disillusioned old man after her marriage to Rupert. So it had been with Madame Lubokova, distant and unfriendly since her star pupil had thrown over such a brilliant career. Why was it that people expected more of her than she was able—or willing—to give? Was it her fault, or theirs?

Suddenly Helen saw before her a face grown familiar in these last troubled weeks, a face from which light candid eyes gazed at her in youthful admiration. Francy! Francy! She felt her heart beating quicker; unconsciously her hand went to her lips. Was there any reason to believe that the pattern of the past would not repeat itself again? Francy was in love with her, that she knew, and what future was there to that love? She should break things off now, while there was still time, before she hurt him, as she had hurt Pahlevi! She knew at that moment that her duty was clear; she must write to Francy and tell him not to visit her again.

"Why, Helen! What on earth are you doing in this gathering spot of

114

mediocrity? Now don't look at me as if you didn't recognize me, or I shall be mortally offended."

"Of course I recognize you, Justin," Helen said, climbing out of the ditch of the past with an effort. "I've just been looking about for a present for Mama Konrad."

"So have I," Justin said. "Only my great devotion to our mother-in-law would make me set foot in that abomination of abominations: a department store. Usually I leave buying to the Konrads: like all nouveaux riches, they are buying mad. Cecilia's idea of a morning well spent is to fit half a dozen incredible dresses, of which she will wear only the two worst. Speaking of bad taste, don't tell me that you've toyed with the idea of acquiring that atrocious lithograph?"

"Don't worry," Helen told him, "I am still perfectly sane."

"Now that is really good news," said Justin as they strolled over to the water-color section. "After a fifteen years' marriage to Rupert, I think you have done nobly. Oh, damn it, I have made another tactless remark. Don't be angry with me, Helen."

"How could I be? You are an irresponsible bad boy, and you know it. You have never wanted to grow up."

"Too much trouble," said Justin, stopping to examine some Cape Cod landscapes that Helen thought she had seen ten times before. "Too troublesome and too painful, and I get on very well as it is. Of course Cecilia's an ass—stubborn too—but I know how to manage her. If ever I lost that knack—believe me, I would fly the coop. That's the trouble in your case, dear Helen: you have never really understood the Konrads. Of course you are too good for that lady's man, Rupert—that goes without saying—still, you might have managed him better if you'd thought of him as a spoiled second-generation product (one of the 'no-good generation' as old Adolph calls them), rather than an attractive individual in his own right."

"But I happen to have been in love with him," Helen said.

Justin looked at her with a funny smile, quizzical or commiserating, she could not tell which; because she liked Justin, she decided it must be the latter.

"I am glad you put it in the past tense," he said. "We are such old friends, Helen, that I can admit to you now that your marriage gave me some uneasy moments. To tell you the truth, I was a wee bit in love with you myself. This seems a funny place to make the confession."

"I have never believed a word you said," Helen assured him, smiling. "But that being as it may, it's high time we picked out our presents."

"Ah, never taken in earnest! That's the penalty for acting the fool," said Justin with a sigh. "Pagliacci, the clown with the broken heart, that's me. But speaking seriously, Helen—*really* seriously—you were asking for trouble when you became Rupert's wife; he wasn't the man for you."

"And who was?"

"Ah, that's the question. You are a difficult person, Helen, you really are! You've read Goethe's *Faust:* two souls in one breast, *zwei Seelen in einer Brust,* or something like that. It describes you."

"It describes many of us in this year 1920," Helen said, picking up a framed picture and at once laying it down. Again her thoughts flew irresistibly to Francy.

She settled finally on a miniature landscape she did not particularly like, and Justin bought an expensive etching, charging it to his wife's account. They left the store and drove together in a taxi to Drexel Boulevard, traversing on the way one of Chicago's black belts. Adolph's big house was now isolated in what had become an unfashionable section of the city, sprinkled with automobile salesrooms and Negro mortuary parlors and speakeasies of the cheaper sort. When Justin pointed out Adolph's stubbornness in clinging to a house which should have been sold ten years before, Helen found a chance of steering their conversation into quieter waters. It was a relief, for she had had enough of his analyzing of a situation grown familiar—yes, all too familiar, with the years.

three

They found that everyone except William and his family had already arrived. In her favorite chair, by the large center table, sat Mama, beaming and matriarchal in one of her black taffeta dresses,

116

every one of which looked exactly alike; her thick white hair was brushed back and drawn into a topknot, as she had been wearing it all her life. This was Mama's great day, and by family tradition it was celebrated by a "chocolate party," for there was nothing Mama enjoyed quite so much as hot chocolate with mountains of whipped cream. Though she had plenty of opportunities to indulge her craving (as witness her spreading girth), it was understood in the family that she and everyone present should on this day consume as much chocolate with the thickest whipped cream as they possibly could manage. Helen went up to Mama and gave her a warm kiss on each cheek.

"Happy birthday, Mama," she said, laying her gift on the table.

"Oh, you are sweet, Helen dear," said Mama, reaching out and squeezing her hand.

Helen looked in Mama's eyes to see whether or not she liked the miniature but, as usual, it was impossible to read her thoughts. Then Helen saw on the table a huge silver bowl laden with whipped cream, inscribed: "To Mama from Rupert, so that she will get good and fat in 1920." With a pang she realized that she had not even asked Rupert what his present would be. How far, far apart the two of them had drifted!

"You all spoil me," Mama was saying. "But what I wonder is how this whipped-cream story ever got started. Land's sake, I don't like whipped cream any better than the next person! What would my figure look like if I ate all the whipped cream that's been brought me today?"

She pointed at another huge bowl, this one of china, likewise filled to the brim with frothy whipped cream.

"Bee gave me that," Mama said. "And my Francy—he gave me this."

She picked up a book and turned it so that Helen could read the title: *Spoon River Anthology* by Edgar Lee Masters. Typical of Francy! Helen thought, as she watched Mama clumsily fingering the pages. Because he loved Masters so much, he wanted Mama to share his pleasure, forgetting the fact that she had scarcely read a line of poetry in her life! Helen's eyes met Francy's across the table, but at once she forced herself to look away. She found herself staring into the eyes of a huge china bear, hollow and filled with whipped cream. The bear's surface was glazed and painted over with a violent pattern of forget-me-nots

117

and pink roses. There was no need for Helen to ask herself who had given that. Who else could it be but Cecilia, she of unfaltering bad taste, who stood chatting with Rupert at the far end of the room? They were standing by a life-sized statue of the deceased carriage horse, Bismarck I, which Adolph had had cut in marble. On the horse's broad back rode Cecilia's three children, Cecil, Harry, and three-year-old Mabel.

"Gee up! Gee up, Bismarck!" Cecil was shouting. "Make him go quickly, Uncle Rupert, please!"

Rupert stepped up and administered a lusty slap on Bismarck's marble quarters.

"Better hold on tight, kiddies!" he warned them. "Mark my words, this is an ornery beast!"

Screaming with delight, the children waved at their uncle. From the expressions on the faces of all four of them, it was clear that children loved Rupert and that Rupert loved children and by every right should have had several of his own.

They could hear the front doorbell giving out an eloquent ring that sounded like a long peal of laughter. A moment later there were shuffling footsteps in the vestibule. The velvet curtains parted, and in the entrance appeared, first the back of Hauptman, then the faces of William and Gladys. They were carrying between them a huge wooden tub, large enough in which to bathe a baby, and filled to its very edge with billowy white foam. Whipped cream! Enough whipped cream to satisfy the cravings of a score of Mama Konrads!

William's children, Bill, Jr., and Suzy, were hopping about the tub, clapping their hands gleefully.

"Happy birthday, Grandma! Don't eat too much, Grandma!" they were shouting.

Mama Konrad gathered them in her arms, shaking with laughter; her voluminous bosoms quivered beneath the black taffeta. Now she was completely and unreservedly happy! All fifteen of the family were present, which naturally was not nearly as many as she would have wished, but at least it was a respectable number in this age of neuroticism and birth control. If only, thought Mama, Bee would forget her political career long enough to get married, and if Rupert could persuade Helen to have a child! But she was not going to let such thoughts bother her today.

"You sweethearts, all of you," she said, beaming from one to the other. "You've made me so terribly happy!"

Rupert was leaning over the great tub, examining the contents with a frown. William had got the better of him today, there was no doubt of it. And he didn't like it.

"Where d'you get that whipped cream, William?" he asked. "It looks—sort of loose."

"Loose? What do you mean lose?" William took a spoon from the table and dipped it into his tub. "You sample it, Mama, and then tell Rupert if it's loose. Come on now! You're the expert."

Mama leaned forward and put her mouth to the spoon. Then she smacked her lips.

"Perfect," she pronounced. "I have never in my life tasted more wonderful whipped cream."

"Ah, smarty! You see!"

William did a victory dance around his tub, his big face above the stiff collar wreathed in smiles. It was not often that he scored a clean-cut victory over Rupert.

"But then Rupert's whipped cream is real dandy too," Mama added a bit unexpectedly. She could not bear to hurt the feelings of any of her children.

Helen strolled over to the green plush sofa where Adolph and Bee sat looking at the family album. Gladys' Susan had joined them, standing gawkily behind the mammoth sofa and craning her neck as the pages were turned. Adolph gave Helen a grin, Bee sent her a smile almost cordial enough to hide the fact that there was very little sympathy lost between them. Bee had become an even better politician than she was as a child and it remained her first aim in life not to make enemies.

"Come on," she said, moving over on the sofa. "Join the family group, Helen."

Helen sat down a little diffidently, for though she had now been a Konrad for fifteen years, she still felt that she did not belong here.

119

Had she had a child, it might have been different; as it was, she was still considered an outsider who happened to have married Rupert.

"Who's that funny-looking man in the big straw hat and the clothes that are too small for him?" Susan asked, reaching a long skinny arm over the back of the sofa to point at a picture.

"Why, child, that's your own papa," Bee said, laughing. "And his jacket's not really too small. Men's clothes always looked like that 'round about 1910."

"No, honest, is that really Papa?" Susan giggled. "And who's the lady in that terrible dress, Auntie Bee?"

"Why, your mother, of course," said Bee, a little embarrassed, for Cecilia wore dresses just as terrible nowadays. "Ladies' styles keep changing, you know, Suzy."

"Not that much, they don't change," said Adolph, leaning over to examine the picture. He winked at Helen good-humoredly.

"Oh look! There you are, Auntie Bee! I can recognize you."

Bee, to be sure, was easily recognizable, for she wore on her dress her favorite emblem since childhood: a huge honeybee. Invariably a bee appeared on her person, whether embroidered on her dress, stuck in her hair, or, as in this picture, clinging to her in the form of a brooch. The bee had become with the years her badge of authority—a reminder to people that she really was "Bee" Konrad, a woman of means, a spinster by inclination, and one of the vice-presidents of the Illinois Women's Political League.

"Auntie Bee, show me some of those funny old pictures of Gramps and Granny, the kind you showed us at Christmas," Susan begged.

"They're in another book, darling. Papa, can you find the old album?"

"Sure. Vhy not?"

Adolph went to the cupboard where various articles of value were stored, unlocking it with a key taken from his vest pocket. Inside were sheafs of contracts and other legal documents (some, yellow with age, relating to the construction of Sans Souci almost thirty years ago), a bunch of newspaper clippings and a few miscellaneous articles, such as an old knife with a broken blade, once used for whittling, and a cigar box full of medals won at Chicago horse shows. From under the lot

120

Adolph pulled out an album marked "Photographs" and rejoined the group on the sofa.

In the meanwhile Hauptman had entered the room to draw the rep curtains. To be sure, it was still full daylight outside, but five was the appointed hour for this ceremony, and Hauptman had a Teutonic devotion to schedules. Apart from that, it delighted him to shut out the hideous view visible nowadays from the windows. Built on a knoll, Adolph's house had once overlooked green fields and farmhouses; it had taken a real buggy ride to get into town. Thirty years later this section had been not only built up but ruined, so that all to be seen now were the decaying buildings of a typical Negro slum.

"Serve us the chocolate ven you're ready," Adolph said as he walked past his butler. "Und look out vhat it's good und hot."

Hauptman gave a nod, his usual form of communication with his master; it was not the nod of a modern trained servant, rather that of a Teutonic retainer for whom disobedience to the leader, or even the questioning of an order, was unthinkable. Clumsily he stamped about, turning on the table lights, most of which had been destined for use with kerosene, and had mammoth bronze or ornate china bases; their great silk shades, adorned with tassels, cut off all but a glimmer of light. When the last curtain had been drawn, the vast room with its massive furniture was plunged into semiobscurity, but here and there cozy centers of brightness stood out: one by the round table, where Mama sat with three of her children and the bowls of whipped cream; one by the blazing log fire before which the three youngsters giggled and played; one by the sofa, where Adolph sat turning the pages of the family album.

Here was the procession of his life, he was thinking, as he showed little Susan pictures of Wilma and him taken soon after their marriage (Wilma still looking like the country girl she was, in a broad hat and plain gingham dress)—other pictures of the young pair after their first child, after their second child, after their third child—finally the photograph of the family group taken the year they moved into this house. As usual Adolph dominated the picture, corpulent and confident-looking—and indeed, why should he not have been, having made enough money at thirty-two to launch his own company and build a mansion on

121

Drexel Boulevard? Wilma, beginning to look matronly, sat beside him, with little Bee on her knees. And already then Bee (only three) was wearing a bee, this one made of celluloid and stuck in her hair!

Yes, here was the procession of his life, thought Adolph again as he turned to a page with photographs of the Stock Yards: the shed where he first sold pigs and cattle, slaughtered by his own hand; the brick building marked "Konrad and Heinrich, Dealers," with Adolph and Max Heinrich in butchers' aprons standing before it; the much larger structure with a tall chimney, still functioning nowadays as Building No. 4; the Konrad Office Building on the afternoon of its inaugural, with him standing amongst managers and floor bosses (Angus Mc-Kenna the least conspicuous of the lot!). And then, at the foot of the page, a large photograph of the heads of the "Big Five": Harold Hastey, Ben Armitage, Silas Woodrow, John Cudason, all confronting the camera in their morning coats and striped trousers, with Adolph standing beside them in hip boots and shoestring tie. Harold Hastey, that pirate from Massachusetts, who had tried to slice his throat on more occasions than Adolph could remember, had his arm through that of Adolph, become a relative since William's marriage to his daughter.

Ah yes, the procession of his life, and a good life it had been! Ever since the day he built that first shed with the help of a hired carpenter, he had had an objective in mind, and that was forty years ago. Forty years? Oh no, he had had it much longer than that! He had had it even as a boy in Schwabenland, kissing his mother good-by, with the contractor waiting outside the cottage to take him to America. Ever he had struggled closer to this final attainment: the big house; the possessions; the children and the grandchildren; the feeling of security. It was all his now, and neither McKenna nor the labor unions could take it from him. The victory was his, and the memories of the struggle—they also were his. Perhaps, thought Adolph, his glance going from the pictures to the faces of his children, spoiled, dissatisfied, ineffectual, perhaps in giving them so much he had deprived them of the most precious birthright of all: the driving incentive to establish themselves in a competitive world.

Hauptman had appeared in the entrance, a huge pot of steaming chocolate held out before him. The maid followed with a cake, a glori-

122

fied birthday cake, but baked in the shape of a heart, with Wilma's name and the date inscribed thereon in German script. That was Adolph's birthday gift and when Wilma saw it she felt the tears of happiness come to her eyes. Better than the etching and the silver bowl, better than the china bear and the book of poetry, Wilma loved this cake, because it was Adolph who had given it to her. She had a deep feeling for every one of her children, but her feeling for Adolph, ah, that was a different thing! And after all, it really was Adolph who had given her all the other presents as well. They had been bought with his money, amassed by his sweat and his brains. She had the primitive woman's feeling for the progenitor, the provider, but for whom this beloved family of hers never would have come into being. In Wilma's mind there was not the slightest doubt that Adolph was the greatest man alive.

And now she was pouring out chocolate into cups the size of small pails. In matriarchal fashion she dispensed the thick liquid, capping each cup with a ladleful of whipped cream. Everyone had gathered around the center table. The children, wearing bibs and seated on pillows to gain height, consumed their meal messily and with gurgling noises. William, next to his father, finished his cup with record speed and handed it on to be refilled; a mustache of whipped cream clung to his lips. Cecilia, as always thinking of her figure, sampled her chocolate daintily with a spoon; but Francy, who had the appetite of a sparrow, gulped his down so as to please Mama. As to Bee, she finished her cup with an absent-minded expression, then slipped out of the room; a moment later she was back with a camera and flash apparatus in her hand.

"Please, all of you, just stay where you are. I want to have this for the album."

A blinding flash, screams from the children and, amidst laughter, Bee resumed her place at the table.

"Mark my words," Justin whispered to Helen, "that family group will appear in the papers about the time Bee gets ready to run for Congress. Bee Konrad's never done anything for one reason only!"

Rupert, seated beside Mama, began tapping his cup with his spoon. When silence had been achieved, he said:

"Listen, boys and girls, this is Mama's day. We're all here together and Lord knows when that will happen again. We're all happy today, and that may not happen so soon again either. Now, as this is such a very special day, I think we all want a speech from Mama."

"Hurray!" "Speech by Mama!" "Speech by Mama!" cried her children, rattling their cups against their saucers. Rupert, self-appointed master of ceremonies, made signs for her to get up.

Mama, flustered and red in the face, hoisted up her bulk from her chair. She really was delighted at this chance to speak to her children all at the same time, but of course it would never have done to admit it. She began by shaking her head in vexation.

"Land's sake, I don't want to speak. I'm no public speaker, like our Bee, and I reckon Rupert. But anyway, now that I am on my feet I'd better say something. And come to think of it, there is something I want to say. It's about the family. Yes, the family. As Rupert just said, we're together today, every single one of us. And we're happy. But he didn't say that we were happy *because* we're together. Well, that's a fact, children, and there's a reason. It's because when people are together, they feel strong, and it's a good thing. That feeling of being strong, I mean. A mighty good thing.

"We ought to try and keep feeling that way, because a lot of things can happen to a family. I've seen it and I know. A family can just fall to pieces, like a rotten apple fallen from a tree. But that's not what's going to happen to our family! No, it will never happen, because our family is a good family and it will remain a good family. That means that we must be kind and honest with one another, and try and love each other even when we get to feel pretty mad sometimes. For a family like ours is really like a whole little village in itself, isn't it? And it's how people behave to each other that makes a good village or a bad one. I want this village called Konrad to look sweet and clean, and that means that we've got to keep our houses in order, so that we can open our windows and let anyone peek inside. For remember this, children, don't ever forget: a village, any village, is going to be judged by the looks of each single house!"

four

Next afternoon Adolph had a directors' meeting at the Chicago and Midwestern Trust Company. This bank, among the city's largest, had been founded twenty-two years before with capital supplied by Adolph and other Chicago businessmen. That, of course, accounted for his position on the board of directors, but the truth was that Adolph was no banker and understood little about finance. For two hours now he had been listening to company reports and to discussion of such matters as investments and compound interest, carried on by cocky little bank officials, most of them thirty years his juniors. He felt as exhausted as if he had put in a hard day's work quartering hogs.

"Pretty fine showing, eh, Adolph? Who'd have guessed, back in the nineties, that our little bank would blossom into a financial giant?"

The speaker was a man in the early sixties, that is to say, about Adolph's age. And, like Adolph, he was one of the original founders of the trust company. But whereas Adolph wore hip boots and a shoe-string tie, this gentleman was more properly clad for a board meeting, in black morning coat and a dazzling white stiff collar that bit into his neck. He looked what he was: a really solid citizen.

"Who vould have guessed? Vhy, I vould have guessed," replied Adolph indignantly. "D'you t'ink I vould have risked my good dollars if I hadn't thought this vas an A-1 investment? Vhat d'you take me for—a nitvit?"

"No, Adolph, I guess no one does that. I've heard a lot of things said about you—but not that you didn't have your wits where they belonged."

"What's this about Adolph's wits? Smartest man in the room, and don't let them tell you anything different!"

A second member of the meeting had joined them, a patriarchal type with Prince Albert sideburns and a florid face. It would have been hard to guess that this pleasant fat man had built up a fortune in pig iron through business methods more questionable even than those of

125

Adolph, or that the Illinois labor organizations considered him their enemy No. 1.

"Hello there, Jacob Kurtweis. I only see you about vonce every year at these meetings," said Adolph, shaking hands.

"Meaning that that's enough?"

"Vell, it stops us from qvarrelin'," said Adolph noncommittally.

"Come on out and have a drink on me," said Kurtweis, laying a pudgy hand on Adolph's shoulder. "I'll treat you too, J.H.," he said to the wearer of the stiff collar. "I've got my car downstairs and we'll nip over to a nice speakeasy on West Randolph."

"Speakeasy? No thanks. Never been in vone in my life," Adolph answered. "I don't vant for to get held up by gangsters."

"That's all right, Adolph," J.H. said. "This here speakeasy is a real family place. Why, I've seen people turn up there with their kiddies and their wives. It's as respectable as the Palmer House."

The three men left the board room and walked through the marble corridor to the elevators. Adolph wondered if any of the employees whom they passed realized that this trio of aging men had been responsible for the very existence of the institution. Here they were now, with their hip boots and sideburns and wing collars, eccentric relics of another age (though all three still had their feet planted pretty firmly in the present one). Yet it was they and their likes who had built this city out of a sprawling village, and later had built it a second time out of charred ruins, still smoking after the Great Chicago Fire. They, the pioneers, had prepared the way for these sweaty bank clerks, with their pinched faces and thick spectacles through whose ordered and staid breeding Chicago had become the fifth metropolis of the world.

Out on La Salle Street they climbed into Jacob Kurtweis' limousine and ripped through the Loop with the chauffeur's horn scattering the pedestrians like frightened sparrows. Kurtweis lit a cigar and blew out the first cloud of smoke with a sigh.

"The city's outgrown us, Adolph! It's become—inhuman. Even ten years ago Chicago was a nice little place where the elevator man knew your first name and asked after the missis. Did you notice the look that fellow gave us today? He paid us as much attention as one of your Stock Yard workers would pay to—three old steers."

126

"Okay," said Adolph. "That's vhat ve vorked for, isn't it—that this place should become vhat it is, bigger und bigger? That's vhy ve sveated und toiled. It's our baby! Und it's going to grow bigger yet!"

"I hope not," said J.H., casting a look through the window at congested Clark Street. "If this traffic gets any worse . . ."

"Ach, you two—old conservatives! You make me sick. I remember the time vhen you, J.H., vas forvard-looking, progressive. Vasn't you vone of de first to invest in land values on the far North Side, vhen it vas no more than a svamp? You made a fortune out of it, too! Vell, you vouldn't have got far mit your nowadays mentality. You're old, both of you—old!"

They stepped out of the Cadillac in front of a tobacconist's and made their way through the shop to a locked door at the rear. At once an eye, bloodshot and wary, appeared at the peephole, and when Kurtweis mentioned a fictitious name, the door opened sufficiently for the three to slip in. Escorted with deference to a table near the bar, they ordered gin rickeys before casting about their eyes. Adolph's nervousness vanished as he realized that there was but little chance of his being recognized; the three elderly men were just another group in the crowded room. It is doubtful if anyone would have looked twice if told that their combined fortunes amounted to well over a hundred million dollars.

"Well, what's the business outlook, J.H.?" Kurtweis asked, passing a handkerchief over his benevolent wet face. "Real estate values going to keep climbing in 1920?"

"Why not? We're just at the beginning of a boom period and there's no reason for it to come to an end. The city's growing, growing! I see half a century of prosperity before us, and fortunes for everyone. The world outlook's never been brighter."

"Now I don't know about that. Those damn Europeans are constitutionally unable to live in peace. Besides, the Bolshies in Russia are going to cause trouble, mark my words."

"Ridiculous!" J.H. said. "Perfectly ridiculous! Russia's a weak nation —always has been. Why, it'd take them fifty years or more even to become self-sufficient! What do you say, Adolph?"

"I say that vhere there's a vill, there's a vay," Adolph answered. "A poor man don't alvays stay poor. No, by Gott, he doesn't! As Americans, ve sure know that."

"You're just looking for trouble, Adolph! I don't see that Russia can give us cause for alarm."

"That," said Adolph calmly, "is because you have no eye for the future. It chust so happens that I have."

Kurtweis gave a chuckle. Though he disagreed with Adolph in principle, he had to admit that his old friend's hunches were more often right than wrong; he himself had profited from them more than once in his business life. Now there came into his eye a sly twinkle as he remarked:

"Still, Adolph, it seems that you are not *always* right. I remember talking with you just about a year ago, and you made another prediction then."

"My Gott, I have predicted to so many people," said Adolph, laughing.

"Well, Adolph, you told me that afternoon that Konrad and Son was going to remain a family business, the way it always had been in the past. I guess you were wrong, weren't you?"

Adolph threw a sharp glance at his questioner; his sure instinct told him that in a moment he would have to hide both anger and surprise. On the screen of his mind a face flashed for a moment and was gone: the sallow, expressionless, long-hated countenance of Angus McKenna.

"Vhat are you getting at, Jacob Kurtweis?" he cried. "Spit it out!"

"Come on, Adolph, you can't kid me. Why, it seems that the whole thing's as good as settled. You're going to float a stock issue, and a mighty big one at that, and you're going to do it through Chicago and Midwestern. You know, you can't keep things like that secret in Chicago!"

"Und who told you that cock-und-bull story?" Adolph forced out a smile.

"Why, if you want to know, I heard it from Al Peterson at the bank, no longer ago than this afternoon. I understood Peterson to say that he's been talking matters over with your manager, McKenna."

McKenna! So his suspicion had proved right! For years McKenna had been advocating this idea of a stock issue, which would transform the very nature of the Konrad packing business. It was clear now that the campaign had passed into a new stage, with McKenna intriguing and bargaining behind his back. Adolph knew in a flash that this was the signal for that long-postponed showdown as to who really ran Konrad and Son.

But when he spoke there was no more than a hint of irritation in his voice. Was he going to let on to these two that he had been placed in a false, a humiliating position?

"Peterson talks too much! I've alvays said so. A big bag full of vind! Vhat if I did send down McKenna to the bank to feel out the ground? Does that mean ve're changing our policy? Gott demn, ve grossed more these last years than any time in our history! Our export trade's shot up like a rocket since 1914. Ve're all of us very happy down at the plant."

"Well, I'm glad to hear that," said Kurtweis. "In this age of corporations and trusts, it's good to think that a few of us old-timers are still holding out. It's better to keep a company's individuality than to expand —expand."

"Oh, ve're expanding too—alvays have expanded," Adolph pointed out. "But by Gott, ve've done it mitout losing our individuality. Konrad und Son is still the old Konrad und Son. Ve've let novone chisel into de firm."

"Good for you," said J.H., but with a trifle less conviction. "I'm all for you, Adolph, but the time's going to come when you'll have to decide. You can't have it both ways, you know: either you stop expanding and retrench; or else you transform into a stock company, like Armitage and Hastey (though I think the decision broke old man Hastey's heart). It's the trend of the times, Adolph! Individualism is dead. Dead as a doornail!"

Adolph took up his gin rickey and drained the last drops; it gave him an extra moment before he need answer. Perhaps in principle J.H. was right, but was he going to let the plant erected through the sweat of his brow pass into the control of a bunch of stockholders— anonymous citizens he had never met who knew less about running a packing business than illiterate Chippy, his office boy? No, no, he wasn't a has-been yet! *He* was the company—neither William, nor McKenna, nor anyone else—just he.

"Don't you vorry about my company, J.H. Haven't you got enough vorries of your own?" he said, scowling from beneath his bushy eyebrows. "I'll handle my company, like vhat I've always done in the past. Und I don't need no interference."

"Sorry, Adolph. I was only talking generalities," J.H. ventured. But now Adolph was off, and nothing could have stopped him.

"Cheneralities? Bah! Vhen a man vants to find fault, he alvays claims he's talking cheneralities. You didn't build up no business, J.H.! You come to this city mit a fat vad of bills und invested in safe real estate. It's I vhat sveated und toiled, und took the risks und built up a business. Und I'm not goin' to have any smart alecks come tellin' me vhat to do mit it now!"

J.H. started to say something, but Adolph pushed back his chair and jumped up; he was determined to hear no more. As he nodded to Jacob Kurtweis and strode out of the bar, he had the strange impression that he was fleeing—fleeing not from his enemies, but rather from those indefinable forces of change which were bound to defeat and humiliate him in the end. And in the curious glances of the other guests that sought his outlandish hip boots, his corduroy jacket, his shoestring tie, he was aware of the same indulgent scorn that he had heard in J.H.'s words, "Individualism is dead, Adolph! Dead as a doornail!"

He hailed a Checker cab and gave the driver the address of Sans Souci. Inching through the streets of the Loop, past Marshall Field's department store, and Carson Pirie Scott and Company, he kept remembering that painful conversation. These businesses, too, had been started by men who had given them their names and bestowed on them their special individualities; but in the process of expansion that individualism had been lost, and they had become vast impersonal concerns, like the great Stock Yards companies that bore the names of Hastey and Armitage and Woodrow and Cudason. These former rivals now produced identical products, priced identically, packed identically; they might have been called Businesses A, B, C, and D, for all the individuality that was left them. Of the original "big five," only

Konrad and Son retained its status as an independent, privately owned concern.

But now they were planning the same fate for his firm as well! Konrad and Son, the child of his brain, in whose plant every last brick and rafter, every knife and conveyer belt, was impregnated with his personality, was to become Business E in the chain of interlocking packing concerns. Its policies were no longer to be directed by him, but rather by the managers and stockholders' representatives, no doubt headed by Angus McKenna, his former paid employee. And in the end even its name might be forgotten, should McKenna and those others find it expedient to merge with another firm!

He paid the cab and stamped up to his front door, advancing a stiff angry finger towards the bell. When Hauptman opened, he strode by without a word. In the deep leather sofa in the sitting room O'Grady was lying fast asleep, his feet on an armchair, his mouth half open in blissful abandon. For the sake of comfort he had taken off his jacket and flung it on the floor; his solid chest rose and fell beneath the bright checkered waistcoat.

Adolph stood looking down at him for a moment, his first sensation of annoyance making way for far more complex emotions. He knew that O'Grady was a wastrel and a parasite and a liar, a man who came to his house to drink his liquor and smoke his best cigars and put his feet on the upholstered armchairs. Yes, those were the facts, evident to anyone. But there was something else about O'Grady which put the lie to superficial judgments. For O'Grady, whatever his faults, was an *individual,* a man unique in temperament and personality. Like Adolph himself, he belonged to an age when people dared be themselves: the checkered waistcoat attested to that, and the torn, pink silk shirt, and the jutting chin, obstinate and self-willed and independent. Sean O'Grady was not one of these modern machine-men who seemed to have been turned out wholesale, like Ford cars.

Adolph felt that in some strange way O'Grady was his ally in a standardized world, a world run by managers and head clerks who threatened to turn Konrad and Son into an impersonal factory for the benefit of nameless stockholders from coast to coast. Perhaps men like O'Grady were anachronisms; they were referred to as "characters," a

131

word apt to evoke indulgent smiles. Well, as to him, Adolph, he preferred O'Grady, lazy and irresponsible, to Angus McKenna with all his cold mechanical efficiency. He understood O'Grady in the same way that he understood his own packing business that they were trying to take away from him. In a way, perhaps, he even loved him.

Adolph took off his jacket and threw it over O'Grady's knees. Then he tiptoed heavily from the room.

five

"Run for your lives! He's broken loose!"

The cry sounded through the killing room, a primitive cry that might have been heard in a factory or in a mine, in a jungle or on a cattle range: in any place where men find themselves in danger. Still holding their bloodstained knives, the Stock Yards workers scattered to the walls, eyes set on the runaway steer.

For a moment the animal stood motionless, but for the swaying motion of his head; a stream of crimson gushed down his forehead from the slanting hammer blow he had received. Then with a bound he charged onto the floor, scattering the blood and the manure to either side. Up the length of the floor he galloped, then back again, bellowing in panic, knocking blindly into the carcasses of the dead steers dangling from the ceiling; his frantic eye sought vainly for an avenue of escape. And at each charge the terrified workers ran for a new coign of safety.

A shot rang out. The steer stopped in his tracks, threw back his head, as though surprised, then keeled over and lay still on the concrete floor. One leg gave three feeble kicks, before stiffening into immobility. From one second to another the steer had ceased to be an object of terror, a renegade and a killer. He had become just another dead animal in the Konrad plant.

"Get that carcass out of here!" yelled the foreman, laying his rifle aside.

Francy, feeling faint, his legs trembling, made his way out of the

visitors' gallery. It was the first time he had seen a steer break loose
on the killing floor, and though he had come here today for the purpose of gathering impressions, he had not bargained for this. For a
moment he felt that he was about to retch, and looked about for a
secluded corner. Gradually the sensation passed away, and he walked
down the stairs and out of the slaughtering building.

Ah, that was better, he thought, letting the spring breeze blow in his
face. It would have been too embarrassing to get sick right there, on
the steps of his father's plant! Now that it was all over, he decided that
he was glad to have witnessed that brutal scene after all; it would fit
perfectly into his *Stock Yards Ballad*. Here was atmosphere with a
vengeance, the very atmosphere that his poem lacked and in search of
which he forced himself to make these visits to the Yards! Taking out
his notebook, he stood with his back to the building to jot down impressions while the scene was still fresh in his mind.

"Remember the look in the eyes of the big Polack worker just before
he turned to run," Francy scribbled in haste. "The hunter become
hunted. . . . Remember blood and manure flying in men's faces as the
steer swerved. . . . Remember the ugly short fellow crossing himself
as he huddled by the wall. . . . The terror, the all-pervading atmosphere of terror, not so much because of the crisis at hand as because of
hazards, fears, dangers remembered or forming part of their racial
heritage. . . . Note: the whole incident should be made symbolic: life
on the rampage, about to gore its victims and trample their starved
bodies in the muck, when the Konrad foreman brings it to terms, because nothing—no, nothing, must be allowed to interrupt the industrial
process leading to the accumulation of more wealth. . . ."

Francy realized that one of the guards was watching him, so he
slipped the notebook in his pocket and set off in the direction of the
main gates. He had secured a visitor's pass from William, but knew
that if he were asked to produce it he might become involved in a long
conversation. Francy feared new contacts with people almost as much
as he feared breakaway steers with blood in their eyes.

As he walked along he tried to figure out how to fit that bloody scene
into his poem. Theoretically he knew how to describe the steer's charge
so as to portray the crass violence of the Stock Yards world and show

the lot of the worker, brutalized and broken. Yes, he knew how to do it, but he knew also that he would not succeed. Once he put pen to paper, the scene would simply fall to pieces, and he would lose himself in a mass of irrelevant details: he realized that there was drama in the moribund herds, in the brutish workers in bloodstained aprons, in the great factory chimneys belching smoke. Yes, there was drama here, but he could not portray that drama.

The fault is in myself, thought Francy, halting before a pen full of squealing, terrified hogs. It is because of my inadequacy as a human being that I cannot write with conviction, even though I feel everything so deeply. I am horrified at the Konrad fortune and the way it was amassed; I am indignant about the exploited workers, and die of shame when I remember such things as that consignment of rotten meat sent to the soldiers in the Caribbean. Yet I am still living on Konrad money in the house of my father, of whom I heartily disapprove. No, I will never be a good poet until I break away from him and make an honest life of my own.

It was at this point in his reflections that Francy perceived the subject of them less than a hundred feet away. His father was standing beside the neighboring pen, talking with a stout fellow who looked what he probably was: a professional dealer in hogs. Apparently he had not yet noticed his son, but just as Francy was preparing to slip away, he turned his head—and then it was too late.

A painful embarrassment seized Francy. How explain his presence in these hated Yards, that he had been shunning since a boy? How avoid confessing that he was gathering circumstantial evidence to condemn his father's whole way of life? As he walked towards Adolph he knew that his lips had twisted into that vacuous smile which with him was always a sign of intense embarrassment.

"Hello, Dad," he said, as though it was the most natural thing in the world that they should meet here.

"Vhy, hello, Francy!" answered Adolph in a cordial voice, and then the surprised Francy understood that his father meant to play along with him. With his birch stick Adolph designated his fat companion. "Francy, dis is Joe Simpson, vhat I've known since you vas knee-high to a grasshopper. Have you met my boy Francy, Joe?"

"Nope." The hog dealer focused Francy with a pair of eyes as materialistic and humorless as those of the animals he was selling. "Of course I know William, an' I remember Rupert from when he used to come to work with you. But I didn't right know you had another son, Adolph."

"Ya, ya. I haf dree sons," said Adolph sourly, no doubt remembering that only one of the three had consented to follow in his tracks.

Francy stood by as the two men discussed the animals, and then the dealer walked off, leaving father and son alone. Seeking for the right thing to say, Francy hit on the innocuous statement, "Fine specimens, those hogs!" Whereupon Adolph leaped at the opening and assured Francy that they were indeed the best hogs in the world, being Iowa bred and certain to tip the scales at three hundred pounds apiece. He pretended to take Francy's interest for granted, and Francy entered into the game, scrutinizing each hog in turn, as if he really saw the difference between one and the next.

They left the hogs after a while and strolled on between the pens, Adolph halting occasionally to explain why some group of cattle was of special value, or to tell him an anecdote from the days when he himself selected every animal destined for the Konrad plant. Adolph was a different person here than in the luxurious house on Drexel Boulevard. This was his real world; this male world of livestock and cattle drovers and of rough men who smelled of hogs and of manure. It was a primitive world, thought Francy, and the only rule of conduct was to push harder than the next fellow. He gave an involuntary shudder as he caught sight of a great hog standing at the feed trough, barring the way to others who were pushing to get at the swill.

From the roof of the Konrad Office Building a whistle sounded, announcing the hour of one. Adolph put a hand on his son's shoulder.

"It's lunchtime, Francy. Vhy not stay und have a bite mit me at de Saddle und Sirloin Club? They serve a pretty good meal there nowadays. Ve'll phone Mama that you're not coming home."

Francy knew that he was caught. He did not have the heart to hurt his father, even though the prospect ahead utterly appalled him. It was rare indeed that they found themselves alone together, and Francy had always felt that Adolph avoided such occasions as carefully as did he.

135

Besides, was not this club the one place where he was bound to meet every figure in the Stock Yards world? Stepping in there with his father was like a public announcement that he belonged to the Konrad clan, approving of their marauding tactics and sharing their brutal and unethical mode of conduct. As he accompanied Adolph to the Stock Yards Inn Building, there swept over Francy that oft-recurring longing to flee to some faraway spot where he would be judged not as a Konrad but as a free and independent individual.

The lunch room was beginning to fill up. At one large table Francy recognized his brother William, Angus McKenna, and several other officers of Konrad and Son; at another were people from the Armitage plant; at still another sat a delegation from Hastey's, including George Hastey himself, William's uncle by marriage and the head of the firm since old Harold's death. In his usual decisive way, his father headed for a small table by a window, scarcely acknowledging McKenna's gesture of greeting as he passed. William, of course, was too absorbed in his food to take any notice.

Installed finally at their table, Adolph tucked a corner of his napkin under his collar and reached for the bill of fare.

"Now vhat'll you haf, Francy? A nice steak, big as that plate, or a thick slab of rare beef? Hope you are good und hungry!"

"Oh, sure," said Francy, trying to forget the charging mass of live meat he had seen only a brief hour before, and to close his nostrils to the all-pervading Stock Yards smell.

He glanced around the room, filled with masculine-looking men, endowed with husky voices and prodigious waistlines. By all the rules he should have felt himself one of them, for he, if anyone, belonged by heredity to this Stock Yards world. Yet how alien it all was! And how distasteful! The virile atmosphere of the huge room, the bustle and confusion, the red dripping meat carried past on platters, all sickened Francy and made him long for the company of people of his kind: artists and writers searching for the inner meaning of things, rather than preoccupied with the sordid business of daily living.

But then a disturbing thought struck him: did he really fit better among Andy Bogarty's crowd than he did here? Wasn't his position there just as false, or perhaps falser? What, after all, was the difference in deceit between his wearing a torn jacket at Andy's, and his feigning an interest in Iowa hogs today? He had always been an outsider, Francy thought, an outsider longing to be where he was not. And again he told himself that his only hope of becoming a whole person was to take a stand against one thing, for another, and thereafter to live his life accordingly.

"Vhat you thinking of?" Adolph asked, peering at him from beneath his bushy eyebrows. "You look vorried, Francy. Perhaps you're afraid you made a mistake ordering steak und not roast beef."

Francy laughed and shook his head.

"No, Dad, that's one decision that I shan't regret. Here she comes now! And what a steak!"

It was, indeed, a sensational hunk that might have turned a stronger stomach than Francy's, especially if one associated it with a wounded steer pounding through a sea of blood and of manure. Francy, forcing meat into his mouth, tried to chew and swallow automatically, and in the meanwhile to tame his galloping imagination.

"Ach, now you're dreaming again!" Adolph complained. "Alvays dreaming, dreaming! Vhy, Francy, you vas a million miles avay from me!"

"No, Dad. Only about three feet."

Francy forced himself to joke, for he knew what his father was thinking. It was what he always thought when Francy fell silent and the specter of the past rose between them, reminding them that father had transgressed against son. Fifteen years back had Adolph's thoughts raced, to the time when the boy Francy lay sick of rheumatic fever and Adolph, overbearing and tyrannical, had told O'Grady to order him out of bed. It was on that very day that Francy's heart had been ruined for life! How, then, was he to assure his father that he harbored resentment neither against him nor against O'Grady, the tool of another man's will? It simply was not in his nature to blame anyone, but that, of course, Adolph would never understand.

"I got to admit something to you, Francy," his father was saying, as he wiped his mouth on the ample napkin covering his chest. "These here are Armitage steaks. Vell, Armitage is a good firm too und they're chust as chuicy as if they had the Konrad label. You ought to come here for lunch real often. I bet Mama doesn't feed you like this at home."

"Don't worry, Dad," Francy said. "She does her best to stuff me. I guess it's her ambition to make me as fat as William by the time that I'm his age."

Adolph's expression grew serious. He chewed in silence at a mouthful of food, then leaned across the table to fix his burning eyes on his son.

"That's not vhat ve vant, Mama und I," he said. "I mean, that you should become like Villiam. Not in fatness—nor in other t'ings either. Naturally I vished for you to follow me in the business. That is for vhy I sveated und slaved. But things turned out different, und now I see that it vas better so. For I am proud of you, Francy. I am proud of you for being chust vhat you are. I vouldn't vant you to be different, in no vay!"

Francy put down his knife and fork and gazed at Adolph, unable to frame a reply. Not once to his memory had his father spoken so intimately before. Their relationship had never been close; since his earliest years it had been undermined by memories of an injustice impossible to obliterate. And now suddenly in this crowded dining room, before the remains of a porterhouse steak, they had attained a moment of complete honesty!

"Thanks, Dad, for being so understanding," he said at last, and took a sip from his water glass, because he felt awkward, talking like this with his father. "I know that I've hurt you—and hurt Mama too—by turning out so differently than you'd hoped. But I couldn't help not liking the Stock Yards, could I? I couldn't help not liking—a good many other things."

"No, naturally you couldn't help." Adolph looked out through the window at the busy world that he had created—and that two of his sons had renounced. "You are you, und Rupert vas Rupert. Let me tell you somet'in', Francy: fifteen years ago, vhen Rupert left his chob here to become a diplomat und marry a professor's daughter, it almost broke my heart. I'm viser now. A person's got to do vhat he's got to do. You go ahead, Francy, und lif your own life!"

Francy reached across the table and gave his father's hand a quick squeeze.

"Thanks, Dad," was all he could say.

"That's all right, Francy." Adolph's knife bisected his last bit of steak; thrusting the huge forkful in his mouth, he ground it up between his perfect white teeth. "I'll alvays help you—you needn't vorry. I've set up trust incomes for your brothers und sisters. There's no reason for vhat I shouldn't do the same for you."

Francy, who for a moment had felt so warmly towards his father, shrank away at those words; again he had the old feeling of talking to a stranger who happened by a queer fluke to have engendered him.

"But, Dad, I don't want your money," he protested, knowing in advance that his father could not understand. "I want to make my own way. I'll never ask for your help."

"Ya," said Adolph, and wrinkled his big eyebrows. "But to make your own vay, Francy, you need money in this world. Mit the sveat of my brow I've made a fortune. It's your fortune too! Mit my money you can do vhat you vill, but mitout it vhat are you? A pauper! A nogood punk vhat anyvone can spit on. You don't know the vorld, Francy, let me tell you! Life's a dirty battle from the vord 'go.' I fought the battle und von it, so that you vouldn't have to fight it again. You're not strong enough, Francy, take it from me. Und I say that mit love."

Francy looked down at the tablecloth. He understood the truth in what his father had said—at least the truth for his father. But it was not *his* truth. For him, Adolph's whole conception of life was false, being based on a noxious lie. The survival of the fittest, big fish eat little fish, devil take the hindmost—those were concepts he refused to acknowledge, that he always would refuse to acknowledge.

"In that case, I'd rather fight my own fight and go under," he murmured, counting the flowers in the pattern of the cloth.

An exasperated look swept into Adolph's face; his lips pouted.

"Ach, you talk, you talk," he said impatiently. "You don't even know vhat you're talking about. Go on like you vant und see vhat happens. Chust vait till you get a little sense knocked into you." He looked about abruptly and snapped his fingers for the waitress. "Cancel the pie!" he shouted at her. "I ain't got all day to sit here vaitin' und vaitin'. The service in dis place is chust terrible! Come on und let's have the check. I don't know vhat's the matter mit everyone today."

139

six

Francy took leave of his father before the Stock Yards Inn and boarded the trolley in a depressed mood. The recent conversation, with its moment of intimacy, its disturbing revelation of parental affection, had ended by making him still more conscious of the abyss between his family and himself. It was not the ghosts of the past that stood between Francy and his father: it was their contradictory attitudes towards life. If he really respected his talent, he must let it develop in a more congenial atmosphere than that of the dark over-furnished mansion that represented everything in the world that he disliked.

In the hallway the mounted animal heads glared down at him from their posts. He had always hated those steers and bulls, which were a constant reminder of the origins of the family fortune. Today it seemed to him that the dead animals returned his hatred in their glassy suspicious stares.

I am an enemy in the house, he thought. Even the dead bulls know it. There is no doubt. I must get away!

As he began to climb the stairs, Mama hurried out of the parlor to intercept him.

"Oh, Francy, you look tired! You ought to lie down and take a good nap. Did you and Papa have a nice lunch together?"

"Yes, very nice," Francy answered to please Mama, whose ambition it was to bring all members of her family closer together. "We talked over a lot of things."

"Well, isn't that dandy!" Mama beamed. "You go and have lunch with Papa as often as ever you like. You two men don't see nearly enough of each other. Remember this, Francy," she said, and into her voice had come that note of gravity which Mama knew how to summon on occasions, "remember that Papa loves you with all his heart. It isn't always easy for him to show his feelings—sometimes a body's just got to sense them. But his feelings are there—never doubt it."

140

"I know, Mama," said Francy. "I know."

He had reached the first landing, on which stood the armored figure of the crusader. Yes, he really was tired, Francy thought, as he paused for breath. His clothes were soaked with perspiration, as always happened when he had overtaxed himself, and he wanted only to throw himself on his couch and sleep. But as he was about to tackle the second flight, Mama spoke again:

"Oh, Francy, I almost forgot. There's a special delivery letter for you. I put it in your room."

"A—special delivery?"

There was a quaver in Francy's voice. That letter could be from one person alone: Edgar Lee Masters, to whom he had given parts of his "ballad" for criticism the week before. If the great poet had written him by special delivery, it showed that he was genuinely impressed! And his opinion mattered to Francy more than that of all other people put together.

In a flash he was up the stairs, had torn open the door, and was sending his eyes about in search of the letter. Yes, there it was, propped up against the bookcase, with the blue special delivery stamp standing out like an emblem of merit. But what a small envelope to have come from a man like Edgar Lee Masters, whose vision was broad as a Midwestern plain! Then Francy's glance went to the handwriting, and a sinking feeling came over him. Tearing open the envelope, he drew out Helen's letter from inside.

"Dearest Francy," he read. "I know that this is going to hurt you . . ."

And then he need not have gone on, for he knew (and had known before opening the envelope) that Helen was asking him not to see her alone again. He sank down on the couch, aware of the chirping of a sparrow in the elm tree outside his window, aware also of the wild pounding of his heart; instinctively he pressed his hand to his breast, behind which that sick organ lived such a wild and frightening life of its own. For a moment life seemed to have come to a full stop.

The grandfather clock on the stairs gave a whir and then began striking the hour. One-two-three, Francy counted, and unconsciously listened for the second whir which always signaled the conclusion of the operation. And as he listened his mind went back to his early child-

141

hood—to that long period of illness when he had lain in this very room, often on this very couch, and kept waiting for the recurring whirs that punctuated the hours of his loneliness. Now, fifteen years later, he was just as lost, just as terrifyingly lonely as then: nothing had really changed. He felt himself a failure as a poet and as a human being, and Helen, the one person who could have helped him, had withdrawn her support. He did not blame her, knew only that he was as desperate today as that small boy had been, waiting for terror to descend on him like a marauding wolf.

Now the black pictures were coming! As always when he was weakened by despair, a vacuum seemed to have been created into which the dark thoughts could rush. Life, crude, brutal, and ugly, reared itself before him. He saw the wounded steer tossing his bloody head from side to side, while his terror-stricken eyes sought frantically for a path of escape. The workers cowered by the wall, and they, too, cast about desperate glances. But there was no escape, Francy knew, neither for the steer, nor for the workers, nor for himself. They must all go on to the bitter end! And at this thought, that there would never be escape, Francy shuddered and closed his eyes.

The clock struck again, one solitary note this time that fell on his head like the blow of a giant fist. He could not stay here any longer! He must get out of this room, where he had spent so many miserable hours, out of this house which he should long since have left forever. Better wander about the streets in solitude than stay here waiting for that clock to strike again!

He hurried down the stairs, grabbed his hat from the rack in the vestibule, and rushed out of the house as if demons were after him. And suddenly he thought, I am going to Helen after all! It may be weak of me, even shameful, but I cannot stop myself. If I look just once into her face, the terror will go away and I will be able to live again. Tonight when I go to bed I will not see that bloody steer's head before me. . . .

When Helen heard the ring, she knew at once that it was Francy. There are many ways of ringing a doorbell; Francy rang as if he regretted the action even before it was completed. Abruptly she broke

142

off her playing and jumped up from the piano stool. Her first idea was to have the maid say she was not in, for it had been difficult enough to write that letter, without going through the further ordeal of telling him to his face not to call again. Then she realized that he must have heard her playing, so would recognize the lie for what it was. How was it, thought Helen, as she went to open, how was it that she was never allowed to get out of things the easy way?

On the stoop outside the door Francy was standing. But what, she wondered, could have happened to him since she saw him last? He looked as if he had been through an illness. His cheeks, his high forehead, even his lips were pale. On his sensitive face lay a beseeching, unhappy look. And suddenly it seemed to Helen that she was again standing in a darkened room beside a bedstead in which lay a sleeping boy, his face wasted with fever. Like on that long-distant day, she felt an affinity with this lonely being, so ill equipped to cope with crude life; like then, she wanted to enfold him in her arms to protect him from brutality. And, like then, she knew it was impossible for any one person so to protect another.

"Francy, my poor darling! What is the matter?"

"Oh, Helen," he said, still standing in the doorway, not daring to walk in. "I know I shouldn't have come here. It was wrong of me to come. Very wrong! But this has been—the most awful day of my life."

"My poor boy! Tell me what has happened," she said, forgetting all that she had planned to say, knowing only that it would have been inhuman not to help him.

"I—I had lunch with my father," he said, and his big eyes stared at her in misery.

That came as such an anticlimax that Helen had to laugh. She took his arm and led him into the sitting room, made him sit down on the sofa.

"Now tell me what's really happened. Let me order you tea, Francy. Don't look so distressed!"

"Ah, if you'd seen what I saw!" Francy sat staring before him, as though he were seeing it all again. "I was at the Stock Yards this morning. A steer got loose on the floor. I'd always heard of that happening, but I'd never seen it before. It was a hundred times worse than anything I could have imagined! Oh, the brutality and ugliness!" He shuddered. "I'll never forget it."

Helen reached out and patted his hand.

"Francy, I do know how you feel! Didn't I tell you how I became a vegetarian after seeing someone cut the head off a chicken? Well, I'm not a vegetarian any longer. You've got to come to terms with life, Francy!"

"Do I? Who says so? The day I come to terms with life, I'll stop writing poetry. I'd just as soon stop living too! If ever I come to terms with life, then I won't mind so terribly—not being able to see you, Helen!"

She was touched. His youthful intensity, his striving for the absolute, his purity of spirit all reminded her of the girl called Helen Mason who had ceased to exist long years before. She had turned into another person, as the boy Francy probably would turn into another person under the hammer blows of life. But just now Francy was very much Francy.

"Has it meant so much to you then—being able to see me?" she asked him gently.

"What do you think? It has meant everything. Of course, you were right about my not coming here—I'm sure you were right. But I did need so much just to see you today! And now that I have"—He looked up at her and she saw that the despair had gone from his face —"everything is much better."

"Is it, Francy? If that's really so, then you must pay no attention to that letter. Let's pretend that I never wrote it."

As she smiled at him, she tried to remember her feelings of such a short time ago, and how important it had seemed that she bring their too close friendship to an end. Now other things had come to seem to her much more important.

"Do you mean that, Helen? You really will let me come?" His whole expression had changed: he was a young man again now, in love with life. "Oh, if only I had the feeling that I could come here—once in a long while. I wouldn't take advantage of it, I wouldn't come very often, but it would change everything for me."

"In that case," she said, "I will always be here, Francy—always when you want me."

144

"Is it a promise?"

"Yes," she said. "It is a promise."

seven

Bismarck II was feeling his oats this spring morning. Gelding though he was, his blood had quickened with the melting of the snows, and he was conscious of pleasurable feelings, in his case but vaguely connected with the mating instinct. Now as he pulled his master's spick-and-span buggy down Drexel, he lifted his dainty feet high, scornful of the motorcars that swished past in an unending stream. Unlike his predecessor, high-spirited Bismarck I, this twentieth-century steed had seen more automobiles than carriages in his lifetime, hence had developed towards them the nonchalant, if not supercilious, attitude suitable to a thoroughbred.

His master, on the other hand, felt moody and out of sorts as he steered the buggy down the familiar road to Packingtown. No joy did Adolph derive from the thought that another spring had burst upon the city; somehow, he no longer enjoyed springs as he used to do. Indeed, he found it singularly exhausting to adjust his sensibilities to the sounds and smells of this season of rebirth, recurring with what had come to seem alarming frequency.

The heavy spring motor traffic, ignored by Bismarck II, likewise jarred on Adolph's nerves. His was perhaps the last buggy in Chicago, and he realized that it, too, would eventually be forced off the streets. Already he caught people laughing at him and pointing meaningfully to the region of their own empty craniums. There was no room left for an individual! The depressing thought struck Adolph once again. Soon he would have to let Hirsch drive him to business in the Pierce-Arrow limousine. And this awareness of the individual's submergence in the modern world, this knowledge of his own inability to cope with the violence of spring and of the Chicago traffic, all swelled the feeling of malaise with which he looked forward to his coming interview with McKenna. In McKenna's stereotyped features, in his machinelike gestures and his impersonal way of speech, Adolph detected the enemy who meant finally to smother every manifestation of nineteenth-century individualism.

Now he was turning in at the Stock Yards gates, and the gateman was touching his cap and smiling. (Was it a smile of affection? Adolph thought. Or just the grin reserved for the harmless crank, the unorthodox eccentric?) The raucous cries of the cattle buyers reached him from the pens beyond the railroad tracks and, as always, these sounds were soothing to his ears. Much as the packing business had changed since the turn of the century, much as workmen and officials alike had taken on the character of automatons, these shrewd appraisers of beef had managed to retain their individuality. So specialized was their knowledge, so responsible their work, that the cattle buyers were not yet expendable. As they shouted out from horseback code words that implied bids for hundredweights of beef, Adolph recognized the familiar weather-beaten faces beneath the brown or black ranchmen's hats. Whether they were his own men or the agents of competitors, he had come to think of these tough tobacco-spitting individuals as friends.

Another friend was Chippy, though no one could have guessed it from hearing Adolph's gruff bark in reply to the little man's "Fine morning!" In the back of his mind Adolph still resented the fact that he had been forced to give Chippy a salary, as well as a regular, if rickety, seat in the corridor just outside his office. Here, decked in a hand-me-down suit and a strangely inappropriate stiff collar (a castoff of William's), the aging office boy presided in some degree of dignity, his bald head and thick glasses giving him the air of an aloof savant; a comic paper usually protruded from his pocket, for the sad fact was that Chippy had not yet learned to read.

Apart from the advent of Chippy's chair, few changes had occurred in or about Adolph's office during the last fifteen years. There was the same brass cuspidor on the floor, what looked like the same picture calendars on the wall, and by the window, under the unshaded bulb, the same roll-top desk, which had acquired the somewhat terrifying habit of folding up without notice. Several times McKenna had hinted that new offices, or even a new office building, would not be amiss for the staff of a multimillion-dollar concern, but always Adolph had pretended not to understand. What, he would have liked to know, was the matter with this sound brick building, with its iron staircase, its roomy corridors, its big uncurtained windows? A little outdated perhaps? Well, one could make just as much money in a drafty, old-fashioned building as in a highfalutin modern one.

Damn McKenna anyway! Adolph was thinking, as he sat whittling away on a birch stick, drawing the knife moodily towards him. Damn him for always wanting to change and modernize and increase efficiency, when things were running quite well as it was. Certainly no one could accuse him, Adolph, of not being progressive-minded! Hadn't they always said that he was half a jump ahead of the next fellow? But this McKenna's notion of efficiency was—well, simply on a different plane! With him efficiency meant production pushed to the nth power, with the producing unit becoming ever vaster, more highly mechanized, less and less marked by the stamp of any one man's personality. And now that the firm had outgrown the framework of a private enterprise it was to be turned into a stock company because McKenna so decreed! How was it, thought Adolph, giving the stick a fierce slash with his knife, how was it that he had allowed this outsider, who knew less about meat than Adolph Konrad had forgotten, to elbow his way into a policy-making position in the firm? Yes, how was it that McKenna's clammy fingers were now reaching out for the very reins of control?

His resentment turned into hot anger as he sat chiseling away at the birch stick clamped between his knees. He wanted to call to Chippy to summon the Scotchman, but at the last moment checked himself. Now, as always, Adolph preferred to go to see McKenna, rather than having that alien character intrude into his sanctum; he did not want those icy eyes to appraise the brass cuspidor and condemn his frayed carpet. He did not want McKenna's impersonal personality to invade the room! Snapping his knife shut, he rose from his chair, and as he did so, the roll top of his desk slid down with a resounding clatter. It sounded like the opening salvo of artillery.

Angus McKenna was dictating away in his office. Typically enough, he employed no human medium for this task, but sat with his lips

147

glued to the mouthpiece of a machine, into which he was pouring an unaccented flow of words; the murmur of his voice was like the purr of a well-adjusted gasoline engine. On catching sight of Adolph, he at once switched off the dictaphone and pivoted about in his swivel chair.

"Good morning, Mr. Konrad."

"I vant for to have a vord vit' you, McKenna," said Adolph, striding up to his manager's desk. (He was glad that the tall McKenna was seated, for this hid the discrepancy in their heights.) "Is this right, vhat I hear about your talking mit Al Peterson at the bank?"

"Oh, you mean that little chat we had about the stock issue?" said McKenna, with the implication that only details remained to be arranged. "It was qiute useful, I'm glad to say. We covered a lot of ground."

"Oh, you did, did you?" Adolph's lips shot out and in. He wanted to spit, and cast his eye about for a cuspidor, but there was no such convenience in McKenna's frugal office. "And you didn't t'ink it necessary for to ask me first?"

"But this was only an exploratory talk we had," McKenna answered. "Nothing was decided."

This was too much for Adolph.

"Not'ing vas decided, eh? Vell, that's too bad! Say, who d'you t'ink's goin' to decide anyvay? Who owns this business, McKenna, you or me?"

McKenna shrugged.

"I'm sorry you take it like that, Mr. Konrad. I assure you that I acted for the good of the firm."

"For me to decide!" shouted Adolph.

"But seeing that you've been unable to decide," said McKenna blandly.

"Who says that? I have decided! I have! I decided against this proposition years ago."

"I'm afraid I can't accept your decision," McKenna said after a little pause. "I'm sorry, Mr. Konrad, but you know how I feel. The company became overexpanded during the war: overexpanded and undercapitalized. Now that the postwar slump's upon us, we've got to change our whole financial policy. I wish you'd reconsider the situation."

Adolph's fist landed on the table with a hefty thump. It made the inkstand tremble and almost toppled over a framed photograph which was the sole indication that the inhabitant of this room had a personal life, unconnected with dictaphones, telephones, and filing cabinets; for a moment the likeness of Maureen, McKenna's daughter, swayed precariously, and the expression of her laughing face seemed to grow quizzical, as though she realized that the stability of many a thing apart from her own picture hung in the balance.

"Vhat d'you take me for, a—a nitvit?" Adolph spluttered. "I never change my mind, vonce I've decided. I built up this business from the bottom, vit'out your help nor anyvone's. I managed myself, and this has alvays been my business—chust mine!"

"Yes, Mr. Konrad," said McKenna, and then he pointed at the calendar that formed part of his writing pad. "But this happens to be the year 1920, and we find ourselves in a changing world. Better not forget that, I'm telling you!"

"Und I tell you to shut up!"

There was a small silence, punctured only by the sound of Adolph's angry breathing and the whir of the ceiling fan; from beyond the open window came the distant lowing and bleating of frightened animals, but to the two men this was as little noticeable as the pungent, ever-prevalent Stock Yards smell.

"Well, Mr. Konrad," said McKenna finally, "you leave me no choice. It's your business, as you say, and I am your paid employee. I've worked for you for twenty years, and during that whole time my first loyalty's been to this firm. I'm sorry, I really am, but I shall have to offer you my resignation."

"Accepted!" Adolph shouted, and he banged his fist on the table again.

But then a strange thing happened to him. It had happened before at moments of crisis, and might have been compared to the ringing of an alarm bell. An instinct almost primeval, certainly unconnected with reasoning, warned him that he was in danger, grave danger. Whatever happened, dislike McKenna as he might, he simply could not allow him to leave the firm!

"Vhat's up anyvay?" he went on, and he was still carried away by

149

fury, but had managed in a matter of seconds to bridle that fury and direct it towards a calculated goal. "They've made you an offer from another firm, is that it? Spit it out, McKenna! Spit it out!"

But McKenna shook his head.

"I have had no offer," he replied, his voice as flat and expressionless as ever. "I shouldn't have considered one while I was in your employ. You ought to know me that well, Mr. Konrad."

"Okay," Adolph shot back. "Now look here. I'll raise your salary fifty per cent, retroactive to January first. Is it a deal?"

Again McKenna's head went from left to right.

"I'm not interested in a higher salary. This matter has nothing to do with salary or anything like that."

Adolph looked up quickly. Peering at McKenna, he knew that the man spoke the truth: he was simply incapable of this sort of lie. So was he really resigning as a matter of principle—because it went against his curious code of business ethics to manage a firm dedicated to a mistaken policy? Adolph Konrad was taken aback. All he had ever heard about the inflexibility of the Scotch race came back to him, and he understood now why its members had won positions of such high trust throughout the world.

"So you von't reconsider your resignation?"

"Only under one condition," said the manager. "And you know what it is. There's no point discussing it further."

Adolph had a moment of panic. He saw defeat staring him in the face: either a personal defeat inflicted by McKenna or a business defeat inflicted by imponderable factors with which he was unable to cope. He could not run the business without McKenna, of that he was painfully aware; and apparently he could not run the business *with* McKenna, at least not the business as now constituted.

Confronted with a choice of disasters, his thoughts suddenly flew to that Sunday fifteen years before, when McKenna had come walking to his house to inform him of the settlement of the pickle-room strike. He had had a presentiment even then that he, like Gogerty, the union boss, might one day suffer defeat at the hands of this astounding McKenna. Well, it hadn't happened yet! Perhaps his enemy had won a major victory, but in every war there is the element of the unforeseen.

"Okay, McKenna," he heard himself saying. "I'll t'ink it over again. There may be somet'ing in vhat you say after all."

The shadow of a smile passed over McKenna's face—no, not a smile really, just the faintest expression of satisfaction. It lasted only a split second, but Adolph had never seen the phenomenon before. As he turned to leave, he was aware that he hated Angus McKenna with an unquenchable hatred. He hated him more than any man alive.

eight

The days that followed his talk with Adolph marked a period of crisis for Francy. On waking in the morning, his first thought was of Helen, and a wave of elation would sweep over him as he remembered the great friendship between them, and then realized that he would be seeing her again that day. But even this perfect apple of happiness had in it the worm of destruction. Seeing Helen meant also that he would be seeing Rupert, and of late he had begun to experience for his second brother an irresistible feeling of dislike.

Who was it who had made use of her to satisfy his own driving ambitions? Why, Rupert, of course, who understood Helen as little as a vainglorious jay could understand a nightingale! And yet was he, Francy, ever torn between desires and counterdesires, never sure of his own mind for more than a few moments at a time, the right person to judge or to condemn anyone? Most certainly not! Suddenly and inevitably all the old doubts and conflicts would be stirred up again, and with a shock of dismay he would remember that the whole structure of his life was wrong.

Yes, it was wrong for him to live in this mansion, built from the sweat of dead workers, wrong to eat three great meals every day, wrong to own six suits and the accouterment that went with them. Wrong, doubly wrong, it was for him to lead a life of pleasant idleness, dabbling with poetry from which he would never make a living, when he realized so keenly that a great effort was called for to build a better and a fairer world. He might condemn his father as a pirate of industry

151

and Rupert as a wastrel and philanderer, but neither went against the dictates of his conscience. And he, God help him, did it every day of his life!

It was not till he was seated beside Helen in the quiet room on East Cedar that the struggle within him subsided. He was happy just to be there, conscious of her sympathy and understanding; it assuaged his inner torment, quieting the disharmonies inside him. Nowadays she often consented to play for him (which he rightly considered a great compliment, because she never played before anyone). As he sat listening, with the dusk of the Chicago evening settling outside, a feeling of peace would settle over Francy. At such moments he no longer worried as to how to resolve his life, and when. He breathed easily in the world of beauty surrounding Helen, and harsh thoughts would have been intruders in that private world.

"It's really curious," she said to him one day when, having played for some time, she came and sat down beside him. "Six weeks ago we scarcely knew each other; I remembered you only as a little boy lying sleeping in a strange house with an unhappy look on his face. Now suddenly you've become an important part of my life, and I don't yet know how it happened. Well, perhaps that doesn't matter too much. It was nice of fate to send you in my path, for the fact is that I needed you badly."

"*You* needed me? Oh, Helen, you know that it was I who needed you. Desperately! Yes, desperately!"

He reached out to lay his hand on hers, and she turned her palm up and clasped his. Shy as both of them were, they had had no closer physical contacts in their many meetings.

"Oh, I—I am easily replaceable," said Helen, speaking very frankly, as she was able to do only with Francy. "A woman well on the wrong side of thirty, not very beautiful, not very remarkable except that she once used to play the piano pretty well. Oh yes, Francy, you'll find many more interesting than I," she went on without giving him a chance to interrupt. "But as to you, that's a different matter. You're a very rare person, my dear, and I ought to know, for if I've learned anything in these years, it's to judge people correctly. There is no evil in you, and that alone sets you apart from almost everyone."

152

Francy, blushing scarlet, had jumped up from the sofa, but Helen laughed and said, "Yes, you'd better hear the truth about yourself at last, whether you like it or not. You have a talent, Francy, and I don't mean your talent for poetry. It's a very special talent: a talent for goodness. It's more important than all the others."

"Don't say such damn stupid things," spluttered Francy, snatching up a cigarette from the table but forgetting to light it. "You don't know me, Helen, though you ought to. I'm not a strong person—far from it. I'm struggling to find my way."

"Because your instinct tells you that it's wrong to live like most people, selfishly, regardlessly. Don't ever be ashamed of rebelling, Francy! The time to be ashamed is if you stop rebelling. I have great confidence in you—as a human being."

"I wish I had."

"Perhaps you will one day. But in the meanwhile, remember this"— Helen stretched out her hand, and Francy walked back slowly and crouched on the floor, leaning his head against her knees—"remember this, my dear—you mean a great deal to me. The idea of Francy Konrad, one pure person in this dirty world, means a great deal to me. I know we Anglo-Saxons are never supposed to say things like that, except in jest. Well, I do say it, and I'm not jesting. No, I'm not jesting, my dear. . . ."

She let her fingers play in his thinning hair and travel down his boyishly smooth cheeks. For some reason she felt very much like weeping. Aware that their relationship was by its very nature transitory, tenuous, she nevertheless recognized it as one of the most precious of her life; these hours spent with Francy had a bland innocence which took her back to her earliest girlhood, to walks across meadows in the company of her father, to early morning awakenings in a sun-bathed room. She felt refreshed by them and absolved of the past. Her repeated failures as an artist, as a daughter, as a wife, were momentarily forgotten (she knew, oh, she knew all too well, that her reprieve would be brief!) and she lived for the hour in a changed world where one could meet one's friend's candid gaze, and return it.

There were other days when they spoke lightly and joked through the hours of the afternoon. There was no longer any question of their not seeing each other alone; Helen seemed to have forgotten all about that famous special delivery letter which had caused him such pain; now she urged him to come and always made him feel welcome. Re-counting anecdotes of diplomatic life in the world capitals she had known, she used to make him chuckle or burst into laughter. He thought her very witty, and reserved for her the veneration suitable for a young man towards a much older woman who has introduced him to her own adult world; it seemed to him that his horizon was broadening even as they sat talking and that his new insight would enable him to write better and to give new scope to his unachieved *Stock Yards Ballad*.

Unachieved with a vengeance. The moment he had left Helen, to hurry back to his writing desk, his stirring of inspiration subsided; seated before the blank sheet of paper, he would feel frustrated and poor, a prey to doubts and self-accusations. He had now heard from Masters, at last, and while the great man's criticism was kindly, it told him what he already knew: one could not write good poetry with words and meter alone. He had failed to express the love and hatred that burned in his heart, and he had failed for one reason above all: because he was living a false life. He was unworthy of his art, as he was un-worthy of Helen's friendship, while subsisting on blood money whose very touch soiled the fingers! And suddenly he would be gripped with his old longing to flee away; to flee from this house, where the stuffed animal heads glared at him from the wall, from this family which un-derstood him so ill, from this city which was his, though it was as alien to his spirit as a city of the moon. He would half rise from his chair, then subside in alarm as he grew aware of that racing heart which was ever a sign of insoluble inner conflict.

On his twenty-fifth birthday Francy received from his father a beauti-ful cigarette case, with his initials stamped on the gold. (Or rather, it was from Hauptman that he received it, for Adolph, always shy of emo-tions, had left it with the butler before he drove off for the Yards early in the morning.) Ever since that day when they lunched together alone, Francy had been aware of his father's desire to draw closer to him, a desire that he appreciated, even knowing that it could never be ful-filled. And now came this cigarette case as further evidence, saying through its golden beauty the words which Adolph could not bring himself to pronounce!

As Francy held it to the light, letting the sun glint upon it, he experienced an emotion which was novel to him: the joy of possession. He loved at first sight this exquisite case which was the first article of real value that he had owned. But at almost the same moment the cancer of doubt had begun to gnaw, that cancer whose existence could be forgotten only for moments at a time. What right had he to own such a precious object? Had not this case, like everything bought by his father, been paid for with blood? In accepting it, was he not countenancing a crime?

That afternoon when he went to see Helen he was in an absent-minded mood that did not escape her attention. For several days she had been practicing one of her favorite pieces for his birthday—Chopin's difficult Prelude in F minor—but now as she played she felt that Francy was not in a receptive mood. Having noted that his hand kept sliding to his breast pocket, she later on asked him jokingly if it was his tongue that he was keeping there. He laughed and took out the golden cigarette case.

"Oh, it's beautiful, Francy!"

"I know it is," he said, almost complainingly.

"And to think that all that I gave you was an inadequately played prelude!"

"I liked your present much better! It was a perfect gift. And I don't feel that I ought to give it back, as I do with this other. You know, if it weren't so hurting to my father, that's what I'd do tomorrow."

"But why, Francy?"

"Because I disapprove of gold cigarette cases! Especially for me. And especially when bought with Konrad money!"

She looked in his face and was struck by his earnestness, by his obvious desire to achieve truth, according to his lights.

"You mustn't always want to do things and not do them," she said spontaneously. "I can tell you that from my own experience. I don't mean that you should give back this cigarette case, but I do want to see you take some decisive action at last."

"You would respect me more?"

"No, Francy, I respect you so much already. But I think you would respect yourself more. And you would be happier."

He strode over to the bay window and stood looking out into East Cedar. A lady with a little girl was strolling by, the lady dressed in the long tight skirt and wearing one of the picture hats popular in that year; the little girl had on a sailor suit and carried roller skates. Francy, staring at them, thought, I shall never forget this lady and her child! When I die, the picture of them will be engraved upon my brain. For this very moment is the most important of my life! I always knew that one day I would find strength to act. Thanks to Helen, it has happened, and as simply as all the big things in one's life.

Swinging about, he said aloud, "Birthdays are good days for decisions. I agree with you that I have hedged far too often. Well, twenty-five is not too late to decide—that I shan't be dependent on Konrad money any longer. You have helped me to make up my mind, and I am very grateful. My shilly-shallying is over at last."

She smiled at him without answering, for it was not in her nature to persuade or to dissuade.

"I shall be leaving Chicago," he said suddenly.

That was a shock she had not bargained for. The thought of his leaving her alone in Chicago sent a pang through her heart; in a flash she realized how accustomed she had grown to these pleasant afternoon visits and how much she would miss them. Thanks to Francy, she had been happy these last weeks—yes, happier than she had been for many years. Gradually she had built up her whole life in Chicago around Francy.

"You must do as you think best," she said, having too much respect for his hard-won decision to suggest that he could live an independent life right here in Chicago.

"Yes, I will go at once," he hurried on. "And the farther the better. New Mexico or Arizona—they are places that I've always longed for. The beauty of those great gorges and deserts would push me on to produce something worth while. I have to get the air of the city out of my lungs. . . ."

"Then do go, if you feel that way," she said. "Your father will understand."

156

"Oh, I shan't be asking my father for anything! I shan't accept Konrad money any more, no matter what happens. If I can't earn my own living as a poet, then I'll give up writing and sell shoelaces instead. But I shan't live on money that I abhor!"

"But, Francy, how are you even going to get out to Arizona?" she said, loving him for his impetuousness and his brave youthfulness. "Besides, you can't start a new life on five dollars."

"Why not? My father did, as I've been hearing since I was a toddler. I'll manage all right, Helen. Don't worry."

"Won't you let me make you a loan?"

"No, no." He brushed the suggestion aside. "Oh, I can't tell you what a relief it is to have come to a decision," he cried, pushing his hand excitedly through his thin hair. "It's taken me so long to make up my mind, but now it is made up—irrevocably. I'm not minimizing the difficulties. I know how hard it is going to be to hurt my family and to cut off from the whole past for good. I'll have to do it."

"And is it going to be a little hard to say good-by to me?" Helen could not help asking.

"Oh, Helen, what do you think?"

He made three rapid strides across the room and took her hands in his. He stood looking into her eyes, which met his gaze warmly and openly; never had she said so much to him, without uttering a word. But she knew she must not try to stop him. Francy being Francy, even his "irrevocable" decisions were subject to change. She disengaged her hand and asked him jokingly if he would like her to play the "Victory" aria from *Aida*.

Francy could not bear to have Rupert spoil his mood, so he left earlier than usual, promising to return and say good-by on the morrow. Riding to the South Side, he passed near the pawnshops on Halstead Street, and on the spur of the moment decided to dispose of the case so as to raise his train fare to Arizona. The little man who waited on him had the casual take-it-or-leave-it manner of all pawnbrokers; Francy's one desire was to get out of the shop as soon as possible. Certain that he was being roundly cheated, he still felt relief on ridding himself of his possession, which seemed to represent the whole ill-gotten Konrad fortune.

But as he was leaving the pawnbroker's shop, he almost bumped into

157

a ragged fellow who stood coughing, with a blood-flecked handkerchief at his lips. At once the futility of his gesture was borne home. By the symbolic act of selling the cigarette case (and at a lower price than it was worth), he merely had pampered his own conscience, without the least benefit to any victim of Konrad greed. The foolish action had mortified him, and no doubt it would hurt the feelings of his father, but it was hypocritical and unworthy. Not thus could he make up for the long history of exploitation connected with the Konrad name! Shamefacedly, he peeled off five dollars from the roll in his pocket and pushed it into the hand of the astonished consumptive, before hurrying off as if the police were after him.

Next afternoon he appeared at Helen's house with a suitcase, and when she saw it she knew that the die was cast. Until then she had half expected Francy to change his mind, hoping that he would and at the same time hoping he would have the tenacity to stick to his resolve. Now she stared at the suitcase miserably, feeling that yet another episode in her life had come to an end: a meaningless and inconclusive end which left her not even a concrete memory to carry into the future. So it had been with Anton Holbein in Vienna and with Pahlevi Azad in Teheran. These young men, also, had meant something to her once upon a time, but because of cowardice, or for what other reason she could not imagine, she had stopped their relationships with her from coming into flower, as human relationships must do. Anton and Pahlevi were but misty memories now, to be evoked by a snatch of music or the sight of an imitation Persian lithograph in a department store. Would the time come when Francy would be dead for her, except when she happened to hear poetry read aloud?

"You are off?" she said, so unhappy she could scarcely get out the words.

"Yes, I am off," he said confidently. "Wish me luck, Helen. I shall write you from Santa Rosa."

"What did your parents say?"

"Oh, I have left a letter. It was easier that way," Francy told her, and then Helen knew that this was the old Francy after all.

"Well, bless you, my dear. Please send me a batch of your poetry when you get some into shape. And you must make me a promise: you will take care of your health, won't you? Don't forget that you have a heart."

"I'm not apt to," said Francy. "But I promise."

His detached tone had a curious effect on Helen. All along she had been telling herself that it was the absence of sex that made their relationship so perfect, but now that he had chosen spiritual peace rather than her company, she felt slighted.

"I wonder if I shall ever see you again," she said, gazing at him from her sofa and suddenly longing to touch his blond hair, which was as soft and fine as a young girl's. "We are sailing the end of next month, Rupert and I. I don't suppose that I shall be coming back to America for years."

"It will be terrible not seeing you," he said, and suddenly the old lonely look flashed into his face, as though he had just realized what this decision of his implied. "You've been so wonderful to me—more wonderful than anyone I've ever known. I could never tell you all that I feel about you, Helen."

"But you have never tried!"

The words were out before she knew it, and then it was too late to take them back. She was not sure she wanted to take them back.

"Francy," she said, "you must do me a favor. I have never asked you a favor before. Kiss me before you go! You haven't kissed me in all this time, and soon you will be far away. . . . No, not on the forehead, that's not what I mean. Kiss me just once on the mouth. Perhaps, my dear— perhaps I love you far better than you will ever know."

nine

Rupert was pleased at the change come about in Helen in these last weeks. Chicago seemed to be having an exemplary effect on her—or perhaps not Chicago so much as Francy. After fifteen years' marriage, Rupert had come to recognize the symptoms accompanying the entrance of a new young man into his wife's life. Having no reason to doubt her faithfulness (nor indeed her frigidity), he had taken a benign attitude to these impermanent attachments which produced such beneficial results for Helen.

For one thing, she drank less, which of course was a relief. With Helen, drinking had never become a habit; it was, thought Rupert, merely a means of escape from insoluble inner conflicts. Through association with artists, she was able to believe that she, too, was still an artist; her guilt feeling was momentarily absolved as she plunged back into her piano playing, and even convinced herself that she would one day give that public concert which she had been postponing for fifteen years.

Of course, he benefited from the situation in a way. Helen, having a new interest of her own, bothered less about her husband's activities, and that was particularly lucky at this time. The truth was that Rupert had discovered an attraction in his native city, and as was to be expected, the attraction had female form. Strange that he had never noticed when he was young that Gladys Hastey's screwed-up little face had a bizarre charm of its own! Perhaps Rupert's taste in women had changed with the years, perhaps there was in his character a perverse streak which drew him irresistibly towards Helen's old enemy number one. If ever he had wanted to conceal anything from his wife, it was this present infatuation! She possessed a knack of making him feel shabby, even when there was very little cause.

So he was complaining to Gladys during one of those charming afternoon calls at his brother's lake-shore house, a stone's throw from his own.

"Helen's a difficult woman," he was saying, as he rested his shapely body in the settee. "A fine character, of course—a truly sensitive being. But she's—well, so abominably moody! You can imagine that life with her hasn't always been easy."

"Poor Rupert!"

"I'm not complaining," Rupert lied, uncertain whether or not he had heard an ironic undertone. Could anyone guess what thoughts were passing behind those squinting eyes of Gladys'? "Helen and I have loved each other, and she's certainly made a fine diplomat's wife," Rupert went on. "It's neither her fault nor mine that we've grown apart—and perhaps discovered that we never did have much in common."

"I could have told you that fifteen years ago," Gladys said, peering at Rupert over the top of her long cigarette holder.

"Why didn't you?"

"You know why. You never gave me the chance. You should have married me—that's where you made your first mistake."

"Perhaps you're right," said Rupert.

She began to laugh.

"My God, the man really took me seriously! Is this the sophisticated diplomat I've been hearing about? Is this the breaker of countless hearts?"

"Don't make fun of me," Rupert said a little sourly. "I've often thought, since coming back to Chicago, how ill suited you were to William, and," he added as he reached for her hand, "how very attractive you were."

"Oh, Rupert, that isn't going to get you anywhere! I have a mirror that I can look into, you know. What's more, I haven't forgotten how you used to snub me fifteen years ago. I think it's only because you have a chance to thwart William that you're wasting time on me now. And it is a waste of time, I assure you," she said, withdrawing her hand from his gently but quite firmly.

And none too soon. The doorbell gave a ring, and almost simultaneously there was the sound of swishing skirts and of Cecilia Judson's overcheery voice:

"Gladys, darling, are you at home?"

Gladys pushed Rupert away from her, just as her sisters-in-law, Cecilia and Bee, burst into the room.

"Why, hello!" she cried enthusiastically. "Hello, girls! This is getting to be quite a family party."

"It is at that," said Bee, catching sight of her brother on the couch. And at once her spinsterish nose gave a twitch; her sharp eyes traveled from him to Gladys and back to him. "What fair wind blew you in here today, Rupert?"

"As a matter of fact," Rupert said, thinking quickly, "I only got here this minute and I haven't yet told Gladys why I came. Seeing that you're all here, I might as well break the news now. It's sensational."

"Well, it had better be," said Cecilia with a giggle.

"I've just had a cable," Rupert announced, "from the lady in waiting of the Princess Xenia. During our two years in Molenavia we got to know Xenia quite well," he proceeded in an airy tone suitable for the enlightening of these provincials. "Helen and I were often asked out to her country palace for week ends. Since the end of the war Xenia's put her whole heart into the rebuilding of her shattered country. What she's done is really inspiring! Now she's planning a tour of America to raise money for the Molenavian Red Cross, and her travels are going to take her to Chicago."

Rupert paused to let his eye pass over the faces of his listeners. He had the advantage now! They were waiting on his words with bated breath, each trying to guess at what was coming, each asking herself how his "sensational" announcement would affect her personally. Cecilia, the inveterate party-goer, sensed festivities in the air and gave a poke at her elaborate hair-do; Bee, presently caught up in state politics, wondered if the impending royal visit might somehow benefit the Illinois Women's Political League; even Gladys had for once dropped her sarcastic smile and looked interested.

"So I have decided to form a Chicago committee to welcome Her Royal Highness," Rupert went on, having tantalized his audience. "And I came to ask Gladys here to suggest some suitable names. Of course I want her and William to go on the committee themselves."

That "of course" must have sounded strange to his sisters, knowing how well William and Rupert got on. Watching Cecilia's mouth tighten in envy, Rupert reflected that this paid her back—she and that smart aleck Justin—for not inviting him to their last dinner party.

"Well, we'll do our best," Gladys said. "How large a committee did you have in mind?"

"Ten or twelve, I suppose. We'll have to ask the mayor to act as honorary chairman. There's bound to be a civic reception, and it goes without saying that everyone who is anyone will want to arrange something for Xenia. My own place is too small for entertaining, but I thought we might fix up a dinner party here one night—that is, if you and William are willing."

"Justin and I would be very pleased to entertain Her Highness,"

Cecilia put in, swallowing what little pride she possessed. But Rupert shook his head.

"Afraid it would look bad if we Konrads monopolized the show, Cecilia. You'll have plenty of chances to meet Xenia, you needn't worry. And I think you'll like her, all of you. She's an amazing personality! But now I've really got to be leaving." He glanced at his watch. "I've got an appointment with a young man I'm thinking of hiring as secretary. He's been strongly recommended to me by Senator Brenn."

"Must be something pretty fishy about him in that case," Bee shot out. "Anyone whom that cheap politician recommends . . . But why in heaven's name do you want a secretary, Rupert? I thought you were going back to Europe fairly soon."

"Ah, well, I may have my reasons," said Rupert mysteriously. "Now please don't say anything about Xenia; I'm keeping it out of the newspapers for a couple of days. And give a thought to that list, Gladys, if you don't mind."

"I will," she promised him.

Rupert left his brother's house, feeling gleeful. He had handled a ticklish situation with consummate skill, and through the same maneuver made old Cecilia turn green with envy. Moreover, he knew that Gladys had savored her moment of triumph. All in all, he had executed a diplomatic master stroke.

In the house on East Cedar a young man was waiting for him in the study. Ruppert at once noted the way this presentable young man was seated; not precisely deferential, it at the same time conveyed the impression that he knew he was here only on sufferance; he seemed to be expecting a call that would oblige him to dart off at a moment's notice. Efficiency was stamped on his pale face and marked the quick motion with which he rose to greet Rupert; but it was not an efficiency that one might believe had been devoted to major operations: it was a petty, insignificant, rather pointless efficiency, like that of an engine still running smoothly in an overturned automobile.

"Mr. Hapgood, I presume?" said Rupert, putting out his hand and experiencing as he did so a curious feeling of fatality: for the fraction of a second he could have sworn that this stranger was destined to

163

play a role in his future. "It was good of you to have come. My friend, Senator Brenn, said some very fine things about you, young man."

"Well, that was nice of the senator," Hapgood answered, his voice suiting his manner ideally; faintly jocular, it was at the same time respectful to a degree. "My dad and Senator Brenn have the same home town, you know; in fact, they went to school together. I've looked up to the senator since I was a little shaver."

"I believe you've practiced photography, is that right?" Rupert asked, finding this suave, well-brought-up fellow more and more to his liking.

"Why, yes, sir. I had a studio in Los Angeles before the war. Art photos and that sort of thing, you know."

"So the senator was telling me," Rupert said, and he began to pace the room while pulling worriedly at the lobe of his left ear; it was almost as if he were trying to pull a decision out of his ear. "I am speaking to you in strict confidence, and even Mrs. Konrad doesn't yet know what I'm going to tell you. It is quite possible (though the matter hasn't been decided yet) that I may return to Europe as minister or ambassador of the United States. I am not at liberty to disclose the country to which I'll be accredited, but it's a fairly important one. Would you consider accompanying me as private secretary?"

"Well, I am very much honored," Hapgood answered after a second's pause. "I would like to think about it for a little while."

"By all means. I believe that I can promise you an interesting life, and as to salary, you need have no worries on that point. I require someone a little special, and I really believe you'd do. So did Senator Brenn," he added, and at once regretted the tacit admission that this senator had Rupert's interests at heart.

But if Hapgood had noticed the slip, there was no indication of it in the bland smile with which he murmured, "I would try to satisfy you, Mr. Konrad. Believe me, I would."

A single bar of music drifted in from the drawing room, then a series of chords struck with a sure hand: Helen must have come home as they were talking and gone straight to her piano.

"That is Mrs. Konrad playing," Rupert said, putting his hand on Hapgood's thin shoulder as he escorted him to the door. "She is rather a fine musician, almost concert standard, in fact."

"I can well believe that," said Hapgood, listening to Helen as her fingers began moving over the keys. "I hope I shall have the pleasure of hearing her perform one day."

Rupert smiled.

"That I can't promise you. I'm afraid my wife is very difficult about playing before people. It may sound strange, but she hasn't even played for me in a good many years."

"Oh well, we must respect people's individualities, mustn't we?" Hapgood remarked, with just the right tone to imply both sympathy and discretion.

"Yes," answered Rupert feelingly. "Yes, we certainly must."

ten

Adolph had called together a family council in his library, presumably to discuss the matter of the stock issue. It was true that not even William knew of Adolph's latest talk with McKenna, yet an atmosphere of tension pervaded the musty library of the Drexel Boulevard house. The four elder children waited nervously in the overstuffed armchairs beside the statue of a winged Walküre; neither Adolph nor Wilma, nor Francy, their younger brother, had as yet put in an appearance.

"Have you noticed that this room smells of death?" remarked Bee, wrinkling her long nose. "Pew! It's really disgusting. I feel like someone waiting for a will to be read out."

"And yet as far as I've heard, nobody is dead." Cecilia tittered.

"Oh yes, my dear: a whole era is dead. And we're about to bury it, with the help of McKenna. What makes me sick is that it needn't have happened—not if the country had thrown out the Democrats in '16. Well, there's a new election in the offing, but it may already be too late to repair the damage."

"The damage? What damage?" William declared stoutly. "Everything's just as it's always been. If Adolph Konrad and Son becomes Konrad and Company, well, that isn't going to change things much."

165

"And besides," added Cecilia, rather inconsequentially, "Justin says that the Democrats are almost sure to be beaten in November. Then everything will be much better."

Bee's fingers flew to the golden bee that she wore on her blouse.

"I wish, Cecilia, that I shared your optimism," she snapped. "Unfortunately, we responsible women in the League realize that private enterprise is threatened, and the sooner the whole country wakes up to the fact, the better. At least I have enough private enterprise left to order a drink, which is more than I can say for you others. Rupert, please ring the bell for Hauptman."

"Father won't like that," William warned. "This is his house, after all."

"Is it?" Rupert rang emphatically so as to annoy William. "I thought it was *our* house. And I thought that the business was ours too."

"I guess it's going to be everybody's business in a few days," Bee said dolefully, "that is, if McKenna gets his way."

Hauptman appeared in the doorway, his face stamped with the disapproving expression they all remembered since their early childhood.

"Bring us some more whiskey and soda," ordered Bee. "And listen, make sure that there's more than half an inch of liquor at the bottom of the bottle."

"The whiskey may be locked up. I'm not sure," said Hauptman sourly.

"Oh yes, you're sure, all right. And don't forget the ice, as you always do. By the way, it's past five o'clock. Hasn't Mr. Francy come home yet?"

"No. And he's not going to either," said Hauptman.

"Not going to? What do you mean, 'not going to'?"

"Mr. Francy went out more than two hours ago, and he had a bag with him. He left letters with me to give to the boss and the missis."

"What's this? Why didn't you tell us all this before?"

"Because you never asked me," said Hauptman, shutting the door behind him.

The brothers and sisters looked at one another in silence.

"D'you suppose he's joking?" suggested Rupert, at last.

Bee snorted.

"Did you ever know that sourpuss to joke? Do you suppose he has one joke in his big clumsy body?"

"Then what in God's name does it mean?"

"Mean? It means that little Francy has flown the coop, that's what! Haven't you noticed that he's been acting queer lately—even queerer than usual? This is what he had up his sleeve."

"The little son of a gun!" said Rupert. "That's a nice way to behave, isn't it? What's Mama going to say? She's always been so stuck on Francy. I think she likes him better than all the rest of us together."

"Perhaps that's why she hasn't come downstairs," Cecilia said.

Rupert shook his head sadly, overcome with that quick sympathy for another's misfortune which was one of his most likable characteristics.

"Poor Mama! You know, I think I'll run upstairs and have a word with her. Yes, I will! Send up and let me know when the old man arrives."

"What about your drink?" Bee called after him, but Rupert was already hurrying past the armored figure, mounting the steps two at a time.

He found his mother sitting by the open window with her darning bag on her lap. On her knees was a shirt that he recognized as Francy's, but Wilma had not yet taken out thread and needle; she sat there with her hands on Francy's shirt, as though it were a little animal that she was caressing.

"Hello, Mama," said Rupert, coming up to kiss her on the forehead. "We're all waiting for you downstairs."

"I know," said Mama absently. "Has your father come back yet from the Yards?"

"No, he's almost half an hour late. Tell me, Mama, what's all this about Francy? Has he really gone off and left you a note?"

Wilma remained silent, whereupon Rupert burst out, "So it is true then! Oh, I'd like to have him here right now to tell him what I think of him!"

Wilma reached out to pat Rupert's hand. "I wish you didn't feel that way about it, Son. Francy's a good boy. I felt lately that he was troubled inside, badly troubled, but he isn't the sort of person who gives one his

167

confidence. If he felt that he had to go—well, then it was right for him to go."

"Now, Mama, that's a funny way to take it, I must say. I've never known anything so inconsiderate in my life!"

"Haven't you?" She gave him that placid smile that was so typically Wilma. "What a bad memory you have! Or perhaps fifteen years is a pretty long time. Too long to remember—that Francy isn't the first young man to go off without telling his family good-by!"

Rupert gave an uneasy tug at his ear. This mother of his had such a quiet way of saying things: she never condemned, rarely even stated an opinion, and yet one could not help sensing that she had definite and strong feelings upon all matters.

"My case was entirely different," Rupert said. "I don't see how you can compare it. For one thing, I was madly in love."

"I see." Wilma threaded her needle and began to darn the collar of Francy's shirt. "So you think that makes all the difference? You were in love, and Francy isn't. You're quite sure he isn't, I suppose."

"Francy? Why, I should think not!" Rupert burst out laughing, if a trifle hollowly. "Who would little Francy be in love with, anyway? Ridiculous!"

"Yes, Rupert, I reckon it is," Wilma agreed. "It just struck me how goldarned sure we are that we know why people act the way they do. Now when you ran away when you were less than Francy's age and went off to find Helen, everyone said you were behaving like a spoiled brat. But I thought you ought to have the benefit of the doubt. That's why I followed you; I wanted to meet the young lady and see for myself why you'd done it."

"Oh, Mama! And I thought you saw her only because I kept begging you."

"It didn't do any harm for you to beg, Son," said Mama airily. "Anyway, I liked Helen, as you know, though I did advise you pretty strong not to marry her. Once you'd made up your mind, I never said another word against it. And look—I guess it's all turned out for the best."

Rupert began to feel ill at ease, as always on the rare occasions when his mother touched on his private life. In comparison to the long and close relationship between his parents, his own marriage was, he well

168

realized, a failure. Nor could he expect his mother to understand the psychological factors in Helen's make-up which had contributed to this situation with no responsibility on his part!

"Oh yes, it all turned out all right," he said, trying to put conviction in his voice. "Of course Helen's a complicated person, difficult to understand and not always easy to live with. She isn't a happy person by any means."

"No, that she ain't, Son," Wilma said thoughtfully. "I reckon we can't all have happy dispositions. Your Helen's what I'd call a person torn in two, and that doesn't make for a body's happiness."

"How do you mean, a person torn in two?" said Rupert, astonished, as he so often was, by the comprehension of this simple mother of his.

"Why, wanting two things at the same time, like. One part of her hankers right back to her father's little yellow house in Cambridge. And I guess if you lived in a palace (as you both might one day), she'll still be hankering back to that house and all that went with it. But if she lived in a shack, why then, sure as can be, she'd be eating her soul out for a palace. And she ain't the only one, Son: Helen is a woman of these times. That's one reason why people are less happy nowadays than they used to be, say when I was her age."

"You're right, Mama," Rupert said. "Absolutely right." He did not enjoy this discussion, finding it embarrassing and in a way humiliating, yet at the same time he did not wish to end it. His mother was wise and it was difficult for a man of any age to find a wise person to go to for advice. "But seeing that she can't have the shack and the palace at the same time, what's the answer?" he pursued. "Don't you think that if Helen finally had a child—it would sort of settle things for her?"

Wilma sewed on for a moment without answering. Now it was she who seemed embarrassed, and Rupert regretted his question. Could it be that she, who scarcely knew the meaning of the word "psychology," guessed that Helen's refusal to have a child stemmed from her non-acceptance of her present life—her desire to leave open an avenue of escape? When Mama spoke again, her voice was noncommittal, like that of a person urged to touch on a field beyond his scope.

"I can't tell you about that, Son. I don't know. I had five children myself, so who am I to understand a woman who wants to have none?

169

But as to a child's settling all Helen's problems—no, I'm afraid that's being mighty hopeful. These conflicts in Helen—they go deeper than that. . . ."

Through the open door could be heard the sound of voices, and then William's husky tenor floated up the stairs.

"Oh, Rupert! Rupert!"

"Excuse me, Mama, for a moment," Rupert said, and stepped out onto the landing, where he could see his brother beckoning to him from below. Making his way down the stairs, he noticed that William looked unusually excited; his neck craned upwards behind the wing-tip collar and he did not wait for Rupert to descend the last flight before calling out in a loud whisper:

"Something's happened. Something pretty bad! They've just called up from the Yards."

"It's—Dad?"

"That's right. He had an accident this afternoon. They're bringing him home on a stretcher."

Moody at the prospect of defeat, Adolph Konrad had left his office earlier that afternoon and gone tramping through his great Stock Yards plant. As a rule he enjoyed nothing better than these long tours of inspection. He liked to watch the sheep and pigs being driven into the death rooms, and then the knife's flash and the life stream pouring from the stricken animal's throat; he liked to stand by as the skilled workers cut up the carcasses with knife thrusts that seldom missed their mark by even the fraction of an inch. Today all his thoughts were on the hateful change which was to come about so soon in this colossal organization. The sight of the bisected carcasses suspended from the conveyer belts reminded him only that this involved machinery and the animals it handled soon would be his no longer. The stamping machines that imprinted on the hides the words "Adolph Konrad and Son" would have to be scrapped; in their place would be machines that spelled out the impersonal appellation "Konrad and Company." The same fate awaited the labeling and stenciling devices. The whole establishment was destined to pass into the hands of an investors' club, to be headed by a scheming Scotchman bent on wresting from its rightful owner the last vestige of control.

Moving from building to building, his wanderings took him finally to the refrigerating plant, where hefty workers, carrying whole sides of beef, staggered down the slippery runways, to range their loads on hooks studding the frost-coated walls. As he stopped to watch them Adolph experienced his old irritation at the ineptness and laziness of these present-day workers. Here these union men were earning many times the salaries of their predecessors, yet in spite of the eight-hour day, their movements resembled those of actors in a slow-motion film! He had half a mind to kick out this whole useless shift, but of course that would have been impossible, considering the agreement negotiated by McKenna with the unions. In fact he wasn't at liberty to kick out a single worker without adequate grounds! Those damn unions! thought Adolph, his resentment against McKenna and the bungling workmen both finding expression in this muttered invective aimed at his old archenemy.

Suddenly Adolph had a desire to act. He'd had enough of standing by without protest and watching the firm go to the dogs! It was true he couldn't kick out his own employees any longer, but at least he could shame them, if such a sentiment was still possible for a union worker. He was over sixty, sixty-one, to be precise, but he was not too old to show them how their work should be done.

"Hey, not like that!" he shouted at a big fellow who was swinging a hundred-pound load onto his shoulder. "You'll never get anyvhere that vay, you idiot. Vatch me!"

He stepped forward and, to the man's surprise, grabbed the side of beef away from him. Bending down, Adolph gradually edged it onto his shoulder, then with a deft motion swung it on his back, while raising himself to a standing position. A feeling of accomplishment flooded through him as he stood there supporting the vast load. Yes, he could still manage it, as he used to forty years before! It had taken more than brains to build up this business, he had always told them. It had taken also grit and muscle, and of these he likewise possessed his share. No, by God, he wasn't a has-been yet!

He took one step down the runway, took a second, a third, with his load seeming to grow heavier every second. And it was then that it happened. He felt his foot giving way beneath him, knew that he was about to fall, and attempted to save himself by flinging the side of beef off his back. As he did so, a sharp pain flashed through his shoulder blade, almost like the stab of a knife. The next Adolph knew, he was lying on the concrete floor with a lot of people hurrying towards him. Two thoughts formed in his mind: that he was going to be out of commission for at least a while; and that this might enable him to postpone the decision about the stock issue. Perhaps he would get the better of that shrewd devil, McKenna, yet!

As they carried him out of the refrigerating plant, and then up the iron stairs to his office, a sly grin lay behind Adolph's grimace of pain.

eleven

Santa Rosa at first view was very different than Francy had imagined. This hick town in the desert, infested by tourists and by people who lived off tourists, was a far cry from the dream city of the prospectuses, where noble Indians rubbed shoulders with pistol-toting cowboys. Both Indians and cowboys appeared mercenary to a degree, and it depressed Francy to realize that he was considered fair game by everyone from the shoeblacks to the real estate dealer who offered to rent him a shack in the canyon.

But his mood changed next afternoon when this fellow drove him out of town and into the desert country to the west. The sight of the great rock formations, looming up like mirages out of the sand, amazed and delighted him; yellow and brown and gray they were, and every shade of red from ocher to deep scarlet. Not a vestige of human habitation could be seen for mile after mile, scarcely a sign of animal life, barring a few lonely chipmunks who watched them nonchalantly as they sped by. Once they saw a great eagle coasting overhead, and its shadow, magnified tenfold, passed across the naked sand, the blood-colored rocks, the clumps of cactus, finally to disappear in the direction of a distant mountain range. Francy told himself that this was a country that

172

would call forth the best in any artist, and he rejoiced in his decision.

The shack itself was perched on the side of the canyon, whose wall dropped sheerly to the gully below. As they drove up, the late sunlight fell on the stone wall opposite, delineating each gash and fissure, highlighting the jagged points, adding an orange overtone to the fantastic coloring of the rock. It was a majestic and rather eerie spectacle, something like an unexpectedly perceived glimpse of the moon.

"Well, is it a deal?" said the real estate man, as they stood gazing across the chasm at the unbelievable color drama unfolding itself on the natural stage opposite.

"Yes," said Francy. "Yes, I guess it is a deal."

Next day he bought a great basketful of groceries in the general store, paid his bill at the hotel, and hired a car to drive him to his shack. As he was leaving, the hotel owner, a half-breed Mexican, ambled up and said:

"Excusing me, mister, but I guess you are related to that Adolph Konrad, eh?"

"Well yes, I am," said Francy, taken aback.

"That's what I thought when I see you from Chicago. My old man in Mexico did a deal with Adolph Konrad about twenty years ago. My family, they owned big cattle ranges in Chihuahua State then. My old man never got gypped before—never met anybody smart enough to gyp him. Some guy, that father of yours, boy!"

So I shall have to travel farther than New Mexico to shed my identity, thought Francy. And he wondered if his blown-up hotel bill had anything to do with his bearing the golden name of Konrad.

He moved into the shack above the gully and began a life quite different than anything he had known before. From morning till evening, day after day, he saw no one. His nearest neighbor lived something like four miles distant; communications with the outside world were, to say the least, difficult. Once every week a man called Fred would deliver provisions from the general store, together with any mail arrived for him at the post office. But for that fact, Francy would have dreaded his visits, which interrupted a solitude grown dear to him. Yet he was never really alone: all day he had the company of that breathtaking view; he woke up with it and went to bed with it at night, and if in the darkness he started out of sleep, his first thought was always of the canyon, perhaps lying there invisible, if the night was black, but nevertheless making its presence felt, almost like a living creature.

Not a week passed that the messenger did not bring him a letter from Helen; usually there were two or three. She wrote that she missed him more than she would have thought possible, and that her life in Chicago had become more difficult, more dreary, since he went away; her health had been poor and she seemed unable to shake off a fierce flu, which of course did not help her depression. She urged him to work hard on his poetry, and not to forget her before they met again. There was always the implication that somehow, somewhere, they would meet again, and Francy, lying on his rickety couch in the crazy shack above the gulch, would smile happily and press the pale blue sheet of paper against his cheek. For there was not an hour of the day that he did not long for her, and the feel of her farewell kiss (the only one she had ever given him) still burned on his lips. And it happened sometimes that he asked himself what he was doing in this out-of-the-world hut, when Helen and he could have been seeing each other in the last brief weeks before she sailed off across the water.

But that thought only arose at moments of discouragement and at first such moments were far between. He worked hard; he felt that he worked well. The long *Stock Yards Ballad* seemed finally to be taking shape and he was in a happy mood. It lasted until the day he sat down to analyze his poem, not line by line, but as an integrated whole—and that day his new feeling of confidence fell to pieces like a house of cards.

Now for the first time he perceived the glaring inadequacies of the stanzas sweated through in Chicago: their artificialty, their labored structure, surprised and appalled him. The Stock Yards of Chicago were not a subject that lent itself to abstract symbolism: they were a gruesome and majestic aspect of modern industrialism, and as such they demanded to be written about in concrete fashion. It was because he had never really smelled the breath of the Stock Yards, had never let himself be splattered with blood and manure, or looked deep into the harsh faces of the drovers and the killers, that these stanzas remained empty words that would move nobody. If it were possible to imagine

William writing poetry, even his inarticulate brother might have done a better job of it, for he at least had a feeling for the subject! Suddenly it seemed to Francy that he had never yet written at all, that everything accomplished until now had been in the nature of more or less proficient finger exercises.

That was his frame of mind as he strode off into the canyon, aware that he must grapple with the gravest decision of his life. He had believed that day in Chicago that he had decided everything by selling his cigarette case and giving Hauptman the two farewell letters to his parents. He remembered the pitiful conceit with which he had told Helen that if he could not make his living by selling poetry he would sell shoelaces instead. Now he understood that this trip to Santa Rosa was a gesture of bravado and nothing more. How could he think of making his living off poetry when at the age of twenty-five he had earned from it exactly fifty dollars?

No, if he were to carry through his revolt, it meant that he must find a job, and there were very few jobs that he was capable of filling. If he applied to the boarding school where he had prepared for college, it was just conceivable that he might obtain a post as assistant instructor in the English department. For once his *summa cum laude* degree would come in useful! Such a job would give him sufficient leisure to work on his poetry in spare hours, but what a far cry from the independent life he had dreamed of for himself! In his mind's eye he saw a picture of the dreary classroom, filled with strange boys with whom he would have to establish contact; he saw the dining hall, crowded and noisy, with himself sitting at the head of one of the long tables, his uncongenial fellow teachers (who would undoubtedly despise him) sitting at the heads of the others; he saw the box of a room where he would be spending his nights, with a single armchair, a hard cot in the corner. Involuntarily he gave a shiver. As easily write poetry there as to leap from wall to wall of this broad canyon!

And then Francy saw before him his own room in Sans Souci, with the dappled sunlight falling in through the branches of the elm. It was so quiet and so comfortable and so clean! He saw the sofa up by the window, on which he had spent so many hours of his days. How pleasant it was to lie there and watch the evening shadows lengthen on the lawn below! For a moment only, but with startling intensity, there swept over Francy a longing to be home again, back in that quiet room in Sans Souci where all problems would be settled by the infallible method of never making a decision.

His steps had taken him far along the base of the canyon. The vestiges of an old Indian trail still paralleled the gully, but there was no indication of when last it had been used; were it not for the lack of soil in the canyon, it would long since have been grown over. Here the two cliffs rose even more precipitately than in the vicinity of the shack; almost perpendicular, they towered above him, and seen from below, their summits seemed infinitely far away. The sun was directly overhead and at this time of day both walls lay in shadow, with the floor of the canyon brilliantly lit, as though by a spotlight projected from above.

Suddenly Francy stopped short. An object lay in his path, but an object so strange that at first he thought he was the victim of some sort of optical illusion. It was a turtle of the ordinary box variety that abounded in the region, living, it would seem, off pebbles and cactuses, for of other vegetation there was none. Yes, this was just another such turtle, unique in only one particular: the animal had two heads! There was no doubt about it, decided Francy as he stepped closer and leaned over the freak animal, which made no effort to draw away. Or to be more precise, an effort to escape was being made, but with no result visible to the eye; for while the left legs of the animal strained to push its box body to the right, the other pair with equal intensity shoved in the contrary direction. The result was that the turtle, instead of scurrying either to the left or right, remained stationary, both of its slotlike mouths opening and closing from the strain of its efforts.

Fascinated by the weird sight, Francy crouched down on the trail to watch the animal's struggles. The heads, he saw, were quite independent of one another, equal-sized and pivoting on two separate necks joined only at the base. At the moment it was clear that the animal's twin heads were each gripped by a single thought: how to escape. But whereas they were united on this end, co-ordination was lacking on the means of attaining it. For a moment it looked as if the right-hand brain were winning; the turtle, against the opposition of its weaker half, began to veer off the trail towards the comparative safety of a cactus

176

clump. At that, the other brain, seized with panic, called forth a new effort on the part of the resisting limbs, and a few seconds later the animal had pushed itself back into the middle of the track, where, gasping, blinking, exhausted, it came to a frustrated halt.

For at least half an hour Francy sat watching the animal, noticing with absorption how each time one pair of legs began to move, a counterimpulse was set up that robbed it of any ground gained. He did not know why the strange spectacle fascinated him so that he could think neither of helping the luckless beast nor of trying to resolve the very real problems besetting his own life. Somehow he felt that this schizophrenic turtle was of special import to him personally, but for the moment he failed to grasp its nature. He observed the travail of the turtle as one observes the conflicts of people on a stage, of which the significance in terms of one's own life will only later become apparent. It was not till the changing position of the sun caused a shadow to stripe the animal's back that Francy got to his feet.

On the spur of the moment, he decided to take the turtle back with him as a pet.

Next morning the first thing Francy did was to run to the enclosure he had rigged up behind the shack. He half expected that his new friend would have escaped, using that uncanny knack of wild animals to find an opening in almost any barrier. No, there was the turtle, squat in the middle of the sandy patch, it's two necks craning forward in opposite directions, its right legs fighting the left in another inconclusive struggle! Francy the night before had thrown in some withered cabbage leaves, and it happened that two of these leaves lay on different sides of the animal. Unable to decide which of the delicacies to capture, the two-headed turtle now found itself in its usual predicament.

More amazed than amused, Francy helped it out by spearing the leaves and holding out one in turn before each of the turtle's mouths. At that the animal snapped at the food with an eagerness that was a good indication of its semistarved state; no doubt its congenital neurosis had further complicated the problem of nourishing itself in this inhospitable region. Francy was transporting the rest of the cabbage leaves within range of the turtle's heads, when he heard in the distance the wheezy honk of the deliveryman's Ford. He straightened up quickly and went to meet him. He would have found it difficult to explain why he was loath to have this crude fellow see the turtle.

"Hello, Frank!" the man called out with what struck Francy as undue familiarity. (Besides, he had always hated being called Frank, a name he considered harsh and unpleasantly conclusive.) "I've got two letters for you today."

"Is that right?" said Francy, the usual embarrassed grin spreading over his face. "From Chicago?"

"Oh yes, from Chicago," said Fred. "And in the same handwriting," he added with a guffaw, no doubt meant to be good-humored, but which to Francy sounded insinuating and presumptuous.

As he watched the big clumsy man search through his pockets he had to control an instinctive feeling of antipathy. He reminded himself that the fellow had never been anything but obliging and friendly—in fact a good bit too friendly. If he, Francy, did not get on with him, it was because of his constitutional inability to get on with the "common man," whom he nevertheless had made the hero of his *Stock Yards Ballad*.

Unable to locate the letters, Fred was now removing his sombrero to scratch his perplexed head, whereupon the two letters dropped out from under the sombrero. Francy picked them up quickly, because somehow the idea of those blunt, oily fingers touching the envelopes addressed in Helen's own hand was abhorrent to him. Now he only wanted the man to go away, and he waited impatiently for him to start up his Ford. He knew that the fellow expected a chat after his long drive here, and that he would feel cheated if he went off without it. Well, it couldn't be helped! He really hadn't the time to stand talking to half-baked louts, with two letters waiting to be read and a very long poem waiting to be written!

His blunt features expressing reluctance, Fred started up his Ford, but Francy had not even had time to open his letters when he saw the car backing towards him again. This time his enemy was waving a yellow envelope from the window.

"I'll be goldarned! I clean forgot about the telegram. What d'you know about that?"

178

Francy ran up and took the envelope. He did not wait for the Ford to be out of sight before splitting it open.

"Leaving tomorrow for rest cure in California," it read. "Should I stop off in Santa Rosa?" And it was signed "Helen."

Francy let himself sink down on a rock. His heart was pounding, pounding so hard that he thought Helen might hear it all the way back in Chicago. In three short days he would be seeing her again, looking into her eyes, hearing her laugh, and—yes, kissing her! If he begged very hard, perhaps she would stop over for two or three days and stay with him in the canyon. He imagined standing with her on his shack's rickety veranda, his arm around her waist, while together they watched the sun painting the rock wall in those fantastic colors. He imagined . . . he imagined . . . Francy put his hands before his eyes, and he sat there in the blazing sun, feeling entirely happy.

No, not entirely! In a back compartment of his mind a thought was already forming, disturbing as an insistent mosquito. Was it right for him to persuade Helen to stay? Was it conceivable that he should make carnal love to his own brother's wife? And other thoughts, too, sprang to life in that hinterland of the mind where things happen even against one's will. Was Helen's feeling for him primarily the affection of a sister, or was it a mature woman's love? Might the fire kindled in Chicago blaze up into a conflagration? And was he, Francy, the sort of man who longed for a conflagration that would consume his life?

Francy took away his hands from before his eyes and let his glance travel down the rock-strewn trail and beyond the brush barrier. There the two-headed turtle lay, straining futilely towards the cabbage leaves that would remain forever beyond its reach.

twelve

Atlantic City was a hell of a spot for a meat packer. So Adolph Konrad had decided the day of his arrival, and nothing had happened to change his mind since. He was supposed to be having a complete rest because of his wrenched back, and O'Grady had insisted that he couldn't get that in Chicago. Well, probably O'Grady was right; the man understood him better than he understood himself. He only wished that Wilma hadn't picked Atlantic City for their first holiday in forty years; and he wished that he hadn't pampered her whim, even though one whim every forty years ought, perhaps, to be pampered.

Fortunately a change was in sight at last, for O'Grady himself was arriving on Adolph's invitation. *Gott sei dank,* the daily routine would be broken for a little while: those interminable morning pushcart rides down the "boardwalk"; the thrice-daily massaging of his injured back; the finicky four-course meals (at least they called them meals, although back home they wouldn't have served roast beef like that to servants); the long afternoons spent rocking away on the veranda in the company of other decrepit guests.

That last was the worst of all. It was then that the bad thoughts assailed him, and he felt unable to fight them back: thoughts of his growing older (Gott demn it, had he not just had proof of it?); thoughts of the monkeyshines McKenna might be up to in his absence; thoughts, above all, of Francy, disappeared into the wilds of the West. He would sit there in his rocking chair, wrapped in a dark blanket, wrapped also in these dark heavy thoughts. So sunk away was he that not even Wilma dared disturb him; in silence she sat crocheting near by, trying without words to convey to him her love. It seemed to her that Adolph had grown visibly older since the day they brought him home in an ambulance from the Yards; there were new grooves in his face and even his hair seemed to have gone a shade whiter. Some days when his back pained especially, or perhaps after getting the weekly business letter from William, he really looked like quite an old man.

"Don't worry, Adolph," she would tell him when he roused himself at last and raised his glance to meet hers. "It ain't ever done nobody any good."

"I'm not vorryin'," he grumbled. "I chust don't like this demn Atlantic City or anyt'ing about it."

"Then let's go somewhere else, Adolph. We don't have to stay here."

"Every other place'd be chust the same. Every place but Chicago!"

"I know, Adolph. Don't think I don't know. Well, your back will be well soon. We've had a nice holiday and I think we're both feeling the better for it."

"Do you?" said Adolph. "Personally I am feeling like hell."

He was sitting on the veranda one afternoon, whittling at a stick, when up drove O'Grady, effervescent and boisterous as ever. A single look at that florid face made Adolph feel a little better.

"Top o' the mornin' to you, Adolph!"

"Gott demn, O'Grady, I am glad to see you!" Adolph gave his friend's hand a good squeeze. "Didn't know you'd come to visit Job Konrad on his ash heap, did you?"

"Sure, Adolph, I'm afraid ye're a failure in them biblical roles. Ye're too rich, for one thing. An' yer sackcloth is cut by the best tailor."

Adolph looked down at his suit glumly.

"Vilma insisted that I get a new outfit for this swell resort. Said I'd shock people if I stomped about the hotel in hip boots. I should think that if a man pays the prices they ask here, he'd be allowed to go barefoot if it pleased him! Vell, how are you, O'Grady?"

"Fit as a fiddle," said the doctor, taking one of the wicker chairs and fanning his hot face with his Panama. "Ye're not lookin' too badly yerself, young fella."

"Don't give me any of that Irish blarney of yours! This demn accident has got me down. Und vhat have I got to be happy about anyvay, mit de business goin' to hell an' that sour-faced Scotchman tryin' to steal it avay from me? Have you seen Villiam, by the vay?"

"Sure, I look in on him now and then at the Yards." (Thanks to Adolph, O'Grady held the lucrative position of company doctor, which necessitated his presence in the Konrad plant three mornings of each week.) "William's getting along fine, Adolph."

"I don't give a demn how he's gettin' along," said Adolph impatiently. "Vhat I vant to know is how the firm's gettin' along. Villiam's letters are so Gott demn evasive, make me vonder if somet'ing is up."

"Why, Adolph, whatever gave ye that idea!" cried the doctor, blinking his deceitful eyes and giving a rather hollow laugh. "Seems to me everything's goin' just fine at the Yards. Business is humming, so they tell me."

"You're holding somet'ing back on me, O'Grady!"

181

"Holding somethin' back! Just listen to the man!"

"You haven't heard any rumors, have you?"

"Rumors? Of course not! Say, come to think of it, I did hear one rumor," the doctor admitted. "But ye're not to get excited now, Adolph."

"Spit it out, O'Grady! Spit it out!"

"Well," said O'Grady, "it seems to me that I did hear tell that Angus McKenna had popped off to New York—somethin' to do with seein' some banker or other. Now I don't know if that'd be connected with the stock issue by any chance."

"Go on. Vhat else?"

"No, nothin' else, Adolph. McKenna's back now. I know that for a fact, 'cause I caught sight of him day before yesterday stepping into the Office Building, that buttoned-up face of his sure as glum-looking as ever. He couldn't have been gone for more'n a couple of days."

"Und the dirty dog didn't even look me up here when he vas only a couple of hours avay! Gott demn him to hell!" Adolph's fist came down on the rocking-chair arm with such a thump that an old lady who had been reading jumped up and hurried into the hotel. "Dis is the end, O'Grady. The end! I'll kick him out of his chob, O'Grady, no matter vhat happens."

"That's right, Adolph. It's yer firm," O'Grady declared, but it was obvious from the way he said it that he was just playing up to his protector; he knew, as Adolph, too, knew, that the time for kicking out McKenna had passed.

Adolph threw away his stick and began to pace the veranda; his back hurt him at each violent step, but he didn't care. His big lips were working in and out like steam pistons.

"They're all going back on me, O'Grady!" he cried. "They're all double-crossing me, the dirty sons of bitches. I made McKenna vhat he is. Who vas he anyvay, vhen he valked into my office? A clerk, that's all—a penny-pinching little Scotch accountant. Look at him now! He won't be happy till he's broken up my business, so that not even the name's left. There's not a body in Chicago that I can trust, not even my children: I've alvays said, dey belong to a no-good generation. Rupert's a stranger, out of touch mit his own country. Villiam's a good boy, but he's chust not got vhat it takes. He's scared of McKenna, O'Grady! Scared!"

"Oh, come on now, Adolph! Don't see everythin' so black."

"How should I see it? Vhite? Gold? Pink? I tell you that they're all going against me. Look at that third boy of mine, Francy. Now he goes und double-crosses me too!"

O'Grady looked up quickly. A queer change had come into his face at the mention of the name "Francy"; in one second the bravado had drained away and the weak mouth sagged towards the chin; his shifty eyes met Adolph's and swerved away like the eyes of a cowed dog. For a second there was silence, a silence loud with unspoken words.

"The boy loves you," O'Grady said finally. "Now don't you go thinkin' anything different. Youth will have its fling, Adolph."

He gave an uneasy chuckle, but Adolph answered nothing at all. He kept walking up and down the veranda, his heavy brows knit, his lips pouting. And it was then that O'Grady understood what really was biting Adolph. More than the hateful business developments, far more than McKenna's insubordination, it was the desertion of his youngest . son that had distressed and unstrung Adolph Konrad! And O'Grady understood why. Perhaps he alone was capable of understanding the complex pattern of love and protectiveness and—yes, of guilt, that overlay this father-son relationship.

"Sure, the prairie air'll do him a world o' good," O'Grady went on. (It struck him as he spoke that he was like a conspirator assuaging the conscience of his accomplice.) "Nothin' like those big open spaces for someone who's sufferin' from a constitutional weakness. Why, the very grandeur of those Western plains—the sun, the quiet, the pure air— they're a health cure in themselves."

"Do you think so?"

Adolph tried to make his voice sound uninterested, but a little note of hope had crept in all the same.

"Sure! Sure, Adolph! There's no question about it at all. In fact it's what I'd have prescribed for Francy if he'd come to me for advice. So as far as your boy's health is concerned"—O'Grady made an expansive flourish with his Panama—"you have no cause for worry."

Adolph leaned against the balustrade of the veranda. His burning eyes searched O'Grady's face, as if to find confirmation and assurance; his fingers behind his back clasped the balustrade so tightly that the knuckles showed white. Rationally he knew that O'Grady was a bad doctor and that what he had just said was drivel. He knew it, yet did not want to know it. He had wagered so heavily on O'Grady's skill that it was impossible to face the naked truth now; to do so would have been tantamount to an open admission that the two of them had sinned sorely against Francy.

Suddenly he burst out, with a violence that to anyone but O'Grady would have seemed incomprehensible, "I don't care vhat becomes of de demn fool! I don't give a Gott demn. If he vants for to go off mit a nickel to starve to death on some Vild Vest plain, vell, it's okay mit me. I vash my hands of him from now on. Positively!"

"That's right," O'Grady said. "You've done all ye could by the boy. No man could have been a better father than you, Adolph."

Adolph grunted. It was what he had wanted to hear—there was no doubt it was what he'd wanted to hear. O'Grady, as usual, had defined his wish in that regard. Yet somehow the trite words did not bring him the customary satisfaction. He thought of Francy, with his ruined heart, living on a few cents a day in that Godforsaken desert—and why? Simply to get away from him and from his millions! To be sure, the letter left behind said that he had gone off "so as to find himself," but Adolph was not taken in by that highfalutin language.

He remembered the lunch they had had in the Saddle and Sirloin Club, and his vain efforts to get a little closer to this gentle son of his whom he had never understood. As always, he had had the feeling that day that Francy thought of him as a guilty man. Guilty, but guilty of what? Of having been a bad father? No, not that! Of final responsibility for his weak heart? Well yes, but that was not the full answer. After all, it had been for Francy's own good that he had overridden Wilma's objections and ordered him out of bed that winter day so long ago. He remembered his feeling at the time that if only he got Francy on his feet, if only he got him out of that sickbed where he was wasting away, he could *will* him to get well. As events proved, he had acted foolishly—brutally too, some people might think. But he had acted according to his lights.

According to his lights! Ah yes, that was the crucial phrase. In the last analysis, he stood accused of no more than of being the sort of person that he was. And how, he asked himself, standing there with his back to the balustrade, yes, how in the name of *der liebe Gott* was a man to defend himself against such a charge.

His thoughts fly back, backwards in time, backwards in space. As happens so often, he sees himself climbing that marshy hill that leads to the lace factory in Schwabenland. It is not yet dawn. In the chill darkness he cannot discern the other workers, who each day mount their calvary, weighted down with the invisible cross of servitude. In the suffering world he and Franzy seem to be all alone. As always, the little boy's arms cling to his older brother's neck, but today the dead weight of the sleeping lad seems even heavier than usual. How long has he been climbing? Ten minutes? Half an hour? Time has ceased to exist; the only reality in this world of darkness is his great fatigue, and the indomitable will inside of him which says, Go on!

And suddenly he feels himself falling. His foot has slipped and, handicapped by his load, he cannot right himself. (Through Adolph's mind there passes the shadow of another memory evoked instantaneously by the first: the floor of the refrigeration plant; the sensation of falling, again; the weight of the side of beef pressing mercilessly upon him. Oh, will those patterns of the past never cease to repeat themselves? Is a man's life no more than a series of recurring themes?) He is lying on the marshy ground, the sour-smelling water drenching his clothes and creeping into his nose, his ears. In a daze he looks about, and then he sees lying near by a bundle darker than the darkness. Franzy! His brother Franzy!

The little boy has hurt himself. He lies half submerged in a pool of water, almost motionless, whimpering weakly. Only one foot in its worn boot beats the surface of the water, rapidly, then more slowly as Adolph crawls nearer, to seize the weak little hands in his. In vain he tries to drag Franzy out of the water, then distractedly begins jerking at his brother's arms.

"Franzy, you must get up! Get up, I tell you! I cannot help you if you will not help yourself."

185

Still Franzy lies there, whimpering in pain.

"*Ich habe Angst,* Adolph. Adolph, I'm afraid," the tiny voice floats up through the darkness.

And at that he is possessed by that wild urge towards life, away from death, which is part of his very make-up—the urge that three years later sent him walking towards the burning potatoes as his father lay dying, that thirty years later caused him to order his son out of a sick-bed and back to life. Seizing a stick, he strikes out at his brother, strikes him brutally on his arms, on his head, on his face, until Franzy, shriek-ing with pain, scrambles out of the pool. Only then does he throw the big stick away. He has won! It has cost him a price that he never can measure, but Adolph Konrad has won the first skirmish in his never-ending battle for life.

"I hate you, Adolph. I will hate you for as long as I live!"

He can hear the voice of his brother, weak now no longer, but charged with the same passion, the same pain, as the voice of Francy, his son, when he told him that day in the luncheon club:

"I don't want your help, Father. . . . I'd rather fight my own fight and go under."

He roused himself. O'Grady was watching him with those sly eyes of his, eyes used to spying out weaknesses in another man, eyes that saw everything and sent the knowledge to a brain that knew how to put it to tawdry use. There was devotion in O'Grady's eyes, but it was the devotion of a clever dog—or, perhaps, thought Adolph, of a person with whom one shares a dim secret.

"And he didn't even leave an address," he burst out again, as though to dispel any doubt that he, Adolph, was the wronged party. "That's a nice vay to behave, Gott demn, O'Grady! Going off to the end of the continent and not even leaving an address!"

"Ye shouldn't expect gratitude from yer children," said O'Grady. "Ye're a good psychologist, Adolph. An' haven't ye read *Lear?* How comes that ye haven't yet understood whom ye should trust—and whom not?"

O'Grady shook his head and, using his Panama, slowly fanned his perspiring face. Strange, thought Adolph as he watched him, strange that that big, easygoing face, disappearing and reappearing behind the grease-stained straw hat, should strike him today for the first time as being utterly ruthless. Had he not known better, Adolph could have taken it for the face of a pitiless extortioner.

thirteen

Francy stood shaving himself in the little alcove behind the curtain. His face, reflected in the wavy mirror, seemed to be two faces at the same time, for the left half was covered with shaving cream, whereas the other side was clean-shaven, its skin fresh and boyish. As he pulled down the corner of his mouth to shave his upper lip, it struck him that the soap-covered portion looked like the tragic white mask of a circus clown. That was his night face, he thought. In it were reflected all the worries and doubts which assailed him as he lay tossing restlessly on his bed; in his day face there was disclosed another Francy, blithe, youthful, and confident.

"Oh damn," he said suddenly and looked away.

Thanks to that travesty of a mirror, he had cut himself again, and quite deeply this time; a thin line of crimson was running down his chin. The sight of blood, particularly his own blood, had always made Francy feel sick. He was about to pull aside the curtain to go and look for the styptic pencil, when he sensed in advance the sharp, stinging pain associated with it. Perhaps it was typical of Francy that he at once found another reason for not fetching the pencil—and a cogent reason at that. For in the room beyond the blue cotton curtain Helen was lying, still sound asleep!

Francy sat down on the little stool and held a damp towel to his cut. The thought of Helen lying sleeping so close to him made him feel happy and gay. What a fool he was to stay awake, worrying for hours, when he had the thing he most wanted literally within reach! Sitting there by the sunny window with an exciting day ahead, Francy could almost scoff at his night doubts. Everything would come out all right, he told himself. He and Helen loved each other, and that was the important thing. As to making a living, that problem would settle itself, insoluble though it had seemed only a few hours earlier. Hadn't Helen hinted time and again in the last week that all she wanted in the future was a simple life? Yes, yes, he must talk to her today, and right after breakfast! There were all sorts of things to be decided. Ridiculous that he had been putting off so long a conversation they should have had the very day of her arrival!

He heard stirrings beyond the curtain. Towel in hand, he rushed into the room, to find Helen sitting up in bed, stretching. How terribly young she looked! Francy thought as he hurried towards her. She had lost at least seven years in these seven days, and as she sat there, holding her arms out to him, he thought that anyone would have taken her for a young girl, silvery-blond hair falling down her back, soft full mouth curling in laughter. She had become the Helen Mason he remembered from his childhood, the young girl who was engaged to Rupert and who used to come into his sickroom to laugh and to cheer him up.

"Oh, Francy! Francy darling!" she cried gaily. "If you could see your own face, you'd wonder why I want to kiss you so much."

"Oh, God! My shaving cream!" said Francy, wiping his cheek with the towel.

"It doesn't matter. Come here! Come here quick! I can't wait."

They dropped in each other's arms and lay on the bed, kissing and laughing. The sun, coming through the open doorway, fell straight on Helen's hair, and gave it that silvery sheen which was the special mark of her beauty. It struck him in the midst of his kisses that this startling change in her looks, her voice, even in the expression of her eyes, were the outer signs of an inner rejuvenation. He was a little proud to think that this was partly his doing.

Afterwards they sat having breakfast on the moldering veranda, with the sheer drop of the canyon beneath them. The opposite wall looked very close on such a clear day, and they could see every fissure on that great rock, scratched on its surface by the receding glaciers millenniums before. How positive and inflexible was the canyon! Francy thought. Just having it as neighbor was comforting in his moments of doubt.

188

But this morning, sitting opposite Helen in the sun, he felt almost as strong as the canyon!

The sun was in her eyes. She put up her hand to shade them and gazed at him across the table through the fan of her fingers. Sitting there in her pale blue dressing gown with the pale hair falling down her back, she looked like a beautiful child, Francy thought. And there was about her a childlike innocence.

"Are you happy?" she said, her mouth making as if to kiss.

"I have never been so happy before."

"Nor I. I have never, never been so happy before!"

"Not even as a kid?" asked Francy. "I think that one's happiest as a kid. There are no decisions to be made then. One is a whole person."

"Oh, Francy, decisions aren't so difficult when one knows what one really wants of life. That's the important thing: to find out what one wants. Because there will always be alternatives."

Francy nodded, with feeling. Ah, this is the time for us to talk about the future, he thought. Now, now at once, while I *do* know what I want, and before those many questions re-form in my mind. It all seems so clear to me this morning. This is the most important thing, the only important thing: being with Helen. Nothing else counts, not my youth, nor my finances, nor the certainty that my family are going to hate me for what I do. No, not even the fact that Rupert (who has done Helen so much harm) is my brother! I cannot hesitate any longer. She has given me my cue.

Still he said nothing. It was such an incredible morning. Wasn't it enough just to live in this moment, not trying to unravel the confused future? There would be plenty of other occasions to talk. This very afternoon, right after lunch, I will speak to her! Francy promised himself.

There was the wheezy honk of a motor horn. Francy recognized it as the deliveryman's Ford, and he told Helen not to disappear into the blue while he went to collect the weekly groceries.

"No, I can't guarantee that," said Helen. "You'd better take me along with you if you want to be safe. One mustn't take anything for granted when one's happy. Remember that, darling."

"What'll the man think?"

"Does it matter in the slightest what he thinks? Besides, do you really believe he doesn't know you have a lady guest, after your telling him to bring half a dozen mousetraps? You're a poet. He expects you to have mistresses all over the place, so don't disappoint him."

They walked down to the end of the trail, where Fred was sitting on the running board of his car, fanning himself with his frayed sombrero. He jumped up when he saw Helen.

"Hello there!" she called to him. "It's a fine morning, isn't it?"

An expansive grin spread over Fred's face. Perhaps he sensed that this morning he really was going to get in his chat.

"Every morning's a fine morning in this part of the world, ma'am," he replied with almost exaggerated politeness.

"And what part of the world do you come from?" asked Helen, whereupon Francy knew right away that they were in for the worst.

"Why, I come from Paradise, New Jersey," said Fred eagerly. He stood beside his Ford, one foot on the running board, upon his face the expression of a man who has not had a chance to talk in a long time. "Only lived there till I was old enough to know better. Terrible town, Paradise, New Jersey. Never been back since I joined a vaudeville troupe at seventeen."

"A vaudeville troupe!" exclaimed Helen, as Francy stood there smiling embarrassedly and waiting for the ordeal to be over. "What in the world did you do in a vaudeville troupe?"

"You want to know what I did?"

Fred's mouth began to work, and a concentrated look came into his eyes. But not a sound issued forth. Instead there came to them from the case of beer bottles inside his car a cracked voice, like that of a little boy in puberty.

"I am a ventriloquist," it said. "And I am a damn good ventriloquist too, even if I do say so myself, what shouldn't."

Helen burst out laughing, and Francy joined in, although he still hoped that the man would get into his Ford and drive off. It was strange, it occurred to him, that he had known this deliveryman for almost two months, yet had never imagined until now that there could be the slightest thing of interest about his life.

"I was on the circuit for forty years, folks," Fred went on, his voice

190

reverting to normal. "Forty years! That's a long time. My wife was in vaudeville too—a female comic—and we had an act that used to bring the house down. 'Fred and Friede,' we called ourselves, only Friede wasn't her real name, mind you. Her real name was Gertrude, folks, and she was some gal. Well, five years ago my wife fell sick. Funny to think of such a big hefty gal (hundred and eighty stripped) coming down with t.b.! We came here to the mountains for her lungs and after she died, folks—well, after she died I didn't feel much like going back to vaudeville. I took this here job as deliveryman in Santa Rosa."

"Oh, I'm sorry that your wife died," Helen said.

"Yes," sighed Fred. "Things are pretty different now, folks. Pretty different. But I got a cat. Sweetest cat you ever seen! Pretty, he is, too, but he's skinny. Don't seem able to fatten him up, no matter what I feed him. He waits for me every night, and when I come home— would you believe it?—why, he jumps right on my shoulder and rubs his nose up against my cheek. . . ."

Much to Francy's relief, Fred finally took his departure, and Helen and he walked back to the shack. On the way they stopped to say hello to the two-headed turtle, which was looking none too sprightly these days. Its twin heads drawn into its shell, only the tip of its scaly feet protruding, it looked like the very embodiment of frustration. Six inches before its nose lay a lettuce leaf that it no doubt had been unable to reach.

"Cheer up, pal," Helen said to it, as she moved the leaf up to its left mouth. The turtle blinked two of its four eyes, but it seemed too far steeped in depression to take further notice.

Leaving the animal to its morbid meditations, they carried in the groceries, together with the Chicago newspapers Fred had brought them. Francy had pointedly avoided ordering newspapers, those un-wanted links with the outer world, but now it had been impossible to refuse them, seeing that they were a present from Fred. ("Thought you might like to know what's going on in your home town, folks.") Francy threw the pile in the corner, but after they had ranged the groceries on the shelf he picked up one of them and scanned the headlines.

"None of that now, Francy! This isn't a day for newspapers," Helen said, and she laughed and took it away from him. "You remember what you promised me for this morning. You're going to read me through your poem right from the start!"

"Oh, not this morning!" Francy demurred. "It's far too wonderful a day."

"Never too wonderful when it's a question of work," said Helen, which caused Francy to smile, because he knew that that was Professor Mason speaking through his daughter's mouth. Actually he had been waiting for this occasion ever since Helen's arrival, so he did not need much persuasion to fetch his manuscript. Helen stretched out on the wicker sofa, apparently prepared to concentrate to the full, and Francy began to read.

And almost at once he grew aware again of the shortcomings of his poem. More strongly than ever he had the feeling that his work was meretricious, lacking in depth and perception. It was so very far from what he had tried to do! In embarrassment he tossed the manuscript on the table.

"No, Helen, I can't go on. It's tripe—pure tripe."

"It certainly is not!" She sounded genuinely shocked. "I think it's splendid," she said, handing the manuscript back to him. "Now be a good boy and go on."

In a disturbed mood, Francy complied, but now that he had received her praise, the ballad sounded extraordinarily much better. Why—why, he could almost imagine that, with extensive revisions here and there, he could save it after all. He had seriously thought of burning it in the grate!

"Yes, yes, it's fine," she said when he had concluded. "You are a real poet, Francy. Congratulations on a good job."

"But it isn't a good job," Francy said. "Don't I know it! There's something missing—there's a lot missing—apart from that flowery symbolism that chokes up my meaning. What's the real fault, Helen? Be brutal now!"

"Well, a critic's got to be brutal to be of any use," said Helen, getting up from the sofa. She walked over to Francy's table and sat down on the board floor beside him. "You've said it yourself, Francy: there is something missing. I felt it in Chicago when you read me those stanzas: I still feel it today. I don't quite know how to put it. I love your poetry, but it's—well, it's a little too abstract. One does feel your indignation at injustice, and that's fine. And yet one doesn't feel that you really care about the happiness of the individual. Humanity's made up of persons, after all! You have a big heart and you love the human race, but you don't love—no, you're not even interested in—say Fred, the delivery-man!"

"Why what do you mean?" Francy laughed nervously. "Didn't I listen to the man's life story for half an hour this morning? I almost got a sunstroke doing it."

"Only because you had to, darling. You listened but you didn't like to listen. You didn't try to picture to yourself Fred's life—his past happiness with his blowzy Gertrude, his present loneliness with that scrawny cat. If you had, darling Francy, your poetry might be even better than it is. Remember, you asked me to be brutal."

"I'm glad you were," said Francy, pressing her hand to his cheek. He did not quite understand what Helen meant, but he was always grateful for being told what to do. "In the future I shall listen to every Fred who wants to speak to me, and I'll do everything else you tell me. You must try and help me, Helen, if you will."

"Oh, Francy, it's not only a question of my helping you. You have more to give me than I have to give you—much more. When I think of how shamefully I've treated my own gift, my talent for the piano . . . If I help you with your work, then you must help me with mine. Promise me, Francy!"

Francy brought his face close to hers and he kissed her on the mouth. Now is the time to talk about the future, he thought as their lips were still joined. Helen has given me a second cue. He knew that if he asked her at that moment to leave Rupert and join her life to his she would not hesitate. Why, then, did *he* hesitate? Could it be (the thought flashed through his mind and was gone), could it be that what she had just said frightened him a little? He wanted to be helped; that lay in his nature. But was he strong enough to assume the responsibility of helping Helen, as she expected him to do? Was he capable of such a mature give-and-take relationship, or would he in the end disappoint her miserably? Ah, there was no hurry, he thought. Better put off that irrevocable talk till tomorrow.

193

"Now you are going to sit there and *work*," said Helen, drawing away her lips and getting to her feet. (Was it Francy's imagination, or did he hear a little change in her voice, as though she had read his thoughts and withdrawn herself from him a trifle?) "There's been much too much laziness about this shack. I'm going to make you work at least five hours a day from now on."

"Oh, but not today!" Francy cried, and he jumped up and put his arms around her, as though to reassure himself. "I thought we were going to take a ride down the canyon."

"The horses will wait," Helen said, casting a glance off the veranda to where the two hired animals stood swishing their tails in their improvised enclosure. "Apart from all else, I want to wash my hair; there's no need to look like a golliwog, even if one does live in the wilds. We'll have our ride this afternoon, but this morning you stick right to it."

"Well, all right, if you say so," Francy agreed, and obediently he sat down at his table. He rather liked it when she gave him orders like that and wished she would do it more often; it established the sort of relationship in which he felt most at ease, for it obviated the necessity of his making decisions himself.

As he pretended to work, Francy watched Helen slide herself off the edge of the veranda and walk over to the well near the horses' enclosure. She was holding soap and an orange-colored towel in her hand, the orange and the pale blue of her dressing gown and the ocher of the rocks forming a color combination that delighted his eye. Beside the well she let the blue dressing gown fall to the ground, and he saw her nude body outlined against the rocks. Again it struck him how like a girl she looked, how little like a woman of thirty-five. The thin hips, the delicately upturning breasts, the long pale hair, were all attributes of a young girl. As she knelt at the edge of the well, turning the handle to bring up the pail, her every movement was youthful and free. Could one believe, Francy thought, that under slightly different circumstances this happy naked girl might be playing hostess to a smart diplomatic gathering?

Assured that she could no longer see him, he left his table and ambled over to the corner where he had tossed the pile of newspapers.

Avoiding the too definite step of picking one up, he let his eye wander down the front page of a *Tribune,* ready at any second to scurry back to his work if he heard Helen approaching. It gave him a guilty sensation, not altogether unenjoyable, reminding him as it did of youthful disobedience to commands. Well, the big world had not changed, he thought, studying a McCutcheon cartoon that depicted the League of Nations tumbling down a mountain. His glance passed to a headline announcing the sinking of a rumrunner off Florida, and that made him reflect that Helen had not taken a single drink since coming to Arizona, though back in Chicago he had often been surprised and a bit shocked by the amount she quietly consumed in the course of a conversation. And then, just as Francy was about to return to his work, his eye caught the name Konrad standing out in a subheadline. "Konrad gets diplomatic post," he read, and then bent down to decipher the small type which said that Rupert Konrad, of the well-known packing family, had just been named minister to a central European country and would be sailing for abroad shortly.

Francy straightened up and walked back to his table. His first inclination was to leave the paper where it was and put off telling Helen. He even thought of tearing out the item or of hiding the paper, but deceit was not in his nature. As he seated himself at his table he wondered how this unexpected news would affect her. Probably very little, he decided. Being ready to leave Rupert before he became minister, she would be equally ready to leave him after. And yet . . . And yet . . . In the back part of his mind, where things went on which he could not control, a secret thought was forming. Might Helen's loyalty force her to stay with her husband, now that his official position made it imperative that no hint of scandal be connected with his name? Might this not be the best solution after all, seeing that he was so unsure of his ability to give Helen what she needed?

After a little while he picked up the paper and walked with it towards Helen, kneeling by the well. She raised up to smile at him, and as their eyes met he remembered for some reason an occasion when, as a boy, he had given away a whole sackful of beautiful marbles because he did not dare compete in the game.

fourteen

Hapgood was an unqualified success. A month after he entered Rupert's employ his chief could not understand how things had been managed without him. Not only did he cope with the mass of detail connected with Princess Xenia's visit, not only did he assist in delicate negotiations with Senator Brenn, but he was ever ready to serve as confidant and adviser—an adviser, moreover, who was cheerfully prepared to have his advice rejected. But Rupert soon began to rely on his secretary's judgment, which in many instances had proved sounder than his own. Were final proof required that Hapgood was the world's best confidential secretary, it was furnished by his handling of the ticklish situation created by Helen's departure for the West.

Without Hapgood's help, Rupert would have been hard put to it to explain away her absence on the very eve of the Princess' visit. Officially, of course, she had gone to California for a health cure (as a matter of fact, Hapgood had actually telegraphed ahead for rooms). That was what Helen had told him, and he had not questioned her too closely, preferring to believe this, or at least not to learn for certain that it was untrue. Once or twice he had thought seriously of telephoning to the California hotel to find out if Helen really were staying there, but somehow that call had never been put in. Hapgood it was who gave Rupert his cue by going out of his way to tell people that "Mrs. Konrad was having a fine holiday," and by making frequent comparisons between the rainy Chicago spring and the fine California weather, about which Rupert presumably had received latest information via Helen. So skillfully did Hapgood pursue this line that even Rupert came near to believing that Helen was bombarding him with a series of weather reports! It needed a barbed hint from the incorrigible Gladys to shatter the pleasant illusion.

"What did you say was Helen's address? I'd like to write to her," she remarked one day, gazing at Rupert innocently from her sofa.

196

"What about?" Rupert countered. "You certainly never found much to say to her when she was here."

"Why, I want to tell her to be sure to be back for Xenia's arrival. Seeing that William and I are on your welcoming committee, it's become almost my duty to see that she is present. So few of us provincial girls have the habit of mixing with royalty, like Helen."

"That was catty," Rupert said. "You needn't worry, Gladys. She'll be back."

"Oh, thank goodness! That's a weight off my mind—if I can trust you, that is. But I wonder if I can. Should I tell you something, Rupert, in strictest confidence?"

"Only if you insist."

"Well, you ought to know it. I've been wondering, (and I think others have too) if Helen wasn't a tiny bit jealous of Xenia, with her decayed sex appeal and her pasteboard crown. Perhaps that's ridiculous."

"I should say it is," declared Rupert hotly. "The very idea! Why, Xenia and Helen were the best of friends. . . ."

"The perfect setup! Come on, Rupert, be a sport and admit that you did have something with that glamorous royal trollop. Remember those cosy stolen moments in the ducal glass coach—or was it in her boudoir? Remember the pink flesh (a bit overscented perhaps) under the ermine! We're good pals, Rupert. Better own up."

Frowning, Rupert lit a cigarette. He did not like being teased.

"Your insinuations are disgusting," he said acidly. "If I didn't like you so much, and didn't understand your queer sense of humor, I'd be pretty well annoyed. If you don't take me seriously, there doesn't seem to be much point in our going on seeing each other, does there, Gladys?"

"But I've told you already," Gladys said, "that I don't want to have an affair with you. Seeing that we're going to remain just friends, we might as well have a good giggle together over your dallyings with Xenia."

"I don't feel towards you like 'just a friend,' " Rupert answered. "And I don't think you do towards me."

She looked up at him quickly and the mischievous smile vanished.

197

No, she did not think of her handsome brother-in-law as just a friend —she never had. Under her bantering manner she was as much in love with him as an embittered rich girl could be with anyone. And she knew that he knew it.

"Too late, Rupert," she said. "Much, much too late. You should have thought of all this fifteen years ago, instead of falling for Helen. I don't like messy situations, my friend, and I haven't the slightest intention of deceiving William with his brother. I think that one example of incest in a family is quite enough—in fact, too much."

Rupert choked over his cigarette smoke. He had never discussed Francy and Helen with Gladys or with anybody else, and now he knew that he was going to get hurt. In his pleasure-filled life he had left little time for pain, but, as with everyone, pain always hovered in the background, waiting only for the opportunity to pounce. Its turn was at hand.

"What do you mean?" he said, braving fate a little longer.

"Rupert, you know very well what I mean. It's because I do like you that I don't want us to play this hide-and-seek game. We both know what Helen is up to, so don't let's try to fool one another."

Rupert shook his head. It had come now, this tussle with reality that he had been putting off so long; there was no possibility of fleeing.

"It's not for you to judge Helen," he said earnestly. "No more than it is for me. Helen is a very fine person, a very noble person. Despite all her faults, she's worth half a dozen ordinary women. A person like Helen lives by her own rules."

Gladys looked at Rupert sharply. Her mouth hardened and he could see hatred glinting in those narrow eyes.

"In other words, Helen Konrad can commit no wrong. Is that it? Oh, I've got to congratulate her! She's done what all her type try to do: built up a legend about herself. She's too good for Chicago, too good for you. She is the great misunderstood artist, oh so sensitive, oh so pure! Well, Rupert, you might as well hear the truth: your precious wife is more damn selfish than you and I put together, and that's saying something! She is no artist, no sensitive soul: she's just a run-of-the-mill product of our times, dissatisfied with whatever she's given, and drinking to console herself. No one will ever get anything out of Helen —perhaps because she has nothing to give."

"I forbid you to speak about her like that!" Rupert's eyes circled the parlor, as if looking for a point of escape; his fingers tugged desperately at the lobe of his ear. "I know that you've always hated Helen—yes, ever since the first time she came to Chicago. That's your prerogative. But I absolutely refuse to listen to you maligning a fine woman whom you can't possibly understand! Whatever our misunderstandings (and God knows there've been many), I have never stopped looking up to Helen."

"Precisely!" Gladys' hard little laugh rang out in the room. "You've put her on a pedestal and it's disrupting to have the tin goddess knocked down. I understand, Rupert: you're prepared to accept her drinking, her flirtations, even her adultery with your own brother, but you are not prepared to accept the fact that Helen Konrad is—a hollow sham from beginning to end."

Jumping up from the sofa, Rupert strode over to the window and stood looking out; he did not want Gladys to see his face. He had been hurt badly at a vital point. He was like a man who has invested all his money in a company, to be told casually one day that it's very organization is unsound.

And he thought, What if it is true? Perhaps Helen has been fooling me all these years—or rather, I have been fooling myself. I have always known that she was cheating me, if not in her actions at least in her thoughts. What has she ever given me, after all? Neither a real home, nor a child, nor all of herself. And now it is perfectly clear that she has gone off to live with my own brother! How can our marriage continue after that? It can't! A divorce—yes, a divorce is the answer!

But at the very moment that he reached this inevitable conclusion his thoughts were interrupted by a knock at the door. The maid entered, to inform them that Mr. Hapgood was on the telephone, asking urgently for Rupert. Feeling like a little boy who has been let off in the middle of a scolding, he hurried into the hall.

"Sorry to bother you, Mr. Konrad," the pleasant voice hummed over the wire. "I shouldn't have done so, but I have really exciting news.

199

Bully news! There's just been a phone call from Senator Brenn in Washington."

"Yes? Yes?" said Rupert, not even asking himself how Hapgood had guessed that he could be reached in Gladys' house. "What did the senator say?"

"He said that you could count definitely on your new appointment. Allow me to congratulate you, Mr. Konrad. I think you'll agree that it was worth disturbing you."

Rupert did not answer; the surprised Hapgood at the other end must have wondered if the good tidings had brought on a stroke. He did not know that a curious process was taking place in his employer's brain. As Hapgood spoke, assuring him of the realization of his lifetime's ambition, a picture had flashed before Rupert: a picture which his whole life long he had associated with success. It was a vision of the glittering dinner table that he saw again, just as he used to see it back in college days, with elegant ladies and gentlemen flanking their hostess, who was clad in a dress of shimmering green silk. To be sure, the appearance of Rupert's guests had changed with the years: they were older now, more dignified, some of the men wearing decorations, the ladies with tiaras and sumptuous earrings. But the face of their hostess was the same. It was Helen Mason's face! She, and she alone, belonged at the head of that table, once seen in a dream, but which had become reality thanks to their joint efforts.

And at that moment Rupert knew that he could never divorce Helen, despite Francy, despite a dozen Francys. Perhaps Gladys was right in calling Helen a sham, but then a dream, too, is a sham, its characters mere figments of the imagination. Suffice that it be real for the dreamer. What man in his sane mind would spoil his life's cherished dream by engaging in the vicious process of logic?

After that, life for Rupert grew strangely hectic. What with preparing for Xenia's visit and for his own imminent departure, he would have been lost without Hapgood. Fortunately Hapgood was always there when he was wanted (and not there when he wasn't), cool as a cucumber, efficient as an adding machine, cheerful, respectful, resourceful—and invariably to be counted on to agree with Rupert, unless his own opinion happened to be asked. Truly, he must have been conceived and born for Rupert Konrad's special benefit! He was like one of those small fish who swim about near the mouth of a shark, receiving protection, and in return warning the monster of the presence of baited hooks.

"He's a gold mine," Rupert confided to Senator Brenn, who unexpectedly had popped up from Washington. "I can't tell you how grateful I am to you for recommending the young man."

"Oh, that's all right, Mr. Konrad," said the senator, pulling grumpily at his long cigar. "Always happy to be of use—to a good friend."

That last remark, and the way it was uttered, gave Rupert pause. The truth was, of course, that he had to thank the senator for far more than his acquaintance with Hapgood; he had in the first instance to thank him for the luscious diplomatic appointment that had fallen into his lap. While a sizable contribution to the Brenn campaign fund had been proffered already, it was clear that a second was in order, now that the goods had actually been delivered.

So much Rupert understood; he was no novice at this game. But as the lion's share of his income was derived from an irrevocable trust which paid out semiannually, he happened to find himself short of funds. As had become his habit, he turned to the indispensable Hapgood for counsel.

"I feel," he said, employing his favorite indirect approach, "that it would be a great loss to the country, as a whole, if Senator Brenn failed of re-election next fall. There aren't many such capable and honest legislators in Washington."

"That's right, Mr. Konrad," said Hapgood feelingly. "There certainly are not."

"I'd do anything I could to help. I hope the senator understands that," said Rupert, groping his way. "I think that a concrete manner of showing my appreciation—I mean admiration—would be to contribute to his campaign fund."

"Oh yes, sir. I'm sure the senator would be very pleased," said Hapgood, not only agreeing, as usual, but employing his gift of making the other person feel that he had made an original, if not brilliant, suggestion.

201

"Unfortunately, I am not able to do so for another month. I happen to have numerous commitments. A month from now I shan't fail to make a suitable gesture."

"Well, that's very thoughtful of you, Mr. Konrad. That's bully," said Hapgood, bringing out his favorite exclamation. "After all, the election is a good ways off. I know the senator well enough to feel that he will understand."

That was all that was said at the time, not a word more. But somehow Rupert felt relieved, as if he had received assurance that this worry, too, would be lifted from his shoulders. And events proved that he was right. Next time he met the senator (it was a couple of days later at the Cliffdwellers' Club) Brenn was noticeably more affable, and went so far as to offer Rupert one of his special long cigars. As he accepted the senator's light Rupert reflected that there is a right way and a wrong way of doing everything, and that this fellow Hapgood had a sure instinct for the former.

That same thought came to him a month later (he was in Europe then), the day he asked Hapgood to send off the check. For once the ever-assenting secretary voiced his discreet disapproval.

"If you don't mind, Mr. Minister, make the check out to me. I'll substitute a check of my own. A man in public life, you know, simply cannot be too careful."

Rupert, nodding his assent, gazed curiously at his secretary. Again he had had the intuition that his path and that of Victor Hapgood were fated never to part.

fifteen

Just before dawn Helen started out of sleep. Through the uncurtained window beside their bed she could barely make out the opposite canyon wall: a dark block outlined against the lightening sky. Seen from that angle, the great rock seemed to be bearing down on her, and for a moment she had the thought that it was about to topple, burying the flimsy cottage and its occupants beneath its mass. There was something ominous, vaguely terrifying, about the canyon at that hour of the morning, and Helen shivered and turned her back on it. How was it, she thought, lying there in the darkness and primeval quiet, how was it that when she first came to this shack, that cliff had seemed so secure, so comforting—a symbol of strength that would last through the ages? If ever she awoke in the night, she had enjoyed looking at it, drawing strength from its primeval strength. Yet today, a few short weeks later, there was no comfort to be had from the cliff!

Her eyes turned to Francy; they rested on his delicate countenance, illuminated by the moonlight. It, too, had once seemed to her so firm and reliable, but now she could see in it the vacillation and weakness that undermined his character. She had come here three weeks ago with the hope that they could go on together into the difficult future. Her life with Rupert had reached an impasse; without blaming him (for people were as they were), she had realized that slowly but surely he was dragging her down to his level.

And now through Francy a miracle had occurred! She had sloughed off the years, becoming once again the old Helen Mason of Cambridge days, with light on her forehead and eyes set on a distant goal. With her hand clasped in his, she would gladly have lived the life of a Madame Lubokova, sharing an apartment no larger than this shack, giving piano lessons to help earn their bread. She had been richest during the poorest years of her life. Why should she fear poverty now? All that she had hinted to Francy, but delicately, as one must hint things to a delicate person. And she had seen a tiny drooping of the shoulders, a lowering of his eyes, as if the anticipated burden of responsibility already weighed too heavily upon him.

So it had been each time she gave him the chance to tell her what she longed to hear. Always that drooping of the shoulders, that embarrassed lowering of the eyes—and then some excuse to put off this talk that had been hanging over them almost since she stepped off the train. Talk? No, a talk was not necessary. All she wanted was to see a lifting of the head, a sparkle in the eyes. Knowing and loving him as she did, the smallest gesture on his part would have conveyed to her as much as a long conversation.

But now as she lay gazing at his high, smooth forehead, at his soft cheek which pressed into the pillow like a child's, she asked herself if she might be mistaken after all. With the generosity of a woman in love, she was ready to give him the benefit of every doubt. One more chance he must have to show her that he was a man to trust, a man to whom one could confide one's life! And if he failed her—ah yes, if he failed her once again? Well, then she would know where she stood and what to expect of the future, thought Helen as she pressed shut her eyes and tried unhappily to recapture her lost sleep.

When she awoke again the morning sun was on her face. From the quality of the light, she knew that the day was already far advanced, and now the canyon no longer had that ominous look which had frightened her at the hour of dawn; its contours softened by the haze, its rocky surface taken on a pastel coloring, it looked like the kindliest of mountains. On the veranda Francy was sitting with his manuscript before him, and when he bounded up and held out his arms she fell into them with relief.

"Hold me! Hold me tight!" she whispered, letting her body go limp so that perforce he would have to embrace her, rather than to let her embrace him, as was his wont.

"You're late, darling. Didn't you sleep well?" he asked, putting his arm about her waist as they walked over to the table which he had laid for their breakfast. "Luckily there's no such thing as time in paradise. To tell the truth, there isn't even a clock."

"That's just what makes it paradise," said Helen. "It wouldn't be, if it had a beginning and an end." But she knew that her voice sounded as if she were trying to reassure someone, perhaps Francy, perhaps herself.

She lay on the sofa after he had gone back to his work, her gaze on the canyon, but ever and again wandering to him. If only, she thought, he did not keep rousing in her the protective instinct, which had never found normal expression because of the absence of a child! He was so young, so vulnerable. How could she blame him for not filling the role that she herself had cast for him? The very fact that he had made this brave revolt against a hated way of life proved him to be one person in a thousand. Would it be his fault if he failed to carry it through to success?

204

No, no, she thought as she watched him struggling with that poem that showed all the weaknesses of its author. Whatever happened, she must never allow him to believe that he had failed her. A person like Francy could be so easily hurt, and once hurt, he might never recover from the blow. Somehow she must find a way to take the responsibility on her own shoulders. He had enough to contend with in his character without going through life feeling guilty and insufficient because of her.

Francy, at his table, crumbled up a sheet of paper and flung it angrily into the wastebasket. She met his eye and smiled.

"Hard going, Francy?"

"Like climbing Everest."

"I know," she said. "That's how I used to feel when I couldn't master some movement of a piano concerto. It's hell."

Francy sighed and reached for a new piece of paper, and as he sat frowning and biting his lips Helen's heart went out to him. She it was who had told him to revise his work, but could one successfully revise a poem that rang as hollow as this *Stock Yards Ballad?* Had she retained her own integrity as an artist, she might have asked him that question, rather than encourage a compromise which appealed to him because of his very nature, but which in the end must bring him only pain and disappointment.

"Oh, Helen, I am knocking off for the day," he cried at last, hurling another sheet in the basket. "I am not going to torture myself—and you —any more this morning. Come on, darling, let's take the day off and go for that ride down the canyon. Let's find out today where the two forks of the trail lead to."

"Oh, darling, darling!" said Helen, smiling but shaking her head. As she thought of what Francy had said, it seemed to her that she could hear the grave voice of her father, could see before her his fine face, with the heavy grooves by the mouth, the ascetic forehead. "Daughter," he was telling her, "the life of a man must be dedicated to something beyond himself. Such a life doesn't consist of flashes of exultation, but of a succession of laborious hours, lived through with pain and with joy, one's goal but dimly perceived. Read Emerson, daughter. I advise

205

you to read Emerson." She went up to Francy's table and let her hand pass over his soft blond hair.

"I don't like those words 'knocking off,' Francy," she said, and though she was still smiling, her voice had taken on something of her father's earnest tone. "I don't think you like them either. They belong to a vocabulary that is not ours, Francy—a vocabulary that I've known far too well in the last fifteen years. Let's cut out that vocabulary altogether! Let's make a vocabulary of our own—for the future!"

She was a little surprised at the gravity of her own words, at the feeling of anxiety that gripped her while she spoke them. Then she realized that this was the moment of decision which she had promised herself. It had come naturally and inevitably, as she had known that it would. The thing that she really had said to him just now was, Shall you and I go forward, Francy—or backwards? It is for you to decide, because no human being can ever stay still. Which shall it be? Which shall it be, Francy? She willed him with all her strength to take up the challenge, now—now before it was too late.

She was watching him for the slightest tremor of an eye, the smallest movement of the head. Nothing was unimportant at such a moment. And she saw what she had dreaded to see, what she had convinced herself that she would not see this time. There it came, as inexorable as fate itself, final, decisive: the slumping of the shoulders, imperceptible to anyone but her; the lowering of the eyes that was equivalent to a negation. A silence raised itself between them, one of those silences that are far louder than speech. Then Francy's voice, charged with unnatural excitement, but in it also the tone of relief of a man who has been rescued when he was about to drown.

"Oh golly, Helen! There's that darn deliveryman. Don't you hear him honking his horn?"

Yes, it was indeed Fred, arrived with his weekly groceries. She could hear his Ford wailing like a chorus of demented cats. But not even the fear of wasting a few moments of Fred's precious time would have warranted the alacrity with which Francy sprang to his feet. So she had had her answer, and sooner than she had expected! She would know what to do. In a voice that was as different from Professor Mason's as

206

Francy's voice had been different from the one she wanted to hear, she cried out:

"Listen, Francy, I've changed my mind. You're right—it's just too wonderful a day to stay here. Do let's go for our ride! Let's have fun!"

It struck her even as she said it that she had not pronounced that word "fun" since coming to Arizona, though it was here that she had spent the nicest days of her life. She felt that she was speaking not to Francy at all, but to one of those young men she had known in the past —to Pahlevi Azad or Anton Holbein or to some junior attaché of a legation in Berlin or in Cairo. "Let's go for a picnic on the Wansee— or on the Nile—or in the Wiener Wald. Come on, let's have fun!"

At the end of the trail Fred was standing, waving a letter in his grubby hand.

"Mornin', folks!" he cried brightly. "I've got somethin' here—somethin' real interesting, if I can find the right person to give it to. How about it?"

Whereupon a little voice could be heard piping from a cactus bush: "Give it to me, Fred! Please give it to me."

The ventriloquist's face took on an expression of outraged indignation.

"I will not! I certainly will not!" he shouted back at himself angrily. "I have a letter here, forwarded from ol' Californie. It's addressed to Mrs. Helen Konrad, General Delivery, Santa Rosa, and I shan't give it to anyone else."

"Good for you, Fred!" said Helen. "I wish all my letters got treated with that much respect."

"Aw gee!" came the little voice from under the bush. "Gee willikens! Don't I ever have no fun at all?"

"You get out of here!" Fred shouted back. "Stop that now! You stop trying to grab that letter away!"

Fred, making a horseplay of warding off the imaginary imp, finally handed the envelope to Helen with an elaborate flourish of his sombrero.

"That ornery kid! Will you believe it that I got to keep my eye on him every second . . . ?"

They carried the case of groceries back to the shack between them, and then Francy, tactful as always, said that he would go to have a look at his ailing turtle. She tore open the envelope and pulled out three sheets scribbled over in an untidy, loose hand. Glancing at the foot of the letter, she saw that it was signed "Justin," and began to read it, her back leant against the cottage's splintered wall. As she read, it seemed to Helen that the canyon before her faded away, and in its place she saw a vista of Justin's world—the world of smart people and sneerers—the two-dimensional social world that she thought she had left forever.

"Your husband, my esteemed brother-in-law, certainly is squeezing the last drop of publicity value out of your friend Xenia's coming visit," Justin had written in part. "A month ago the name Molenavia meant nothing to two out of three Chicagoans. They probably thought it was a soup or a new game of cards. Now the newspapers are running editorials pointing out its importance (if any) in world politics. For some reason Rupert's name always figures in those articles. You'd think he was the lamented royal Prince himself, instead of just the Princess's . . . Oh, I'm sorry. This damn fountain pen writes so fast, it actually got ahead of my thoughts.

"Anyway, Rupert's present interests aren't directed towards royalty, so I understand—unless you call these Stock Yards aristocrats royal. I beg to report that he was seen attending the opera with that bitch of a sister-in-law of ours, Gladys, with William in tow. Now figure that one out for yourself, not forgetting Rupert's natural affinity for William. The upshot of all this is—shouldn't you come back to Chicago soon, beautiful Helen? I am the soul of discretion and I love you very much. Far be it from me to ask what you are doing out in California, or even if you are in California (which I doubt), but I hope, yes, I *hope* (you see, I am underlining!) that you are not contemplating any follies. Someone once said that thirty-five was 'the dangerous age.' Please remember, dear Helen, that it is a very wicked thing to burn bridges behind one and that Rupert Konrad is sailing off to his post abroad in ten days' time. Do I need to remind you that it is your post too, and that you've been working for it for fifteen years?"

So that was that, Helen thought. Gladys and Rupert! She might have known it. The news affected her remarkably little. It was almost as if she had been reading about the doings of a man called Rupert Konrad whom she had known at some former period of her life—oh, much further back than the Cambridge period with her father! But then she remembered that Rupert was her husband. Re-reading the last sentence of that letter, she understood how to carry out her resolution of such a short while ago.

"You know, Francy, that letter was from Justin," she said when Francy walked back on the veranda. "He wrote that Rupert's leaving for abroad in ten days' time."

"Is that right?" Francy said, and she could see from his face that he was once again urging himself to embark on that long-deferred conversation. Instead his eyes traveled to the case of groceries and he pushed it nearer to the wall with his foot. "Rupert must be feeling pretty elated," he said, his back half turned towards her. "This is what he's wanted all his life."

Helen took advantage of that indecisively turned back to walk off a few steps. It would be easier to put on her act if she did not have to look into Francy's eyes.

"Yes, Francy," she said, "that's just what I want to speak to you about—I mean about Rupert's getting this post. As you say, he's wanted it all his life. I can't say that he's exactly worked for it, because it was others who did most of the work, but he certainly has schemed for it, and I suppose that's one kind of work too. Well, now he's got it—a legation!"

"He certainly has!" Francy said, and he pushed the wooden case even nearer to the wall. Sitting down at his writing table, he gazed out over the canyon, but Helen saw that his eyes were blinking distractedly.

"A legation isn't what you might think, Francy," Helen went on. "It's not just a place with a lot of official papers lying about and where some work's done in connection with Americans abroad. No, when Rupert, and people like Rupert, think of a legation, they see a drawing room filled with elegant people; they see bowing servants in livery; they see a whole row of engraved invitations wedged in their dresser mirror—not invitations from fellow citizens, sons and grandsons of immigrants, like themselves: those invitations are from people with titles or else from wealthy expatriates who own palaces in Venice or winter houses in St. Moritz. And when Rupert thinks of a legation he sees a dinner table too. He told me that he's been seeing that dinner table in his imagination all his life. There are glittering guests at Rupert's table, but the guests aren't really what's most important. There's a hostess at its head in a shimmering gown with her hair worn like a crown of silver. Well, Francy darling"—Helen gave a smile—"believe it or not, that glamorous figure at Rupert's table is—Helen Konrad!"

Her rather ridiculous speech was over! It had not been easy to carry it off. Another moment, Helen felt, and she would have broken down and sobbed, or perhaps just burst into laughter. Now she summoned all her will to walk over to Francy and lay her hand on his shoulder, as simply and affectionately as she had ever done before.

He raised his head slowly, and she saw that his face had gone pale; his light eyes were fastened on her with the same frightened look as that day he came to see her on East Cedar, after receiving her letter telling him not to call.

"And what—what does this all mean, Helen?" he asked her.

She found the strength not to weep, not to throw herself in his arms with the cry, "Francy, Francy, let us save ourselves before it is too late!" She found the strength to smile at him in the most natural way as she answered:

"Why, Francy, it doesn't mean anything, really. I was just telling you about Rupert's dream of success, which has come true at last. It's a darn silly dream, *I* think. But at least"—she gave a laugh—"it warrants my taking a little trip to Chicago to talk things over. Don't you think so?"

He jumped up from the table. His eyes were focused on her, and in them was that look of fright that always made her want to take him in her arms to comfort him. Perhaps it still is not too late! Helen thought, a last hope flickering in her breast. If now, even now, he told me to stay—oh, it is certain I would not leave him!

"A little trip," he said, and she could feel how the two halves of his mind fought against each other. "Oh, Helen, I hate having you leave here! It is going to be awful without you! But at the same time, if you feel that you really ought to go—I don't want to stop you."

"I think I should go, Francy," she made herself say.

210

"Well, if you feel that way, then perhaps you really should talk things over with Rupert. I shan't persuade you against it. After all, you could be back here in a few days, couldn't you?"

"Oh yes, I could be back in a few days," she said, and now there was only lead in her heart. "So, let's say that it's decided like that, and now for heaven's sake, let's stop talking so seriously!" She walked over to the veranda's edge and threw out her arms towards the canyon in what she tried to make a gesture of joyful abandon. "Come on, Francy!" she cried. "Let's go for our lovely ride!"

Into Francy's face came a look of relief—relief that the final decision had been once again postponed, that the door was still open. Poor Francy! said Helen to herself. Oh, my poor, poor darling!

They started out shortly after noon, packages of sandwiches in their pockets, and both pretending that they felt as gay and carefree as on any other day. Francy was whistling as he led the way, but his tune soon dwindled into silence, perhaps because it really was too hot to whistle. The desert heat had been growing fiercer every day, and the midday sun beat down upon them, its rays not yet deflected by the canyon wall. Only when they neared the point where Francy had picked up his incredible turtle did a welcome shade fall across the path. Francy was wiping his forehead when they stopped to rest, and it seemed to Helen that his face looked drawn.

"Sure you are feeling all right?" she asked him. "You don't want to turn back, do you, Francy?"

He shook his head.

"No, no. I'm feeling splendidly."

"You mustn't overdo it," she said, searching his face and then leaning over the side of her horse to give his arm a squeeze. But, like everything she had said since making up her mind, this, too, sounded theatrical and false. Tomorrow or the next day she would have left here, and who then would look after him and encourage him to work and see to it that he did not overstrain his poor heart?

They continued slowly, their horses picking their way along the rock-strewn path, instinctively aware that one misstep would send them crashing down the bank. Across the chasm, the opposite mountain wall seemed to grow taller, more rugged; here and there fissures appeared to view, like wounds cut into the red flesh of the mountain. This was the heart of the canyon, which stretched for many miles in the general direction of the New Mexico border. And in all their explorations they had not yet found a single evidence of human habitation.

Now they had come within sight of a fork in the track, one prong veering diagonally downward, while the other zigzagged towards the summit. Francy, on the lead horse, halted just before reaching the branch, and Helen drew up alongside him. The moment that she saw his face she knew that something was wrong.

"Oh, Francy, you are feeling badly! We shouldn't have come so far."

He turned his head then and gave her a long look, half frightened, half puzzled, it seemed to Helen; it was as if he were trying to remember something.

"It's strange," he murmured. "The fork—the two trails. I have been in this spot before."

"Oh, but there are many places that could look like it!"

"No, no." He shook his head stubbornly. "It was this very spot—this very spot. I recognize it so well: the zigzag trail, the dried river bed below. And I recognize my own feelings too: the need to decide, the knowledge that I can't decide. It's—it's so dreadfully familiar, Helen!"

"You dreamed it all!"

"Yes," he agreed, still looking dazed, "perhaps that's it. Perhaps I did dream it all. And yet it's more than a dream, Helen. Much more than a dream! I simply cannot decide which fork to take, just as I can't decide anything in my life. And I am never going to be able to decide."

"Then I'll decide for you," she said decisively. "We'll take neither the up trail nor the down trail, but ride straight back to the cottage. Please now, Francy! You really aren't yourself."

"Very well," he said, so meekly, so unresistingly, that it was clear he had only been waiting to be told. And he at once turned his horse's head homewards.

They rode back in silence, refreshed by the cool of the late afternoon, and both feeling somehow relieved after that moment of tension. Yet an aura of defeat hung over them. Yet one more decision had been put off! Perhaps it would have been better, Helen thought, had they found the courage to go on, along one track or the other. There were, she had learned, worse things in life than meeting disaster on a mountain trail.

They dismounted finally beside the shack, and as Helen went indoors, Francy led their horses to the improvised corral. Waiting for him on the sofa, she felt overcome by a profound weariness, a numbing of the senses which precluded all emotions. One thought alone existed in her brain, and she clung to it with the strength of desperation: twenty-four hours from now, all this would have slipped into the past! She knew that the scar left by this separation would be with her until the day she died; but she knew, too, that the pain of it would merge gradually with the pain of all those other wounds which had been inflicted on her, or (if she were to be quite honest) which she had inflicted on herself.

At the entrance of the shack stood Francy, and he was holding an object in his hand. At first Helen thought that it was a large stone, or perhaps a block of wood; then she saw that it was Francy's turtle, but its two heads hung limp and the scaly legs protruding from the carapace drooped dismally in a gesture of defeat.

Her gaze moved upwards above the lifeless body, to find Francy's gaze upon her. And for a moment it seemed to Helen that she could read panic in his eyes.

sixteen

It was a long time since Chicago had seen anything like it. Being host city to a royal princess is exciting under any conditions, but when the visitor is as dramatic a personality as Xenia, when she has been publicized as a war heroine and the prospective savior of her country—well, then there is nothing for it but to go all out in a public welcome. To be sure, there were some bad tongues who maintained that Xenia was more popular outside her country than within it, and that her subjects despised her as a publicity hunter and something like a gold digger on an international scale. These unheeded skeptics could only look on cynically as Xenia was whisked from party to reception, the cortege of limousines whirling through the Chicago streets to the accompaniment of shrieking police sirens and thundering motorcycles. From the minute she left her palatial suite in the Blake Hotel until she dropped into her scented bath at night, there was scarcely a moment that she could call her own. Xenia loved it, Chicago loved it, and needless to say, Rupert loved it more than all of them put together.

Those days formed for him a fantastic and altogether delightful period. His diplomatic career sensationally advanced, his social prestige sent rocketing, he had attained his long-standing ambition of showing Chicago that he was the most important Konrad of them all: more important than his father, who had made the fortune, or his two sisters, who were spending it; more important a hundredfold than William, who was doing nothing more important than trying to preserve it. He alone could hobnob with crowned heads, chat cozily with mayors and senators, accord or refuse to accord interviews to the press. As if kind fate had determined to sweep the last cloud from his sky, there arrived a wire one fine morning to say that Helen was returning to Chicago.

"Look here, Hapgood," he said, having summoned his lieutenant, "you'd better call up the Cunard Line and have them reserve another stateroom. Mrs. Konrad may be sailing to Europe with us after all."

"Oh, isn't that bully, sir! I do hope she's in the best of health now. What about the dinner at Mrs. William Konrad's tomorrow night? Do you suppose that Mrs. Konrad will be attending?"

"I hope so," said Rupert, "but it's not certain."

"Wouldn't it be just bully if she could!" Hapgood exclaimed feelingly and, as had become his habit, Rupert looked for the inner meaning of the words. He found it. Yes, it would indeed be "bully" if Helen showed up for William's dinner, thus disproving any suppositions already formed as to the cause of her absence. Then and there he determined that Helen *would* show up.

It was not easy for him to arrange to be at the station to meet her, seeing that her arrival coincided with the Stock Yards tour that had been arranged for Xenia's benefit. In one way that was a relief, for Rupert had always been a bit ashamed of his connection with the Yards, and but for Xenia's insistence, never would have put the tour on her program in the first place. Unfortunately it would now devolve on William to escort the famous visitor, a pleasure which Rupert naturally begrudged him. William had already got far more than he deserved in being allowed to give a dinner party for Her Highness, and with this added honor, his fat head might begin to swell!

This fear was in Rupert's mind as he waited for Helen's train, but the excitement of the moment robbed it of urgency. He was, Rupert realized, more excited this minute than he had been forty-eight hours before, when he came to the station to meet Xenia. Helen was coming home! Strange how the thought delighted him, considering the rather special circumstances of her absence! It was needless for Gladys to point out that Helen was irresponsible, selfish, and weak, that she drank too much and did not even love him. That all was in some way beside the point. The point was that Helen was part of his life! He felt the need of her now, as much as he had that night in the Cambridge inn, when he had tried to explain his feelings to Mama. Now, as then, he knew that there was on one who could take her place. How was any outsider to appraise the subtle and mysterious relationship between two people who had been married for fifteen years?

Then he caught sight of Helen walking down the platform, with that airy gait of hers which always made it seem as if her feet were barely touching the ground. He watched her for a second, remembering his old feeling that the day might come when she would float out of his life for good. Well, she had, indeed, floated out, but here she was, floating right back again! Perhaps the same thing that made her indispensable for him made him indispensable for her, Rupert told himself. Perhaps in the course of the years his dream had become hers as well, and she knew that, without him, it was bound to explode like a bubble of air.

"Hello, Helen," he said. "I am glad to see you."

"Hello, Rupert."

"Did you have a good journey?" he asked, walking beside her towards the barrier. It seemed a rather absurd thing to say.

"It was quite hot on the train."

Her responses came automatically, and it seemed to him that she was moving almost as in a daze. When the porter put her two suitcases in their car she stood by, watching, as though they were not her suitcases at all, nor this the same old railway station into which their trains

215

had steamed so many times. And for some reason his thoughts flew back to that other morning when he, young, eager, and in love, had driven down to meet her on her very first visit to Chicago. How much water had flowed beneath the bridges since that day! How bitterly they had disillusioned one another!

They did not speak while the car edged its way out of the Loop district, but as they were passing the river on their way to the North Side, Rupert said to her:

"Helen, I am glad that you are back. Let us not mention the past, for that will get us nowhere. The present and the future are more important."

"Very well," said Helen, but it was in the same dead voice with which she had announced that it was quite hot on the train.

"Xenia will be glad to see you," Rupert said. "She's asked after you several times. William is giving a dinner party for her tonight. We all hope you'll come."

"If you like," she answered.

At the house there was a telephone message awaiting Rupert—a most important message, said the butler as he handed it to him on a salver. It proved to be from Hapgood, transmitted from the Stock Yards. There had been a serious incident and Rupert's presence was demanded as soon as possible.

He found that pandemonium had broken out. Even before entering the Konrad Office Building, he sensed an atmosphere of unrest and wondered what the little groups of workers were talking about so excitedly during what should have been their lunch hour. Not till he stepped through the door of William's office did he realize the full gravity of the situation.

A number of people were gathered here, among whom he recognized William, squeezed into an extraordinarily tight-fitting morning coat, as well as Hapgood, dapper and collected. The Princess Xenia was seated on William's sofa, clad in an attractive gray velvet dress, or rather, a dress that had once been attractive. Now Rupert saw to his horror that the material bore stains in various places, some red, some yellow, some of an unpleasant greenish color. Could it be that these were the marks of eggs and of tomatoes? Kneeling beside the sofa was little Chippy, attempting to remove the spots with the help of a bottle of benzine. The Princess' face, once strikingly beautiful, still handsome, bore a stony look that Rupert had never seen there before.

"Good God!" he cried. "What has happened, Your Highness?"

Hapgood came hurrying up, to spare her the anguish of explaining.

"There's been a most unfortunate happening, Mr. Konrad. Most unfortunate! A group of rowdies, egged on by instigators, waylaid Her Highness as she was passing through the plant. Nothing like this has ever happened before. It's inexplicable!"

"Not inexplicable at all," said the Princess in her perfect English. Each word sounded as if it had been allowed to marinate in vinegar. "There was no police protection. I have always heard that one needed police protection in this gangster city. You might have seen to it, Mr. Konrad. . . ."

As she spoke, there mounted to the room a murmur of voices from outside; there were shouts in a foreign language which Rupert thought he recognized as Molenavian. Going to the window, he saw a group of perhaps twenty workers standing on the lawn before the office building. They were obviously very much excited. Some bore banners which read, "You have sucked the lifeblood of our people!" or "We, the Molenavian workers, denounce you, Jezebel!" and there was one little man who, when he saw Rupert, brandished his fist and shouted out a Molenavian word which happened to be one of the five Rupert had learned during his two years' residence in the country. It was not a very pretty word.

"My own people!" declaimed the Princess theatrically. "Oh, this is the saddest moment of my life! Could I have imagined that here in Chicago this dreadful thing would happen to me? My poor deluded subjects!" said Xenia, resting her fine forehead on the back of her pale hand.

"A bunch of rabid socialists! They all ought to be hung!" It was the voice of William, and he was striding up and down the room in his tight morning coat and too high stiff collar. "I don't know what the country's coming to," he cried. "This damn administration . . ."

A series of husky cries from the demonstrators drowned out his words, and now Rupert felt that the time had come to assert his own authority.

"Don't worry, Your Highness," he said in his best official manner. "This unpleasantness will be over in just a minute. Accept my apologies. Hapgood, hurry up and put in a phone call to the police. Tell them to send over a couple of patrol cars right away."

"Yes, sir. And they'd better hurry," said Hapgood, looking at his watch. "We're expected at that civic luncheon in half an hour."

But before Hapgood could reach the instrument the Princess herself had stepped in his path; she laid a restraining hand on the telephone.

"Do nothing of the sort!" she cried. "Those simple people down there are my friends. They don't understand that yet, but I shall tell them. I am going to speak to my poor confused compatriots."

"Your Highness!" "Just a moment, please!" "Step back, Princess, this is serious!"

These simultaneous shouts crowded the air as Xenia moved up to the window and with a magnificent gesture threw it open. Immediately a different series of cries came up to them, but, undaunted by either chorus, Xenia stood in the open window with her head up and her tall figure silhouetted against the background of factory chimneys belching smoke. She looked so precisely like a musical-comedy princess in a mob scene that she might have been rehearsing the role.

An egg flew through the open window and splattered against the wall. She never budged. But when the shouting had subsided a little, slowly, very slowly, she lowered her head and gazed down sadly, yet with infinite understanding, at the people below. And then she began to speak.

Rupert had no idea what she was saying in that outlandish language that he had never mastered, but just listening to her voice told him that everything would be all right. Sentiment was thick as treacle in her words, and at times they had that semihumorous lilt that had bewitched him and so many others. Rupert was no royalist at heart, but he felt a stirring of emotion as he watched and listened to this titled personage who in a sense could be called his protégée.

The cries of protest had subsided. Not a jarring sound was to be heard as Xenia's voice rolled on, now sugary and appealing, now fiery and inspiring, and she stood there with her back against the window frame, her stately head held high. The people in the party, mostly members of Rupert's welcoming committee and Xenia's two ladies in waiting, had relaxed in chairs or on the sofa; they were watching her with the enthralled air of individuals witnessing a memorable performance. Of all those present, perhaps only Rupert understood why Xenia had taken her courage in her hands and risked this gesture. When again would she have such a chance to gain publicity and capture the heart of the great American public?

Now the shouting outside had recommenced, but its nature was entirely different. Hurrahs reached them, mingling with cries of acclamation, and when Rupert looked through the window he saw people throwing their caps aloft and others waving their arms in enthusiasm. The little man who a few minutes before had sworn with fiery obscenity could now be seen wiping away a tear with a large colored handkerchief.

Rupert whispered in the Princess' ear, "Xenia, I admire you."

"Yes," she answered aloud, "yes, you are quite right. We feel," she added, turning to the others, "that it would be a nice gesture if, before leaving, I went down there and shook hands with some of my dear compatriots. You agree with me? I'm so glad! What's that you're saying, Mr. Konrad? Oh yes, if you think the people of Chicago would be interested, I have no objection to a few photographs being taken. . . ."

Before evening Xenia was a Chicago heroine. There were accounts in all the afternoon papers telling how, singlehanded, she had quelled the violence of a mob of Molenavian thugs, led on by anti-social organizers. Two of the sheets ran photographs of the royal personage shaking hands with her reformed compatriots, and there was one snap of Her Highness being presented with a large egg, originally destined to be exploded on her head. Rupert knew that she had established herself for once and all in the hearts and minds of Chicagoans, and that now she could murder the city fathers themselves and get away with it.

An atmosphere of triumph prevailed at William's dinner party that same night. The guests felt doubly gratified at being asked to honor someone who not only held a genuine European title of nobility but had proved herself a personage in her own right. Before the entrée was served, there had been three separate offers of donations to the Molenavian Red Cross, and it became clear that Chicago's quota, as set by the welcoming committee, would be handsomely oversubscribed. All of which, of course, redounded to Rupert's credit. It was almost as if he himself had quelled the rabble, thus heroically saving the honor of his native city!

Only for Helen, seated opposite Xenia at the long table, the whole dinner party had about it an air of unreality. She could not figure out what she really was doing here. Two nights before she had been lying in a lonely shack with Francy, whom she loved as she would never love anyone again; outside there had been the canyon and the stars, and within the room a raging silence that was like a mute cry of pain. And here she was tonight, playing her usual role of woman of the world, being charming to Rupert's royal guest and frigidly polite to Gladys, whose green eyes squinted at her from the end of the table. So it was true, then, that all that other was but an interlude!

"Come on, Helen! You've done your duty on that side. Talk to me for a little while."

It was Justin Judson, on her right, with whom she had been avoiding conversation all evening. Now, calling forth her insipid smile, she turned in his direction.

"Well, Helen, how does little old Chicago strike you after the great open spaces of the West?"

"I think a city is as nice as its inhabitants," she hinted broadly.

"*Touché!*" said Justin, stroking his mustache. "I shouldn't have asked. But don't worry, Helen, I am the very soul of discretion. Besides, you know that I have always liked you very much."

"If that is so," answered Helen, "please don't ever ask me about this last month. You are an old friend, and I beg you, as a special favor."

"I promise you," said Justin, as nearly serious as he could be. "May I just say, though, that I am very glad you *did* come back? In fact, very! Frankly, I don't like your husband, as you know, but the other alternative would have been—disaster. Let us drink to your happy future."

220

He raised his glass, but Helen did not respond to the toast, so Justin drank his wine down alone. His life had conditioned him to rebuffs of various sorts, and now his voice was quite cheerful as he resumed.

"I bet you are remembering that I am the first man who encouraged you to take a drink. Do you know where? At Jane Atwill's birthday party, just fifteen years ago! Rupert was furious with me that day, but in my humble opinion there are plenty of worse things to do to a woman than just pouring her a drink. What do you say, Helen?"

"What do you want me to say? I suppose that you are right."

With a thoughtful air Helen took up her champagne glass and, still thoughtfully, drank it down to the last drop.

After the dinner party broke up they adjourned to the drawing room, which had been prepared to receive a number of guests. At one side rows of chairs had been drawn up before a grand piano, because Xenia was fond of music and a recital was scheduled for later in the evening. Thanks to Hapgood's efforts, a well-known pianist had been procured to entertain the guests. In every corner were elaborate flower decorations, these and the well-dressed ladies and the distinguished gentlemen all serving as background for the stately Xenia, who in her sweeping black velvet dress looked, as Justin put it, "every square foot a queen."

"This party is costing our brother-in-law William a pretty penny," he said, while perching on the arm of Helen's brocaded chair. "Isn't it good that we Konrads are so rich? It's a shame the old man isn't here to enjoy it, though on second reflection, perhaps it's just as well he isn't. I don't see him striding in here in his hip boots and lumberman's shirt, do you, Helen? Besides, he'd hate every second of this. Money for him was something to be used to make more money, not something that you exchanged for social prestige."

"Is he still in Atlantic City?" Helen asked, seeing that she was expected to open her mouth from time to time.

"Yes, but he's due back almost any day now. Afraid he's in for a nasty shock. It seems that McKenna's as good as taken over the company while the old man's been away. For all practical purposes, it's become Konrad and Company already, with McKenna at the wheel. The agreement for the stock issue is drawn up, and there's no opposing it any longer. But speaking of the devil . . ."

221

Glancing towards the entrance, Helen saw to her surprise that Angus McKenna had just come into the room, accompanied by an extremely attractive-looking young woman. Even more astonishing than his presence here was the man's total lack of embarrassment in what for him must have been very strange surroundings. To be sure, he wore his tail coat rather as if it had been fancy dress, but there was complete confidence in McKenna's manner as he shook hands with Gladys and then introduced the young lady at his side. At first Helen wondered if the extraordinary Scotchman had taken a new wife (he had been a widower now for several years). Then she realized that this must be Maureen McKenna, his daughter, whom she had not seen since Maureen was a little girl.

Cecilia came bustling up, distress written over her smug countenance; even the frilly, salmon-colored dress seemed to have turned a shade darker out of indignation.

"Have you ever known anything like it? If this isn't the very limit! Imagine William's inviting that man to a royal party! Whatever do you suppose induced him?"

"Just common sense, my dear," Justin answered in the bored tone he always used in speaking to Cecilia. "After all, it's really McKenna who is his boss. And William knows it. He'd better look out for *his* job."

"Don't be nasty now. The man's still our paid employee."

"That's what *you* think," Justin said.

Gladys was taking McKenna up to the Princess, and again his composure was such that he might have had the habit of meeting royalty every day of his life. When pretty Maureen curtsied to Her Highness, it struck Helen that she did it with more natural grace than had any other woman in the room.

Other people were beginning to arrive for the soirée, some with the happy expression of people who know they are in the right place at the right time, others looking a bit offended, as though they felt they should have been asked for the dinner itself, and not only afterwards. In the latter category Helen recognized her sister-in-law Bee, excluded so as not to make the table topheavy with Konrads, as well as Gladys' old friend Jane Atwill, who had been left out because her husband was not sufficiently important. There were many others whom she recognized, or thought she recognized, but she still had that feeling of unreality that had been with her the whole evening. This Chicago drawing room, with people curtsying and bowing, had a quality of grotesqueness that was growing more marked every moment; and the people themselves, whether familiar or unfamiliar, were like odd characters in a puppet play.

Then from one moment to the next it became clear that something had gone wrong; it was as if the strings that manipulated the various dolls had all got tangled up behind the backdrop. Hapgood had come in, had whispered some words in Rupert's ear, and then the two of them had slipped out together. They were gone for a long time. Helen, making conversation with Justin, so as to escape talking to anybody else, wondered vaguely what had happened. She caught Gladys' eyes fixed anxiously on the doorway and knew she was worried for the success of her soirée.

Suddenly Hapgood was back again and standing by Helen's chair; he was still flashing his amiable grin, but it had become as meaningless as the grin on a Halloween pumpkin.

"So sorry to bother you, Mrs. Konrad. Would you mind very much stepping into the library for a moment? Mr. Konrad is anxious to have a word with you."

She got up and followed him automatically, passed through the door that he held open for her—and found herself alone with Rupert. He was pacing up and down his brother's library, in his eyes the look of a man who has given himself over to the task of worrying. He halted when he caught sight of her, and his fingers, which had been tugging distractedly at the lobe of his ear, motioned her into an armchair.

"I am in trouble, Helen," he said. "Bad trouble. And you are the one person who can help."

She stared at him, not knowing what he meant, yet feeling instinctively that something evil was about to happen to her. A frightening premonition swept over Helen: she must pay now, pay for her brief happiness.

"Yes, Rupert," she heard herself say, and she thought that her voice sounded like that of a prisoner awaiting sentence.

"Hapgood's just had a message," said Rupert, still pacing the floor, "from that fellow Schoelkopf, who was to play the piano this evening. He's had an attack of some sort—appendicitis, they think. He would have it, just this evening! Now there are sixty people waiting in there, to say nothing of Xenia."

Helen looked at him silently. Suddenly she understood that this was an ultimatum.

"So you want me to play in his place?"

Rupert nodded. "It's too late to get anyone else, otherwise I'd not think of asking you. I know how you feel about playing in public, and I've always respected your idiosyncrasy. But all Chicago is here! What will they think if the evening turns out to be a flop? I'd be the joke of the town. Now listen, Helen, I haven't said a word about everything that's happened. But I do ask you to help me! In fact I insist on it as a condition to our going on as before."

For a second everything went black before Helen's eyes. She was overcome with a feeling of panic, like that of a man who knows he is about to drown; she actually had an impulse to call out for help. She knew, she had always known, that if once she betrayed her piano she would never want to play it again. Why else had she been so adamant about not performing before anyone in all these years? And had not Madame Lubokova warned her that what Rupert now demanded was an act of betrayal? But it no longer seemed to matter very much; tonight nothing seemed to matter. The feeling of panic passed, to be succeeded by an icy calm.

"It's all right, Rupert," she replied. "You don't have to insist. There's no need to threaten. I will do what you want."

"So you will play? Really?"

The relief in Rupert's voice was so vast, so deep-seated, that it would have told Helen, had she not known it before, how much people's opinion meant to him. At that moment of self-abasement she despised him more profoundly than ever in her life before.

Her calm did not desert her as she preceded Rupert into the drawing room, nor as she listened to his announcement that his wife, in spite of her long lack of practice, had consented to play in place of the ailing Schoelkopf. It did not even desert her as she sat down at the piano and ran her fingers tentatively over the keys.

224

So this was it at last! the thought occurred to her before she began to play. This was that first public concert for which she had begun practicing twenty years before; the concert for which Madame Lubokova had prepared her so lovingly and on which her father had pinned his fondest hopes. But she was playing under very different circumstances than the three of them had foreseen: for an audience of social celebrities, instead of discriminating critics; with death and not hope in her heart.

As she brought her fingers down on the keys for the opening notes of the "Appassionata," the face of Francy sprang up before her, panic-stricken and beseeching as he gazed at her above the dead turtle; and because she did not want to see it she closed her eyes. But now, instead of Francy, it was the canyon wall she saw, and it was leaning towards her, just as when she used to look at it from her bed. Forward, ever further forward, swerved the wall, until suddenly it collapsed upon her with a crash that sounded like a mighty chord of music.

seventeen

"Oh, Francy, how can you say it! You, a worry for me? If you knew how happy I was just to have you back!"

Francy, lying in bed in his own little room, smiled up at his mother warmly. Perhaps he wanted to tell her that he was happy to be home, but the words seemed to stick in his throat. What he did say made her every bit as pleased.

"Mama, I feel so much better today! I'll be up now before you know it."

"That's what O'Grady tells us!"

Wilma beamed at him, trying to exude confidence in her smile and finding it far from easy. How things kept repeating themselves! she was thinking. She could have sworn that she had heard those same words fifteen years ago, sitting beside this same bed on this very same chair. She had given Francy the same answer too, hoping then, as she hoped today, that O'Grady had not spoken to please Adolph.

225

"You look like a different person," she hurried on, lest he sense the fright in her heart. "You've got color in your cheeks today. Why, my skinny Francy has even taken on weight, I do declare! You were a sick boy, good and sick, when you came home two months ago."

"Nonsense, Mama! I just came home for a little pampering, that's all. And if you want to know the truth"—he pulled down her head to give her a kiss on the cheek—"I've made myself out much sicker than I was because it's so nice to be fussed over."

They could hear the doorbell ringing down below and then the sound of a girl's voice speaking to Hauptman. A gay burst of laughter drifted up the stairs.

"That's Maureen," Wilma said. "I've never known anybody who could laugh quite like her. Come to think of it, I've never known anybody in these last twenty-five years who could even work up a smile while talking to Hauptman."

"You're right," Francy said as he lay back on his pillow. "Somehow Maureen McKenna has more laughter in her system than any two other people together. It's really strange, when you think of her glum father! She's made me laugh too—laugh a lot."

"That's a good thing. You need to laugh a lot, Francy "

Wilma went out on the landing to greet Maureen as she came up the stairs. It always refreshed her just to look at the Scotch girl's face and to hear her voice, so gay, so vibrant with youth.

"And how are you, Mrs. Konrad?" It came to her now up the dark well of the staircase. "Hasn't it been a wonderful day?"

"Just fine," Wilma said. "Francy's waiting for you, Maureen. He's feeling much better today."

"Is he? Oh, but that's simply gorgeous! Don't you think he'll be able to get up soon, Mrs. Konrad?"

"So Dr. O'Grady says. I think you've laughed him back to good health! I want to thank you," she said, and gave Maureen a hug, because the girl was so appetizing that it really was difficult not to do so.

But a little later, darning socks in her room, Wilma felt little of the confidence she had simulated. Francy's health seemed better, it was true, and he put on a great show of cheerfulness; but there was something about his whole attitude towards life which both puzzled and frightened Wilma. He seemed so resigned, for one thing. Ever since he had turned up that night, looking more dead than alive, and asked meekly if he could go to bed, he simply had—well, let things happen to him. Not once had he protested or complained; scarcely had he made a suggestion of his own. He gave the impression—it broke Wilma's heart to have to admit it—he gave the impression of a defeated man.

She sighed deeply and let the sock that she had been darning drop to her lap. Sitting there with her glance set through the window on the elm tree in full leaf, she thought back on that night of his return. She had been sitting with Adolph going over household accounts (for they had returned from Atlantic City only recently and things had had to be straightened out), when the doorbell gave a ring. Even at the time it had struck her that it was a diffident sort of ring, as though the person out there was not quite sure whether he would be admitted. A moment later Hauptman had come into the room, his phlegmatic face for once enlivened by emotion, and had announced:

"Mr. Francy has come home!"

She had run out into the hallway, to find Francy sitting on one of the two big chairs that flanked the doorway. He looked so sick, her first thought had been that he was actually dying. Pale and drawn was his face; his eyes stared out from deep sockets; he did not even rise from the chair, but just looked up and gave her a smile. And then it was that he had spoken those words that she knew she would never forget; she could hear them now, pronounced in the shaky voice of a little boy asking a favor that might not be granted:

"Please, Mama, may I go to bed? . . ."

Wilma took out her handkerchief and dabbed at her eyes, for the tears came a little quicker, now that she was no longer young. All her life she had been a dry-eyed woman, and she had prided herself upon it. Yet are there not times, she thought, when a woman has a right to weep, and surely one of those times is when she sees a loved one broken! A bare week before, when Adolph returned from that fateful bank meeting where the old Konrad and Son had passed out of being, she had read defeat in his eyes also. But that was not total defeat; Adolph would fight on for a long while to come. With Francy there

227

was no hope of recovery from the blow he had been dealt, and she understood that with her mother's heart that was as incapable of reasoning as it was incapable of error.

Weeks had passed since then, desperate weeks, painful weeks. Slowly, oh, so slowly, Francy's body had struggled back to health, almost as though it were unaided by any effort of the will. A double heart attack it was that had lain him low in Arizona and there were times when Wilma wondered if Francy were not just waiting for the third attack which would release him from the battle. Sick as he was, he had wanted to see no doctor except O'Grady, had even declined O'Grady's own suggestion that a specialist be called in. Was it, thought Wilma, because he wanted O'Grady to feel that he did not hold him responsible for his condition? That would have been so like Francy! Or perhaps, she thought, there was a deeper motive in his refusal: that half-understood desire to complete the circle that is inherent in all human beings. By ending his illness under the ineffective care of the man who had created it, he would, in a certain sense, have given unity to his life.

Then came the night when she learned for the first time that it was not only the failure of his poetry that was tormenting Francy. He had passed a restless day, and it was with feelings of misgiving that she had bidden him good night. She woke up suddenly, hearing him moaning and calling out in his sleep. Hurrying to his room, she found that he had thrown himself out of bed; he lay on the floor, still moaning and mumbling, and the name that he was speaking was "Helen." Then Wilma knew. In fact she realized that she had known all along, but until now had refused to accept the knowledge. The whole past formed itself into an understandable pattern.

She had realized then that she was too weak to fight alone for Francy's recovery. He himself did not help her; nor could Adolph give help, for between him and Francy stood the old wall of misunderstanding. She must seek an ally on the outside, and as luck would have it, there happened to be an ally handy. Through what strange chance was it that she had just met Maureen McKenna for the first time? In McKenna's house it had been, which likewise she had seen for the first time, since McKenna never had invited them there previous to his appointment as general manager. But no sooner had she heard Maureen laugh than

228

Wilma understood her potential usefulness and, at the risk of Adolph's displeasure, asked the girl to drop in on her at Drexel Boulevard.

She did not know to this day if Francy had been taken by Maureen or if he let their friendship develop mainly in order to please Wilma. One never knew anything about Francy. At any rate he seemed to like the girl, and Maureen certainly liked him, and there was no doubt that Francy's health had improved since she had taken to dropping in on him in the late afternoons.

As Wilma listened to them laughing and chatting away, a new hope had germinated in her heart: a hope whose realization would benefit not only her darling Francy but the family as a whole, whose position of late had been so decidedly weakened. And it was the good of the family that always had been Wilma's first concern! Just as William's marriage to a Hastey had given the Konrads prestige in 1905, so might Francy's union with Maureen serve the same purpose in 1920. Reasoning instinctively, as ever had been her way, Wilma knew that the days of power of the big families were already over, and that the future belonged to the managers, to the technicians, to those who ran the businesses conceived by the geniuses of another day—in other words, to men like McKenna. . . .

There were footsteps in the corridor and then a knock sounded on her door: firm, confident, hopeful. She went to open and saw Maureen standing there, a warm smile on her face.

"Oh, Mrs. Konrad, Francy has something to say to you. He thinks that it's quite important."

She took Maureen's arm and walked with her the few steps to Francy's door, a feeling of expectancy struggling with her inner disquietude. She knew that this was what she had wanted, but now that it had come, could she be sure that it was for the best? Did one ever really know what was for the best for one's loved ones? Her thoughts flew back to that far distant evening in a Cambridge inn, when she had promised another son that she would support his marriage. That very decision, she now saw, had brought tragedy into the family.

From his bed Francy stretched out his two hands, and Wilma took the left one, Maureen the right. His gentle gaze went from one woman to the other as he told them:

"I hope we three will always remain such good friends, for we shall be seeing a lot of each other in the future. . . ."

Wilma looked deep into Francy's eyes. What did she see there? Happiness? Resignation? Despair? She did not know. Perhaps she would never know.

part three 1950

THE BUYERS

one

"Good gracious, Frankie! If you were just sixty-five years older, I swear I would have taken you for your grandfather!"

Frank Konrad moved his glance from the club car's window, first to a leather portfolio with a bee stamped on its surface, then to the owner of the portfolio, Bee Konrad herself. He leaped up and held out his hand.

"Why, I didn't know that you were on this train, Aunt Bee! I didn't even know that you were in the East."

"Yes," Bee said, shaking hands in her efficient way, "I had to make a trip to New York for the Illinois Women's Political League. William called me up there to give me the bad news about your grandfather. I can tell you, it was a shock, Frankie, even though he is ninety-one years old! He's always been so full of life, I never got used to the idea that he'd have to die one day, like everybody else. I suppose you're going to Chicago to say good-by to him?"

Frank nodded, his glance through the train window set on a herd of cattle, the same sort of herd that had contributed to the build-up of the family fortune.

"I had a phone call from Uncle William too, and just made the Capitol in Philadelphia. It's six years since I've seen Grandfather. And come to think of it, Aunt Bee, it must be about six years since I've seen you."

"That's right," said Bee. "You passed through Chicago in '44 on your way to becoming a hero in the Pacific."

"Aunt Bee, now listen," said Frank, watching her as she stood there with a brief case in hand, on her face the harassed expression of *a woman who does things*. "You are not making a political speech today. Do me a favor and lay off that hero stuff."

233

"Well, you *were* a hero, whether you like it or not. That's how we think of you, Frankie Konrad, and you'd better know it." (Bee always sounded as if she was trying to catch a vote, and as a matter of fact, she usually was.) "Anyway," she went on, "I'm delighted that you are traveling out to Chicago. All of the family are coming home. As soon as I heard about your grandfather's stroke I called up Rupert at the embassy in Santo Pedro; he and Helen had already booked space north on Pan American. Cecilia and her two sons are motoring east from California. The Konrads are gathering from the four corners! Your grandfather was a great man, Frankie—a great man and a great Chicagoan," Bee concluded, still sounding as though she were persuading a vacillating voter to support her party.

But just then Frank happened to glance at her, and he caught in Bee's face a look which was not that of a professional politician in the least; it was a look of pride and honorable satisfaction which made Frank want to squeeze her arm and smile at her. Perhaps his Aunt Bee did make herself a little silly with her hysterical political activities, but she was a person to be respected, a person who had dedicated her life to something outside herself!

"How about having a cigarette with me?" he suggested, and pointed at the next chair.

"Oh gracious, no! What would it look like for a woman in public life to be seen smoking in a club car with a young man, tall, dark, and handsome, with flashing eyes and bushy eyebrows? You know, Frankie, you don't look one iota like your father! My brother Francy had such a delicate face—almost like a flower. But yours is all determination and fire, just like your grandfather's face in those early photographs! We're counting on you to live up to the Konrad tradition of success. But what I don't see"—Bee fixed her nephew disapprovingly—"what I don't see is why you had to take this job in the East—in Philadelphia. If you'd asked your cousin, William, Jr., I'm sure he'd have found a place for you in his laboratory, not half an hour from the Loop. Everyone says it's one of the finest private laboratories in the country—and I can't imagine anything more inspiring than to work for a real genius like William, Jr., a man recognized as one of the leading inventors in America."

234

Frank's heavy eyebrows drew together.

"Don't worry about me," he said, a little curtly. "I'm getting on all right. I'm in no immediate danger of starvation, I promise you."

But then he saw that Aunt Bee was smiling, and he made himself smile too.

"Yes, you really are Adolph Konrad's grandson, there's no doubt of it!" said Bee. "If there was one thing that made him hopping mad, it was having somebody tell him what to do, or even volunteer advice. I can just hear him yelling, 'I run my own business, and no one's going to tell me how to do it!'—those big lips of his working in and out. I guess no one's going to tell you how to do things either, are they, Frankie?"

"Well, I'm afraid they are—for a while yet," said Frank, laughing now. "My chief in the chem lab at Snyder's, where I work, keeps telling me every day. There's no maybe about it either! I'm one of a dozen chemists working in a room about five times the size of the parlor at Sans Souci, and it's only after hours that I can do research on my own. Since Mother's death, I've had to think of the little problem of making my living."

"I understand, Frankie." Bee's voice took on the confidential tone befitting the elderly female relative who is in on all the family secrets. "Your mother, Maureen, was a darling—a gay little darling—but she just had no idea of the value of money, did she? Strange, when you remember that she was the daughter of Angus McKenna! Your Scotch grandfather would have turned in his grave if he'd known how she threw dollars about. It shocks me—yes, it does—to think of one of Adolph Konrad's grandsons going through life with scarcely a cent that he can call his own."

"I wouldn't be too shocked," said Frank, patting her shoulder. "Seeing that everyone's always telling me I'm like Grandfather, there's no reason to think I couldn't make money too, if I wanted it enough. It just happens that my interests are in a different field. This job at Snyder's is a springboard to big things ahead, and my work there's darned interesting. If only I could move the whole lab to Chicago, lock, stock, and barrel, I'd be perfectly happy. I do miss Chicago, believe me. What's more," he added, a little shyly, "I miss all of you a lot."

235

"And we miss you," said Bee, looking gratified. She cast a glance at her watch. "Oh gracious, I must be getting back to my drawing room! I've got my secretary along with a bunch of letters to be signed before we get into Chicago. You can't imagine," she said, sighing voluptuously, "the constant burden on a woman in public life!"

"In that case," suggested Frank, "why not sit down and relax?"

"Oh, the very idea! Get thee behind me! Get thee behind me, I say!" And tucking her portfolio beneath her arm, Bee was about to charge down the aisle, when a thought halted her. "Oh, Frankie, I'd better warn you. There's someone on this train you certainly won't want to see; I've just made a point of cutting him dead. Do you remember a man who used to work in William, Jr.'s laboratory called Smedlin—a Jewish refugee from Czechoslovakia?"

"Jan Smedlin? I should say I do! Why, Jan and I were great friends once upon a time—when I was about fifteen, to be exact, and used to come out to Chicago and stay with Grandfather."

"A lot of things have changed since then," Bee remarked dryly. "One of them is your friend Smedlin. Neither William, Jr., nor any of us in Chicago, speak to him any more. He's become insufferable! And to think of all that William did for him—apart from actually snatching him out of a concentration camp and bringing him to Chicago! Take my advice and give him a wide berth, Frankie."

Frank, left alone with his cigarette, decided at once that he would track down Jan Smedlin and say hello. He could not imagine Smedlin as "insufferable," even though he remembered now having heard that the little Czech inventor had gone lamentably to seed. There had been some sort of quarrel or misunderstanding between Smedlin and William, Jr., with the result that William had thrown him out of the Konrad Laboratory, where he had been working ever since Frank met him in '39.

Frank had always felt that he owed Smedlin a great debt, for through him it was that he had first been introduced to science as an abstract conception; speaking to Smedlin, the boy Frank had come to share that half-mystical emotion which was destined to play so prominent a part in his later years. Smedlin, scarcely heard of for six years or more, was still the driving influence in the adult life of Frank Konrad.

236

He finished his drink, left a tip for the waiter, and made his way out of the club car. Pleasantly excited at the prospect of the meeting, he sent his glance over the Pullman, expecting at any second to catch sight of a wiry little body, a narrow high-domed head, pale eyes whose glance seemed to penetrate through solid objects. That was Smedlin, as Frank remembered him, and when, in the third Pullman car, he caught sight of the Smedlin of today, he realized that there indeed had been a change.

Not so much on the outside, to be sure: on the outside this was the same old Smedlin, all his black hair still there, on his back one of those green gabardine suits so favored by central Europeans. And yet somehow this *was* a different Smedlin! The way he sat gave it away (slumped in his seat, like an old man), and the harsh lines by the mouth, and the unshaven chin. He was, thought Frank, like a bombed-out town that one has known in its sunnier days. And aware of this, Smedlin hid behind a pair of large dark glasses and held up before him a tall magazine as a second shield between the world and himself.

"Jan!"

No movement from the little figure seated bolt upright by the window: Smedlin's attention was still concentrated on the open pages of the picture magazine. Below the black glasses the thin mouth seemed to harden a trifle; it formed a bitter line in the ash-gray face, cruel and impersonal as a knife wound.

"Come on, pal. You can't get away with this. Don't say you don't remember Frank Konrad."

Then Smedlin moved his head a little and the black circles were focused upon Frank. The mouth moved, but the voice issuing forth was lifeless; it had nothing to do with the vivacious foreign voice that Frank remembered so well. Even the accent had vanished, and Smedlin now spoke in careful, correct English.

"I remember all the Konrads," he said. "And they remember me. What's more, they turn their back because they recognize me as an enemy. They're right! You shouldn't underestimate anyone—not even me."

Frank might have smiled, had he not known that a smile would offend Smedlin. "Persecution mania," he decided, thinking of the dark glasses, the hostility, the way Smedlin sat shrunk into his corner, like an animal at bay. And he thought of the Czech's tragic past: the Nazi concentration camp, the loss of a beloved family, the long years of suspense. He was sorry for the unhappy fellow, and with an instinctive gesture reached out to press the thin arm beneath the gabardine.

"Come off it, pal! Let's get this straight: I'm not your enemy—I thought that we were pretty good friends once upon a time."

"Friends?" Smedlin repeated the word doubtfully, as though it were a long time since he had had occasion to use it. "Why yes, we did use to be friends," he admitted, and though his expression had not changed, his voice sounded less flat, a bit more like the voice of a living man. "If you want to know the truth, I was thinking of you only this morning and wondering if you might be coming to Chicago because of the old fellow's stroke."

"Ah, so you keep up with the news!"

"Yes, everything to do with you successful Konrads interests me. Anyway," said Smedlin, "I didn't have to be much of a sleuth. 'Stock Yards King Stricken at 91,' is how the *Mirror* had it."

"Just how they would have it! 'Stock Yards King'! What a way of describing a great man, God damn it!"

"Don't blow your top now!" Smedlin gave a laugh. "I see you've still got that old Konrad temper. But there's no need to get mad: no one as rich as Adolph Konrad gets dismissed in just five words. They went on to string out the usual line. You know: last of the Chicago pioneers, man of vision, great public benefactor—though who Adolph Konrad ever benefacted except himself, God only knows. You're looking shocked, Frankie. Have I committed lèse-majesté?"

Frank bit his lips as he fought down his feeling of outrage. He was determined not to let his temper get the better of him with Smedlin, and he well realized there was no cause; nowadays one had to be a prig to think of one's kin as a little superior to most other people. And yet, despite all reasoning, that sense of family loyalty persisted: it formed an integral part of his character.

"So you're still living in Chicago?" he said, without answering Smedlin's question. "If you don't look out you'll become one of the city's oldest inhabitants, Jan."

238

Smedlin for the first time took off his dark glasses, and as he gazed at Frank the faintest of smiles curved his lips. Now Frank saw that that farseeing look was still in his eyes, the look which he had always associated with men whose talent it is to invent. Smedlin never seemed to be looking *at* an object, but through it and beyond. Without glasses he was much more like himself: his face looked less desperate, less ravaged. It was almost kindly.

"Yes," he said, "I guess I've become a real Chicagoan, Frankie. I have a house—I even have a housekeeper. Do you know who? My own sister Katrine from Prague!"

"But, Jan, I thought that your sister . . . wasn't Katrine . . . ?"

"No, she wasn't," said Smedlin, still smiling vaguely. "That's the strange thing. As you know, I always believed that all my family had been wiped out by the Germans. Well, after the war one day, I got a letter from the IRO saying that there was someone in a DP camp who was looking for Jan Smedlin. Believe it or not, it was my own Katrine, who by a miracle had survived a whole series of camps and prisons! I managed to arrange for her to join me in the States."

"Gosh, that is swell!" cried Frank, and in his voice Smedlin could not have failed to detect delight at another person's good fortune. "And what are you doing with yourself, Jan? Still inventing?"

"Hell no!" Smedlin gave a little laugh, meant to be casual, but which sounded more like a broken sob. "I gave all that up years ago. I don't invent. I don't even invent excuses for not inventing."

"Oh, I'm sorry to hear that," Frank said, regretting his tactlessness. "I saw my cousin William in New York not long ago, but he never said a word about your having given up inventing."

"Oh, he didn't?" Smedlin shot out the question like a projectile. "Well, he ought to know, if anyone. He's what one might call an expert on the subject."

From one second to another the short-lived amiability had fled, and Smedlin's pale, harassed face began to work. Frank remembered now that Jan had always had a nervous twitch in his right eye, though when he had known him as a kid, before the war, it had been much less noticeable; with the years this nervous disability had become aggravated, so that now it looked as if his old friend were winking at him violently and continually. The effect was unpleasant to an extraordinary degree.

"But what the devil really happened between you and William?" The words burst out spontaneously. "Why, you two used to swear by one another! I remember how William was always telling people that you were the best man in his laboratory, and I thought of you as close friends. I wish you'd give me the dope, Jan. What's the great secret anyway?"

"The secret?" Smedlin echoed the words in a curious, tense voice, as though he were putting a question to himself. His right eye gave another violent twitch that for a moment contorted his whole countenance. "Well, why don't you go ask the great William, Jr.?" he demanded abruptly, slipping the dark glasses back on. "He's the proper source of information, not I. There are certain situations that one does not go into, out of respect for one's own feelings. Yes, let us put it that way: out of respect for one's own feelings. I forbid you to ask me again —that is, if we ever meet again, which is doubtful."

The train was sliding past the first buildings of Chicago. Houses, monumental in their ugliness, reared themselves directly beside the track, and through their uncurtained windows one could see people eating their breakfasts or scolding their children or dressing to go out to work. The porter passed down the aisle, calling out in a bored voice, "Getting into Chicago, ladies and gentlemen." One felt that had he been announcing their arrival in Valhalla or at the river Styx he would have used exactly the same tone.

Frank said good-by to Smedlin and walked back to his car with a feeling of relief. And yet their inconclusive conversation had left him with an unpleasant taste in his mouth, gripped by a vague uneasiness. For a second he experienced something like apprehension as he remembered Smedlin's look of hatred while pronouncing those words, "the great William, Jr." But then Frank asked himself how this derelict of a man with the spotted gabardine suit could possibly injure his former employer, not to mention the rest of the family. What was Smedlin, after all, but an unsuccessful inventor consumed by envy of a famous colleague, and probably laboring under some imaginary grievance? The psychopathic wards were full of people like that! Little harm could they do a family as powerful as the Konrads, respected by all, who had won the fame and success that they deserved.

two

So here was Chicago again, just as hot, just as noisy—just as crowded and dirty and lusty as Frank Konrad remembered it! He was happy to be here. Oh, there were other cities much pleasanter, like Baltimore, for instance, with its faded charm, and Washington of the monumental avenues, but Chicago was *his* city and he loved it. He loved the violence and confusion of it, loved its lake front and its parks, loved the wind that blew across the water from Michigan, and even that other wind which blew from the southwest and carried with it the odor of the Stock Yards. His family had helped build this city into what it was today, and he was proud of the city because he was so proud of his family.

As he taxied down Michigan, and then southwards towards Drexel, he asked himself why he had not come back here in all these years. He had told his aunt that it was because his job kept him in the East, but that was not really the reason. He had stayed away, he decided, because he did not want to be taken as the poor relative, come to see what he could get, or as the war hero, expecting to be specially favored. He had wanted to make his own way, as his grandfather had done three quarters of a century before, and only now, after proving to himself that he could do it, did the thought of returning here for good appeal to him.

Sans Souci, Frank discovered, had not changed with the years. The surrounding district had got a little blacker, a little poorer, but the big house itself remained in excellent repair and the driveway was as well swept as ever. Hauptman, answering the doorbell, stared at Frank as if the summer heat had gone to his head—or as if a ghost had stepped out of the taxi.

"Glad to see you, Hauptman! Is there anything wrong?"

"No, Mr. Frank. Nothing wrong." The old man came out of his daze. "It's just your looks, Mr. Frank. So like the boss!"

"Well, it's I, all right," Frank assured him. "How is the old gentleman, Hauptman?"

"A little better today. But he is a sick man, Mr. Frank. Mighty sick," said Hauptman, and the senile tears came to his eyes.

Frank picked up his suitcase and, despite Hauptman's objections, carried it to his old room on the first floor, the room that had belonged to his father before him. As he let his glance pass over the white dresser with the lace cloth, the lithograph of Goethe and the glass-fronted bookcase (its shelves still filled with Francy's books), he felt, as always, strangely moved. Between these four walls his father had spent most of his short life, and then, as now, the morning sunbeams had slanted through the glass, and in the branches of the elm the sparrows had sat chirping and preening their feathers. New leaves, new sparrows, and a new Francis Konrad watching them from behind the window! Life went on, repeating itself, without monotony.

When he had unpacked, Frank made his way downstairs to the parlor, stopping on the landing to raise the visor of the armored crusader, which had fallen down over his face. He had not taken five more steps when he heard a clatter, and looked around to see that the visor had fallen down again, just as it had been doing for the last sixty years. In the parlor, too, everything was the same. The huge armchair and sofas stood guard in their old places; the ornate bronze lamps weighted down the consoles and tables upon which they had been placed decades before; in its usual corner stood the marble statue of that great carriage horse, Bismarck I. The silence of the grave reigned in the parlor, and Frank found himself tiptoeing across the heavy carpet, as though a single sound might disturb his dead grandmother eying him from the wall, or enrage the prize bull, from whose mounted head a pair of glass eyes followed his every movement.

But then there reached him the sound of quick footsteps, a laugh, a bright voice calling out his name. The sliding doors were pushed open and into the parlor stepped as fantastic a being as if the armored crusader had come to life and clattered down the stairs. A pair of scarlet Chinese trousers encased her legs below an orange sash, while the

242

upper part of her costume consisted solely of a band no wider than
necessary, tied tightly about her breasts. On top of her head the young
woman's black hair was piled tier after tier, resembling a miniature
Chinese pagoda. It was, indeed, an amazing getup, considering the
morning hour, the Edwardian setting, and particularly the fact that
the master of the house lay stricken in the room above. But once he
had got over his first shock, Frank was not surprised; he knew that his
cousin Cosima, ever since she was a child, had done exactly what came
into her head.

"Holy smokes!" he said, and began to laugh. "If it isn't my favorite
clown! What on earth are you doing in this house, Cosima? And what
on earth are you doing in that garb?"

She snatched his two hands and pressed them delightedly; it was
clear she had achieved the effect desired.

"It *is* sensational, isn't it?" she said, looking down at herself in admiration. "But if you live in a morgue, as I've been doing this last
week, you've got to dress up as a buffoon or as a corpse. It happens that
a shroud doesn't suit me. Besides, I must live up to my reputation, or
my friends, and visiting cousins like you, might be disappointed. I
might even disappoint Rupert and Helen, much as they disapprove of
their daughter. It seems to have become my profession: shocking people, I mean."

"Isn't it rather an old-fashioned one?" asked Frank. "Gay twenties
and *Green Hat* and all that."

"Ah, that's the trouble." For a moment Cosima's attractive countenance clouded over. "I really was born out of my era, as you say, but
it doesn't matter too much. We Konrads have to make a roaring success at something, and as I couldn't attain the intellectual level of you
and William, Jr., nor cared to scale social heights like Aunt Cecilia and
Gladys, I decided to make what the French call a *succès de scandale*.
You must admit that I succeeded, though, believe me, it gets a bit
wearing at times. Now let's ask Hauptman to bring us two nice cool
drinks, and tell each other all about ourselves."

She rang the bell and, when Hauptman appeared, told him to bring
a whiskey and soda for her cousin and an orangeade for herself.
(Cosima was a strict teetotaler, a fact which could have surprised no

good psychologist who knew she was Helen's daughter.) Drinks ordered, she made Frank sit down on the damask-covered sofa near the statue of the lamented Bismarck.

"Frankie, you're looking wonderful!" she cried, studying his face in the light sifting through the heavy lace curtains. "Handsomer than ever. I bet those Philadelphia girls are crazy about you! Now tell me, is there anyone—in particular?"

"Well, yes. I guess you'd call Harriet Roberts someone in particular. Chances are I'm going to marry her."

"You're *not!* Oh hell, just my luck!" Cosima groaned. "It seems my fate to meet people too late. I've always been dying to marry someone like Grandfather, and you certainly fill the bill, with those flashing eyes and bushy eyebrows of yours. I am passionately in love with Grandfather, you know."

"Isn't he a bit old for you?" asked Frank. He knew the remark was in the worst of taste, but Cosima had a knack of making another person's speech as irresponsible as her own.

"Oh, I don't believe in age!" She leaned back in the sofa, a flirtatious smile on her lips. "A man like Grandfather hasn't any age; he's sick and dying now, yet in his lucid moments he's younger than you or I. But, Frankie, you must tell me about this Harriet person. Is she beautiful? Is she clever? Is she chic?"

"Yes, she's all of those. She happens to be a very successful businesswoman too—got a beaut of a job in an advertising agency at about double my salary. The best way I can describe Harriet is by saying that she'd get on here—with the family, I mean."

"I'm all for her, in that case. You know, Frankie, the more I see of people, the more I appreciate us Konrads. We have our faults, but blood's thicker than water and I've become terribly family-proud since my third marriage. If all my husbands had been Konrads, I'd be a happier woman today."

Frank laughed, but those remarks of Cosima's had struck a responsive chord. He felt suddenly quite close to her, despite her erratic behavior, her amazing garb, her obvious desire to shock him and everybody else. They were both Konrads, and they understood that the Konrads were somehow different from other people: not more intelligent, perhaps, not necessarily more talented, but certainly possessing a special quality of their own! Since childhood he had had a love and veneration of his relatives that was typical of a fatherless boy.

Hauptman had not yet arrived. Cosima, growing conscious of the long delay, jumped up and gave another jab at the table bell. It was an old-fashioned bell depicting two cherubs whose kiss produced an electric contact when their heads were united, and this time Cosima kept them kissing for a good fifteen seconds.

"What on earth is Hauptman doing with those drinks?" she cried irritably. "Hatching them out of eggs? He's always been the worst butler in Chicago, but since Grandfather's sickness, his standard's sunk even further."

"How impatient you are!" said Frank, catching her arm to pull her back to the sofa. "Haven't we got all the time in the world?"

"Yes, but I'm used to getting things when I want them. If I don't get things when I want them, well, then I don't want them at all." For a moment Cosima's pleasant face took on a determined, almost aggressive expression that reminded Frank of old Adolph—or of himself. "Hauptman may be living in a senile daze, but the fact remains that he gets a good salary. We have the right to expect service."

"Be a good girl now," said Frank, a bit shocked at hearing an old friend spoken of so heartlessly. "You haven't even told me yet what you have been doing in Chicago in the middle of July, and living here, rather than in your own house."

"Oh well, it's because of this damn divorce of mine," said Cosima, her immediate compulsion forgotten. "The case is coming up in court this week."

"Divorce! My God, Cosima, another one?"

"Yes, isn't it the limit? Stan and I used to get on so well, too; we could laugh together at any old time. Then he loses his sense of humor and goes suing me for divorce! Can you imagine that he's even asked for the custody of the child, that steamship purser that I turned into a playboy! I don't think I'll marry my lovers in the future, Frankie. Too exhausting, too expensive. And what's the point?"

"I quite agree with you. I don't know why you should."

"Oh, you always were such a help, Frankie!" She reached out and squeezed his hand. "I've made enough genuflections to conventionality. You agree with me?"

Frank put back his head and laughed. He roared with laughter.

"Oh, Cosima, you are wonderful! Genuflections to conventionality! Wow!"

The more he thought of Cosima's marriages, the more he had to laugh. One of her husbands having been a boxer, another a jewelry-store clerk, the third a ship's purser, those genuflections of Cosima's must have been accompanied by an energetic thumbing of the nose. All in all it would have been more conventional for her to live in sin, which no doubt was why she chose marriage.

Cosima jumped up for the third time and gave a jab at the bell. It was clear from her expression that her patience, if any, was at an end, and Frank was relieved when Hauptman at that moment walked into the room. He was carrying a tray, but Frank saw that he had forgotten both the orangeade and the ice; somehow he had been almost sure this would happen.

"Good Lord, Hauptman, what *have* you been doing?" Cosima's voice was taut with exasperation. "We've been waiting for you half an hour."

To Frank's surprise, all the good humor had drained from Cosima's face; her eyes flashed almost menacingly at the old butler. However, Hauptman, being hard of hearing, did not seem greatly impressed.

"Lunch is at one o'clock," he said, having misunderstood her. "Cook says she can't get it ready before. There's no point insisting."

"I didn't say anything about lunch. I asked why you took half an hour with those drinks."

"Half an hour? Lunch can't be ready in half an hour," said Hauptman surlily. "We've always had it at one as long as I've been in this house."

Now there actually were tears in Cosima's eyes; Frank could see that she was biting her lips to keep them back.

"*Ya, ya,* always one o'clock sharp," Hauptman mumbled. And he walked out of the parlor.

"The fool!" Cosima shouted. "Oh, the blithering old fool!"

She took two steps after him, then stopped dead, her eyes on his retreating, bent figure. She was shaking with anger; her lips were working and Frank would not have been surprised if in another moment she had burst into tears. She carried her finger to her mouth and bit it hard.

"Cosima, for heaven's sake, what's the matter? Was it you who was talking about a sense of humor a moment ago?"

She turned her head slowly, and then slowly, very slowly, a smile crept into her face. Her tense posture relaxed and she walked back to their sofa, swinging her hips.

"And believe it or not, I don't really want a drink at all," she said, making fun of herself in her old way. "Take a lesson, Frankie. It's not always easy to be a Konrad—and at the same time to act like Mr. or Mrs. Jones."

A little after noon Uncle William arrived, looking very much like "the man of distinction" in his dark business suit, black necktie, and carefully groomed gray hair. William had recently been made first vice-president of Hastey Amalgamated, the giant packing concern which had absorbed half a dozen competitors, including (just before Angus McKenna's death) Konrad and Company itself; the new honor seemed to have accentuated the qualities of solidity and conservatism that he had possessed since he was a baby. He was accompanied by Aunt Gladys, who had fetched him at the Stock Yards in their Lincoln limousine and who, on catching sight of Frank, burst out with the usual:

"My goodness, Frankie, you certainly do take after your grandfather!"

"So it seems," said Frank, a little impatiently. But then he laughed and said, "I have my work cut out, all right. Everyone's expecting me to be another Adolph Konrad, and it isn't going to be easy."

"Well, mind you don't disappoint us," said William, looking his nephew up and down. "We're counting on you, and according to Bill, Jr., we've put our money on the right horse. It seems you've got a promising career ahead of you in science. Bill, Jr., was much impressed with your academic work at M.I.T. (Swell job, your walking off with that science award, by the way. Congratulations, my boy.) And he liked the paper of yours that they printed in the *Journal of Chemistry* —thought there was a lot of interesting possibilities there. That reminds me," went on William, depositing his dignified bulk in an armchair that looked as if it had been fashioned to his measurements, "he's very anxious to see you and show you over the laboratory. Wants to talk to you about something important. I suppose you know that he's doing confidential war work now, with government backing?"

"Yes, I am not a complete ignoramus," Frank said. "I'd very much like to see the lab, Uncle William—and to see William," he added, with as much conviction as possible, for he knew that his uncle was aware the two cousins had never got on very well.

"Good. Then how about driving out to Hadon Heights tomorrow? I'll tell Bill to expect you for luncheon about one o'clock. And now I suppose we'd better go upstairs and see the patient. Quite a surprise it was, his taking this turn for the better. When I sent you that telegram we thought it was all over—and as a matter of fact, O'Grady did too."

"O'Grady! Don't tell me that old horse doctor is still looking after Grandfather! He must be over eighty himself!"

"Eighty-two," said Aunt Gladys. "And he doesn't know more than he did half a century ago!" Her eyes narrowed, giving her that Chinese look which had always made one wonder what thoughts were passing in her head. "It's strange that your grandfather won't see another doctor—won't even let us call in a specialist. Why, it's almost as if that O'Grady had some power over him!"

"Stranger still," put in Cosima as she gave a hitch at her silk trousers, supported only by a sash, "stranger still that he hasn't yet managed to kill Grandfather off. It seems that when he woke up this morning—Grandfather, I mean—he yelled for his breakfast as if his whole illness was a joke. Gives you some respect for the Konrad constitution, doesn't it?"

"Er—yes," said William, who quite obviously disapproved of Cosima. "Well, should we go upstairs?"

In his old room on the second floor Adolph Konrad was lying in bed: in the great double bed where he had slept for the last sixty-odd years, in which three of his children had been conceived and in which his wife had died. There was, thought Frank, an aloof expression on his powerful old face as the four of them filed into the room; it was as if his thoughts were far away and came back only reluctantly to the present. And yet he looked remarkably virile for a man who had been given up for lost two days before. True, his skin was the color of old parchment, but in the eyes turned on his visitors was some of the old fire, and his great white eyebrows seemed to bristle with vitality.

"Hello there," he said (and if it was an old man's voice, it still had a great deal of body to it). "Come to see the corpse, eh vhat?"

Frank was keenly conscious of his aunt's and uncle's discomfiture at this unexpected greeting, and even Cosima, that *enfant terrible,* looked a bit put out. He was the only one who smiled at his grandfather's words, whereupon old Adolph's eyes circled the group to rest on him; as the light of recognition came into them, Frank thought he saw a pleased look appear in the old man's face.

"Vhy, it's Frankie! I'm glad to see you again, Frankie," he said, and slowly his hand moved forward across the counterpane.

Frank took it and held it in his a moment. It was weak, very weak. And cold. That was the first time since he had come into the room that he realized his grandfather did not have many days, perhaps not many hours, to live.

"They tell me you're a scientist—a chemical engineer. Is that right?" the old man asked.

"Yes, that's right," said Frank. "I have a job in a chemical laboratory in Philadelphia."

"You have, have you? Vell, dat's very interesting."

The old eyes were still on him, shrewd and merciless; they traveled down the length of his body and back to his face again. They were the eyes of a man used to dealing with many people, used to forming judgments and risking everything on the basis of his findings. His grandfather had built up the Konrad fortune through the shrewdness of those eyes.

"Tell me chust vhy you made up your mind to become a scientist," he said at last.

Frank had a hard time hiding his surprise. Adolph Konrad was on his deathbed, and he knew it. How was it, then, that he could have interest in a grandson, disappeared from his life six years before? But it was a serious question, deserving of a serious answer.

"I decided to go into science because our world's become a scientific world. Fifty years ago, or even twenty-five, I'd have gone into business, like you, Grandfather. Applied science is carrying on from where business management left off."

He was picking his words carefully, not sure how much Adolph could grasp, yet hoping to convey to the old man a true impression of himself. Time was short; he might not see his grandfather again. He had come to Chicago not only to say good-by, but also, he now realized, in the hope that this old man and he might get to know each other in the eleventh hour—seeing that everyone said they were so much alike.

But now William stepped forward, his face expressing dismay because of the tenure of the conversation. Conventionalminded as he was, he had expected a classical sickroom scene, with assurance to the patient that he was on the road to recovery, possibly a few suppressed sobs, stiff upper lips. He tapped Frank's shoulder with a meaningful shake of the head.

"That'll do for today, Frankie," he whispered to him. "Father's pretty weak."

Adolph's glance swerved from Frank to his eldest son, and suddenly into his face flooded a look of unmistakable boredom and irritation. His great eyebrows hunched together in that ominous frown.

"Get out of de vay, Villiam! For Christ's sake, leave us alone!" he shouted so categorically that William took a few steps back, the long habit of filial obedience asserting itself even at that moment. He stood beside Gladys, unhappily fingering his black tie, like a little boy who has been reprimanded.

"That vas very interesting, vhat you said," Adolph went on after a moment, for his concentration had been disturbed. "I mean about science going on from vhere business management left off. I'd like to have a good talk mit you vone day, vhen I'm feeling a little stronger. Vill you come und see me?"

"Of course, Grandfather," said Frank. "I'm living in the house."

"Oh, you are? Fine. Fine. You come und see me vone morning alone. D'you understand—alone!" His glance sought William, standing by the wall, then returned to his grandson. "I've got an idea ve've got a lot to talk about, you und I."

Frank did not know why those words of his grandfather caused him pleasure. He had a feeling (it had come over him since he stepped into this room) that he had something to learn from this old man whom he took after in so many ways. From the moment their eyes met, he had felt that there was an understanding between them; and that his grandfather had felt it too, he was certain. Why, otherwise, should he have expressed a desire to see his grandson, knowing that his hours were numbered, knowing also that his children had come to say good-by from remote corners of the earth? Frank understood all at once that Adolph Konrad had something of importance to say, and that he had chosen him, rather than all the others, to whom to say it.

three

They drove up to the airport at midnight, just before the departure of the plane. As Rupert loathed waiting, and especially so in a public place, Hapgood had arranged for the car to call for them as late as possible. When they stepped out of the Packard with the United States coat of arms on the door, the loud-speaker was blaring:

"Pan American flagship for New York! *Avión Pan Americano para Nueva York!* All aboard, please!"

Hapgood came hurrying out of the waiting room, exuding an atmosphere of frenzied efficiency; his pale face gleamed in the southern night.

"No hurry, Mr. and Mrs. Konrad. No hurry at all. The luggage is on board and your passports have been stamped. That's what I'd call bully timing!"

He made a move to relieve Helen of her overnight bag, but she shook her head and began walking across the field. Hapgood slipped the ambassador's portfolio beneath his arm instead, and a moment later they were mounting the departure platform, Helen first, her husband and the secretary following.

"There's a photographer from the *Independencia* down to take your pictures, sir. I gave him the tip-off. You know how they appreciate these little scoops."

The aiming of the camera. The flash. *"Muchas gracias! Muchas gracias!* Happy landing, Mr. Ambassador!" The photographer faded into the night as Helen stepped onto the plane and looked about for the empty seats. She had made a plan of campaign as the pictures were being taken, and now she sat down quickly in a single seat in the rear of the cabin.

"Helen, there are two places together up in front. Let Hapgood here change seats with you."

"But I want to go to sleep right away." She did not look up, knowing that he could detect her lies. "Let me stay here, Rupert. We can change about in the morning."

She closed her eyes, precluding protests, just as the starboard propellers began to churn. Through narrowed eyes she saw Rupert and Hapgood taking the seats up forward, and in relief reached for the robe to drape about her knees; the end of it she threw across the overnight bag.

"Should I take care of that for you, madame?" It was the flight stewardess speaking. "It might be in your way there."

"No thanks. I like to keep it where I can get at it."

The other motors started with a roar and the lights in the cabin went out. Soon the big plane was moving down the runway in that cautious way that always reminded her of a duck waddling over dry land. Through her window she could see the lights of the Santo Pedro terminal glittering through the night and the shadowy forms of three men standing on the roof. Then the plane began to move faster, still faster, until suddenly the ground fell away and the great ship, become airborne, rose upwards with a roar of triumph.

Helen Konrad closed her eyes and relaxed in the comfortable seat. She tilted it slightly backwards. She was pleased to be off, and relieved that their departure from Santo Pedro had taken place so suddenly and on the whole painlessly; no last-minute change of plans, no farewell parties, not even any final arguments with Rupert. Last night that cable about his father, and here they were already, putting miles between themselves and a city she hoped never to see again. Not, to be sure, that Santo Pedro was an unattractive town; it was even charming in its haphazard way. But loneliness had been her portion there, loneliness and boredom, in spite of the unceasing round of entertainments which kept the diplomats rushing to each other's houses. Strange that, of all the contacts she had made, not one had ripened into friendship! No person really cared that she had left, nor was there a single man or woman in Santo Pedro whom she wished to see again. No wonder that she had backed Rupert's decision to take advantage of this forced trip to the States to apply for another post. Helen Konrad had not yet understood that her inability to find friends stemmed not from lack of opportunities but from causes deep within herself.

Helen moved her foot and touched the night bag lying underneath the robe. That brief contact gave her pleasure. The thought of the blue bag and its contents, lying there within such easy reach, was as reassuring as a mother's promise to her child. Reaching down beneath the robe, she felt its bulging surface, then withdrew her fingers quickly. No, the time had not come yet; it was pleasant to tantalize herself with the thought of the happiness to be found at the moment of her own choosing. Casting a glance forward, she reassured herself that her explorations beneath the robe had gone unnoticed. The position of her chair was strategically superb!

Rupert, she saw, was tugging at the lobe of his ear with that nervous gesture she knew so well, the gesture which meant that he was worrying, as usual, scheming for the future, planning how to make this unexpected journey work in with his private plans. His father never entered his thoughts, that was certain, though there was a perfectly good chance that they would arrive in Chicago to find him dead. No one entered Rupert's thoughts except Rupert Konrad, with whom he had been in love his whole life long! All the world might crumble away under a hail of atom bombs, but if Rupert Konrad survived as a leading citizen of the blasted planet, he would not give two thoughts to humanity's fate.

As Helen sat looking at the well-shaped head with the still thick gray hair, spotlighted in the tiny beam shining from the wall, she was overcome with a violent hatred. Her hatred for her husband was so intense that she pressed shut her eyes so as not to see him. She hated him for that nervous mind of his, ever turning in a spiritual vacuum, for his constant scheming to bring about his own petty advancement, for his detestable assumption that everyone and everything could be had for the buying. But in the last analysis she hated him because she herself was one of the people he had bought. Had she not hated herself so much, she could not have hated Rupert with the unbridled violence of an embittered woman.

Ah, now the moment had come, sooner than she had expected! She felt an uncontrollable desire for the medicine that would assuage the burning pain inside her, for the trustworthy ally that would deflect the dagger pointed at her heart. Reaching beneath the robe, she unzipped the night bag and drew forth the flask with the brown liquid showing through the slot in its cover. No one was watching. Most of the passengers were asleep; the stewardess had gone behind a curtained alcove, where she could be heard turning the pages of a magazine.

She drank. Tilting the flask upwards and controlling the flow with her tongue, Helen let the harsh spirit run into her mouth, and swallowed it in tiny gulps, growing larger as her palate accustomed itself to the shock. She drank long and deep, watching from the corner of her eye as the level registered through the oblong slot sank to the three-quarters mark. Then she drew the flask away, capped it, and slipped it underneath the blanket. Not a person had seen.

A pleasant feeling of lightheadedness gradually took possession of Helen. Those first draughts of liquor were like an antidote to the poison of hatred which had seemed to be gnawing at her internal organs; now she felt relieved, fortified, almost serene. She could gaze at her husband without experiencing that fierce revulsion of a moment earlier, could study his profile impersonally, and even reflect that, despite the hardness that had crept into his face, Rupert at sixty-five was still a good-looking man. Far from befuddled, she actively enjoyed this preliminary stage of inebriation, when her thoughts were clear and the pictures that sprang into her mind were sharp as a finely executed photograph, light and shade juxtaposed in harmonious patterns.

She drew apart the curtains and for a long moment sat gazing into the night. Their plane was sailing through a sky smooth as a black sheet sprinkled with powder; there was not a cloud to be seen, only the stars, thousands and thousands of them, forming intricate, cabalistic patterns. For a moment she could have believed that the plane was picking its way among those stars, so near did they seem in the clear southern night! They were like a shower of sparks from an exploding rocket . . . or like a handful of petals thrown up into the air. She imagined the white petals drifting silently down to earth, spinning and dancing as they fell. They landed in the fields and on the housetops. And a few of them settled in the black hair of a little girl, running laughing across an orchard and calling out "Mama! Mama!" as she ran. . . .

Cosima! She drew in her breath, concentrated her whole being on preserving the happy remembrance, on retaining before her eyes that charming scene which gave her pleasure each time it reappeared. When had the incident occurred? She could not remember. They had lived in so many countries, had seen blossoming fruit trees in so many parts of the world! And what had been Cosima's age? Six? Eight? Ten? That, also, she could not recall. She knew only that her memory was a true one, that sometime in the interminable past (which stretched behind her like a jumbled cinematograph film with its sequence hopelessly confused) there had been a smiling girl called Cosima running towards her across a meadow, with a shower of apple blossoms falling in her hair.

The airplane gave a lurch. They must have hit one of those unexpected air pockets which, she had often been told, were no source of danger, though she used to find them exceedingly alarming. The jolt shattered the picture before her eyes, sending the fragments flying into the night. Cosima was still there, still smiling. But what a different Cosima, and what a different smile! From one moment to another an oft-remembered scene built itself up around this new Cosima who stood gazing at her mother with that too knowing, too clever smile.

They were standing in Helen's bedroom, the two of them, and Helen had just confronted her daughter with a discovery she had made by the purest of chance: the discovery that the fourteen-year-old girl was carrying on a full-fledged love affair with the gardener's son. There was not the slightest doubt of it; indeed, Cosima herself made no effort to deny the accusation. Instead of protesting her innocence, she stood smiling at Helen, who, unable to make Cosima understand the monstrosity of her action, in final desperation announced her decision to divulge the unsavory facts to Rupert. And it was then that Cosima, still smiling—smiling straight into her mother's face, had said in her cold voice, which was not a little girl's voice at all:

"And what about those bottles, Mother—those bottles in your dresser drawer? Do you want *me* to tell Father about *them?*"

Today, in the plane, Helen's eyes closed in pain as she remembered her sensation of horror, remembered, too, her certain feeling that Cosima had already chosen the erratic path she was to follow throughout life. How had she guessed Helen's secret? Impossible to tell. She must have divined the existence of the bottles with the sure instinct by which she seemed able to guess each person's weakness and see how it could be turned to her own advantage. So here was yet another failure to be added to her past failures as an artist and as a daughter, as a mistress and as a wife! As a mother she had proved the worst failure of all. For what was to become of a child who resorted to blackmail, a child who cold-bloodedly let herself be seduced for the sake of the sensation, a child who never had shown respect for anything except money, and the power that money could buy?

Well, the intervening years had given the answer, thought Helen, still seeing Cosima's face with its cold smile, still hearing that voice, sarcastically cruel, yet bewitching also, as were so many things about Cosima. In those years their daughter had fulfilled the doleful promise of her youth. They had never been able to count on her, except to do the thing that was least expected, the thing that was most hazardous and in the worst of taste. As the years passed and scandal had followed scandal, Cosima had been a constant source of worry to them both: in Rupert's case because his daughter's behavior often threatened his own reputation and career; in her own case because each new proof of Cosima's wildness, each new escapade and love affair and sensational divorce, seemed a further indictment of herself as a parent and as a human being.

Helen roused herself with a start. She was aware of the stewardess standing by her chair, glance fixed on Helen in solicitude. No doubt the girl was wondering why this solitary passenger had not yet found sleep, but sat rigidly, staring out into the night. Perhaps she had seen something in Helen's face that made her aware of the nature of the comfort that was needed.

"Are you all right, madame? Would you like me to get you something to eat—or to drink? A little glass of sherry perhaps?"

"No, no," said Helen, coaxing a smile into her face. "I am quite all right. I have everything that I need."

She watched the stewardess as she busied herself rearranging someone's blanket, and she thought, Sherry! My God, sherry! That girl must have noticed my beautifully waved gray hair, my well-cut traveling costume, and somehow it struck her that a little glass of sherry would settle all my problems. If she only knew of the raging flames that are burning me inside, she'd realize that all the sherry in Spain couldn't quench the conflagration! But perhaps she is too young to understand—too young and too pure.

The girl disappeared again behind the partition, and when she had left, Helen took out her flask and drank deeply of the raw liquor that her whole system craved. (Wine and even champagne had come to disgust her in these last years.) As the new liquor took effect her painful feeling of tenseness vanished; she could feel her body relax. For a moment, but a moment only, a delightful sensation of well-being flooded over her, and the harassing thoughts were gone—gone, it would seem, beyond recall.

Suddenly she saw Cosima seated at the piano: Cosima, the child, again, age indefinite, locality of the scene also indefinite. There was a white bow in her black hair, and each time she jerked her head forward to study the notes the bow quivered, like the wings of a great butterfly. One-two-three, one-two-three, Helen could hear herself counting, and now once again she experienced the old feeling of excitement and expectancy. One day, perhaps, this little girl whom she was initiating into the world of music, this little girl whom she had baptized with the name of Wagner's wife, would grow up to be a pianist of note! That would make up for everything; it was her one remaining ambition. She could still see the child Cosima's hands moving stiffly, uncertainly, over the keyboard of the piano.

The piano . . . the piano. As always when she saw a piano, in reality or in her mind, Helen could hear a tune playing, but so distantly, so faintly, that she knew it might fade away at any moment. It was Beethoven's "Appassionata," once her favorite composition, in whose rendition she had perfected herself through years of hard practice. When she was preparing for what was to be her first concert, Madame Lubokova, her teacher, had selected it to head the program. How long ago had that been? Forty years? Forty-five? She had stopped remembering. In her head the melody ran on, weaving in and out of the hum of the motors like a fine golden thread. It seemed to her that the noise of the airplane was like background music—background music from that orchestra before which she had never played.

The features of Cosima faded. The tall girl seated at the instrument, hair down her back, white linen dress open at the throat, was not her daughter. It was herself. She saw her own fingers traveling over the keys and experienced again the tenseness, the ecstasy, the uneerie sensation that this music was issuing *through* her, almost without intervention on her part.

And now there was commencing the last movement of the composition, building up slowly to that perfect climax in which it seemed that all the music of the spheres had been let loose. Silence succeeded: a silence so heavy, so portentous, that the very air of the room seemed to weigh on her, as if charged with the power of the expended notes. Then at last the voice of Madame Lubokova, no longer critical today, no longer the solicitous voice of the beloved teacher, but the voice of an artist, moved by the performance of a fellow artist.

"That was beautifully played. Yes, Helen, you are . . . a true musician. Oh, my dear!"

The airplane was roaring in her ears. Now she could no longer hear the tune, not even faintly, and the sound of the motors had ceased to be the crashing of a mighty orchestra and become—just noise. She wanted to beat at those great metal cases so that she could listen to her music again. How could she be expected to make out such a distant tune behind the thunder of this mechanistic age? Was there no way to drown out the sound made by ten thousand iron horses so that one woman could listen to a melody?

258

Then she thought of the bottle. She brought it out and drank fiercely, until the brown liquid sank almost to the halfway mark. Even so the melody did not return. Only that incessant pounding of the motors, each throb a tiny hammer blow upon her brain. The music had fled, as it once had fled out of her own life. Whatever happened, she must bring it back, if only for a little while! She felt she could not go on living without it. She raised the flask and drank again, swallowing the crude liquor in gulps that burned her throat and stirred her blood into a tumult.

And at last she did hear the music! It was the "Appassionata" she heard, but it was not really the "Appassionata"; the music in the air sounded as tinny and mechanized as a tune issuing from a barrel organ. Yet there was the piano, and herself seated at the piano, clad in a shimmering evening gown! Who were these people sitting before her in rows, they also dressed in smart party clothes, their vacant glances focused upon her? They looked like an audience of dummies, their movements mechanical, their painted faces lacking in all expression. Then suddenly she recognized the scene, recognized also the profound feeling of defeat associated with that solitary occasion when she had played in public: the evening of the reception for the Princess Xenia in Chicago.

The music had ceased. In its place there now came another sound: the hollow sound of polite clapping. The dummies were striking together their hands in approval—not in approval of her playing (whose merits or demerits were far beyond their comprehension), but in approval of the fact that she *had* played, and played before them. They were applauding this token of her final surrender! Until that evening her music had been sacred: it had belonged to that small part of her life she had not allowed Rupert to touch. By playing before this audience of gaping fools she had done what Madame Lubokova had begged her not to do: she had profaned her art. Never again—no, not to this day—had she seated herself before the keyboard of a piano!

But yet one more act had been needed to commemorate the death of the soul. Its execution was not long delayed. That very night it took place, not in a drawing room, but in a bedroom, which is the proper

259

place for deaths—or for conceptions. Both were implicit in the surrender of her body to Rupert, in the shameful embrace that ended that shameful day. Was it an inherent longing for self-destruction that had caused her to leave her bedroom door unlocked, that had silenced her protests when Rupert begged once again that they should have a child? Always in the past she had denied his pleadings, because the thought of flight still lay in her mind. Now she knew that she would never flee, for a dead person cannot flee. In bitterness and in despair had her daughter Cosima been conceived. Was it a wonder if the fruit of such an act bore the seeds of new evil in itself?

The tears were pressing out beneath her quivering eyelids. She tried to force them back. She knew that those were tears of drunkenness, tears of weakness; in moments when she really was herself she was dry-eyed and hard. Why weep about the past, about those years when she was alive and still had the capacity to suffer? It would be more fitting to mourn the present: the dead present, the shameful present. If she had a sincere tear left in her body she would remember to shed it tomorrow. As to tonight . . . She picked up the bottle and carried it to her lips. She knew there would not be a drop left in it by morning.

four

Next day Adolph was worse again, decidedly worse. Cosima, meeting Frank at the breakfast table, told him that the patient had had a troubled night and that the nurse had instructions that he was to see no visitors today. Dr. O'Grady had already called, and had gone away shaking his shaggy head.

"Well, I hope the old boy lasts out a few days longer," said Frank as he sliced his cantaloupe. "I'd like to have that heart-to-heart talk he promised me."

Then he realized that his words must have sounded callous, though he had not meant them that way. Adolph was going to die; there was nothing to be done about that. While appreciating his grandfather, he could not shed many tears over this aged man whom he had not seen for six years; however, he did know that Adolph had something to tell him, something that would remain unsaid if death struck too soon.

"Wait and see," Cosima answered. "This has been a seesaw tussle all the way. I wouldn't be a bit surprised if Grandfather rallied again tomorrow. Between you and me, Frankie, I wonder if the shock of seeing Cecilia in her incredible getup didn't have something to do with the relapse."

Cosima, clad at the moment in a sheer dressing gown that looked as if it were made of cellophane, was scarcely the person to speak of unorthodox attire. But at least she was attractive, thought Frank, glancing at the curves she made so few efforts to hide. And the same could scarcely be said of his aunt, who had arrived in Chicago the afternoon before. Age had not improved Cecilia's taste in clothes, whereas it had ravaged her looks; her pink organdy frock had suited her lifted face no better than the picture hat swaying on her dyed mauve hair.

"How is it," Frank said, "that Gerald Foyles, an Englishman whose clothes, hair, and nails have obviously been cut within spitting distance of Savile Row, lets his wife keep doing that sort of thing? He may not be the dominant type, but he still has a foot to put down."

"Has he?" asked Cosima. "Don't you know, my dear Frankie, that putting down a foot is intimately related to footing a bill? Let's be honest now: Gerald didn't marry Cecilia for her organdy frocks—or what lay beneath them. Not that I begrudge him one grain of his imported caviar! He's rather a darling and absolutely safe: he'll never run off with his wife's jewels, like Justin Judson, his predecessor. And I don't think he's venturesome enough to put down one toe, let alone a whole foot!"

Frank laughed, because Cosima always made him laugh, but he could not help feeling shocked, as he had the day before when Cosima had complained that old Hauptman was not earning his keep. Rather unpleasant, this assumption that everything was to be had for the buying, from a spouse's obedience to the services of an old retainer with tired legs! It wasn't to keep Cecilia and Cosima in husbands that his grandfather had put together the Konrad millions.

The telephone in the other room began to ring. Without giving Hauptman a chance to answer, Cosima jumped up and darted from the breakfast veranda, her transparent dressing gown flying out behind her. Ten minutes later she was back, a satisfied grin on her face.

"You look," said Frank quizzically, "like that proverbial cat. Did you enjoy your canary, Cosima?"

"Very much so," she answered. "And he's quite a canary, believe me! Name's Billy Cartwright, and he's very respectable, at least for my standards. Believe it or not, he's a wealthy stockbroker. And most attractive! That's why Stan kicked up such a row when he—well, found out the worst. He probably wouldn't have cared if Billy had been just an ordinary fellow."

"Stan? That's number three, isn't it?" asked Frank, genuinely confused.

"Of course, silly. The one who's suing me for divorce. Incidentally, I've had notice that the case is coming up in court tomorrow. It's going to be most unpleasant. Stan's insisting on keeping the child, and naturally I won't let him."

"Where's the little girl now?"

"Oh, Pat's staying with her father in Hadon Heights. Chicago's too hot for a kid at this time of year, and besides, Stan insists on keeping her until the court awards final jurisdiction. He's very upset. Says I'm a bad mother."

"Which you're not?"

"Of course I'm not. Do I look like a bad mother?" Cosima wrapped her dressing gown a little tighter around her. "I'm driving out to Hadon Heights before luncheon to see her, by the way. If you're going out to visit William, Jr.'s factory of science, I can drop you on the way. Try and be ready about noon. . . ."

Actually it was long after noon when they drove away from the house, Cosima's apple-green Buick taking the sharp turns of the driveway at record speed. She was late through her own fault, but now she sat at the wheel with jaw set, pushing the big car through traffic as if her very life depended on lopping minutes off of her driving time.

"My God, Cosima!" Frank cried, as she veered sharply to avoid a truck. "Take it easy. There's no fire, is there?"

"There's always a fire," Cosima said. "A fire in here." She put her left hand on her breast, while there swept into her face the same tense, unhappy look as when she had stood ringing so frantically for Hauptman the morning before. "I have to live at top speed, Frankie—quickly and recklessly—otherwise I don't want to live at all. There's something driving me on, and it's stronger than me. I love speed for its own sake, not because it's going to get me somewhere (I don't know where I want to go, most of the time), but just because it's boring to go slow. Thank God I was born in the age of planes and of speed-cars."

"I guess it's the only age you could have been born in," Frank remarked as they swung into William, Jr.'s well-tended driveway.

His estate (and it really deserved that appellation) comprised thirty acres of the most valuable property in Hadon Heights, which William, Sr., had bought as an investment twenty-five years before. Here it was that Susan Konrad, William, Jr.'s sister, had constructed the glass-fronted laboratory through which she had achieved a certain reputation as an architect. Half a mile away lay the inventor's own residence, an attractive modernistic structure from which William, Jr., supervised the work of his staff of crack scientists. It was before the doorway of this house that Cosima drove up her Buick a little before one.

"Come on in with me and say hello," suggested Frank, as he stood beside the car, his foot on the running board.

"No, no, can't be done. My child's been expecting me for an hour, and then I have to rush back to town to have lunch with my lover. Besides," said Cosima, smoothing the kerchief she had bound around her hair, "William, Jr., depresses me. I don't know why it is. He's a great success, I realize that, and a brilliant intellect, no doubt. He's even convivial in a sinister sort of way. Still, Willy gives me the willies, and that's all there is to it. . . ."

"That's all there is to what?" asked William, Jr., himself. He had appeared unexpectedly around the corner of his house, probably having come walking from the laboratory. For some reason, however, he gave the impression of having spied on their conversation; his little baldish head, with the long nose and the sharp eyes, was the head of a born spy.

"Oh, nothing at all. And I have to be off," said Cosima, racing her engine. "Nice to have had a glimpse of you, William, but I'm afraid it can't be more. I have fish to fry."

"But I've fried them already," cried William, as the car began to move off, "including a big one for you. Stay and have lunch with us, Cosima! Make it a family party!"

But the Buick was already halfway down the drive, scattering the pigeons that were pecking about in the gravel.

"Always so impetuous—Cosima," said William, as he watched the green roadster disappearing. "Sometimes I wonder where all that undirected drive is going to take her." Then he turned to his young cousin and squeezed his arm. "Glad to see you, old man! Awfully glad! You're looking swell. This tragedy with Grandfather has at least one compensating factor, seeing that it's brought the whole family to Chicago. About time, too!"

William was very cordial, almost embarrassingly so, thought Frank, considering that there was fifteen years' difference in their ages and that they had never been in the least intimate. He kept his hand on Frank's arm while ushering him into the house, the whole time chatting away and fairly exuding hospitality. Yet somehow the show of friendliness did not ring true: he was, thought Frank, rather like a dog belying his nature by trying to climb a tree.

"Let me mix you a cocktail, old man, and then we'll have a bite of lunch," he cried, pressing a button. Whereupon the floor opened and a cocktail cabinet, complete with electric shaker, square monogrammed glasses, and even a framed drawing from *Esquire,* shot up through the floor. "Only one cocktail allowed before meals," he exclaimed with desperate joviality. "My chef threatens to resign if I debauch the taste buds of my guests. He's a Cordon Bleu and lived for years in Indo-China. I consider him one of the best oriental cooks in this country."

As Frank knew, everything connected with William, Jr., from his best friend to his ashman, was not only superlative of its kind, but somehow unique. It was not sufficient to be catered to by a Cordon Bleu; it had to be a Cordon Bleu with knowledge of Indo-Chinese cooking. Not even the humdrum best satisfied the fastidious tastes of this specialist in the exquisite.

Frank sat down on the streamlined sofa to enjoy his martini, whereupon a bracket swung out from the wall, presenting beneath his nose a selection of choice cigarettes in whose midst flickered a tiny flame.

"Just a silly little idea of mine," explained William, Jr., smoothing his thinning hair with a gesture which somehow conveyed a colossal amount of self-satisfaction. "Gadgets are my hobby, you know, but I don't have much time for fooling about with that sort of thing nowadays. For the last two years all of us at the laboratory have been concentrating on military stuff: land torpedoes, high-precision shells, and the like. It's no secret that we've been doing some important work, but between you and me, we hope to do better yet. We've had government backing ever since the war, and there's a good chance of our grant being doubled."

"Is that right?" said Frank, wondering why he always doubted the veracity of William, Jr.'s statements, even when he knew them to be completely true. "Congratulations are in order."

"And so they are for you, old man," cried William, squeezing Frank's arm again with what Cosima had termed "sinister" conviviality. "Your paper in the *Journal of Chemistry* was really first-rate, Frankie. Loewenstein, my top physicist at the lab, came across it the other day, not knowing who you were, and later asked me if Frank Konrad was any relation. When I stuck out my chest proudly and murmured, 'Yes,' Loewenstein said, 'Why not try and get him to join our team? He could be pretty useful around this joint.' And so," concluded William, never changing the conversational tone, "I decided to take his advice. As it happens, we could do with another man on the chemical side, and why take a Smith or a Finkelstein when we might land a Konrad? Note that I said 'might.' Now it is up to you, old man."

Frank looked for a table to put down his martini. In this house of gadgets there was nothing so practical, so he ended by placing it on the edge of the cocktail cabinet.

"Am I to take it that you are offering me a job, William?"

"Ah, brilliant! I always knew it." William gave a cackle. "Loewenstein wasn't one bit mistaken. But this is a little more than a job, Frankie. I could have offered you just a job when you graduated from M.I.T. I wanted to wait and see what developed, for there's a hell of a lot of difference between a crack student and a practicing scientist, you know that. Well, you've had your trial period in the chem lab at Snyder's, and the reports I get from there are A-1. (Ah, you didn't know that we ran a little secret service of our own, did you?) So what

I'm proposing to you"—William, Jr., again passed his hand over his hair—"is to step into the lab at about ten thousand a year, with the prospect of eventual partnership in my company. Not for a good while, of course, but that would be the general idea. Time's going to come when I'd like to have some of the responsibility taken off my shoulders and, as I said before, I'm all for keeping things in the family."

Frank was too taken aback to answer at once. He needed a drink to recover from the shock, so reached out for his martini, only to discover that the whole cocktail cabinet had sunk through the floor. He felt cold all over, then hot. Torn between the desires to emit a yelp of joy and to pound William on his skinny back, he restrained himself, remembering what Harriet used to tell him about the importance of selling oneself for a good price.

"Well, I am very, very much honored, William," he decided would be a safe reply.

"So you should be," William, Jr., answered blandly. "Anyone would give his eyeteeth for this chance. I'm sure you'll enjoy the work, Frankie, and I imagine we'll get on. I don't think we'll take potshots at each other," he said in a jocular voice that again brought to Frank's mind that picture of a dog trying to climb a tree. "But we'll have plenty of chances to discuss details before you leave town. There's the clock striking one, and I don't dare to be thirty seconds late for luncheon. After you, old man!"

Luncheon was exotic and choice, but as it happened could not be appreciated by either of the participants, Frank's mind being in a turmoil and William, Jr., having, it appeared, developed stomach ulcers in these last years. How was this sensational offer going to affect his life? Frank kept thinking. He could marry Harriet now, and bring her to Chicago, which was just what he had been wanting for a long time: here he would have opportunities never dreamt of in the East, not only to advance himself in his career, but to build up a pleasant life from every viewpoint. It meant something, after all, to belong to one of a city's leading families! "Ah, you see!" he could hear Harriet telling him when they met. "Didn't I always say that it was crazy to have a family like yours and not use them? Who wouldn't take advantage of a sensational short cut?" Well, that had been Harriet's viewpoint all

266

along, and though he himself was pretty suspicious of short cuts, he realized that no one could afford to turn down such a chance, even if it meant seeing William, Jr., not once every few years but daily.

It was fortunate that Frank did not have to take an active part in the conversation, his cousin being only too pleased to monopolize it. Seated at the kidney-shaped aluminum table, he discoursed with authority on the composition of the intricate rice dishes that he could not eat, on the culture of the Moselle grape which had gone into the wine he could not drink, on the special process, invented by himself, for maturing figs in the Illinois climate. In the meanwhile he munched concentratedly on some dry rusks, washed down with buttermilk. He really knew everything, and was only too anxious to share his knowledge; he was scintillating, witty, erudite; his brain sent out globules of knowledge like sparks from a revolving Catherine wheel. There was scarcely a subject that William, Jr., did not know from the ground up and that he could not discourse upon with originality and brilliance.

After coffee (decaffeinized) they strolled down the path between the trees which led to the Konrad Experimental Laboratory. Frank had never seen this building, constructed since his last visit to Chicago, but he could not have failed to see some of the publicity it had been accorded. He knew that the construction alone had cost William, Jr., a cool half million, Susan Konrad having spared no expense in constructing a sensational monument to her brother's inventive, and her own architectural, talent. Luckily, William, Jr., could afford that sum, for the income from his various inventions had made him a wealthy man in his own right. Frank had heard that two of them alone had netted him a small fortune: the revolutionary "Konrad turbine" used by the United States Navy in the last stages of the war, and the rudderless motorboat in whose perfecting Jan Smedlin had collaborated.

"Oh, I forgot to tell you," said Frank, as they approached the huge structure whose glass front could be seen glittering through the trees. "I ran into Jan Smedlin yesterday on the train. It would be untrue to say that he sent you his regards."

Frank could sense the stiffening of William's whole body; he realized all at once that this was the one subject his cousin had been avoiding since his arrival.

267

"There are no regards passing between us in either direction. God, how I hate that double-crossing little son of a bitch!" William burst out so hotly that Frank was taken aback. He had never guessed that this cold, impersonal scientist was capable of so much emotion.

"But what on earth happened between you?" he asked, just as he had asked the same question of Jan Smedlin the day before. "When I knew him, he used to be your chief assistant. You thought the world of him, William!"

"That's just it! I gave him my friendship, the more fool I! Why, before I ever met the little runt I used all sorts of influence to get him out of a concentration camp, and then brought him to America. And how does he repay me? By spreading a web of dirty insinuations all over Chicago. Do me a favor, old man, and don't mention that name Smedlin again."

Frank would have liked to find out more about those insinuations, and more about Smedlin generally; his curiosity had been whetted by that talk on the train. However, there was no point in annoying his future employer by pursuing the subject, and besides, here they were at the laboratory, perched on the steep hill ahead.

Frank decided at once that none of the descriptions he had read did justice to this fantastic structure. Cigar-shaped, with both ends projecting into space, it looked like a colossal Zeppelin hovering in mid-air. It was, literally, a glass house, with outer walls and roof composed of beautifully fitted concave panes. William, Jr., had his own theories about the beneficial effect of sunshine, and his great glass Zeppelin had been set on a revolving pedestal controlled by high-precision machinery so as to keep his own offices in a direct line with the sun's rays. In the morning the ends of the tube-shaped building pointed east and west; now in the afternoon they pointed north and south.

"Well, I can see you like it, old man," said William, grinning like a magician who had produced an exceptionally large rabbit out of his top hat. "We used ten thousand square feet of glass in the construction, so if the health of any of us breaks down it's not going to be for want of sunshine. We've got fifteen top-flight men at work there at the moment, including some of the finest European scientists alive. There's more gray matter employed in the Konrad Laboratory than you'd find in an average city!"

As they were making their way down the main corridor, flanked on either side by private laboratories, one of the doors opened and there stepped out a tall man with grayish hair and an exceedingly high forehead; Frank, meeting his eyes, had the same impression that he used to have with Smedlin, that the man's glance passed *through* objects, rather than resting upon surfaces. How different, he reflected, were the eyes of William, ever flitting from object to object, with their nervous, calculating stare!

"Hello there, Loewenstein! How's work getting on?" the inventor called out. But then, without giving the tall man a chance to answer, he hurried on. "Loewenstein, this is Frank Konrad, my cousin, whose paper in the *Journal of Chemistry* impressed you. D'you remember? I've taken that advice you gave me, and he's coming to work with us this fall."

"Ah, is he? Well, that's good news," said Loewenstein. "Your cousin is right, Mr. Konrad. Your paper did impress me a great deal."

"Nice of you to say so, Mr. Lowenstein."

"Oh, it is my sincere opinion." Loewenstein made a little European bow. "Perhaps I will have a chance of talking it over with you someday."

That bow, the accent, the clipped speech, all reminded Frank of Smedlin when he had first known him. Smedlin, too, had been a refugee, brought to America by William, to become before long his principal assistant. The duplication of circumstances was really curious, and for some reason made a disagreeable impression upon Frank. He decided that he would reflect upon it later, for now they had come to the inventor's private office, whose ray-controlled door swung open at their approach. Disclosed was one of the most amazing rooms that Frank had ever seen. Like the outside of the building, everything here was of glass: the tables, the chairs, the wastepaper basket, the typewriter, and the telephone; even the curtains and the carpet were made (he was informed) of very fine spun glass. One could see through every article of furniture, including the filing cabinets. On one glass table stood a mechanical object which Frank would have taken to be a television set, had not William, Jr., enlightened him.

"That's what I've called a colograph: a little invention I've been perfecting with the help of two members of my staff. It interprets musical compositions in terms of color. Let's see it work."

He pressed a button, whereupon the strains of Stravinsky's "Sacre du Printemps" filled the office, while on the colograph screen there appeared a procession of arcs and lines which took the form of geometrical designs varying in shape and color as the composition progressed. William, Jr., pressed another button, and the screen was filled with swirling many-colored ribbons winding themselves in and out like agitated worms. No doubt the shapes and colors did in a vague way interpret Stravinsky's music, but the utility of the operation was, thought Frank, somewhat beyond him.

"This fellow Loewenstein," he said, as they watched the writhing ribbons, "tell me how you got hold of him, William. He's quite a find, isn't he?"

"Quite a find is right. Why, Loewenstein's one of the top physicists in his field! Will you believe it that he was moldering in a DP camp in Austria when I tracked him down? I got him to sign on the dotted line before bringing him to America; now I've got him under contract for five years."

"Didn't you find several good men in the same way?" asked Frank, remembering what he had been told about William, Jr.'s "scouting expeditions" to Europe before and after the war; Jan Smedlin had been included in the bag of the first of those expeditions.

"Oh yes. Four of my best men are ex-DPs, and I picked up others in various corners of Europe." William passed his hand over the back of his head with that self-satisfied gesture of his. "As a matter of fact, Frankie, I might tell you that there are no more than half a dozen native-born Americans in my whole team."

"And everyone's under contract?"

"Oh yes. I'm no altruist, my boy. Every one of my workers has signed a long-term contract (by the way, you'll have to do it too), and believe me, everyone gets paid very well. But now they're working for me, and what they produce here is my property. There's no two ways about that! I'm not the grandson of Adolph Konrad for nothing."

Frank's eyes passed from the face of his cousin, calculating, over-clever, to the screen of the colograph, on which those colored snakes were twisting themselves in and out of anguished knots. It struck him that the snakes were like the workings of William's mind, devious and complex beyond the possibility of simplification. Yes, William, Jr., was Adolph's grandson, as he'd said, but in two generations how different a type of brain had been evolved, quite unaccustomed to old Adolph's direct, clear thinking! Was this an advance, thought Frank, an advance called forth by the sophisticated nature of modern life? Or was there already apparent here a degeneration, a perversion of genius whose material expression was to be found in the incredible Zeppelin of glass?

William's nervous fingers were toying with the knobs of the colograph, now turning one forward a few notches, now moving it back to its original position. On his clever face lay an expression of torment and dissatisfaction. And the whole time the snakes and the wavering lines raced across the screen of the colograph, giving a visual interpretation not only of Stravinsky's weird symphony but of the disharmonious soul of a twentieth-century man.

five

Strange, thought Frank, emerging from the giant Zeppelin, strange that he should have the sensation of stepping from darkness into light. Actually the exact opposite was the case, for the glass-walled laboratories had been as drenched with sunshine as a Florida beach at high noon, whereas the tree-bordered driveway lay deep in shadow. Nevertheless, he had this sensation of relief, this feeling that there was something somber and vaguely sinister about William, Jr.'s "factory of science," where he himself would be working before too long. How was it, he asked himself, that the prospect did not thrill him? His cousin was right in saying that any young scientist would have given his eyeteeth for the opportunity. He must be sensible and remember that ten thousand a year was ten thousand a year, and the offer of it didn't come every day.

As he drove down the driveway in the smart blue Packard which his cousin had placed at his disposal, Frank's thoughts kept turning to Jan Smedlin. On this very road he had walked with the little Czech eleven years before, he a lanky youth of fifteen, carried away by his first discovery of the magic of physics. He remembered how Smedlin, speaking rapidly with his execrable accent (and never speaking *down* to Frank, though he was only a schoolboy, in contrast to Smedlin, a practicing physicist), had disclosed to him a whole new concept of science, which to him was the means of enriching man's life on earth.

He had taken Frank to his private laboratory in the brick building since replaced by the glass Zeppelin, and shown him the blueprints of the rudderless motorboat on which he was then working. And young Frank, pleased and honored by these attentions from a man who had "Doctor of Science" engraved on his calling card, was struck with what ease he understood the principle of a discovery which had seemed so complex when his cousin tried to clarify it at the luncheon table. After that day physics for Frank had ceased to be merely a pastime involving fascinating experiments in the school lab; it had become a study of the principles governing the functioning of the world. Perhaps it was then and there that he had formulated the decision (crystallized years later) to devote his mature life to science. In the last analysis the responsibility lay with the little Czech whose name William, Jr., had asked him never to pronounce again.

"Where do you wish to go, sir?"

Frank roused himself to find that the car had already left Edgeware Beach behind and was about to enter the upper stretches of Lake Shore Drive.

"Stop where I can consult a directory," he answered on the spur of the moment. "Here, this drugstore will do."

Making his way to the phone booths at the rear, Frank thumbed through the *S*'s in the catalogue, scarcely expecting to find what he sought, and surprised when he saw staring him in the face the words "Jan Smedlin, 17 Pimento Place." Pimento Place! The name evoked pleasant associations from his early Chicago years, when he had lived with his mother and stepfather in an apartment on the North Side. It was, he recalled, one of those few quiet squares which had survived the city's breath-taking metamorphosis. Its houses were old, at least old for

Chicago. They had the touching dignity of survivors, aware that their span of life might at any moment be cut short by the arrival of the demolition squad.

No. 17 was a small two-story house, almost square in shape, its brick front lying back a little from the street. The old-fashioned bellpull gave forth a melodious tinkle that to Frank sounded like the notes of a harpsichord. As he waited, his eye traveled to a calling card tacked to the letter box. "Jan Smedlin," it read. And underneath, in small letters, "Doctor of Science, Prague University." The card looked a bit tired, and Frank noticed that one of the lower corners was torn off. Before he could move his glance away, the door swung open and he caught sight of a young woman standing there.

"Good afternoon," she said. "Have you come to see Jan Smedlin?"

There was a noticeable accent in the voice, and somehow she did not look like an American girl, though it would have been hard to say just where the difference lay. Her brown hair was cut short and lay in a fringe on her forehead; she wore a simple flowered frock that had probably been purchased in some Chicago department store. Perhaps the un-American feature was her eyes. They were smiling and friendly as those of any Midwestern girl, but behind the smile lay a serious, almost tragic expression. It was as he looked into her eyes that Frank realized she must be Katrine, Jan's sister whom he had mentioned yesterday on the train.

"That's right," Frank answered her. "I dropped in on the chance of finding Jan at home. I am an old friend of your brother."

She raised her eyebrows. "So you know already who I am?"

"Yes," said Frank. "I even know your name: Katrine."

She smiled; unconsciously her hand went up to smooth her hair. "Well, sir," she said, "Jan is not yet home, but he should be presently. Please to come in and wait."

The words of refusal were on Frank's lips when he changed his mind. Partly, no doubt, it was because he felt attracted to this young girl with the smiling face and the funny foreign speech. Partly it was because she belonged in the mysterious life of Jan Smedlin and through her he might come to understand better the puzzling little Czech.

He walked to the automobile to dismiss the chauffeur, and when he came back she was standing watching the big car drive off. On her face was an expression of wonder that reminded him of the look on the face of a child peering at a toy through a shopwindow.

"What an enormous, enormous car!" she exclaimed, and gave a giggle. "You know, that must be one of the biggest cars in Chicago."

"Perhaps it is," agreed Frank, amused by her naïveté. "I wouldn't know. It's my cousin's car, not mine."

"Oh, I realized it wasn't yours, sir! You certainly don't look like anyone who'd own such a car. If you had, I wouldn't have dared ask you in."

The Packard had sped out of Pimento Place. Jan's sister opened the door of their little house, and Frank walked through the entrance hall into a pleasant sitting room, curtains, chair covers, carpet, all looking as spotless and neat as Katrine's flowered dress. Apart from the cuckoo clock on the wall, there was nothing particularly foreign about the room, and yet it gave Frank the same impression as the girl herself; it certainly was not American. Through the open windows he caught a glimpse of a tidy back yard, with flower beds and a couple of fruit trees. As Katrine followed him into the room a white pigeon swooped through one of the windows, to alight on the arm that she held out.

"How do you like my lovely pet? His name's *Miláŏķu.* That means 'darling' in the Czech language."

"He's a beauty," said Frank, walking up to the white bird which was pecking at the grain in Katrine's other hand.

Then Frank saw two things that caused him quickly to move his glance away. On Katrine's arm, a little above the wrist, there had been branded a six-digit number, perhaps half an inch in height; and below the wrist, on the hand which now held the kernels of wheat, one of the fingers was broken and twisted out of its normal shape. The discoveries were as startling to Frank as if the girl had suddenly struck him in the face. Now he remembered Jan's telling him that his sister had spent many months in concentration camps, but that grim fact was utterly incongruous in relation to the gay, childish Katrine.

"Where does he live? Have you a cage for him?" he said, sending his glance about the room so as to keep it from going to that branded arm.

"No, no, I shall never keep anything in a cage," Katrine answered,

274

and now her words seemed to Frank to have double significance. "If he wants to go, then he must go. He came to me like that—flying in through the window—he can leave in the same way."

"So you didn't buy him?"

"Oh no, I would not buy an animal. I hate buying of any sort. I have always thought that buying does such bad things to the buyers. And a live animal I would never buy."

The white pigeon flew up from her arm, hovered for a moment in space, its wings beating the air, then swooped out through the window. Katrine followed its flight with a little smile.

"Gosh, I can't say you're not original," said Frank, laughing. "Most American girls go in for buying in a big way. In fact we Americans generally seem to do an awful lot of buying in the course of our lives! Well, I suppose I should have expected the sister of Jan to be unusual. He certainly is!"

"Oh, indeed he is," said Katrine. "One in a thousand."

"One in ten thousand, I'd say! Your brother played quite an important part in my life. If it hadn't been for him, I doubt if I ever would have taken up science as a career."

"Is it true?" She seemed delighted. "I didn't know you were a scientist, sir."

"Yes, I'm an experimental chemist. I met your brother when I was a kid of fifteen, and he was the first person I'd known who was really in love with science."

"Ah yes, so he was! You are right. Not any more though, I'm afraid." A shadow stole into her face. "Jan was a pure scientist, like many men in our family. My father, you know, was a professor of biochemistry in Prague University. My elder brother had a prominent position in the Skoda laboratories—that was in the old days, of course."

The shadow lay deeper on Katrine's face; she looked much older suddenly. Now she was no longer a child who could giggle at the sight of a big automobile, but a mature woman who had passed through the valley of suffering and would bear forever the scars of her journey.

"Jan has told me about the tragedy of your family. And he has told me about you. I am very sorry," said Frank, aware of the inadequacy of words.

275

"Ah, we were just one more Jewish family," said Katrine, and he saw that her right hand moved to cover that row of digits near the other wrist. "There were so many of us, and everyone has already forgotten. Even the few Jews we meet in Chicago are embarrassed when we mention that our entire family was wiped out by Hitler. Yes, everyone—everyone, except Jan and I."

She walked to the rear window and stood looking out, her fingers still clasped over the mark of the camp. But when she turned back to face him, Frank was amazed to see that her face once again was clear and untroubled as the face of a young girl!

"I see that you play chess," he said, taking advantage of the presence of a chessboard with pieces in play, to steer the conversation to other channels. "Chess used to be my passion when I was a student at M.I.T. Are you pretty good at it?"

"Well—pretty good," she said with a frankness that was disarming. "I had an uncle who was a well-known player in Czechoslovakia. He taught me the game. Jan and I used to have great tournaments, sitting at that table!"

"Only used to?"

"Yes. Jan has such difficulty concentrating nowadays. He's—he's quite changed in these last years." Her gaze clouded over again, though only for a second. "I still play quite often," she said, ". . . mostly against myself."

"That can't be very exciting."

"But it is, sir! I was just engaged in the most passionate game when you rang at the door. As you see, I had got black in a ticklish position. White to move."

"Who are you rooting for? You or yourself?"

"Oh, I sympathize with black. Perhaps that's because he's on the defense by tradition. I suppose I've come to associate myself with the defensive position," she said, smiling wryly.

"Perhaps I ought to leave and let you finish your game?"

"Oh no," she cried quickly. And then he saw her blush a little as she added, "I mean, not unless you are in a hurry. A good thing about playing this sort of chess is that you can always get hold of your opponent."

Frank laughed. He was only too pleased to stay on with this pleasant girl, who was so unlike anyone he had met before. I suppose, he thought, watching her walk to the kitchen and take two Coca-Colas out of the refrigerator, she is the very antithesis of Harriet, their only common trait being that they're both decidedly attractive—oh yes, and both intelligent. I can't imagine Harriet playing chess against herself, or for that matter against anyone else, and I can't imagine this quiet little Katrine working in an advertising agency. I suppose they would simply hate each other if they met.

"Well, I have made my next move," he told her when she came back. "I'll let you have black, of course, seeing that you specialize in the defense. Look out for your queen."

Katrine pondered the board for a moment, then unexpectedly moved her bishop. Frank continued the attack, but before he had downed half his Coca-Cola found himself in a quite impossible position and had to resign.

"That wasn't really fair," said Katrine, giggling. "I was too familiar with that game. Besides, I'm in training. I have nothing to do except keep house for Jan, read books, and study chess problems; that's been my life since coming to Chicago. It's funny that I seem to be so busy the whole day long!"

"It must have been strange for you—suddenly finding yourself in this big city, and in a foreign country. You must have felt very lost at the start."

Katrine shook her head. Again he noticed that she hid the branded numbers, putting her arm behind her back.

"No, not so lost as all that! If you've been in concentration camps and DP camps for years, then it doesn't seem to matter much any longer where you live. You're at home everywhere, if you see what I mean. Will you believe that one can even think of Dachau as home! Someone who has lost everything—everything, must find all he needs in himself. Otherwise it is certain he will die."

"And that is why you did not die?" said Frank, looking in her young face, charged with suffering, now that her thoughts had turned to the past, yet at the same time bearing a look of confidence and strength.

"Yes," she said. "That is why they could not kill me."

She looked at the Coca-Cola bottle, and suddenly she smiled.

277

(Strange, thought Frank, that she could glide from mood to mood, like a skier swooping down one hill and then up the next, with only the slightest change of stance; for her the border line between sorrow and happiness must have become tenuous, almost non-existent.) She stuck two fingers in the necks of the bottles and dangled them playfully, making them knock against each other.

"Look! I bet you couldn't do that."

"I don't think I would try," said Frank, looking at the giggling face, the little teeth, the fringe, and telling himself that at that moment he might have taken her for just a kid, had he not known so differently. "Have you got many other tricks?" he asked her.

"Yes, you'd be surprised. I'm afraid that some of them aren't very dignified, though. And, come to think of it"—she was still laughing—"I don't even know your name."

"That's right, I guess you don't. My name is Konrad—Frank Konrad."

Katrine stopped laughing. Her fingers stuck in the bottle necks went limp, so that one of the bottles fell off and went rolling to the floor. Slowly she raised her head and looked at him, and now her eyes were narrowed.

"Konrad?" she said in a changed voice. "You mean, then, that you are the brother of William Konrad?"

"No, William doesn't have a brother. I'm his first cousin, though, and as it happens, I had lunch with him today."

"Ah, so that huge automobile—it belonged to William Konrad?"

"That's right. Everything belonging to William is very big."

The girl Katrine's eyes darkened. A complete transformation had taken place in her since she had heard the name Konrad: she was aloof now, reserved, even hostile.

"And you think that is a good thing," she said, ". . . to own big cars, big houses, big fortunes? You think it is a sign that your cousin is a success?"

"Not at all," said Frank. "I think it is a sign that he might be an unhappy man, losing his hair and cursed with stomach ulcers, which happens to be the case."

He had spoken lightly, hoping to re-establish the mood of a moment

278

before, but Katrine was scowling; apparently she had lost all pleasure in their conversation. Frank, watching her, thought, Hell! Why did we ever get on this tender subject of William? I might have known this would be the result.

"And yet you say that you are a friend of Jan's!" she broke out angrily. "It seems funny that you should come here straight from William Konrad, his worst enemy. From William Konrad, whom he hates more than any man alive!"

"That's what I wish you'd explain," said Frank earnestly. "I hadn't seen your brother for six years, until I met him yesterday on the train. You see, I live in the East—in Philadelphia. What's all this trouble between William and him? Honestly, I don't know!"

She looked at him to see if he was telling the truth. Whatever she decided, her expression did not change. She shook her head.

"Go ask your cousin, if you're interested! Or ask Jan to tell you about the little happening that"—her eyes filled with tears and she turned her head towards the wall—"that has made him into the man he is now. It's his secret." She glanced quickly at the cuckoo clock on the wall and went on, "By the way, sir, I doubt if he will be back for some time. Perhaps you had better call him on the phone if you wish to see him."

"If you think so," said Frank.

He wanted to tell her that, whatever had happened between William and Jan, he had had no part in it, that actually he was no great friend of William's, even though he was about to join his laboratory. But Frank had the feeling that all this would not make much difference; Katrine had turned against him not because of anything he had done or said but simply because his name was Konrad.

"I hope I shall be seeing you again," he said, deciding it was safer not to put out his hand lest she refuse to see it. "I enjoyed our talk very much—and our half a chess game. I'm afraid you could beat me quite easily, even giving me a couple of pawns."

She shrugged her shoulders. "I suppose you weren't really trying."

"Of course I was trying. What makes you say that?"

"Because," said Katrine, not looking into his face, "I understand from Jan (and he knows) that your family *always* win, when there's something at stake."

279

six

Adolph Konrad lay breathing deeply, with an unhappy gasp at the end of each breath. He was asleep and a dream was passing through his mind. Or was it really a dream? Where was he to draw the line between those terror-ridden dreams (during which a part of him knew that he was dreaming) and the waking memories that had all the gripping reality of a nightmare? Imperceptibly he slipped from one to the other, only emerging into short or longer periods of lucidity. True that during those minutes, or hours, his brain worked with startling clarity; he could evaluate his life, coming to conclusions never before reached; in conversations with his children and grandchildren he glimpsed hitherto unknown facets of their characters. But then from one moment to another his concentration would collapse, he would feel himself slipping, slipping . . . and again he would be back in a dismal world peopled by ghosts and shadows, with his conscious and his subconscious struggling for domination. . . .

He is lying in a boxed-in room—can it be a prison cell?—on a bed so narrow that he knows that the slightest movement will fling him to the floor. Nor can he raise his body, for fear of knocking against the upper partition. He lies there motionless, oppressed with a feeling of claustrophobia and sickened by the overpowering smell of vomit in his nostrils. But what is that swishing sound, akin to the ripping of some heavy material? Ah yes, it is the sound of water sweeping against the walls of the ship. Then he remembers that he is lying in a bunk, bound for America, and that there are many other boys in this steerage cabin with its solitary porthole. How many days has he been lying here? It seems as if it had been forever, with the sound of the rushing water always in his ears, the stench of seasickness pressing on his face like a damp cloth.

And now, above the sound of the water, he hears moaning: a weak moaning, as from someone utterly exhausted, or perhaps someone lying close to death. Peering through the darkness, he can barely make out

280

the shape of a body beneath a blanket, can discern the movement of an arm and see a hand as it passes across a forehead to wipe away the sweat. It is his friend Max Heinrich who lies there sick: not sick with seasickness alone, but with another ailment which no doctor has yet diagnosed, because for steerage passengers there is no doctor.

"Ich kann es nicht aushalten! I can't go on!" the words reach Adolph's ears, and he sees Max's arm fling itself up, as in a final gesture of protest; the clenched hand knocks the wooden boards of the upper bunk and drops back onto the blanket. There it lies, still clenched, motionless, like the hand of a dead person. Dead is the hand, dead, too, is the will of Max Heinrich, who became Adolph's friend the day they stepped onto this torture ship, bound for America and their fortunes.

Adolph reaches underneath the pillow. He does not know what he is seeking, but when his hand closes on the hard slice of bread, then he knows. He tears the bread in two, reaches one half across the gap between the bunks, and forces it into the inert fist lying on the blanket.

"Eat!" he commands. "For two days you have not eaten. If you do not eat now, you will die. I have saved you some bread from last night's supper. Swallow it! Swallow it, I say!"

"I cannot swallow it. Let me alone! Dying would be the best thing of all."

"Coward!" he cries. "Don't you realize that one is not *allowed* to die? Eat the bread or I shall beat you with this stick. I promise you (and I keep my promises) that *I shall beat you until you eat!"*

As Adolph takes hold of the stick at which he has been whittling earlier in the day, the ship gives a sickening lurch. He is flung to the side and clutches hard at the rim of the bunk lest he tumble to the floor. . . .

Adolph Konrad woke up with his hand clamped to the post of his bed, and inside him a fierce determination not to let go—not to let go whatever happened. It was the same determination that had kept him alive during the whole of this last week, even though his body wanted to die; the same determination which, in the last analysis, was responsible for his threat to beat Max, as he once had beaten his brother Franzy to save him from drowning in a stagnant pool.

For life was good, thought Adolph as he lay there, feeling the tough veins of the wood under his unyielding fingers. It was good, or if not good, at least it was one's only birthright. Cling to it one must with iron will! The opposite of life was death, was blackness, was oblivion. He had dedicated himself to the battle for life, and somehow the pattern of the struggle had kept repeating itself. Ever and again one of life's weaklings had been thrust in his path, and he had carried on the fight that they were inadequate to wage themselves. Franzy, his brother . . . Francy, his son . . . Max. At different periods he had fought each one's battles, not with the hope of their salvation (for a weakling can never be made strong), but simply because he liked life so much. And for that they had hated him—him, the strong one, the one who never gave in. Well, it did not matter now if they had hated him or had loved him. The important thing had been the struggle, the unending struggle for life that he was still fighting today.

"*Ich kämpfe! Ich kämpfe!*" he murmured, and the sound of those words gave him a strange feeling of happiness. I shall fight on, he thought. I shall fight on till the bitter end. . . .

It was then he realized that there was someone bending over him. A big face, vaguely familiar, hovered near him, features drawn in compassion under the bald dome. A voice in German reached him.

"*Sie brauchen nicht mehr zu kämpfen.* You need fight no more!"

He stared up into the big pale face, vaguely comforted by the German words and the awareness of that German presence close beside him. Still hovering in the borderland of dreams, he tried to place the features, which he both knew and did not know, tried to complete the association between this man and the steaming cup on the bedside table. (The odor of bouillon assailed his nostrils.)

And at last, just before he slipped off again, he realized that the man was Hauptman. How could he have failed to recognize him before? Because of that look of commiseration that transformed the phlegmatic face? Or because Hauptman had addressed him in German, when they had conversed in English for over fifty years? Yes, for all that span during which they had lived together under the same roof, he had insisted on their speaking in a foreign tongue that precluded any intimacy of contact! What a lot of time we have wasted! was his last thought before he fell back into the void where love and comfort were things unknown, and pain was the sole reality. . . .

He is talking with Max Heinrich again, or rather it is Adolph who is shouting at Max, and he can feel rising within him that fiery anger which ever threatens to overcome him in a dispute. In a sense this is the continuation of the other dream, and Adolph knows it even as he dreams. But now he and Max are on a boat no longer; they are standing in a room which must be Adolph's old office in the Stock Yards, for there is the roll-top desk with the shiny cuspidor beside it, and in the crack of the doorway he can see the weasellike face of Chippy, who is listening in.

"I'll do what I like how I like!" he is shouting, his hand pounding the desk top. "I'll God damn well run my own business, and I'm not going to let anyone tell me how. We're not partners any longer, remember, Max! I'm your boss and I pay you a salary now."

But though he shouts and pounds, Max's face retains that gentle smile of his which nothing seems able to rub off. He smiles and smiles, yet in his eyes lies a look of horror which tells Adolph what Max is thinking. He is thinking of those soldiers about to die in the Caribbean because of Adolph's contaminated meat—young soldiers who must meet their death ignominiously, so that Adolph Konrad shall grow richer. This silence of Max's exasperates him beyond endurance. Why doesn't the man shout back, accusing him of his crime—accusing him of murder? Why this silence that is more damning than words?

"What I do or don't do is my responsibility!" he cries again, wild with exasperation. "I'm not asking you to share it. Come to think of it, you'd better get out of here, Max. Two bosses are one too many in this plant. That's final!"

Still Max remains silent, in his eyes that look of horror, on his lips that vague, gentle smile. But suddenly he raises his hand and points a rigid forefinger at Adolph. Now the smile has vanished, and into his face has come the grim look of a prosecutor pronouncing sentence. He speaks at last, but the voice that issues forth is not Max's voice in the least: it has an impersonal quality, like the metallic voice of a radio announcer. It is not Max who is speaking, though his mouth moves; it is the voice of a stranger, perhaps (the thought comes to Adolph) the voice of one of the soldiers who are to die for his benefit on that Caribbean isle.

283

"One can't treat men as you do! Men aren't pigs, Adolph Konrad. Men are men!"

Men are men! The words were still in his ears as he struggled out of his dream. He felt alert, his mind lucid; all of his perceptions seemed extraordinarily acute. Curious, he thought, as he lay there with eyes still shut, breathing deeply—curious that that phrase, once spoken by Max, should come back to him today! He hadn't thought of it for at least forty years, had scarcely thought of Max Heinrich for forty years. Yet today, with half a lifetime of impression intervening, with hundreds of faces crowding his memory, it was the face of Max Heinrich that he saw, of Max whose life he had once saved and at another time had smashed into bits. Men are men! He said the words to himself, conscious that they held a deep significance, offered a clue to a problem that had been worrying him for long. Especially during these hard days of struggle with what he knew to be his last illness, that problem had presented itself ever and again.

It was a problem not easy to define, for in fact it was the problem of his whole relationship with mankind. How was it, he had asked himself, that he, who always had fought the battle for life, should be responsible at the end of the count for so much death and suffering? How was it that he, whose life had been long, colorful, and sensationally successful, should be able to look back on but two satisfying human contacts: one with Wilma, his willing slave, one with Sean O'Grady, a sycophant and a liar? Time and again he had been offered friendship, but he had refused it, because that was not what he had wanted of men. For him they had been the means for his own aggrandization, like the pigs and cattle in which he dealt; he had had no interest in them apart from that.

Adolph lay quite still on the bed, not daring to move lest the nurse come in to disturb him; this problem needed thinking out, and he knew that the time left him was short. With a great effort of will he tried to look at his life objectively, as any man must do to reach an evaluation. Examining his achievements, he experienced his old pride in their worth: he had founded a great business; had built up a fortune; had helped make his city one of the industrial capitals of the world. Adolph Konrad could say truthfully that he had won his battle, but no victory of such magnitude can be attained without heavy losses: losses in terms of human lives, of human happiness, of human dignity. His workers in the Stock Yards had paid for his triumph, but he, their commander, had paid too, though in a different way. He had, in truth, given up part of his humanity, like any great leader for whom personal considerations are surrendered to an all-embracing goal.

Yes, that is what happened to me, thought Adolph (and, strangely enough, there was relief in the knowledge that he, so definitely an individual, had after all been following a universal pattern). Being the man he was, born in a certain period of America's industrial development, he literally had been forced to do all that he had done, from selling contaminated meat to making his pickle workers stand in ankle-deep pools of acid. Max Heinrich had been right in saying that men and pigs should not be treated alike. But how was Max Heinrich, a weakling, to understand the compulsions that governed a person like himself? It was the destiny of the Adolph Konrads to ride over corpse-strewn battlefields with never a companion in sight.

If only the time and strength were left me, thought Adolph, I would use them both to make one last human contact before I died.

Even as this resolution passed through his mind he grew aware again of that familiar yet unfamiliar presence in the room. Opening his eyes, he looked straight into the eyes of Hauptman, who had been standing by the bed during those brief moments that Adolph slept and dreamed. On Hauptman's large pale face lay an expression of pain as he watched the sick master whom he had been serving for half a century; his trembling fingers molded the loose skin of his throat in anguish. As Adolph lay gazing into his eyes, the thought struck him, Perhaps this is the first time we have really looked at each other in fifty years! He has brown eyes—I could not have said that before—and there is a sad, lonely look in them. The truth is that I do not know Hauptman at all! Adolph's lips moved, and the words sprang forth with no effort of the will.

"*Danke, mein Freund,*" he said. "I thank you—yes, my friend, I thank you for everything."

The blood rushed into Hauptman's wax-pale cheeks. The shock of hearing those German words from his master robbed him of the power

285

of speech and movement; he kept staring down at Adolph with quivering lips that refused to obey his commands. A great joy filled him, almost painful in its intensity. He realized suddenly that he had been longing for this moment for years and years—yes, ever since the day that he stepped into this house as a young man and donned the black livery that had been ordered to his measure. On that day, as on every day since, Adolph had spoken to him in English, had even looked daggers when a German word crept into Hauptman's speech. Only this evening beside the deathbed of the man he loved had he received tacit acknowledgment that they were two German immigrants in a foreign land, two Schwabenland boys linked by the bonds of a common tongue and by kindred memories of their impoverished childhoods.

Scarcely aware of what he was doing, Hauptman picked up the empty bouillon cup and its saucer; from force of habit he poured some spilled bouillon back in the cup. Again he sought to say something, but he could think of nothing suitable, nothing that would in any way befit the occasion. At last, staring fixedly into the depths of the cup, he managed to mumble:

"Immer zu ihrem Befehl, mein Herr. Always at your service!"

Without turning his head, cup and saucer held out before him, he stalked solemnly from the room.

seven

Brushing his hair before the dresser, Frank let his eye move to the two messages propped against the glass.

"Mr. Rupert has arrived at the Blackstone and wants you to dine at seven-thirty," Hauptman had written on one chit, his old man's scrawl forming rows of almost illegible hieroglyphics. And "Mr. William phoned and wants you to dine at seven-thirty," he had scribbled on the other. Which was no different than it had always been, thought Frank, and grinned. Those two brothers had been engaged in a breakneck competition as far back as he could remember.

If Uncle Rupert landed a new diplomatic appointment, Uncle Bill (exuding triumph, his big nose shining with pride) was sure to announce his election to the board of the Chicago opera; if Uncle Bill went and bought himself a Lincoln, Uncle Rupert instantly countered with a Rolls Royce. Now, well on in the sixties, they were still at it, and Frank knew that his choice of Rupert's invitation represented for that uncle a symbolic victory. Vain as he was, he would never realize that his nephew had favored him because of the fact that Helen was his favorite aunt, and because Cosima, who made him laugh, would be present.

When he stepped into the Blackstone, a half hour later, the first person Frank saw was Victor Hapgood, his Uncle Rupert's private secretary. His loose-boned body encased in a dinner jacket, his pale face tense with concentration, Hapgood was standing by the Western Union desk, sending off a sheaf of telegrams, as usual. If on Hapgood's tombstone were to be engraved a picture of the deceased engaged in his favorite occupation (as was the custom among the ancient Egyptians), the likeness would undoubtedly depict this harassed individual dispatching messages for his employer to all corners of the globe.

"Hello there!" Frank called to him. "At it again, eh?"

"Glad to see you, Frankie!" The secretary proffered his hand. "Just wait a second while I shoot these off, and then we'll go upstairs."

"Didn't know it was going to be such a gala occasion," said Frank, surveying Hapgood's attire. "Boiled shirt and black tie and everything. And here I am in my old flannels!"

"Oh, don't worry. It's quite *en famille*," answered Hapgood as he passed two more telegrams to the employee. "The ambassador wanted to get some of you Konrads together, but it seems that your Uncle William is giving a dinner tonight too. Not very kind of him, I must say! We're expecting Cosima, of course (she hasn't seen her parents for over a year), but apart from you two, there was no one available. Between you and me, Frankie, I'm glad you could make it; it's a bit of a strain when that *enfant terrible*, Cosima, is with her father and mother alone. Well, thank goodness that bunch of wires is off! Got to hurry upstairs now. Your uncle may be wanting me."

Rupert Konrad had taken a suite overlooking Michigan Boulevard. Here he greeted his nephew with a warmth that made it fairly evident

287

that he shared Hapgood's dread of seeing Cosima alone. In his well-cut dinner jacket, a white carnation in the buttonhole, he looked as elegant as ever, and quite youthful for a man of sixty-five, thought Frank.

"How is Santo Pedro? Speak Spanish yet, Uncle Rupert?"

"Like a native, my boy. Santo Pedro's a very fine place: lot of distinguished people, best society in South America, a dinner party every night. But step over here a moment and let me introduce you. This gentleman's a reporter from the Chicago *Despatch*. Mr. . . . . Mr. . . . ."

"Graham," said the young man, getting up from his chair and slipping his writing pad in his pocket. "Sam Graham's the name. But I shan't take any more of your time, Mr. Konrad. You've been very helpful, and I've got all that I need."

Frank took a good look at the young reporter as he shook hands with him. Sam Graham was about his own age, that is to say twenty-six, with quick but remarkably gentle eyes and a long sharp nose—the very nose that a reporter should be born with. Frank wondered if it was his imagination, or if there had been an implication in those casual words. Was it the tone of voice or the expression in the clever eyes that told Frank that this Graham had summed up Rupert Konrad, with his talk of "distinguished people" and "a dinner party every night," summed him up and found him wanting? Though the reporter had made a pleasant enough impression upon Frank, he could not help feeling resentful. Rupert Konrad might have been outwardly superficial, it was true, but did not the very fact of his successful career bespeak his exceptional capacities?

And then, just as Graham was about to leave, there sounded a knock at the door. Hapgood ran to open, his hands held out before him, as though to capture an elusive butterfly. A strange butterfly it proved to be! Into the room swept Cosima, her curvaceous body draped in an elaborate evening gown, with neckline plunging far, far below the limits of decorum; apart from this, the tight skirt was cut high up one thigh and gave indications of various other apertures here and there. In her hand Cosima held a huge fan of green feathers, which she now waved about gaily as she advanced towards her father.

"Welcome home, Papa," lisped Cosima, affecting a little girl's speech. *"Soyez le bienvenu,* as they would say in diplomatic parlance."

288

Frank could almost feel his uncle wince. It was obvious that reprimands were as ill suited to the occasion as Cosima's dress itself, and in the end Rupert contented himself with a slight frown and the planting of a cool kiss on his daughter's forehead. Whereupon Cosima, having espied the young reporter, bore down upon him with the purposefulness of a woman who has but a single interest in life.

"I think we've met before, haven't we?" she cried, eying him coyly over the upper edge of her fan.

"Oh yes," said Graham unresponsively. "I interviewed you at the time of your last divorce—about six years ago, I believe. And now I hear that you're going to get another."

"That's right. In fact the hearing's tomorrow morning. You know how it is: one gets in the habit of these things."

"I suppose one does." Graham still looked rather bored. "Perhaps you'll let me interview you again this time?"

"But d'you really think my divorces and marriages are still news in Chicago?"

"Everything a member of your family does is news," declared Graham, with a glance at the ambassador. "You've become a civic tradition, if I may say so—something like our windy weather and the Chicago *Tribune*. By the way, Mr. Konrad, I forgot to ask whether Mrs. Konrad traveled up with you today?"

"Oh yes indeed." Rupert gave a tug at his ear. "She's resting in the other room—feeling rather exhausted from the trip and—and from everything."

"Perhaps I had better tell Mrs. Konrad that her daughter has arrived," suggested Hapgood, starting for the telephone. But he had not reached it before the bedroom door swung open and they caught sight of Helen Konrad herself in the entrance. She was wearing a dress of pale green, her favorite color, and it seemed to Frank that the harsh atmosphere of that hotel parlor had been somehow softened by her arrival. She looked, he thought, much older than when he had seen her last, older and more tired. Suddenly he was overcome with that old sympathy which the sight of his Aunt Helen aroused in him; knowing little of her life, unable to appraise the factors that had undermined it, she struck him nevertheless as a tragic and appealing figure.

289

"Hello, Mother," Cosima said, and she put her fan over her breasts in a mock gesture of prudery. "You needn't tell me. You thoroughly disapprove of my beautiful evening gown!"

"Well, seeing that you know it, there wouldn't be much point in my telling you. Would there now?"

Frank saw that his aunt was smiling, and he felt a great admiration for her; he knew what she must be feeling and how hard it was for her to carry off the pretense of not caring. But Cosima, finding the wind taken from her sails, decided for once to act like a normal woman. Going up to her mother, she kissed her, almost with affection, and Frank even had the notion that she regretted having put on that shocker of a dress.

Sam Graham, who had been standing embarrassedly by the door, again prepared to take his departure.

"Good evening, Mr. and Mrs. Konrad. Good evening, everyone," he mumbled, but before he could make good his escape, Rupert intervened.

"Wait a moment, young man. Have a drink before you leave. My secretary here is famous for his cocktails. Better sample one."

Hapgood, Frank now perceived, had produced ice and bottles, and stood rattling a shaker by the window. His smiling face was outlined against the illuminated clock in the Illinois Central Tower.

"Martinis!" he cried brightly. "Martinis ahoy! Oh, it's nice to be back in the land of good gin and free ice! Will you have a martini, Mrs. Konrad?"

"A martini? A martini?" Helen repeated vaguely. "No thank you, Victor, I don't think I'll have one tonight."

"Well, you can give me one," said the ambassador, in obvious relief. "And I'm sure you'll break down and take one, Cosima, just to celebrate the occasion. It's not often that the family's gathered together like tonight. I know that a hotel suite isn't like a home, but the thing that counts is the spirit, isn't it? The spirit of family happiness!" the ambassador elucidated shamelessly. "I propose a toast—to our little circle. Come, Frankie—you, Hapgood—Mr. Graham there, all join in. Though I suppose," he added as an afterthought, "that we really ought to be drinking to my poor father's health—considering."

290

the buyers

The spirit of family happiness had evaporated completely by the time dessert was served. Indeed, there had been something devastating and almost gruesome about that meal partaken of in the ornate sitting room, with currents of antipathy flashing back and forth across the table like electric sparks. As always with his aunt and uncle, Frank was conscious of a profound disharmony which made him wonder what could have brought together these two contrasting personalities and kept them linked for almost half a century. Tonight the Strindbergian quality of their relationship was heightened by the presence of Cosima, the strange fruit of a strange alliance, the very antithesis of either of her parents and a perpetual irritant to both. Hapgood's bland badinages, meant to cover up an intolerable situation, served only to emphasize the uncongeniality of this "family gathering."

But before they rose from table there occurred an incident which, to Frank's surprise, did produce a moment of genuine understanding between father and daughter. As they were finishing dessert there came an urgent ringing of the telephone, and Rupert, who had been expecting a call from Washington, flew to answer. Discreet though he was, Frank could not help overhearing one end of a conversation between his uncle and an unnamed gentleman who, it would seem, was furthering Rupert's interests in Washington; there was mention of other personalities referred to by initials alone, and the name of two European capitals came into this conversation, which had an aura of secrecy and illegality worthy of a talk between gangsters in a grade B movie. Frank's natural embarrassment proved uncalled for, as both Cosima and Hapgood listened with no attempt to hide their interest; Helen, who had been silent and distrait all evening, sat staring into her glass with an expression of strain, as though her husband's preoccupation with his career bored her to the point of desperation.

When Rupert came back to the table, Cosima at once asked, "Are things going all right, Father? Do you think you'll get that new appointment you want?" And then, having noted Rupert's hesitant glance towards Frank, she added confidently, "Frankie here's one of the family. There's no danger in talking before him."

"Oh, it isn't that!" Rupert gave his nephew's arm a friendly squeeze. "Only this whole matter of appointments is so tricky that discretion's the order of the day. Things do seem to be shaping up, though, I can say. My friend in Washington sounded pretty hopeful."

"Isn't that bully now!" Hapgood exclaimed, his enthusiasm sounding as hollow as the applause of a paid claque in a theater.

However, there was no mistaking the genuine satisfaction in Cosima's voice.

"Oh, I am pleased, Father! And it's going to be a really big embassy this time, isn't it? I mean one of the *really* big ones—Rome, Paris, or something like that? It's about time they stopped giving you these second bests, like Santo Pedro. I mean, it's not as if you didn't have powerful friends in Washington—people who owe you a lot. Can't you go down there and put a little pressure on them?"

Frank was watching his uncle's face. He expected him to get angry, or perhaps to burst out laughing as he explained to Cosima that matters were not handled quite like that. Instead, he nodded sagely, as though she had suggested a quite sensible plan that had already received his consideration. And it was at that moment that there passed between Cosima and her father that look of complete understanding. Despite their contrasting personalities, it was clear that they both believed that the best things in life were for sale—and that it was eminently fitting that a Konrad should buy them.

Surprise swept over Frank, surprise and disappointment. Could it be that this was how his uncle had succeeded in his career—not through ability but through the influence of well-placed personalities who "owed him a lot"? Oh, God! thought Frank. And I who've always believed him such a great guy, a real success, in the family tradition! Well, live and learn, I guess. That famous Konrad money seems to be buying a whole lot of things I didn't even think were for sale. Cosima and Cecilia buy husbands, Rupert buys diplomatic posts, and William, Jr., buys up European scientists as if they were bananas in a grocery store. I must be suffering from a case of retarded development. College, army, college again, and now two years in the Snyder Labs—no wonder I've never found out about the facts of life before! Better grow up, Frankie!

But then he heard Katrine saying in her earnest way, "I hate buying! It does such bad things to the buyer." Well, Katrine was not suffering from arrested development, that was certain, yet she would have been more shocked than he by that look of collusion between Cosima and her father. Now if Harriet had been in the room, her reactions would have been different. Harriet took people as she found them. Though honest and loyal, she was aware that this was a competitive world (good God, wasn't she in the advertising racket!) and on the whole she accepted the proposition that the end justified the means. Probably it was better to be like Harriet, rather than to have remained so naïve (she called it starry-eyed) that the morals of an uncle you saw once every five years could upset you!

Dinner was over and the waiter had rolled the table into the corridor. On the suggestion of Rupert, Hapgood unpacked his slide viewer and began exhibiting his collection of colored slides from Santo Pedro; Cosima sat on one side of him, while on the other side sat Rupert, glancing absently at the pictures. They really were brilliantly taken, those photographs of Hapgood's, but Frank did not feel much like looking at pictures tonight. For some reason he did not care to sit too near his uncle either. As Hapgood's flat voice droned on, explaining that this slide showed Santo Pedro from the harbor and that that one had been taken (with permission) at Sir John and Lady Haskel's last garden party, Frank joined his aunt where she was sitting in the window alcove, gazing down at the long stretch of Michigan Avenue.

"What's the matter, Frankie? You look sad and worried, all at once."

Frank shook his head. "Your imagination, Aunt Helen!"

"Oh no, it isn't. It's funny, Frankie: you know, you don't look like your father at all. But just then, for a moment, you had his very expression!"

"Is that right?" said Frank, struck by the strangely intimate way Helen always spoke to him of his dead father. "Tell me, Aunt Helen," he asked, "did my father often look as you said I did just now, sad and worried?"

"What a funny question!" Helen gave him a little smile, and as he smiled back he had the feeling (it had come to him before) that there existed a mysterious and delightful bond between this favorite aunt and himself. "Why no, Frankie," she said, "at heart he was gay. But he did have such terrible inner conflicts! He was a thinker and a dreamer, not a man of action; decisions were difficult for him and, once made, still more difficult to carry out. If psychological terms had been in vogue in those days, I suppose one would have called him a split personality. And yet he was a fine person—an intelligent and fine person."

"Yes," said Frank gratefully, "I know he was."

They sat looking out on the black avenue, along which cars swept past, the swish of their tires mounting to the window like the sound of tearing paper; even from that air-conditioned room one could see that it was a very hot night. Strange, Frank was thinking, very strange that only from Helen did he seem able to find out anything about his father. His other relatives, and even his mother, had always seemed reluctant to talk about the unsuccessful Francy. (Gay and superficial, his mother seemed to have forgotten her first husband on the day she took a second, and Frank used to feel that she was ill at ease when he tried to speak of him.) Only from his father's facial expression on old photographs and from the little collection of his poems printed posthumously by his mother could Frank glean an idea of the sort of man Francy had been. Yet Frank had loved him passionately as a boy, and he still loved him. Unknown to him, half forgotten by others, his father represented for Frank Konrad something precious and very fine.

Rupert jumped up from the sofa and came walking towards their corner of the room. Perhaps it was Frank's imagining, but it had struck him before this that his uncle always made a point of breaking in when he was having a talk with his aunt.

"Go have a look at those pictures, Frankie," he said. "That fellow Hapgood—he's really quite a photographer."

"Thanks, Uncle Rupert, but it's getting late."

"It certainly is," came Hapgood's voice from the sofa. "With your permission I'll be skidding out too, and leave the family to themselves."

Hapgood and he said good night to the three of them, Frank receiving from Cosima an anguished wink which implied that she would have given a great deal to join the exodus. Hapgood was carrying his viewer and the box of slides as they stepped into the elevator; he looked like a man who has just completed a performance that has had countless repetitions.

294

"Don't you live in the hotel here?" Frank asked him while they shot downstairs.

"Oh yes, indeed. But I thought I'd step out for a breath of air before turning in. There's a newspaperman's bar a few blocks down the street. Don't want to join me for a drink, do you?"

"A drink, you say? God, I wouldn't mind a little drink!"

Hapgood left his photo equipment with the night clerk, and they strolled down Michigan, turning off when they reached East Harrison. Hapgood kept wiping his face, which perspired profusely in the humid heat. In the smoke-filled room behind the glass door a piano was being pounded; the trio of men at the corner table looked as if they were preparing a Chicago holdup.

"What'll it be?" said Hapgood, leaning his long arms on the brass bar. "They serve excellent Irish whiskey in this place."

"All right. I like Irish."

"Two double Irish, Teddy," said Hapgood to the little barman.

He unbuttoned the jacket of his dinner suit and leaned relaxedly against the bar. He seemed to have unbuttoned his face at the same time; the expression of forced jollity and respectful camaraderie vanished, to be replaced by the look of a man who had done a hard day's work. He yawned.

"Pretty dull evening, wasn't it, Frankie? Your uncle wasn't really feeling himself, I'm afraid. I think he was upset that so few of you Konrads turned up, and then he's been worrying about this new post —whether or not he's going to get it."

"Well, he's always worrying about something," said Frank. "But tell me, who was this bird that Uncle Rupert spoke to in Washington? They sounded like two conspirators together."

"Oh, nothing like that," said Hapgood with an uneasy chuckle. "But you know how these things are managed, Frankie; a little push in the right quarter is all to the good. And your uncle's very keen on getting shifted."

"I must be simple," said Frank, "but I had the idea that diplomatic posts went to the men best suited to fill them. I didn't realize that anything like baksheesh was involved."

"That's not how I'd put it." Hapgood looked rather shocked. "For a man in your uncle's position, I assure you that it's quite regular to make contributions at election time and to—er—show appreciation in other ways. Your uncle would never do anything dishonorable," he added, for he had always been very loyal to his employer. Then he glanced about, evidently searching for a safer subject. "Nice bar this, isn't it?" he said. "I am a specialist on cheap bars in the neighborhood of swank hotels. There's a beauty in Santo Pedro."

"I've never thought of you as a barfly," said Frank, still conscious of that feeling of disappointment and disgust which he had experienced in the hotel.

"Oh—well," said Hapgood. "Guy's got to let his hair down once in a while." He stared morosely at the ice cubes floating in his glass. "This high life gets to be sort of a strain, tell the truth."

It was as Hapgood spoke those words that Frank had the feeling that their conversation was being overheard. A newcomer had arrived and taken a place near them at the bar. Now as Frank turned about, he found himself looking into the light, penetrating eyes of Jan Smedlin. The curious thing, he thought afterwards, was that he was not more surprised; for some reason it seemed quite natural to run into Smedlin tonight.

Casually the newcomer raised two fingers in greeting. Smedlin, thought Frank, gave an entirely different impression here than on the train: an impression of confidence, or perhaps indifference. He had on the same worn suit, and he was again unshaved, but there was all the contrast between a man caught in alien surroundings and a man installed in his own milieu. Obviously he was not drunk. And yet he seemed almost cocky.

"Who's your friend?" Hapgood asked, lowering his voice. "Am I wrong or have I seen him before?"

"You must have. Fellow called Smedlin, used to work with my cousin William. He was his top man at the lab once."

Hapgood nodded.

"That's right. And they had some sort of quarrel—I remember now. Well, Frankie . . ." He signaled the barman. "I think I'll be toddling along. Tough day tomorrow."

Frank was about to ask Hapgood to have a return drink, then decided against it. Suddenly he wanted to get away from the bar, away from the sarcastic Smedlin! True, it was only that afternoon that he had gone to the man's house for a chat, but a lot had happened since then. He had become quite vulnerable all at once, it occurred to Frank —rather like a snail whose protective shell has been cracked. The shell was still there; nevertheless, that first crack was important.

As they walked out of the bar, Hapgood first, he a little after, Smedlin turned his head and gazed at Frank. He did not nod, nor give any form of greeting, yet somehow Frank had the feeling that Smedlin was beckoning to him! It was as if he had actually crooked his forefinger in the gesture, Come here! Almost against his will, Frank halted his step.

"What's up?" Hapgood said. "Not coming along with me, Frank?"

"No," he answered. "If you don't mind, I'll say good night. I want to have a word with that guy in there."

"Okay. Good night then. And listen, Frankie . . ." Hapgood bit his lips worriedly. "Don't let that phone conversation get you down. Try to keep things in their right perspective. We live in this world, you know, and we've got to take it as we find it."

"Do we?" said Frank. His heavy eyebrows drew together. "Well, I'm not so damn sure!"

eight

Smedlin scarcely turned his head as Frank walked back into the bar. On his face showed not the least surprise at this development, and for a moment Frank could have sworn that Smedlin had *known* he would return. Raising a lazy forefinger, Smedlin muttered a laconic "Hello."

"Hello," said Frank. "I wonder if I left my hat here."

"You didn't have a hat," said Smedlin. "You know you didn't."

Well, how answer that? No point arguing with Smedlin as to whether or not he knew he had been hatless. He confined himself to

297

taking the stool next to him at the bar, but he pointedly did not ask the fellow to have a drink. He experienced at that moment an active dislike for the impolite shabby little man, and was annoyed with himself for coming back to join him. It was humiliating and somehow—yes, somehow it was dangerous! Had not Smedlin himself said he was an enemy?

"So my sister Katrine finally had the honor of meeting a Konrad," were the Czech's first words, as he sat toying with the ice in his glass. "It seems that you had quite a chat with her."

"That's right," Frank answered. "I did."

"I hear that you came straight from a visit to your favorite cousin," Smedlin went on. "You and William, Jr., must have had a real cozy lunch together. What did he give you to eat, by the way? Tripe? It wouldn't have cost him a cent. All he'd have had to do was open his mouth and spit out some of that pseudo-scientific nonsense of his. But I'm forgetting that money's no consideration for William, Jr."

"If it isn't," said Frank, "it's because he happens to be successful." Goaded to anger, he let his eyes rest pointedly on Smedlin's worn suit. "I never knew that it was a crime to be successful. William's made a damn sight more money through his talent than he ever inherited, and don't you believe anything different."

Smedlin gazed at Frank silently for a moment, and then he began to laugh. It was a very bitter laugh, one of those laughs that might at any moment turn into a sob, and as he laughed there lay on his face a deeply tragic expression. As suddenly as it had started, the laughter ceased; his right eye began to twitch.

"Excuse me," he said. "Excuse me for my atrocious manners. But really, my dear Frankie, that line about William, Jr.'s talent! God almighty! If you're a big enough swine, I guess you can buy anything in this world, even a reputation as a genius. It must be easy, in fact, if you belong to a family of buyers."

Family of buyers! Frank felt the blood rush to his cheeks. He had a good mind to punch Smedlin's pale, supercilious face for him!

"You shut up!" he shouted, and perhaps there was particular vehemence in his voice because the remembrance of Uncle Rupert's telephone conversation was still in his mind. "You shut up, damn you

298

anyway! What's biting you, for God's sake? As far as I can see, you owe us Konrads quite a lot. Perhaps you've forgotten that if it hadn't been for William you'd have been snuffed out in a concentration camp about twelve years ago."

Then he realized that he had gone too far, and he was sorry. But Smedlin certainly had gone too far too! There were limits to how one could insult a man's family. Frank didn't want to hear any more. He refused to hear any more! Since this afternoon his future lay with William, so why let this embittered inventor poison his mind against him?

He was about to jump up. He was actually halfway off the chair, when Smedlin said something that changed the whole situation. Looking at Frank with a strange, helpless expression, quite different from the aggressive one he had been wearing until then, he said slowly:

"My boy, if William had let me die in that concentration camp I'd have been spared other tortures that the Nazis never dreamed of. It's not in Germany, but in this rich America of yours, that I was broken in two."

All Smedlin's arrogance had fled. He sat there shattered and shaken, his defenses down, his mask of cynicism fallen to the floor. He looked all at once as Frank remembered him from before the war, a bundle of ragged nerves, held together by devotion to something outside himself: science as an abstract conception. And with the appearance of this familiar Smedlin, Frank's anger vanished. He wanted to take Smedlin's hand and say that he was sorry for him; he wanted to reassure this tortured fellow of his friendship. Because he was a young American brought up in the tradition of discretion, all he did was signal the barman and say:

"A couple of Irish, please."

Smedlin, watching the liquor fall into the jiggers, had in his eyes that faraway look which seemed to traverse the walls of the little bar and rest on some distant vista. His right eye was still twitching, but less furiously now, as if Frank's small gesture of friendship had brought momentary relief. He cupped his hand around the glass pensively and looked down at it in the appreciative way that one looks at a valued gift.

"You mustn't mind me, Frankie," he said without looking up. "I go off the deep end sometimes, as they say. I swear there are times when I scarcely know what I'm saying—or doing. It's a bad way for a man to get. Very bad!"

"Don't give it another thought," said Frank. "I've forgotten."

"Then we are still friends?" There was a pleading note in the voice. "I'd like to believe that. If you want to know the truth, I've thought of you a lot, Frankie, in all these years. I even wrote you a letter once, when I heard you were back from the Pacific, but I guess I never sent it. I never seem to get around to doing anything nowadays. Anyway, I'm glad we ran into each other again—and I'm glad that you got to know Katrine."

"So am I," said Frankie. And as he no longer felt that he had to stop himself, he went on, "I think you've got a wonderful sister, Jan. I mean that. I've never met anyone quite like her. American girls are always wanting something of life, and they go out to get it, which of course is fine too; it's in the American temperament. But Katrine doesn't ask a thing! She's got all the resources within herself. She's—well, a very rich person."

Smedlin looked up from his drink, and there was a warm smile on his lips. It was the first time Frank had seen him looking happy since he had spoken of Katrine on the train.

"If you knew her as well as I do, you'd realize just how rich," he said. "Believe me, she couldn't have gone through what she did otherwise. I'm sorry that you don't live here in Chicago, so that you could get to know her better. Sorry for Katrine's sake too. She hasn't many friends. And you know, Frankie, she liked you the minute you stepped through the door."

"Well, I liked *her*," said Frank, trying to sound casual.

And yet a shock of pleasure had gone through him. Pleasure—and then surprise. For after all, there was no reason why he should feel pleased and, indeed, rather proud that Katrine liked him (in spite of having kicked him out of the house). He had a perfectly good girl of his own in Philadelphia, and no doubt could have had as many others as he wanted. But this Katrine was no ordinary girl! In her he had felt a sense of discrimination which, coupled with the natural shyness of a lonely person, must have made friendly contacts rare and difficult.

300

"I haven't given Katrine the life I would have wished," Smedlin was going on, frowning at his glass. "I live as lonely as a coyote, scarcely see anyone from one week to the next. If I could have brought her over to America a few years before, things would have been different. I had friends then—not many, but a few. I lived a different sort of life before. . . ."

"Before what, Jan?"

"Why, before I shut myself up in my shell," said Smedlin quickly, and took a drink from his glass. But Frank saw that telltale eye of his give a twitch.

"That isn't what you were going to say. Before what, Jan?"

There was a silence which seemed to Frank to last for a long time. Suddenly he felt himself gripped with intense excitement. As he waited for Smedlin's words he could hear the sound of his own breathing, and it seemed to him that the silence grew deeper, deeper. It was a fateful silence: the sort of silence that transpires between the release of the bomb and the cataclysmic explosion.

"Before William, Jr., stole my invention," Smedlin said at last in a quiet voice.

Frank stared at him, without at first grasping the full implication of his words. By now he had got rather used to hearing Smedlin say intolerable things about William. Then in a flash it came to him, and he realized that what he had just heard would be bound to have a profound significance in his life. So it was to learn this that he had gone to find Smedlin yesterday, that he had come walking back into the bar tonight!

"How do you mean, stole your invention?" he heard himself ask, but his voice betrayed the fact that he understood all too well.

"Why, just that: stole my invention, the Konrad turbine. It's really scarcely news," said Smedlin, and he was speaking quite calmly, very differently from his former almost hysterical manner. "After all, William, Jr., steals everybody's inventions—that's his profession. He has about as much inventive talent as a chicken, but he buys up brains wholesale and picks them methodically until there's nothing left to pick. Then he goes out and buys another lot. Don't pretend you don't know."

301

"And I don't believe it," cried Frank, clinging to his last illusion about William. But a strange thought had presented itself: perhaps his own brain was one of these William intended to pick next!

"You don't believe it?" repeated Smedlin. "Well, most people don't believe it, and won't believe it if you prove it ten times over. He does it cleverly, I'll give William, Jr., his due. There's always a long-term contract—a good juicy one too. In fact so juicy that as a rule you don't read it closely enough to find out that he has proprietory rights on every thought that's passed through your head since you lay kicking in the womb! Including, in my case, the rights to an invention I'd been working on years before he ever darkened my life. The original idea of the Konrad turbine came to me when I was still in the university in Prague. Konrad turbine!" Smedlin grimaced. "It's the Smedlin turbine, and that's what it ought to be called."

"Oh, the dirty bastard!" cried Frank, and his eyes blazed up beneath the heavy eyebrows, and he brought his fist down on the counter with a bang. "Why the hell didn't you bring suit against him? Why didn't you give this publicity?"

Smedlin looked at Frank with the pitying smile one gives a child who has asked a foolish question.

"A fat chance! What was the word of an unknown man (not even a citizen yet) against that of William Konrad, Jr.? What proof did I have that I'd worked out the model of that turbine ten years before? He's already taken out patents in his name. Besides, that was the war year 1944, and the only thing that interested anyone was how soon it could be put into production; no one cared a damn who the real inventor was, except William, Jr., and I. And that detail"—Smedlin's eye gave a twitch—"that detail was finally settled in the usual Konrad fashion."

"Meaning?"

"Why, through money of course! It happened that I was badly in need of dough—a whole lot of dough—just then. I'd had news that my mother might still be alive in the Theresienstadt camp near Prague, and that by sending the right sum to the right man, via Switzerland, I might get her out. It was a false rumor, I found that out later, but I was desperate and had to act on the tip. I made a deal with William, Jr., and once made, there was no unmaking it: I got the money; he took credit for the turbine. It was perfectly simple."

"Oh, God, Jan, it's the most terrible thing I've ever heard!" Frank's anger had passed. He just felt sick now, physically sick; his gorge rose, as if he were about to vomit. "And William knew the whole thing— about your mother, I mean?"

"Naturally he knew. For him it was a straight business deal, like any other, and he paid well for what he got. Tell the truth, I've been living on that money ever since—the money he gave me for betraying my talent. But an invention isn't like a pair of shoes, Frankie! An invention's a man's lifeblood, a man's soul. What happens when a man sells his soul? The day I endorsed your cousin's check I knew that I was through as a scientist, that I'd never step into a lab again. And I haven't either—not once. The power's gone out of my fingers. It'll never come back. A layman couldn't understand. You're a scientist, Frankie. You can. I'm—I'm good for nothing any more."

Smedlin laid his arm on the counter and put his head down on it. A mesh of dark hair fell forward, to dangle in a pool of spilled liquor. He looked what he was: a man beaten by life, too demoralized to pick himself up and resume the struggle. And Frank did understand. Because of his own love for science he understood what had happened to Jan—understood also the futility of words.

"Now I know," he said. "Now I know—why you hate us so much!"

Smedlin did not answer. He sat there with his head on his arm, and Frank saw that his shoulders were shaking. Never before had he seen an adult man cry, and the sight filled him with dismay. He knew that there was nothing to say, that there was nothing to do. How console a man so far beyond the reach of consolation? The kindest thing would be to leave Jan in his own tragic world, whose secrecy was the last dignity left him. It would be the crowning insult to try to trespass further on the private domain of grief.

Apart from that, he had his own problems to resolve: problems of deep import. After what he had learned tonight he knew that he must establish a new attitude towards his family and towards the fortune that they represented. And, having established it, he must act accordingly. His Aunt Helen had said that his father had been a thinker, incapable of reaching decisions, or of acting upon them, when reached. He, Frank, was no thinker, but he knew from experience that it lay in his character to decide.

"Good-by, Jan," he said, expecting no answer, and keenly aware that Smedlin only wanted him to go. "Thank you for telling me."

The frail figure sprawled across the counter was motionless; even the spasmodic heaving of the shoulders had stopped. Jan Smedlin was rigid as a statue of stone depicting defeat.

Frank walked to the end of the bar and laid two dollar bills on the counter. Thank God, he told himself, that this was his own money, earned by his efforts, not part of that Konrad fortune which seemed to dominate the lives of its inheritors. Perhaps, the thought occurred to him, his mother had done him the best service she could by squandering the money which should by rights have been his.

The little barman called Teddy sidled up. He was wiping a glass on a towel.

"Good night, Mr. Konrad. Come again!" he called out.

"How the hell d'you know my name's Konrad?" Frank asked him.

"Oh, I know most things about this city. I was born right on this block."

"Well, look after my friend there, Teddy," Frank said to the barman. "He isn't a very happy guy."

"Don't worry. I'll look after him." Teddy, still wiping the glass, threw a glance at Smedlin. "God damn it," he said, "why is it that this town Chicago is so lousy with unhappy guys?"

nine

The green Buick shot up the driveway and came to a halt beneath the portico. Cosima leaped out and rang the doorbell, but when a few seconds passed and Hauptman failed to appear, she dove into her handbag for the key. Not finding it, she dumped out the entire contents on the car seat and picked out the key amongst coins and lipsticks. Then she poured back the other things into the bag, unlocked the heavy oaken door and pushed it open with her shoulder.

On the sofa in the hallway her cousin Frank was sitting talking to a young man whom she recognized as Sam Graham, the reporter from the Chicago *Despatch;* she remembered vaguely having given him an appointment for two o'clock. Both men jumped to their feet when she came in the hall.

"Gosh, Cosima, you look flustered! What's happened?" asked Frank.

"What's happened? Oh, nothing—nothing at all," replied Cosima, throwing her hand to her head in what she realized was a dramatic gesture. "Only that they've decided to take my child away from me. I suppose it isn't very important at this stage of the world's history."

"You mean that the court awarded your husband jurisdiction after all? I'm sorry, Cosima!"

"Ah, but he's not going to get away with it! You see if he does. To think of that so-and-so's saying that I wasn't capable of bringing up a child—but that he *was*. He! Why, Stan Harding was purser on a boat when I first met him, and not even an honest purser! Can you imagine the Court's giving him jurisdiction instead of me?"

"Well, my imagination is pretty good," said Frank, fascinated by the sensational curves of Cosima's figure, which as usual were displayed to best advantage. Whereupon Cosima swung around on Frank.

"That was a dirty crack! I'll know in the future who are my friends and who aren't."

She turned and flew up the stairs, teeth clenched, face dark as a storm cloud.

Sam Graham, who seemed to have made a habit of being present when Cosima was kicking up rough, remarked, "Well, I guess that settles my interview. It doesn't matter too much. I'll write up one anyway and send it for her okay. It'll probably sound more plausible than anything your cousin could say."

Frank gave a grin. He could not help liking Graham, despite the fellow's hard-boiled manner and what at times seemed purposeful rudeness. Beneath his cynical mask Frank had felt a sensitivity and a certain youthful idealism seldom associated with reporters. Perhaps that was why he had struck up this conversation, having run into Graham while about to leave the house after luncheon.

"I guess Cosima's pretty obvious," he remarked. "Too much money, too little control, third generation and so on. Don't need to be a psychologist to diagnose her trouble: she's lacking an aim in life."

"Sure. Sure. I cover the divorce courts; I see dames like that every day. They come a dime a dozen, and as a matter of fact they're of no interest any more. Life's a pretty serious proposition nowadays, and there's no room in this country for people like this haywire cousin of yours."

"Or people like my Uncle Rupert?" suggested Frank.

Graham sent Frank a sharp glance; his long nose gave a twitch, as if he were scenting the ground.

"I didn't say that! In fact I gave my interview with him quite a complimentary twist. Did you read this morning's *Despatch?*"

"Sure. And I read between the lines. I don't say you're wrong, but you sure don't think much of him as a diplomat, do you?"

Graham took out his handkerchief and blew his great nose. Perhaps it was his way of stalling for time, but it sounded like a snort of disgust.

"Oh well, you Konrads have to do something with your money," he said pointedly. "I guess giving dinner parties is as good a way of tossing it about as any other, but it's too bad your uncle got bitten with this diplomatic bug. I happen to like this country, and I hate having those foreigners taking the Honorable Rupert Konrad as the best type of American. Talk of sending ammunition to the Communists! Your aunt, Mrs. Foyles, makes a fool of herself too, but thank God she does it at home. So does your other aunt, Bee Konrad, though I'll give her the benefit of the doubt and say that she means well. At least she's an honorable woman."

"Say, Graham, you seem to know an awful lot about my relatives!"

"Oh well, you're a famous family, you know. It's really part of my job. It's a good thing someone keeps an eye on you rich guys, or you'd be running this city and this country, and I wouldn't like that one bit. Now I guess you'll want to kick me right out of this marble mansion."

"Wrong again. Have a drink!"

"No thanks. I had a Konrad cocktail yesterday and it wasn't very good. Besides, I have to be going; it happens that I've got to work for my living."

306

"All right," said Frank, "but before you go let's get this straight." He pointed his forefinger at Graham. "Don't you go mixing me up with my Uncle Rupert or anyone else. My name's Frank Konrad, and I'm quite a different guy. I happen to be working for my living too."

Graham looked at Frank sharply; his nose gave another of those exploratory twitches. Then he let a good-natured smile come into his face.

"Sorry," he said. "I know I've got the hell of a disposition. Just born that way, I guess! The fact is, you Konrads have always managed to get my goat. I was born on the South Side, right near the Stock Yards, and as a kid I used to have that God damned stink in my nostrils day and night. Perhaps that's what started my anti-Konradism, but it's got a lot worse since I found out about the people responsible for that stink —and a few others. I just don't like the idea of one family's buying up everything from social position to solid fame! Still, I should have known that not all sheep are one color. Well, I'll be seeing you—one of these days."

He reached for his hat, set it on his head at a jaunty angle, and ambled out of the house.

In the meanwhile Cosima, in her room, had locked the door and flung herself on the bed. She wanted to think things out and arrive at conclusions, but it was a bit difficult, considering how her head was spinning. Moreover, Cosima was not in the habit of clear thinking. The thing that had just taken place was so staggering, so momentous, that she felt that the pillars of her world were shaken. Such things simply didn't happen when you were a Konrad, and when, as in this case, you had known the presiding judge since you were a child!

And it was so unjust! Naturally she had been a little wild from time to time, naturally she had a boy friend (who hadn't?), but was either of these a reason for awarding her own child to a nobody like Stan Harding, who had been purser on a Fall River steamer when she made his acquaintance? What if Pat *had* said that she would rather stay with her father? Was a child of five to understand what was best for her? It was a cruel and unnatural thing to separate mother and daughter, thought Cosima, who had never shown herself very averse to such separations in the past.

Cosima jumped up from the bed and began pacing the room. She had to do something. She had to do something. But what? She thought of phoning her boy friend, Billy Cartwright, but Billy was a stockbroker and very conservative by nature; he would just advise her to make the best of it, and to come to his apartment to get consoled. Her own parents were in town, but they were the very last people she would want to consult. She felt deserted and betrayed. The thing in which she had laid unquestioned trust since a child—the power of the Konrad name and money—had for almost the first time proved wanting.

Cosima stopped at the window and stood looking down at the lawn below. One of her grandfather's gardeners was trimming the grass, and the noise of the mower sounded in her ears like the rattle of machine guns; soothing at any other time, it jarred her today, so that she wanted to throw up the window to call to the man to go away. She realized that her arms, resting on the window sill, were trembling; there was a sensation of dryness in her throat. And now, as she stood listening to the mower, she could feel a pounding in her head, as though the rhythmic tattoo were churning up her blood. Cosima experienced a brief pang of fright. Knowing herself, she realized that at times like the present she was capable of absolutely any action, that all notion of moderation and judgment had already been abandoned. She put her hands to her ears and stood quite still for a moment, trying to shut out the noise of the mower. It sounded louder than ever. It seemed to be whirring away inside her head.

Leaving the window, Cosima sat down at her dressing table. She was not thinking, was scarcely conscious of her actions as she made up her face and bound a bright yellow scarf about her head. Leaning closer to the mirror, she plucked out a gray hair near her temple with a movement of instinctive panic. Before leaving the room, she went to get the overnight case which she always kept ready packed in the closet, and she counted the money in her bag. There were about three hundred dollars in clipped bundles of ten-dollar bills.

"Where are you off to?" Frank called to her as she passed through the hall.

"Fireworks," said Cosima tersely. "There are going to be fireworks. Keep tuned in to this station for sensational developments."

the buyers

She slid into the driver's seat of the Buick and threw the car into gear; a shower of pebbles were flung against the base of the portico as she sped off down the drive. Rounding the sharp curves and then speeding down Drexel, Cosima began to breathe freer. The very act of traveling dangerously, too swiftly, seemed to relieve the fierce tension inside her. In this solid black section of the city careless pedestrians were apt to wander into the street, but Cosima never slackened her speed, seeking rather than avoiding close escapes. A Negro boy holding a section of watermelon leaped back as she swept by, and then stood gazing at the rapidly vanishing car that bucked red lights and wound its way among the traffic like a swerving meteor.

As she reached the North Side and sped along the lake road towards Evanston, Cosima's excitement again mounted. In her ears the sound of the mower had come back, a steady whir that seemed to rise or sink in accordance with the speed of the car. As yet there was no fixed plan in her mind; driven onwards by an irresistible force, she knew that at the crucial moment she would see her way and act without hesitation. Thus it had always been in the past. Fleetingly the memory of other escapades flashed through her mind: the time she and Sam Luke (the ex-boxer whom she later married) held up and robbed a car on the highway, just for the hell of the thing; the time she walked out of the Art Institute in broad daylight with a valuable painting under her arm (it had cost her father a pretty penny to straighten out that affair); the time she pretended to be a famous French actress at a lunch party, and the actress herself arrived while they were at dessert. Always she had felt an urge to accomplish actions without any possible benefit to herself, but whose very incredibility lured her. She had not been able to stop herself, nor, if truth be known, had she tried. When worst came to worst, she had counted on her father and Hapgood to pull her chestnuts out of the fire. Rupert, for the sake of his own position, could not allow scandals to break about Cosima's head.

I am an *enfant terrible,* thought Cosima, her foot pushing hard on the accelerator. But then she remembered with a pang that unfortunate gray hair plucked out by the roots half an hour before. Why must she be confronted with these disturbing evidences of physical maturity?

The house where she and Stan Harding had lived since their marriage lay on the northern outskirts of Hadon Heights, not far from William, Jr.'s glass laboratory. Cosima slowed up when she came within sight, and drove her car off the road, to park it in the shelter of some hawthorn bushes. Then she got out, made her way through a break in the bushes, and slipped into the residence through the service door. Having tiptoed across the empty kitchen, she ran up the creaking back staircase and took the corridor which led to the living quarters. Arrived at the door of little Pat's room, Cosima stopped to listen. Thank God! she thought, hearing neither voices nor footsteps. Pat must be having her after-lunch rest. The first part of the adventure had passed off very well!

When she walked into the room, little Pat was lying in bed looking at a picture book. Beside her on the pillow lay the enormous Mickey Mouse Stan had given her for her fourth birthday. When she caught sight of her mother Pat gave a squeal.

"Oh hello!" she said, and even in Cosima's excitement she could not help noting the absence of delight in the child's voice. (Stan's been setting her against me! she thought.)

Cosima put a finger to her lips.

"Sh!" she warned. "Don't make any noise, darling. This is a secret between you and me. I've come to take you for a drive and a picnic supper. Won't that be fun?"

"Ye-es," said Pat doubtfully.

"Oh, it will, darling! You'll see. Now I want you to get up and dress, like a big girl. I'll help you. Then we'll go off together and have lots of fun."

"Ma'amselle said that I shouldn't move till she gets back. She'll be angry," Pat declared.

"Don't be a goose now! I'm your mother. Ma'amselle won't mind."

Pat's clothes were still laid out on the chair. Cosima picked up Pat's jersey and held it out to her, whereupon Pat slowly took off her pajama top and put her arms in the sleeves of the jersey. Cosima slipped it over her head.

"Now hurry up, Patsy! Let's try and get ready before Ma'amselle gets back. That's a good girl."

"So Ma'amselle *will* be mad?" said Pat, gazing up at Cosima with her big eyes.

"No, no. Ma'amselle isn't going to know. Here are your bloomers now, sweetheart. Come, jump out of bed."

Two minutes later Cosima and Pat were walking down the main stairs, Cosima leading her daughter by the hand, because she still seemed reluctant to go along on this strange afternoon "picnic." As they were about to leave the house, the maid came out of the pantry with a large bunch of flowers in a vase. She gave a start.

"Oh, I didn't know you was here today, ma'am."

"I just came to take Pat for a little drive. We'll be back in a while."

"Yes, ma'am," said the maid from behind the flowers. And then she added, "Mr. Harding, he wasn't home for lunch."

"No," said Cosima. "If he comes in, tell him that I'll be back soon."

"I see, ma'am," said the maid. "Should I say where you went?"

"Don't trouble," answered Cosima. "He won't care to join us. Come along, Pat!"

They walked down the driveway, and then along the main road towards the hawthorn bushes where Cosima had parked the Buick. Calm outwardly, she sensed within her a frantic excitement which quickened her heartbeats and caused her throat to feel dry and constricted. She talked a lot and tried to joke with the child; Pat, however, walked along slowly, dragging her steps. On her handsome, expressive face lay a sullen look.

"Well, here we are," said Cosima, unlocking the door of her car. "One-two-three, in you go, darling."

"I want to go home," said Pat suddenly, not looking up at her mother. "Ma'amselle will be looking for me."

"I've told you already that Ma'amselle won't mind," said Cosima impatiently. "We're going to take a lovely drive and then have picnic supper together. Get in now, Patsy."

Pat stood looking down at the road. Her pouting mouth, her brooding eyes, even her knotty little pigtails expressed rebellion; had she been a child given to moods, she would have fallen into a tantrum, or else begun to cry. However, obedience had been drummed into her by an authoritarian Swiss governess, and now without another word she stepped into the car. Cosima took a deep breath of relief. Everything was under control, and it had gone a lot better than if planned to the last detail. To think that she had not known an hour ago that she meant to kidnap her own daughter! That, thought Cosima, was what made her life so fascinating; she cherished the element of incertitude ever present when one relies on one's inspirations.

But before she had time to push the starter Cosima realized that her inspirations were not infallible after all. A gray roadster had appeared around the bend and, without having seen the number plate, Cosima recognized it as Stan's car—or at least the car that she had given Stan. Rapidly it approached and then swept by her, and her eyes met his for the fraction of a second. It was in that moment of fleeting contact that Cosima had a premonition, sharp as a dagger thrust, that catastrophe lay ahead.

"That's Daddy!" Pat cried, turning about in her seat to wave. "Why don't you stop, Mummy? Oh, stop! Stop!"

"No, we haven't got time, darling. And besides, we want to have our picnic supper alone, don't we—just the two of us?"

"Oh, do we?" said Pat. "I think it would be more fun if Daddy came along."

From the tone of her voice Cosima could tell that Pat did not believe a word about that "picnic supper."

The car was ripping along the highway now, its motor out, the tires singing in protest as they dug into the asphalt at the turns. Cosima's eyes, glued to the road, moved upwards ever and again to the surface of the windshield mirror, and presently, sure enough, a gray car came into view, traveling as rapidly as Cosima herself, though several hundred yards behind. Cosima's eyes flashed and she pressed down on the accelerator. The venture had gone on the rocks, no doubt of that! Nevertheless, thought Cosima, it had been successful in a way. Why should one always do things for a result anticipated—why not for the mere sake of the doing? Inside her brain the lawn mower had begun to whir again, making a clattering sound now, as if something had gone slightly wrong with the mechanism. She gave a shake of her head; she smiled. In this moment of wild crisis Cosima was perhaps as near to being happy as she could ever be.

"Why are you going so fast, Mummy? The arrow on the speedometer thing says seventy-five."

"We're having a race, darling," Cosima said. "A real automobile race, like you've seen in the movies. Don't you think that it's fun?"

Pat tried to smile, but her mouth was trembling, and the words seemed to stick in her throat. Her eyes, set in fright through the window, rested for fractions of seconds on trees, houses, and pedestrians as they flashed past. Traveling so quickly, everything seemed to her distorted and queer. They passed a street intersection with a traffic light, and the light was red as they tore past; they went through a village where a policeman waved to them to stop; then they were out in the open country again, and in the dashboard mirror the gray car was still following them, about the same distance behind.

At any moment, thought Cosima, I can stop. I can slow down, and then draw up beside the road, and this mad chase will be over. I'd better do it for the kid's sake, if not for mine. As it is, I'll never be able to throw off Stan. He's as stubborn as a mule, and he's just as reckless as I. Should I put on the brakes now? Yes, now!

Yet even as she toyed with the thought her foot pressed hard on the accelerator. She knew in her heart that she wouldn't stop, couldn't stop, even if she wanted to. On and on she must go, and at breakneck speed. And suddenly, for some reason, she thought of her grandfather, lying dying in his big four-poster bed. He, whom she admired more than anyone, had hurtled on like this right through life, oblivious of his own or anybody's safety. True, he had headed for a well-perceived goal, which certainly was not the case with her. Well, that was too bad, but as she could not speed towards a goal, why not—just speed? The old Konrad drive is still there, she thought, a bit aimless nowadays, a bit degenerate perhaps, but don't I know that it's as powerful as ever!

The whole time the lawn mower was clattering away in her brain. It made a hideous, grinding sound, ever increasing in intensity, and it goaded her on like the rattle of the can tied to a cat's tail. Louder and louder grew the clatter. It was almost intolerable, yet what could she do to stop it? She must go faster, faster! In the end she might leave the clatter behind, together with Stan. A curve loomed ahead. No, she could not slow up even for that! It would let her gain yards on him.

As the tires shrieked in protest on the bend, Pat gave out a terrified scream. Throwing herself against her mother, she seized at her arm in panic. The car veered, and there was a fearful bump as it left the road. So this is it! thought Cosima in the split second before the crash. This is what I've been waiting for all along. Suddenly she knew that she had been heading for this moment ever since she was Pat's age—no, even before that—perhaps ever since she was born. Always inside her had been this fierce impulse towards disaster, wrecking every relationship, overriding every other emotion. As she waited the cataclysm before her, Cosima Konrad experienced a feeling of completion for the first time.

ten

William Konrad, Jr., was sitting in his office, fiddling with the colograph, when they phoned from the police station. As he switched off the instrument, bringing Shostakovitch's Fifth to an untimely end, he had the feeling that there was something very wrong, and when he heard the voice of Johnson, the local police captain, he was certain.

"Good afternoon, Mr. Konrad. I'm afraid I've got bad news. Your cousin, Mrs. Harding, has had a terrible smashup just down your road. I'm sorry to say that her little girl was killed on the spot. Mrs. Harding is suffering from severe shock and they've taken her to the hospital. It's a bad business."

"My God," said William, and to himself he added, Damn Cosima! I always knew she'd end by doing something like this!

"I thought I'd better call you," went on Johnson (his voice low, as if he did not wish to be overheard), "considering the special circumstances. Fact is, Mrs. Harding was trying to kidnap the little girl and Mr. Harding was chasing them in another car, hell-bent for leather. You may not know that he was awarded final custody of the child this morning."

"Ouch! That makes it bad, doesn't it?"

"It sure does. We're trying to keep it out of the papers, Mr. Konrad—I mean that aspect of the case—but it isn't going to be easy. That's why I gave you a call soon as possible."

"Very nice of you, Johnson. I appreciate it."

"Well, you've been very nice to me, sir. Now if I were you, I'd try to get on to Mr. Stanley Harding right away. It's really up to him how much publicity this matter's going to get. You may be able to squelch it, with good will all around. If not—well, I'm afraid it is going to make a nasty stink."

I should say it is, thought William, as he hung up. What's more, the stink is going to blow in my direction. Damn Cosima! Oh, damn her for an irresponsible bitch! What a time to have the name Konrad dragged through the mire, with the grant for the laboratory up for renewal and the wolves ready to tear me to bits. Whatever happens, whatever the cost, scandal's got to be avoided.

He switched on the colograph, which resumed its interpretation of Shostakovitch from the point where it had been turned off; as the instrument played on, the colored snakes and worms traced their eerie paths across the screen, and William sat watching them in absorption. He had found the manipulation of gadgets to be of great help in mental crises. When the third movement had come to an end he turned the off-button, reached for the telephone again, and dialed the number of Cosima's house. After listening to the ringing sound for a good minute, he was relieved when a servant came on the line.

"Is Mr. Harding home?" William asked her. "This is very important."

"Yes, but he can't come to the phone." The woman's voice sounded distracted. "There's been a terrible accident this afternoon."

"Tell him that Mr. William Konrad, Jr., is on the wire. And please say that it's of the utmost urgency that I have a word with him."

"Very well, Mr. Konrad. But I don't think he'll come. Mr. Harding is just terribly cut up."

As William waited, passing his hand thoughtfully over his thinning hair, he analyzed the situation. It certainly was not a pleasant one, whatever way one looked at it. A scandal loomed, a scandal that might involve the whole Konrad family, including himself, and the arbiter of their destiny was Stan Harding, a fortune hunter and adventurer. In

315

his power it lay to divulge the facts of the kidnaping: to have Cosima judged as an unfortunate woman who by chance had caused the death of her own child—or else to brand her as a wanton murderess. It would take negotiations and luck to keep the truth out of the papers, but, thank God, the Konrads had always been good at negotiating. And there was no doubt they had had their share of luck too, thought William.

And here was Stan Harding on the line, his voice sounding quite different from the last time William had heard it, when Stan and Cosima came in for dinner about a year before.

"This is a hell of a time to call up a man. What do you want anyway?"

"I've just heard this awful news, Stan. I rang up to tell you how terribly sorry I was. Believe me . . ."

"I certainly don't," Harding snapped. "I never believe a word from any of you Konrads. The only thing you're sorry about is that you think there's going to be a ruckus, and believe me, you're right. I'll see to that. You know, once upon a time women used to get stoned to death for infanticide!"

"I'm sorry you feel that way about it, old man," said William soothingly. "Cosima's haywire and we all know it. But listen, Stan: just think how she must be feeling at this moment!"

"I haven't got time. I'm feeling something myself," said Harding.

"Oh, I do realize that, old man. I'm sorry as I can be. Such a cute kid too, little Patsy! It's a limitless tragedy, and I'm sure Cosima was to blame a hundred per cent. I only wish," William said, picking his words carefully, "I only wish that we Konrads could make up to you for it in some way."

A silence at the other end. William waited anxiously, hoping that he had not gone too far, hoping particularly that no one was listening in to his conversation. Suspicious by nature, he had of late got the idea that telephone conversations from the laboratory were being tapped. It was a relief when he heard Harding's voice, though there was nothing encouraging about the words, nor the tone either.

"Now what the hell do you mean by that?"

"It's too painful to talk about all this on the telephone," said William, seeing an opening at last. "Would you mind if I drove over to see you, Stan? I could be there in a few minutes."

Another silence, longer than the first. Then Harding's voice, still curt, unfriendly: "Well, if you want to, I guess that I can't stop you."

So that was that, thought William, turning in his seat to switch on the colograph again. The first round was gained, but one thing was certain: this affair was going to run into big money. Fortunately there were others involved far deeper than he, and he saw no reason why they should not shoulder the responsibility. He considered telephoning his Uncle Rupert, but then he hit on a better plan. As it happened, a good many Konrads were in Chicago right now and his own father was the acting head of the family. There was no doubt that the occasion was serious enough for William, Sr., to call together a family conference in Sans Souci.

Tugging frenziedly at his ear lobe, Rupert strained forward in his seat as the taxi shot away from the Blackstone.

"Snap it up, driver! There's two dollars extra for you if you get us to Drexel Boulevard by six o'clock."

"Relax, Mr. Konrad—take it easy," Hapgood advised him. "There's nothing to be gained by taking risks. And a lot to be lost, as we've just learned from your own daughter Cosima."

"I guess you're right," said Rupert, forcing himself to sit back in the seat. "Oh, God, Hapgood, why did this have to happen? And why just now? Cosima couldn't have chosen a worse time for a scandal, what with my father's illness bringing us all right in the news, and my appointment up for decision any day. What sort of an impression is it going to make in Washington, d'you suppose, when those headlines burst out? Hapgood, do you realize that that girl may have ruined my career?"

"Don't let's exaggerate," Hapgood said. "Nothing really bad's happened yet—apart from the child's death, of course," he added hastily. "Let's hope for the best, sir—and just fight like hell!"

Rupert nodded, lighting a cigarette. Strange how this fellow Hapgood could calm him, even when things looked their worst! He had a knack, one might almost say a talent, for soothing, for projecting himself into another person's tortured mind, for finding the one word that would encourage or give solace. After their thirty-year alliance Rupert realized more keenly than ever that he literally could not have got on without him.

"What actually did my brother say on the telephone?" he asked in a calmer voice, noting through the window that the taxi was speeding past Soldier Field. He had not been at home when William telephoned an hour ago, and it was Hapgood who received the message.

"Well, just as I told you," the secretary said. "Your daughter had this unfortunate accident while driving off with the child, and was taken to the hospital suffering from shock. Mrs. Konrad went to join her, feeling very much upset. You know how fond she was of her little grandchild."

Rupert nodded, and into his eyes, usually turned in upon himself, there came a look of profound distress.

"Poor little kid!" he said, shaking his head. "Poor little Patsy! What a horrible tragedy it all is, Hapgood!"

"It is indeed," Hapgood agreed, seeking for words of solace and finding none. "It's—it's most unfortunate," he concluded lamely.

"But what do you suppose got into Cosima's head to do such a thing?" Rupert cried in a tone of bewilderment. "How can a woman steal her own child and try to run off like a sneak thief? I always knew that Cosima was wild, but this isn't just wildness; it's the action of an unbalanced person. Am I to believe that my own child is abnormal?"

"No, no," Hapgood protested. "Nothing like that, sir. Just another escapade, like all those before, but it happened to turn out much worse. The fact is, if I may say so, that your daughter Cosima has never really grown up."

"Well, isn't that in itself pretty tragic?" said Rupert. "After all, Cosima's no child; she's been married three times. When *is* she going to grow up? We've spoiled her, Hapgood—spoiled her horribly ever since she was a baby. Spoiled her and not given her any real values to live by: only money, money—cars, jewelry, clothes. I can see it all now, and I blame myself. I was a bad father, and I suppose I deserve to make the painful discovery that my own child has become a psychological case!"

Hapgood took a long time to reply. For once he did not know the right thing to say, the thing that would re-establish his employer's shattered world and assure him that the important thing in life was the winning of prestige, rather than the solidifying of human relationships. For thirty years he had watched Rupert Konrad devoting himself to the former pursuit, and in that he had been able to help him; but now that he saw his chief bewildered and distressed, face to face with the incontroversial fact that at the age of twenty-nine his own daughter was a stranger, Hapgood felt embarrassed and at a loss for words. Indeed, it seemed to him that the language in which they had always conversed was quite inadequate for this occasion.

"I shouldn't worry too much," he said at last, feeling that he was like a man struggling with a foreign tongue. "In the end this tragedy, painful though it is, may prove a helpful lesson for your daughter. A terrible lesson, I realize, but perhaps the only kind that she could understand. It may even turn Cosima into a mature human being! The important thing now," concluded Hapgood, his practical mind searching for solutions, "the important thing is that we try and save her good name—and the good name of the family. The important thing, in other words, is that we keep this story out of print."

"Ah yes," said Rupert, he also sounding relieved to be back on more familiar ground. "You're right, Hapgood: we've got to see to that, whatever it costs. It's the first and foremost consideration. For the moment let's not think of anything else."

Hapgood leaned back in his seat. He took out his handkerchief to wipe his forehead, which was covered with sweat. Thank the Lord, he thought, that he had managed to steer the conversation away from a painful subject, and one entirely out of his ken. He had acted as father confessor to Rupert before this, but he refused to take (or rather found himself incapable of taking) the place of the family analyst. After all, reflected Hapgood, passing the handkerchief over his pale cheeks and then over his perspiring neck, there were limits even to the duties of a confidential secretary! Now he and Rupert were speaking their own language again.

319

When Bee and Cecilia drove up to Sans Souci they found four cars parked in the winding driveway, which had been laid out for carriages, rather than for high-powered automobiles. The rear of William, Sr.'s huge Lincoln protruded into the rhododendron bushes.

"Ah, there's Cecil's Nash. We drove in it from California," said Cecilia as they alighted. "And, thank goodness, there's William, Jr.'s blue Packard. If anybody can get us out of this jam, it's William, Jr. He's a genius, that boy! Those were Gerald's very words when I told him what Cosima'd gone and done."

"I thought you weren't to tell anyone," scolded Bee, locking her car door with the golden bee on the panel. "Your husband included! Didn't William make it clear that the less people who know about this the better?"

"Ah yes, but Gerald really isn't anyone, is he? And he'd rather die than let out a word. Honor of an English gentleman and all that. A woman should have no secrets from her husband."

"So you *still* believe that," said Bee, which was an allusion to the unfortunate occasion when Gerald's predecessor, Justin Judson, had worked the combination of his wife's safe preparatory to running off with her jewels. "You were always a fool, Cecilia, if you don't mind my saying so."

"Not in the least, dear. You've done far too much speaking in public to be taken seriously any longer. But this isn't the time for bickering, is it? The family's in trouble and we've got to stick together today."

"Yes, there you're right," said Bee as she rang the doorbell. "What a situation—especially for me! If I've stood for anything in Illinois politics, its morality and family unity. My friends in the Women's Political League want me to run for Congress, but if this scandal breaks, I'd have as much chance as Al Capone's ghost!"

"And how about *my* social position? D'you suppose this will help it?" grumbled Cecilia. "You know Chicago: the size of a village and not a very large one at that. In a week, my dear, most people may be thinking of us simply as Cosima Harding's aunts!"

Hauptman opened the front door, bowed to the two elderly ladies, and murmured: "Good afternoon, Miss Cecilia. Good afternoon, Miss Beatrice." Having known them both since they were children, he

320

always found it difficult to remember that one of them was now a grandmother and the other often referred to as "the old queen bee of Chicago."

"Quite a family gathering, isn't it, Hauptman?" said Cecilia, stopping before the hall mirror to adjust the feathered hat perched gaily atop her mauve hair.

"No, Miss Cecilia, you can't go upstairs," answered Hauptman, having as usual misunderstood. "Dr. O'Grady, he says the boss can't see no one today. When I brought him his bouillon at one o'clock he didn't even recognize me."

The old man spoke categorically, but at the same time with unwonted cheerfulness. He smiled to "the children" before disappearing in the direction of the pantry.

"You'd think he was trying to keep Father to himself," Bee said to Cecilia as they headed for the parlor. "He's never looked happier than when he says 'No visitors.' Do you realize that he actually *smiled* at us today? Something nice must have happened to him. I wonder what. Well, well, now for the atom blasts!"

The big room seemed to be crowded with Konrads. By the center table, in Mama's old chair, sat Gladys, between her daughter Susan and Cecilia's married daughter Mabel; she nodded solemnly to her sisters-in-law as they came in. At the other end of the room, near the marble effigy of the horse Bismarck, a male confab was going on, the two Williams, Rupert, and Cecilia's sons, Cecil and Harry, having put their heads together in earnest consultation; Victor Hapgood hovered discreetly on the periphery, available at any moment, should Rupert wish to call him. Of the men present, one alone had failed to join this inner conference: Frank Konrad, who sat on the green plush sofa beneath Mama's portrait, on his face a tense look that Bee's shrewd eye noted the minute she stepped in the room.

"Cheer up, Frankie," she said, walking up to him. "You'll see, it'll all come out right in the end."

He looked up at her then, but there was no answering smile on his face. Once again Bee was struck with the remarkable resemblance between her nephew and old Adolph, lying stricken in the room above. She remembered occasions when she had come across her father ponder-

ing some decision, and on his face had lain that same look of un-
divided concentration.

"It'd take more than this to beat the Konrads," said Bee, wondering
what thoughts were passing through his head.

If his answer was any indication, Bee might have been happier without knowing, for what he said gave her quite a shock. Later she wondered if she had understood him right. Looking her square in the eyes
with that fiery gaze which he also had inherited from old Adolph, he
said in a calm voice:

"That is just what I've been wondering, Aunt Bee—I mean, whether
or not this thing is going to beat the Konrads. Well, I'll wait and see."

Bee would have asked him what he meant, but just then the group in
the corner broke up and William, Jr., and his father came walking towards them. The older man was talking, while William, Jr., listened
earnestly, and once or twice nodded in agreement. Then his father
walked off, leaving William, Jr., standing by the center table, whence
he sent his glance about the company. Gradually everyone fell silent.
Not a sound could be heard except the tick-tock of the old grandfather
clock that stood in a corner of the hallway. Even the horse Bismarck
seemed to be cocking his stone ears in attention.

And then, just as William was about to speak, as he stood there, stroking the back of his head with that gesture familiar to them all, there
came the sound of the doorbell ringing. Everyone glanced about, wondering who the newcomer might be. As far as Bee could make out, the
whole family were present, excepting Cosima and Gerald Foyles, who,
not being a Chicagoan, had not been invited. Adolph's four children,
six of his seven grandchildren, were assembled here today to decide in
a time of crisis the line of Konrad policy.

Suddenly there came to her ears the sound of light footsteps and a
woman's voice speaking to Hauptman in the hall. But of course! How
strange that she should have forgotten the mother of Cosima on this
particular occasion! Or perhaps not so strange after all, seeing that
neither she nor any of these others had ever thought of Rupert's wife as
really belonging to the family. They had never accepted her, and con-
versely, she had never accepted them. As the door opened and Helen
Konrad stepped into the room, it occurred to Bee that she was as much

of a stranger here today as on that winter afternoon forty-five years before when she, the professor's daughter, had come walking into their lives for the first time.

eleven

Helen had driven straight from the hospital to Sans Souci in a taxi. Having found her daughter sleeping under the effects of a narcotic, she had decided to go on to the family conference, rather than to wait until Cosima awakened—awakened to the full realization of her crime. No doubt her decision was a cowardly one, thought Helen, once she was in the cab: cowardly and facile, like so many of her decisions. She had dreaded the moment of truth between herself and Cosima in the whitewashed room, the moment when Cosima would turn to her for comfort, only to find that she had nothing to give her daughter any longer, neither love nor sympathy. The fearful fact was that Cosima today could more easily find comfort from almost any other person— a strange nurse, a lover, possibly a friend. The very presence of her mother would be a reproach, not only for this latest deed, but for a pattern for life of which Helen had utterly disapproved, yet had been utterly incapable of altering.

In the taxi she had begun to cry. She did not know if she was weeping for Patsy's death or because it was Cosima who was to blame; or because she herself had proved so abysmal a failure as a mother. Her sorrow was very bitter, and as the sobs shook her body, she felt that she had that day reached the depth of misery—yes, an even lower depth than the time Cosima first used blackmail against her, or that far distant occasion when she said good-by to Francy in his mountain shack. Strange how there always remained a new stratum of suffering to which to penetrate, even after convincing oneself that one had reached the very end! Would one on one's very deathbed have to face new trials, new ignominy, new spiritual pain? Must one, she thought, kiss the foot of the cross again and yet again?

She was almost at her destination. All at once she had a wild desire to

323

drive back to her hotel, to go into her room—and drink. In her mind's eye she saw that square bottle in her cupboard, the bottle that would bring forgetfulness, if only for a while. What a fool she was to refuse the help of her sole ally in this heartbreaking struggle with life! She thought of the long evening ahead, the conversation with Rupert, the meeting with Cosima (it could not be put off forever), the contacts with sympathetic relatives, ready to plunge daggers into her heart. Already reaching out to tap at the window, she thought better of it and relapsed in her seat. There would always be a tomorrow—a tomorrow and a tomorrow. The bottle would keep. The mere knowledge of its existence made today's ordeal bearable, as with a man in the torture chamber who remembers the vial of poison through which he can at any moment end his sufferings. . . .

And here was the familiar driveway, the rhododendron bushes, the arched portico before the house. As she greeted Hauptman and then made her way through the hall, Helen suddenly felt calm and collected. She had a long experience of attending functions in a suicidal frame of mind without letting anyone guess what she was feeling. Today she was among enemies, and she knew it. She would let no one feel sorry for her, let no one suspect that Cosima's action had beaten her finally to the ground; she rejected in advance the false sympathy of a family who had hated her from the start.

There was a turning of heads following her entrance into the parlor. William, Jr., on the point of addressing the company, gave her an impatient nod, while waiting for her to be seated; several others, including William, Sr., and Cecilia, came up to her quickly to murmur a word of sympathy. One person alone pressed her hand in a warm grasp as he said to her earnestly:

"Aunt Helen, I am sorry! Terribly sorry! I want you to feel that."

"I do feel it, Frankie," she answered, grateful for the note of affection in her young nephew's voice, heartened and revivified by that handclasp.

"Helen, there's a seat for you over there," Rupert broke in (as he always seemed to do when she was speaking to Francy's son). He indicated an empty chair next to Gladys.

She hesitated, then, pretending not to have understood, made her way to Frank's sofa, beneath Mama's portrait. At once she regretted the petty action. How could she at this moment of tragedy even remember her old feud with Gladys, begun forty-five years before? Had she nothing more important left in her life than a meaningless enmity whose very origin had been forgotten?

But now William, Jr., had begun to speak. In a voice whose calm tone was disproved by the nervous twitching of his fingers, he told them: "I'm glad that we're all here—all of us, that is, except Cosima, who for reasons you know couldn't be present. I think we're all very much distressed at what's happened—distressed and worried. That's why Dad and I decided to call you together, knowing that this matter concerns every one of you intimately. I don't need to tell you that it can have serious repercussions. We Konrads are a prominent family in this city, and for people like us there are always enemies ready to do harm. I imagine that there's scarcely one of you who wouldn't be affected by publicity of the wrong sort. I'm quite frank in admitting that my own thoughts are on the government grant for my laboratory, which comes up for renewal shortly."

He paused, while his nervous fingers drummed on the table top. The family group seemed sunk in dejected thought.

Oh, those self-centered Konrads! Helen was thinking. Here a tragedy had occurred involving the death of her own grandchild, but all William, Jr., could think of was how it might affect the plans for his own aggrandization! She let her glance go to her husband, and saw in that face, too, the look of self-concentration she knew all too well. Rupert's thoughts were far from Cosima and the dead child; he was worrying about the new diplomatic post, of which this unfortunate accident might rob him. And in the same way, she was sure, everyone there present was concerned for his own personal ambitions, without a thought given to the larger issues involved. Self-indulgence, smugness, calculation, vanity—those were the Konrad vices that had come to dominate the family behavior.

Suddenly Helen's thoughts winged back to the last occasion when she had seen them thus assembled—that famous "chocolate party" on Mama's birthday, thirty long years ago. The same room, the same faces, but what drastic changes life had brought to the Konrad family and

325

to the world in which they lived! That had been 1920, a year of hope and optimism, when men thought in terms of peace and human progress, and when Mama Konrad had been able to say, "Our family is a *good* family. It will remain a good family." Helen wondered if Mama Konrad would say the same thing today. The Konrads were successful, according to the standards of a disillusioned world. But were they still what Mama would have called "a good family"?

She realized that William was speaking again, though his first sentences must have escaped her, lost in her memories. She was getting to be an old woman, thought Helen, rallying her attention. As she leaned forward to listen she noticed that her nephew Frank, seated to her right, was watching William with an expression of tense concern on his face; his heavy eyebrows were drawn together and his troubled eyes reminded her of Francy's. My Lord, how like he is to his father now, she told herself, feeling that little catch at the heart which always came with the thought of Francy. He is as different from these others as black from white!

"So, as I say, the very last thing we want is a scandal," William was continuing, as he passed his hand over his thin hair. "And it's to prevent one that I took the step about which I shall tell you. Uncle Rupert knows what I have done, and he approves. I was acting for him in the first instance, because as Cosima's father he would be more affected by newspaper muck than anyone else. But really I acted for all of you, so I think I had better tell you just what has happened. I hope you'll agree that the only course was to make a deal. It's going to cost us all money, but by God, it is money well spent!"

"A deal?" Cecilia interrupted blandly. "What kind of a deal, William?"

"Why, a simple money deal, Aunt Cissy. For a consideration, Stanley Harding, Cosima's husband, was willing to forget that he was chasing Cosima in a second car when the accident occurred. There wouldn't be the ghost of a chance of clearing her if that ever came out! As it is, the accounts will simply state that she had a smashup while taking Patsy to a picnic, and no one is going to think more of it. By good luck, we have the co-operation of the local police, and as to the newspapers—I am happy to say that Dad's not without influence in that quarter."

326

"In other words we're paying blackmail money," said Bee. "I don't like it, William."

"Nor do any of us," William, Sr., cut in. "Unfortunately William didn't have any other alternative. It's not the first time this sort of thing has happened, Bee, and I imagine it won't be the last."

"That's right!" Rupert, for one of the few times in his life, supported his brother. "Personally, I feel that William, Jr., did the best thing possible under the circumstances. Time was of the essence. A quick decision had to be made."

"Naturally it did," agreed Bee. "I still don't like the idea of that scoundrel Harding getting away with this, but of course I do support William, Jr."

"So do I," said Cecilia enthusiastically. And she added, sending him a sugary smile, "In fact I *know* now that William, Jr., is a genius."

The older William looked relieved. Sending his glance from one member of the family to the other, he announced, "Well, I take it for granted, then, that we all of us stand by William's action? We don't like the situation, any one of us, but we're forced to accept it. I believe that's the consensus of opinion. Do any of you wish to say anything further?"

A silence in the big room. And then abruptly the voice of Frank Konrad, calm, respectful, but as determined as a man's voice could be:

"Yes, I do, Uncle William."

Helen's heart had begun to pound. For some reason those words, spoken so quietly by young Frank, moved her to the depths. It was not the voice of Francy she had heard, though it had the same gentle quality; it was the voice of a man who knew his own mind, as Francy had never known his.

"Well, what is it, Frankie?" William, Sr., asked, and he glanced meaningfully at his thick watch. "You've got a question to ask before we break up?"

"No question," Frank said, rising to his feet, and still speaking in that calmly determined way. "I just want to tell you all—that I thoroughly disapprove of this whole dirty business."

"You disapprove?" William, Sr., seemed to have difficulty taking in the gist of the words. "Well, of course, Frankie, we all disapprove. I

327

thought I had just made that clear. It's not the way we like to handle matters, that's certain. But there was nothing else to be done."

"You see, that's where I disagree, Uncle William."

"Then what would you have suggested? I know you're a very bright boy, Frankie, but I fail to see how you could have done better," said William, Sr., having decided to jolly along this recalcitrant relative.

"Why, I would have let things take their course," Frank said. "I wouldn't have done anything."

An embarrassed silence followed that remark. Bee had taken off her pince-nez and was polishing them scrupulously; Rupert was tugging frenziedly at the lobe of his ear.

"So you wouldn't have done anything?" William, Sr., repeated, consternation written across his heavy face.

"That's right, Uncle William. I'd have let things take their course. Naturally I understand what this can mean to all of you; still, I don't see why Cosima should be protected, even if it didn't mean getting mixed up in such a dirty deal. After all, she is guilty, let's face it. She deserves her punishment."

"You don't know what you're talking about!" William, Sr., had begun to shout. "You'd better remember, young man, that you're only in the twenties and that there are a lot of things you don't know about life. Do you mean to say that you're going to stand there and set yourself up against the whole family?"

"Well yes, if it comes to that," Frank answered after a pause.

William, Jr., jumped up and walked over to his father. He smiled and patted him affectionately on the back.

"Let me say a word now, Dad. There's no point in our getting mad at each other, is there? Frankie here's got a right to his opinion, and personally I think a hell of a lot of him. I think I've proved it by offering him a confidential position in my lab, and I certainly wouldn't have done that"—he fixed Frank with a shrewd eye—"if I hadn't thought he had his feet on the ground. What I feel is that he's been away from Chicago so long that he's forgotten the sort of people we are. Look here, old man," he said, sending Frank a smile, "we none of us want to whitewash Cosima—and I think I can include Uncle Rupert and Aunt Helen in that statement. She's done a very foolish thing, and who's going to regret it more than she? God help her, she'll have enough mental anguish to go through.

"But this is a long way from concerning Cosima alone," William, Jr., went on, smoothing his hair. "It concerns every one of us, individually and as a group. We Konrads have a fine name in Chicago. I'm proud of it. I think we're all proud of it. There's scarcely a family who's been more prominent in the history of this city, and now, with Grandfather lying on his deathbed, we're in very real danger of having our name dragged through the mire. I don't think that you, old man, would be very happy to have it said that one of the Konrads was a . . . a . . ." He decided to change his sentence, perhaps out of regard for Cosima's parents. ". . . was guilty of the death of her child," concluded William, Jr., his sharp eye still on his cousin.

Steadily and calmly Frank returned that glance. As she watched him standing there, face to face with the whole family, Helen knew that it would take more than glib words to swerve Francy's son. If only his father had been like this, how differently his life—and her life—might have turned! She was struck suddenly with a strange and exciting thought: that this revolt of young Frank's that she was witnessing today was really a continuation of Francy's revolt against a standard of behavior that he could not accept. Now it was being carried on by the next generation, and this boy had the strength to carry it through! His victory would atone in some measure for poor Francy's defeat. She leant forward with beating heart as he began speaking.

"I think," he said slowly, wrinkling his forehead as if he were making an effort to express himself clearly, "I think that everything you have said is—well, simply beside the point! It's not hard to find reasons for doing dirty things. Personally, I don't think any reason's good enough! The point, as I see it, is this: have or haven't we a code of honor? Does or doesn't our family stand for anything? I always thought it did. I thought it was a family people could look up to, and I was proud of it because of that. The family's always meant a lot to me—perhaps more than to most of you. But if we are going to lower ourselves now to pay money to save our skins"—Frank straightened his shoulders and Helen saw his eyes blaze, as old Adolph's eyes used to blaze—"well, then I say, damn the family!"

329

Now it seemed to Helen that everyone had begun speaking at the same time. William, Sr., jumped forward and, red in the face, his stiff collar looking as if it were about to choke him, shouted, "How dare you say that, young man! I forbid you . . . I positively forbid . . ."

"Keep calm, Dad!" His son took his arm. "It's not worth getting excited over. Just let me handle this."

Frank's cousin, Cecil Judson, had leaped to his feet, and he, too, looked as if he had been slapped in the face.

"What's the matter with you anyway!" he shouted. "Are you crazy, Frank Konrad?"

"No, he's not crazy!" It was Rupert speaking. He had taken two steps forward, and Helen could see in his face that the old Konrad temper had got the better of him. "He's just—just a dreamy-eyed idealist!" cried Rupert. "An impractical idealist, like his father, Francy!"

Frank looked at his uncle with those dark eyes of his blazing. His lips were working in and out as old Adolph's used to do before an outburst; his heavy eyebrows were drawn together. But then his expression relaxed. He nodded at Rupert, as though in agreement, and answered deliberately:

"Yes, Uncle Rupert, perhaps you are right. After all, we do take after our parents, thank God! You're wrong in one thing, though: I'm not impractical. I'm a chemical engineer, and who ever heard of a good engineer being impractical? Perhaps what you call my idealism is more practical in the long run than your pursuit of the main chance. Do you mind if I point out that your generation haven't done too good a job of things, Uncle Rupert?"

He nodded again, turned his back, and made his way towards the door. He pulled it open and closed it slowly, deliberately, behind him. The thought struck Helen, That is how Francy should have closed a door! Frank Konrad has made the decision which neither his father nor I could make.

twelve

His face was burning, his mind was in a spin. As Frank strode out of the house and down the driveway, he thought that he could hear angry shouts and pounding footsteps behind him; the very trees beside the road seemed to be leaning forward to threaten the renegade with their branches. Rounding the first bend, he was quite certain that he heard the front door of the house swing open and then bang to. No doubt some member of the family was coming after him to argue or to threaten, maybe to cajole! He felt that he could not face any one of them at the moment.

Leaving the driveway on his right, he cut across the sloping lawn, in whose center stood a great silver ball on a wrought-iron pedestal. The evening sun glittered on one side of the ball, and on the other side Frank saw his own image reflected, but distorted into a misshapen giant, huge curving body, elongated head above. Is that how I really look? he thought. It doesn't surprise me. I am finding out all sorts of things about myself today!

He rejoined the gravel path at the foot of the slope, and found himself in front of the garage, which had once served as stables. In the fading light he could make out his grandfather's ungainly Pierce-Arrow inside, standing next to a modern station wagon; among the deep shadows at the rear stood the ancient buggy in which Adolph used to drive to work and which he had refused to dispose of in the intervening quarter century. There was something peaceful and soothing about that deserted garage, inhabited by vehicles ancient, old, and contemporary: an ideal spot it was for meditating on an action performed on the spur of the moment, but which might well affect one's whole life.

Now why did I do it? he thought, walking to the back of the building and then sitting down in the buggy, as there was no other seat. I had no idea that I would say a word until Uncle William asked us if there were any comments. Suddenly I found myself saying things that I didn't even know were in my mind! No, that's not right either.

They'd been in my mind, all right. They'd been there ever since my talk with Jan Smedlin, when I began to ask myself if William's purchase of talent and Uncle Rupert's purchase of diplomatic posts weren't isolated examples of bastardy, but—well, typical of the Konrads. I guess that what happened today gave me my answer. Jan was right. We've become a family of buyers!

He put his chin on his hand and sat staring bleakly at the floor. The smell of the Stock Yards came in through the open door, carried on that soft wind from the west which had been blowing since early morning: it mingled with the musty odor of the buggy to form a cloying, nauseous aroma. He felt slightly sickened by the smell, or perhaps it was the events of the day that made him feel sick and the putrid smell was only associated with them in his mind.

Over there, two miles to the west, the furnaces of the Stock Yards were burning, emblems of a mighty industry which his grandfather had helped found. But it seemed that the impulse to create, which had activated Adolph and his like, had died with the attainment of financial security; their children and grandchildren had found that they could purchase what they wanted (fame, position, or esteem) on the open market rather than earn these things through honest effort. Sitting there in the deserted garage, on the cracked seat of Adolph's old buggy, Frank made himself a promise that in his own life he would never use money for any other than its intended purpose: the acquisition of material commodities.

It was growing darker in the garage. From where he sat he could barely make out on the walls the framed photographs of the fine carriage horses that had once been Adolph's pride: Bismarck I, Bismarck II, Sehiller, Goethe. Near the buggy was a showcase in which blue, red, and yellow rosettes were laid out in rows, beneath newspaper clippings and faded pedigrees. Frank got out of the carriage to have a look at them.

"Mr. Adolph Konrad's fine team of grays was one of the sensations of the Chicago horse show," he read on a yellowed clipping behind the glass. And above the caption there appeared a photograph of Adolph himself, wearing a long checked coat and holding a whip in his hand.

How old-fashioned that looks nowadays! reflected Frank. But fifty years ago my grandfather's long checked coat was right up to date, and his pattern of life was up to date too: profits and roast beef and devil take the hindmost. Gradually a new pattern evolved, and the second generation decided there were more useful things to do than hang onto a business that had got too large for any one family. They wanted celebrity, so they went out and bought it. Now I am the third generation, and their pattern of existence seems as antiquated to me as old Adolph's must have done to them. Four years in the army gave me a different idea of what I wanted of life, a different perspective, above all a different feeling towards men. I can see now that Uncle William and Rupert and even William, Jr. (who belongs to an intermediate generation), no longer are important in my world. They don't know it, but really they're as antiquated as old Adolph's long checked coat!

He walked out of the garage into the evening dusk, which was falling gently over Adolph's estate. In the branches of the old elm trees birds were twittering sleepily, and from the pond behind the rose garden came the quacking of frogs. It was a melancholy hour, and as Frank followed the driveway towards the massive entrance gates he was overcome with a sensation of loneliness such as he had not experienced for many years. Where was he to go? Certainly not back to the house! He would return there only to pack his clothes and, if possible, say good-by to his grandfather. Ah, how everything had changed since he boarded that train in Philadelphia! He remembered his feeling of pleasure at the thought of going home, remembered his anger at Jan for sneering at people whom he loved and respected. Now all that was a thing of the past. Henceforth anyone could say anything they liked about the Konrads.

He crossed Drexel Boulevard and found himself plunged in the Negro quarter, with small shops and eating houses occupying the former buildings of a middle-class residential suburb. Stepping into a bar, Frank ordered himself a scotch and drank it slowly at the counter. The odor of the Stock Yards seemed stronger than ever, and as he stood drinking in this joyless place his feeling of loneliness deepened. Now that the initial excitement had worn off, he was acutely conscious of his youth, of being one against many, of the fact that he had of his own will kicked away the supports (invisible but reassuring) which had been there since he was a child.

And gradually, irresistibly, the thought formed that he may have acted a bit rashly that afternoon, may have gone further than he should. Hating dramatics, he shuddered at the knowledge that he had made a show of himself. Wasn't it presumptuous, even ridiculous, for a man of twenty-six to get up and upbraid people like his uncle and William, Jr., who were counted among the better-known citizens of the community? They had been so sure that they were right. What if they *were* right—and if he, consequently, was wrong?

A young Negro workman walked into the bar, ordered himself a glass of beer, and stood sipping it while he exchanged small talk with the barman. Now it seemed to Frank that even that tired workman was a person to be envied, for it was obvious that he belonged in this quarter, had roots here, and in all likelihood had a family to which he felt that he belonged. This was Chicago, Frank's own city, but the thing that made it his was the existence of the people he had disowned. Without them, what was Chicago but another great city like Philadelphia or New York, where he was one more grain of sand on the beach? He was a stranger here tonight, and is there anything more devastating than being a stranger in a metropolis?

Katrine, too, is a stranger here, he thought, leaving the bar and strolling northward up Drexel. She is friendless and must find what she needs within herself. But it's quite different for a person like Katrine, who can get from a pigeon who flies in through the window all the company she needs! I doubt if even a year at Dachau would make me so self-sufficient. I need the feeling of belonging to a family, to a city, to a class of society. I am not as strong and decisive as I'd like to appear! I wonder how it would really feel to settle in the East, perhaps marry Harriet and never see Chicago again. Have I enough guts and talent to win the rat race, run on the enemy's field, with only strange faces in the bleachers?

He walked on and on, quite regardless of direction and trying desperately to ward off a feeling of panic. Though he was leaving the Stock Yards behind, it seemed to him that that fetid odor was following him like a resentful dog. He walked on past Prairie Avenue, with its double row of defeated mansions, then down the dreary stretch of Indiana Avenue, which seemed to have sunk to an even lower stage of decrepitude since he strolled there last. Emerging finally on Michigan, he caught sight of the lake to his right, its waters shimmering under the July full moon. Farther down the avenue lay the bulk of the great Stevens Hotel, and beyond it was the Blackstone, where only last night he had sat having dinner with his Uncle Rupert and his Aunt Helen.

The thought of Helen brought a small glow of comfort. She, at least, was an ally, thought Frank. That afternoon, when he got up to speak, he had sensed her eyes upon him, sending courage, urging him on, begging him to say the things that she, a woman defeated by life, could not say. It struck him now that of the whole family it was only his grandfather and Helen who still meant anything in his life: the one because he represented the initiative and power which Frank used to associate with the name Konrad; the second because she had never ceased hating the mentality of Rupert and his kind, even though her hatred had proved ineffectual and weak.

For a wild moment he thought of entering the Blackstone and telephoning her room, so great was his need to hear the voice of a friend in that lonely Chicago night. As he stood beneath the towering wall of the hotel he realized that Helen, even if he could reach her at that hour, could not give him what he wanted. Much as he loved her, he knew that it did not lie in her power to give help to any person.

He began walking on, heading for the North Side. He knew now that he was going to Katrine.

She opened the green door to him, as she had done last time. As soon as he saw her face he knew that he had been right in coming here and that the lateness of the hour did not matter, nor the fact that she had been so curt last time when she said good-by. She realized he was in trouble the moment that their eyes met.

"Come in, sir," she said. "I am glad to see you."

The pigeon was sleeping on top of the bureau, his head nestling between his wings; on the gate-leg table beneath the cuckoo clock was the chessboard, with pieces again in play. It all looked exactly as he had

335

hoped that it would look, and he was glad that Katrine had on the same flowered dress as the day before.

"It's nice of you to let me come in for a moment," said Frank. "My God, can that clock be right! It isn't really past midnight!"

"Cuckoo clocks are never wrong," said Katrine solemnly. "But it doesn't matter. I seldom go to bed so early. You look tired. Have you been walking far?"

"Pretty far. All the way from Drexel Boulevard," said Frank. "That's quite a few miles."

"I should say it is! You look hungry too. I bet you haven't had any supper."

"How on earth do you know that?"

"When you have seen as many hungry people as I, you get to know. How about my beating together a few eggs?"

"Eggs," Frank repeated dully. He could not think of anything more to say, and Katrine must have known that he did not want to say anything at all just then.

She disappeared into the kitchen, where he could hear her using the beater with energetic rhythmic strokes. He imagined her watching the hardening eggs with the same earnest expression with which she had studied the chess game the day before, and he knew the result would be equally successful. When she came back into the room he was not surprised to see that she was bearing the neatest of trays, shakers, toast rack, tall glass of milk, lined up beside the superb-looking eggs like soldiers on parade.

"Now eat," said Katrine, placing the tray on the table, together with a snow-white napkin. "Eat and don't talk. The two don't go together."

Frank ate his creamy eggs with half an eye on Katrine, who sat quietly in an armchair. Not daring to disobey her, he remained silent, but he was thinking, I've never met anyone quite like this Katrine! How can she sit in a chair without doing anything at all, and yet look so occupied and contented? I couldn't do it for a minute! I'd begin to fidget or frown. I can't imagine Harriet sitting still in a chair for even thirty seconds. Perhaps when you have been closer to death than to life, you realize not only the supreme importance of a plate of scrambled eggs but also the importance of being happy when you can.

"They were gorgeous," he said when he had swallowed the last mouthful. "You are a wonderful cook."

She nodded, accepting that as a statement which needed neither modification nor elaboration.

"Food," said Katrine, "is one of the nicest things in life. It would be a shame to spoil it. I learned the secret of good scrambled eggs, and many other things, from our Therese, who was certainly one of the best cooks in Prague."

"Aren't you lucky to have had such a fine set of teachers!" Frank joked with her, grateful that she understood his need to engage in trivial conversation. "Your uncle taught you championship chess— Therese taught you the wizardry of cooking."

Katrine laughed gaily.

"That's right. My family were sort of specialists in nice living; they wanted the food they ate and the friends they saw and the house they lived in all to be just right. We only had a few pictures in our home, and it was sparingly furnished, but every single picture and every chair and table was a darling. We loved each single piece! If ever we got anything new, it was after long and earnest consultations in which the whole family took part. It was strange for me when I came to America and found people rushing into shops and buying, buying—almost as if they didn't care what they bought—just buying for the sake of buying."

Ah, back on that subject again! thought Frank, his smile fading. That's how it always is: one hasn't thought of a thing for years, perhaps has never thought of it, and then it crops up six times in the same day. As he formulated an answer, he felt that he was clarifying his own ideas, rather than trying to enlighten Katrine.

"There's a lot of money in America," he said, "and most of it's been accumulated pretty fast. We like to spend it, because that's just the way we're made, but we don't always know on what. Wise spending goes with an old culture, I guess, and ours is pretty young. That's why we go and buy a second car when one will do, or a too expensive television set. And sometimes we buy things we want awfully badly but to which we don't happen to be entitled. That's the hell of a nasty sort of buying, Katrine!"

It was the first time he had used her name, and he looked at her to

337

see if she had minded (considering how she had said good-by to him the day before). Then he saw that her eyes had clouded over, and that it was the other Katrine who stood before him: the Katrine for whom suffering had become an everyday companion. She was thinking of Jan, he knew.

"When my cousin William paid for the right to put his name on Jan's invention he was doing that sort of buying," Frank said, looking her in the face.

She gave a start. "So you know!"

"Yes, Jan told me last night. I want you to believe that when I came here yesterday, I . . . well, I had no idea of what had happened between them."

"Why do you wish me to believe that?"

"Because I would be ashamed to have you think that I'd knowingly take lunch with such a man!"

She gazed at him for a moment silently, and Frank knew that in those seconds their future relationship hung in the balance. He had wanted to tell her about the family meeting, embarrassing though he would have found it. Now he knew that it would not be necessary; he had let her know where he stood, and she must either believe him or not believe him. Slowly the shadow of a smile crossed Katrine's face— no, not a smile really—rather the look of acceptance given to a person who shares one's beliefs. It was like a handclasp, and he felt fortified and relieved.

"Where did you see Jan?" she said, changing the subject, just as he himself would have done after such a private moment. Only a person far cruder than Katrine would have tried to form a reply to what had been said by the fleeting expression of the eyes. "Did you have an appointment with Jan?" she asked him.

"No. I ran into him by accident in a little place on East Harrison Street."

"A place? You mean a bar." Katrine looked away. "That's one of Jan's hangouts, I know it well, I wouldn't be surprised if he were there this very minute! Doesn't it seem strange that he has to sit in that room alone, eating his heart out, while I sit here alone, playing chess against myself? Most people go to a bar to drink, but that's not true of Jan: he goes there to sit by himself. We love each other so, and yet he can't bear being alone with me during the long evenings. And you know, Frankie, I understand him. There is too much sadness between us. It's best that he goes to the bars!"

"But, my God, you must have some friends," Frank said to her. "You ought to see more of people, both of you—you ought to make an effort. Don't you go to the movies once in a while?"

Katrine smiled, but it struck him that it was the smile of a very old person.

"How American you are after all, Frankie! You understand some things so well, you're so sensitive—and then you tell Jan and me to go to the movies, or worse still, look up people! Always a practical solution to any problem. Don't you realize that for a man like Jan there can be no friends any more? Seeing people is torture for him. And for me . . ." She gave a funny little shrug, and then her eyes went to Frank's face, their expression suddenly candid and childish. "For me it is so rare that I find anyone I like."

He knew that he was blushing like a fool. He was immensely confused. A sensation of pure delight swept over him, as though no girl had ever said (and in more direct terms than this) that she was a bit taken with him. He wanted to tell Katrine that he liked her too, indeed that there was scarcely another person he liked so much. But he already knew her enough to realize that she was like a bird alighted in a tree, ready to take flight at the first strident note.

The clock struck one. Instantly he began speaking, so as not to give her the chance of telling him that it was high time he went home.

"But is there nothing one can do for Jan?" he asked her. "He's still a young man, isn't he? Well under forty. He's got a brilliant mind. I refuse to believe that life is over for him because of this rotten experience. Other people . . ."

"Ah, but that's just it, Frankie: Jan isn't other people. He's himself: a man who suffered too deeply for too long, and who finally broke under the strain. At Dachau there were certain people like that, people whom everybody realized were done for, even if they should be released from concentration camp next day." (As she mentioned those words "concentration camp," Frank saw her hand make that instinctive movement to cover the numbers tattooed on her arm. He wished he could put out his own hand to blot out the ugly past which had left its mark upon her heart.) "You met Jan before the war, Frankie. You remember what a simple, trusting person he was, even after all that he'd been through: persecution and prison and the long years of strain. It was that last blow he couldn't stand: being betrayed by the man whom he admired more than anyone in the world. That's what broke Jan, Frankie!"

She closed her eyes for a moment, as though to press back the tears. When she spoke again, her voice was choked, faltering.

"Four years I've lived here," she said. "For four years I've fought to save Jan. I've given him love—all my love. I've tried to give him my strength too, and the faith in life which I kept like a jewel when the Nazis took everything else from me. And now"—she flung out her ten fingers in a hopeless gesture—"now I know that I am beaten. I feel Jan slipping away from me, further, further into the shadows. He is a doomed person, Frankie, like those poor souls at Dachau waiting only for death. Sometimes it seems to me that he is dead already—and that his murderer lives in this city. And I—I stand here, helpless and alone . . ."

Frank was moved as he had been but rarely in his life. It seemed to him that Katrine in these minutes had opened a second door, behind the shining green door that gave on Pimento Place. Behind it he had caught a glimpse of an inner room that he knew nothing of, and Frank was filled with pity for the inhabitants of that secret room. Perhaps, he thought, in many of these little houses that look so gay and carefree from the street there is an inner room dwelt in by people like Katrine and Jan, who have pushed shut the door behind them.

"You are not alone, Katrine," he said. "I am here with you. If my friendship can mean anything to you, now and for always, let me be your friend."

He left the chess table and took three strides towards the center of the floor, where Katrine stood with arms folded over her breasts, eyes on the carpet. But when he put his arm around her shoulder she looked up at him quickly, and then suddenly, quite unexpectedly, she smiled: it was as if curtains had been thrown wide apart, letting the sunlight pour in.

"I have a friend!" she said. "How wonderful! I have a friend. Now I can never be really alone again. Somewhere in the world there will be Frankie, a person one can respect—a person one *must* respect. Do you know how many people there are in the world of whom one can say that? No, probably you don't. Please, Frankie, make me a promise that you will never change."

"You must help me," said Frank, and as he kissed her on the mouth he could read the answer in her eyes.

thirteen

His suitcase was fully packed. Frank straightened up from laying in his handkerchiefs and took a last look about that little bedroom which he would never see again. With his grandfather's death, Sans Souci would suffer the fate which should normally have befallen it decades before: the dikes would be torn down and that symbol of nineteenth-century capitalism would instantly disappear under the swirling floodwaters. If there were anything to preserve from the inevitable deluge, any memento of his Chicago past to carry into the uncharted future, this was the moment to claim it. In a few minutes he would have left this house and a whole period of his life would have drawn to a close.

He walked over to the bookcase and let his eye pass over the volumes of poetry that had once belonged to his father. "Chicago poets," read the typewritten label above the top shelf, and there stood their works, unopened and unread for the last quarter century. At random he opened a volume of Edgar Lee Masters and scanned a poem or two, then put it back on the shelf; pessimistic fatalism did not appeal to him, and he would have been surprised to know that his father had once shed tears while reading those very lines. He let his eye go about the walls, from the lithograph of Goethe, to the framed college diploma, to the water color of a mountain shack with the sunlight bringing out strange color patterns on the opposite canyon wall. No, none of these would he take with him either. A young man of today had to travel lightly through life.

Frank strode over to the window and threw it wide open, bringing the hum of the metropolis to his ears. Leaning out, he peered through the branches of the elm at the busy city street just visible above the tall wall encircling Sans Souci. Somehow the sight of that street, ugly and crowded though it was, made him want to hurry out of this house, haunted with the ghosts of the past. *That* is what I'll take with me, he thought—the memory of Chicago, kicking and screaming and laughing like a lusty brat. One day I am coming back here to live, but I shan't come back to the Chicago of the Konrads (who are as unrepresentative of this city as its handful of gangsters); I shall come back to the Chicago that belongs to that fat man in shirt sleeves running for his bus and that tall girl with glasses and a bundle of books under her arm. It's they and I who are going to write the Chicago story, not the William, Jrs., in their big houses in Hadon Heights, nor Aunt Bee and her busy political committees. And it is going to be a damn good story!

He lit a cigarette and drew the smoke deep into his nostrils, pleased at the prospect of the exciting future. True, he was going back to a routine job in the Snyder Laboratories, rather than stepping into William, Jr.'s "factory of science," but he knew this was a decision he would never regret. On the table lay a letter from Harriet, written after she had received his wire, and now he sat down on the couch to read it for a second time. As his glance passed over the neatly penned lines Frank felt more strongly than ever that a definite period of his life was over.

". . . so that's why I'm so pleased about your cousin's offer," Harriet had written in part. "You're a clever boy, Frankie, but we all know that the world is full of clever boys. One needs more than brains, or even talent, to get along nowadays: one needs a little push from behind. If this hadn't come up, I could see you messing about with your little test tubes at Snyder's for years to come, taking orders from nonentities and living like a dry-goods store clerk. Now you can go straight to the top! . . ."

Straight to the top! Frank repeated the words, as he stretched out on the sofa to ruminate. But that is exactly what I don't want to do! he thought. When I get to the top (as I shall get!), it won't be by the use of short cuts, in the Konrad manner. It will be by climbing the long hard way. Yes, I am going to keep messing about with my test tubes, dear Harriet, and you know what strange things are apt to happen inside a test tube. I shan't try to concoct gold out of base metals, like the alchemists, but I may find something that is of more use to me, and to the rest of the world, than gold. I'm sorry, Harriet, but it seems that our futures don't lie together. In these last three days I've learned who I am, and the sort of life I want. And I've learned what sort of people I want in that life.

As that thought passed through his mind, he suddenly saw before him Katrine, and she was holding her hand over the tattooed numbers on her arm. "You are not alone," he heard himself saying, and then he saw the sunlight flood into her face. "I have a friend!" said Katrine. "I have a friend. Now I can never be really alone again. . . ."

Frank turned his head on the sofa pillow, aware that someone was knocking at the door. It was a fumbling knock, so soft and weak that it might have been made by one of the branches of the elm scraping against the wall of the house.

"Yes, Hauptman," he said, smoothing his ruffled hair. "Come in."

The door opened a little, and the old butler stepped inside. As he peered across the room at Frank a reminiscent smile came into his face.

"Why, Mr. Frank, do you know that for a moment I could have taken you for your father, Mr. Francy, lying there! *Ya, ya,* he was always stretched out on that couch, hour after hour! When I think back on him, I always see him on that couch."

"Is that right?" said Frank, and quickly he swung his legs to the floor.

"It is right, Mr. Frank. He was always lying there—never seemed able to make up his mind to get off that couch." The old man shook his head, as if to fling off these ever-recurring memories that interfered so seriously with daily life. His large pale face lit up as he went on, "Ach, do you know what's happened, Mr. Frank? Just now the boss asked for you! He wants to see you right away, Mr. Frank."

"Wants to see *me!* Are you sure?" Frank's first idea was that Hauptman must have made a mistake. He had quite given up hope of seeing his grandfather again, for old Adolph had been sinking every day; in the mind of everyone had been the thought that the end was not far off.

But Hauptman insisted, "*Ya, ya!* The boss told Dr. O'Grady he want to see you, Mr. Frank. And Dr. O'Grady, he says okay. Dr. O'Grady never said no to the boss yet," added Hauptman approvingly.

Frank hurried out into the corridor and almost bumped into O'Grady himself, who had just emerged from the sickroom. It was the first time Frank had seen the doctor in at least six years, but he seemed to have changed remarkably little; he was like some long-lived animal—an elephant or a whale—which, never having had any inner life, remains at eighty about what it was at fifty, or at twenty-five. He greeted Frank with the same meaningless heartiness with which he used to greet Frank's father thirty years before.

"Top o' the mornin', me boy—or rather, afternoon. Ye're lookin' swell, Frankie—swell. Be gorry, ye're a healthy-lookin' customer, aren't ye? If yer father had only had yer constitution he'd be with us today."

"Is it really all right for me to go see the old gentleman?" Frank cut in, feeling that inexplicable revulsion that always came over him when O'Grady spoke about his father. (He had never understood why the man took every opportunity to do so, nor why O'Grady had tried to be so nice to him when he was a boy. Frank remembered one occasion when the doctor had given him a giant Meccano set, and he had been punished because he did not want to thank him.)

"Adolph's expectin' ye," O'Grady answered. "He's feelin' chipper this mornin'. There must be damn near a dozen of ye Konrads here in town, an' yet he asked specially fer ye. Now what d'ye know about that? Go in and say hello to him, me boy—an' better say good-by at the same time."

In the sickroom the curtains were drawn and in the half-light it was hard to see the invalid's face. Even so, Frank noticed a great change in his grandfather since he had visited him two days before; the process of disintegration had gone forward at a rapid rate, drawing the life-blood from his face and quenching the fire in his eyes. The once powerful hand which Frank's hand clasped was limp as a wilted flower. There was no doubt that he was in the room with a dying man.

"I am glad you sent for me," Frank told him, sitting down on the edge of the bed.

The old man offered no acknowledgment by sign or word; it was as if he were preserving his remaining strength to say something of importance. As Frank's eyes adjusted themselves to the obscurity he could note the labored up-and-down movement of the chest beneath the covers and make out on the bedside table the framed photograph of his grandmother propped against the lamp; in the darkness the contours of the determined face were almost merged with the background. Then suddenly Adolph spoke, and today again his first words came as a complete surprise.

"Vell, you are the third generation, my boy," he said in a weak voice which was yet remarkably clear. "Now it is you who must go on! Vhen you're an old man, a very old man like me, you can see things like vhat you couldn't earlier. It's like vhat you're looking at them from far avay, the whole past, und vhat's coming later, too. Then vhat happens during tventy, thirty, forty years don't seem so important. There's only vone thing vhat's important, just like vhat used to be important in the stone age: that the fire don't go out!"

Adolph paused. He was breathing deeper, and the covers and the counterpane rose and fell at each breath. In vain Frank tried to understand what the old man was driving at; he knew that he must not interrupt him. With pain his grandfather was unraveling the slender thread of his thoughts, and once snapped, he would never be able to retie it.

"Vhen I came to America," Adolph said, and now his voice was a little stronger, "I brought that fire mit me in my hands. It made me varm vhen I vas cold (und I vas often cold) und because of it I could build the things I vanted to build. I built the Konrad plant und this house, und I built a new family in America. For I vas a builder, like all the men vhat made America vhat she is, und ve vasn't building for ourselves. I vanted my vork to last und for my sons to go forward mit the building. That's vhat I hoped. That's vhat could have happened, too, McKenna or no McKenna. But they didn't have it in them!" Adolph suddenly cried, and Frank could see that his hand on the counterpane was shaking. "It vasn't their fault, those sons of mine. They belonged to that no-good second generation, Gott demn it to hell!"

Frank was going to tell the old man to take it easy, but again he did not dare disturb him. As Adolph spoke, a sensation of excitement had gripped him; he had the same feeling as two days before, that Adolph had something to say of overmastering importance to himself. He waited for the next words with a suspence that made the present pause appear almost interminable. As the old man gathered his strength to continue, Frank sat leaning forward, his eyes on the parchmentlike face, imagining at every second that he heard the pit-pat of the nurse's footsteps, come to interrupt them. He willed Adolph to continue.

"Go on! Go on!" he heard his own whisper in the silent room.

"Your father, he vasn't like the others," Adolph said at last. His hand had stopped shaking and lay still on the counterpane, fingers spread out stiffly, like a dead hand. "Yes, I can see it now. He vas better stuff than the other four. Und yet he vas a veakling, a veakling! A man must be strong, for if not, God Himself cannot help him. I loved Francy, but I could not help him. He couldn't decide. He died because he couldn't decide."

Adolph struggled to raise himself in his bed. The great head with its shock of white hair moved restlessly on the pillow, and the sunken eyes blazed up and fixed themselves on Frank. Spontaneously Frank reached out and hooked his arm around his grandfather's body, to draw it up into a half-sitting position against the pillows. It was like moving a dead weight that responded only to the law of gravity and to outer force. But the eyes were not dead! Glowing like live coals, they remained focused on Frank.

"You must be strong!" he cried again. "Yes, strong! Strong! My father told me that before he died, und my father vas right. You, boy, are not like Francy. You are like me! I thought so already vhen you vere young, und now you have become a man und I am sure. You are like me, who alvays knew how to say yes und how to say no, und to keep saying it even vhen they *proved* I vas wrong. It is a hundred times better to be wrong than not to know vhat you think!" He stopped a few seconds to gasp for air, and Frank realized that he was making a

346

supreme effort. The beads of sweat glistened on his forehead; the shoulders under the old-fashioned nightgown quivered like a live thing.

"Rupert und Villiam are stubborn," he went on, his voice weaker again now, so that Frank had to move close to hear him. "That does not make them strong! Young Villiam, he's clever, but he is a coward straight through. You, Frankie, are the only vone who's like me, the only vone of all my children und grandchildren! You have the fire that I brought with me to this country, the fire that must stay burning if America shall remain America! It's jumped a generation. That doesn't matter. Vhat matters is that it's burning in a Konrad today—the fire that helped build Chicago, und vill help build the Chicago of the future. Listen, Frankie . . ." Adolph's hand made a movement on the counterpane, and Frank saw what he wanted and closed his own hand over it. "Don't let them put out that fire! Go your own vay, even vhen they all tell you it's wrong. Your vay is not the same vhat mine vas. The things I vanted are not the things you vant, und vhat vas important to me maybe isn't important to you. But don't let the fools tell you vhat you should vant! Don't ever listen to them, Frankie. Don't let them put out the fire . . . I tell you, don't let them put out the fire. . . ."

The old man's body gave a violent jerk. His head shot back as if he had received a blow on the chin, and the eyes, still staring at Frank, slowly lost their brilliance to become clouded over. The mouth opened a little, and stayed open, so that Frank could see the tongue falling to the side before he realized that it was only following the motion of the head. It dropped sideways on the pillow, slid forward a few inches, as if seeking a more comfortable position, and came to rest. Gradually the realization dawned on Frank that Adolph Konrad's long battle for life was over.